Caro Fraser was educated in Glasgow and the Isle of Man, before attending Watford School of Art and London University, King's College, where she studied law. She was called to the Bar of Middle Temple in 1979. After leaving Art School, Caro Fraser worked for three years as an advertising copywriter. She then studied law, and read for the Bar, after which she spent six months in pupillage. Before turning to writing, Caro Fraser worked as a shipping lawyer. She is married to a solicitor and has four children.

The Trustees

CARO FRASER

PHŒNIX

A PHOENIX PAPERBACK

First published in Great Britain by Orion in 1994
This paperback edition published in 1995 by Phoenix,
a division of Orion Books Ltd,
Orion House, 5 Upper St Martin's Lane,
London WC2H 9EA

Third impression 1995

A CIP catalogue record for this book is available
from the British Library.

ISBN: 1 85799 059 5

Typeset by Deltatype Limited, Ellesmere Port, Cheshire

Printed and bound in Great Britain by Clays Ltd, St Ives plc.

For Mum, Dad, Sie and Nick

Chapter one

As he surveyed his new room as senior partner of the firm of De Vaut, Montacute & Strange, Geoffrey Montacute felt a deep sense – no, not of pleasure, that was too warm a word – of gratification. It had to be said that he was proud of his recent achievements. They were successes for which he had worked hard for many years. Not only was he now the senior partner of a leading firm of City solicitors, he was also, since last week, a member of Lloyd's, the result of prudent husbanding of his earnings over the years. He felt he had done well, for a man of forty-seven.

He moved slowly round the room, a tall, dark, heavy individual, his dignified figure borne slackly and without athleticism, approving the small touches that made the room his own and which obliterated the traces of his predecessor, Alfred de Vaut, who was now consigned to a token consultancy at the top left-hand corner of the firm's notepaper and a quiet retirement in Esher, Surrey.

At the thought of Alfred de Vaut, Montacute returned to the large mahogany desk which he had transported from home to grace his new office, and slid open one of the drawers. From it he pulled one of the new sheets of notepaper and quietly admired the sight of his own name at the very top of the list of names of members of the firm, a discreet advertisement to the world at large of the eminence of his position.

He glanced at his watch. Ten to ten. Just time for a cup of coffee before his client, Lady Folgate, was due to arrive. Really, he thought, as he buzzed through to his secretary, as senior partner he should not now be dealing with the testamentary dispositions of people as impecunious as Sir Norton and Lady Folgate. Titled they might be, but it was quite ridiculous how these people clung to a sense of their own importance.

'Coffee, Miss Reed, if you please,' he said into his intercom.

In the outer office, Miss Reed received the instruction and went off to fetch Montacute his coffee. She was a grim, conscientious woman who had worked for Mr Montacute for fourteen years and accepted his cold, charmless treatment of her with unflinching loyalty. Neither she nor Geoffrey Montacute had any time for secretaries of the younger, frivolous variety, and they both made it their duty to make the lives of any such unfortunates as might stray into the offices of De Vaut, Montacute & Strange as uncomfortable with disapproval as possible. She found another of the particular objects of her disdain, twenty-four-year-old Richard Ranscombe, articled clerk, whistling beside the coffee machine.

'Morning, Miss Reed,' he said cheerfully. 'First of the day?' He finished stirring his overfull cup of coffee and took a noisy sip, dropping the spoon back on to the trolley that stood beside the coffee machine.

'I wish, Mr Ranscombe,' said Miss Reed, picking up the spoon and rinsing it at the little sink, 'that you would remember not to leave things unwashed. And,' she added, mopping at a pool of coffee on the edge of the machine, 'that you wouldn't make quite so much mess. It is most unpleasant for others.'

'Sorry, Miss Reed,' murmured Richard, taking the cloth from her with a gallant smile, and wiping up. 'Here, allow me.' Apart from his youth, which she naturally held against him, Miss Reed had a special mistrust of this young man's unbecoming air of careless cheerfulness. His manner, she felt, was not suitable for the offices of De Vaut, Montacute & Strange. Certainly there was much in those offices that would have depressed the spirits of a lesser man than Richard Ranscombe. The rooms were grand, grave and forbidding, those of the partners panelled in dark wood, and the rest of the offices painted a sombre green.

All of the equipment, down to the filing cabinets and the typewriters, was of an antiquated nature, but solid and dependable, with no hint of shabbiness. The atmosphere was, as befitted a leading firm of Chancery solicitors, heavy and

2

humourless, and had worn down the spirit of many a chirpy typist. Now, only the dullest and most wordlessly efficient of women worked for De Vaut, Montacute & Strange. No chattering gaggle of girls flocked out of the office door at lunchtime; only middle-aged, grey women who donned their coats and left, returning quickly with their sandwiches, which they ate in silence at their desks, gazing at recipes and knitting patterns and the faces of the Royal Family as they turned the pages of their lonely magazines.

It was in an effort to combat the oppressive atmosphere of the office that Richard kept up his air of levity. Most days it was a bit of a strain. He sighed inwardly as he returned to his room, which he shared with an assistant solicitor three years his senior, called Clive Fry. Clive was everything that Richard was not, and vice versa, so that their relationship, in spite of Richard's cheerful nature, was not harmonious. Where Richard was bustling and energetic, Clive was painstaking and precise; where Richard was disordered and light-hearted, Clive was meticulous and morose. Richard was stocky and well-built with wide, irregular, but pleasing features, and Clive was slender and dark, with thin, white hands and a long, sallow face. Clive admired and revered Geoffrey Montacute, and imitated his manner, which was both insinuating and supercilious, whereas Richard thought Montacute a pompous pain in the arse, and an insufferable bore. He was also aware that Montacute disliked him; being young, Richard did not care to be disliked by anyone, even a pompous pain in the arse, and he tried whenever he could to be pleasant and bright with the man, though he did not especially admire Clive's brand of ingratiating humility. Although he might pretend to himself that the dull monotony of De Vaut, Montacute & Strange was as nothing to him, there were days when its influence was almost more than he could bear.

He set his coffee cup on his desk and sat down, glancing at Clive. He wondered if Clive really was as miserable as he always looked. You'd be miserable, Richard told himself, if you worked until seven every evening just to impress Montacute, and wore the same dreadful dark suit every day of the year.

3

Clive looked up at him as Richard resumed his task of sorting through lists of documents, whistling under his breath.

'Mr Montacute would like to see you,' said Clive.

'Oh? Did he say what about?' asked Richard, a little depression settling on his heart.

'No,' replied Clive, arching his black eyebrows as he looked back down at the originating summons which he was neatly preparing, 'but I wouldn't be surprised if it was something to do with yesterday.'

'Yesterday? What about yesterday?'

Clive gave him a caustic glance. 'You know perfectly well that he isn't keen on you taking long lunches. He certainly didn't seem very pleased when he came looking for you at two o'clock.'

Richard rubbed his hands over his face. 'Oh, God,' he groaned. Not again. He was getting up to leave the room when Clive said, with quiet relish, 'He has Lady Folgate with him just now. I wouldn't add to it by disturbing them.'

'Thanks,' said Richard. 'Thanks a lot.' He sat down again, wishing that the two pints he had had with Derek in the Princess of Wales in Holborn hadn't turned into three, as they always did.

Montacute spent far longer with Lady Folgate than he deemed strictly necessary, but he succeeded in that time in inflicting several wounds upon her nervous sensibilities, and in bringing her, with infinite courtesy, to an unhappy awareness of the smallness of the bequests which she had resolved to add by codicil to her will. She and Sir Norton varied their wills often. To mete out fragmentary pecuniary rewards to friends and relatives and charitable bodies gave them great pleasure.

Montacute managed to deal with Lady Folgate's dispositions with such belittling dismissiveness that she felt quite cowed by the end of their interview. Montacute conducted matters, as ever, with the blandest of smiles and the coolest of voices, his heavy courtesy almost – but not quite – disguising his impatience at her testamentary fussings. From having entered his room with a happy sense of the importance of her

4

business, Lady Folgate left it with an apology for having taken up so much of Mr Montacute's valuable time. He smiled, his large, waxy face a mask of benevolence, and murmured, 'Not at all. Your business is always a pleasure to attend to. Please give my very kindest regards to Sir Norton,' as he ushered her out.

Richard heard Montacute's voice as he showed Lady Folgate out, and steeled himself for his coming interview. He let a few minutes elapse, and then got up and left the room without a word. Clive's gaze followed him, almost happily.

Montacute, thought Richard, as he entered Montacute's splendid new domain, was going to be infinitely worse as a senior partner than he had been before. He gazed at the top of Montacute's head, at his thick, rather greasy hair combed carefully back from his pale forehead, waiting for him to lift his eyes from his work. At last Montacute looked up. He stared coldly at Richard.

'Clive said that you wanted to see me,' said Richard, with an attempt at a cheerful smile.

'Yes,' said Montacute, capping his fountain pen and clasping his hands on the desk before him. 'I understand that you came back from lunch at a quarter past two yesterday.'

'Well, yes – I'm very sorry, but I went to meet an old friend and I rather lost track of time. I didn't think that ten or fifteen minutes would matter too much.' He smiled again. 'Sorry.'

'I had two affidavits which required to be filed urgently,' said Montacute, 'and I expected to find you at your desk at two.'

'Wasn't the West clerk—?' began Richard.

'The West clerk,' interrupted Montacute icily, 'was already out on business.'

'Oh,' said Richard. This was a bit of a fuss about nothing, he thought. Something of this must have betrayed itself in the tone of Richard's voice, for Montacute continued.

'It is much more than merely "oh", Richard. Your constant habit of taking longer lunch hours than anyone else is indicative of a distinctly obreptitious tendency.' Richard wasn't sure what this meant, but he didn't like the sound of it. 'I have spoken to you before about letting your somewhat—'

5

He paused. '—casual lifestyle interfere with your work here. If you wish to succeed, we expect a conspicuous amount of diligence, and a demeanour consistent with the gravity of the business which this firm conducts. You would do well to follow Clive's example.'

'I can't go around being as gloomy as Clive, if that's what you mean,' replied Richard lightly, wishing that the lecture would end.

'Clive is at least punctual and to be found at his desk at the proper hours – and beyond, I may say,' said Montacute. 'I am referring to a facetious attitude which you seem to display towards your work. I sometimes wonder if your general behaviour is all that we might expect of an assistant solicitor with De Vaut, Montacute and Strange. Please think seriously about what I have said.' He waved Richard out.

Montacute's sense of greatness expanded as the day progressed. Important though he had been before, he was now conscious of a pre-eminence which expressed itself in an exacerbation of his coldness of manner when dealing with the firm's more menial members, and in pomposity, barely concealing self-satisfaction, when speaking to his fellow partners. Everyone hoped it wasn't going to last.

Montacute, like all people, found it difficult to don the mantle of new authority without a slight manifestation of pride and some attempt at assertiveness. The problem was magnified in Geoffrey Montacute's case, however, by the fact that he was initially unlikeable, and that he knew no other way of exerting authority over others than by reminding them at all times of his power. He had been so long accustomed to being disliked that it was a factor in people's response which did not even weigh with him.

At five o'clock, however, his serenity received something of a slight shock. Harold Strange came to his room, a copy of the day's *Times* in his hand. He looked tentatively at Montacute and passed a hand over his grey head.

'I don't know if you already know, Geoffrey, but I've just read it, wondered if you'd seen it. I thought you ought to know . . .'

'Know what?' enquired Montacute with impatience; he

6

found his partner's inability to get straight to the point rather tiresome.

'I think he's your cousin, isn't he?' said Harold, folding the paper open at a page and laying it before Montacute. 'Alexander Laing, the artist. He died in Italy at the weekend.'

'Good God,' said Montacute, picking up the paper. 'Alexander. He was only forty-five.' He murmured aloud as he read the article. ' "*Alexander Laing . . . well-known artist . . . works form part of major contemporary collections . . .*" It says he died of viral hepatitis,' remarked Montacute, glancing up at Harold, who gave a sympathetic wince. Montacute looked back to the paper. ' "*Divorced from his wife, Marion, who still resides in England with their two children . . . estate understood to be worth a considerable fortune . . .*" ' He leaned back. 'We have his will here,' he said. 'I drew it up.' He tapped his fingers on the arm of his chair. 'Do you mind if I keep this?' he asked Harold.

'By all means,' replied Harold, glancing at his watch. 'Only sorry to bring you such bad news.'

When Harold had gone, Montacute sat staring at his desk for a few minutes. Alexander. He had not seen him in over twelve years, not since he was divorced from – what was his wife's name? He glanced at the paper again. Marion. He had been at their wedding, he recalled, but he could remember nothing about her.

He rose, took a key from his drawer, and went downstairs into the general office where the locked filing cabinets containing clients' wills stood. He said goodnight to Mr Dibdin, the office manager, who was just leaving, and unlocked the drawer marked '*H to N*'. He found Alexander Laing's will, together with an envelope which he had sent from Italy some years ago, and took them back to his room.

He read the will carefully to remind himself of its contents, for it was twelve years since he had drafted it. He and Oliver Pocock, Alexander's agent, were named as trustees (he would have to ring Oliver), together with Marion, Alexander's ex-wife. He perused the contents again – he doubted if they would please Marion Laing, though that largely depended on her expectations. He would have to get in touch with her tomorrow. He supposed she had already heard.

7

He opened the accompanying envelope and read the contents of the document it contained. No surprises there – merely the disposition of his Italian property, with a few extra bequests. Montacute folded up the documents and placed them carefully in his desk drawer, which he then locked. He sat for a few moments. He felt no grief as he thought of his cousin, whom he had once so envied and detested. Fate had seemed to shower Alexander with every gift that Montacute had been denied; love, popularity and easy success. He remembered when Alexander had first come up to Oxford, when he, Montacute, had been in his second year at Balliol. Good-looking, talented, charming, Alexander had swum effortlessly into the smart set, the one that always seemed to have so much fun, filled with young men who were always laughing and having drinks parties in their rooms, attended by pretty girls with clear, debutante voices and endless fresh linen, silk and time at their disposal. It had always been either summer for them, sunny and gay, or exciting winter, when they would dash through their work to hold witty, drunken conclaves in their softly lit rooms, which Montacute could glimpse across the quadrangle as he sat at his lonely toil.

And here, thought Montacute with grim satisfaction, was Alexander's end. In the comfort of his cold heart, Montacute read to himself the little lesson, that such a dissolute and indolent life must necessarily lead to an early and unhappy demise. He put his large white hands together and pressed the tips of his fingers to his lips, and sighed.

Seven o'clock found Montacute still at his desk. Others assumed that he stayed late through pressure of work, but the truth was that Montacute worked on, or else spun out an hour or two at his club, to put off for as long as possible the necessity of going home. Yet home was always there, waiting.

He heard the cleaners beginning to move around with their buckets and plastic sacks, and then the sound of Clive Fry's footsteps as he left the building. He, too, invariably worked late, in the hopes of impressing his senior partner with his industry. The exigent Mr Fry, thought Montacute with faint contempt, getting up from his desk, locking it carefully, and putting the papers he had been reading into his briefcase. He went over to the coatstand and put on his overcoat, folded his scarf carefully round his long, white throat and tucked it in, fished his gloves from his pocket, and stood for a moment, surveying his new room. Then he picked up his briefcase, switched off the light, and left. Two of the cleaners in the hallway murmured goodnight to him, and he bestowed on them a dignified nod and went downstairs and out into the chilly air of Lincoln's Inn. It would have astonished him to know that the cleaners felt a little sorry for him, toiling till late, lonely hours every night. He did not think of himself as one for whom others could possibly feel pity.

He strode up to Holborn, his head well up and his step brisk, a figure of importance. At the station he bought an evening paper and caught the Piccadilly Line to South Kensington, and thence to Richmond.

He sat throughout his journey, browsing through the paper, magnificently oblivious of those around him, the noisy youths, the tired women, the shabby, middle-aged men. They were mere irrelevancies to Montacute.

But when the train reached his stop, and Montacute folded up his paper and alighted, his step became less brisk and his posture less erect. When he turned into Gourock Avenue his shoulders drooped perceptibly, and when he pushed open the wrought-iron gate of number twenty-seven, 'Innisfree', it was with a heavy and reluctant hand. The gloom and littleness of south-west London suburbia seemed to have settled upon him, the dignified persona of Montacute, senior partner and a name at Lloyd's, discarded somewhere between Kew Gardens and Richmond.

Montacute's home – his home for forty-seven years – was a large, detached house in a long avenue of similar houses, built somewhere around the turn of the century. There were four large rooms on the ground floor, two on either side of the hallway, and a kitchen at the back. The rooms on the right-hand side of the hall had served as waiting room and surgery for his father's medical practice, and had stood cold and empty and unused since his father's death thirty-nine years ago. It was from one of these rooms that Montacute had taken the desk that now graced his room in Lincoln's Inn.

On the floor above were four large bedrooms, but only two of them were used, by Montacute and his mother. The others stood empty, and their windows stared blankly down at him as he made his way up the path to the front door. The garden was a gloomy tangle of depressing evergreens. He never looked at the garden; he hated it, as he hated the house. He should have left years ago, before his mother had become too old to live on her own. Now, he thought – as he thought every evening of his life – he would never be able to leave.

He let himself into the dark hallway, silent except for the dull ticking of a grandfather clock. He took off his overcoat and hung it, together with his scarf, on the hall stand. He hesitated for a moment, wondering whether to go upstairs first. Then a door opened at the end of the passageway and his mother appeared, framed in the light from the doorway. She was an imposing figure, tall and broadly built like her son. She was, however, heavy with age, and bore her bulk painfully, moving slowly from the lighted doorway, her legs bandaged, her swollen feet spilling puffily over the edges of her slippers.

Montacute walked towards her and kissed her, as he always did, on her forehead. She surveyed her son with a cold glance.

'Late.' She shuffled past him towards the sitting room. 'Late every night. But, of course, you would rather be working than be here with me.'

This was a truth stated so often, and at just such an hour, that Montacute said nothing. He followed her into the room, which was lit only by a small lamp standing on a table next to his mother's armchair, and tried to dispel something of her gloom.

'Well, mother, I moved into my new office today.' He rubbed his hands and raised and lowered himself on his heels, as though trying to coax a child into cheerfulness. She looked at him stonily, pain working in her eyes. 'Father's old desk looks very handsome.' He lifted his chin slightly as he thought of his spacious new office. 'Very handsome.'

'You should have left that desk where it was,' his mother replied. 'There was no need to move such a fine piece of furniture. Heaven knows what damage will come to it in that place you work in.' She lowered herself slowly into her armchair. Undaunted, Montacute began to tell her something of his day's doings, but she interrupted him, saying, 'Put on the radio, please. There is a concert I should like to listen to.'

Her son fell silent, and went obediently to the old-fashioned radiogram that stood next to the fireplace. The grate was cold, but on the broad hearth stood an electric bar fire with a plastic shell of imitation coals, black and red. A little fan revolved in a slow and endless flicker beneath this, in some feeble simulation of firelight. Montacute had once suggested that they should put central heating in the house, but his mother had simply left the room at the suggestion, and nothing more had been said on the subject. He was used to cold rooms, after forty-seven years.

He switched on the radio; no need to tune it, for it was always set at the Third Programme, as his mother still called it. The sounds of Beethoven's *Sonata in D* filled the room, the mournful tones of the cello quavering in the dimly lit air. Montacute thought of his club. He had no real friends there, merely a few acquaintances, but at least there was movement and conversation, occasional laughter and an atmosphere that was not as cold as death.

'Sherry, mother?' He moved to the sideboard and took out a bottle of Harvey's Bristol Cream. She said nothing, but her eyes followed his movements brightly and hungrily. This, he knew, was the indulgence that she craved. No matter how late he was, she would never pour out a drink for herself. She would wait for him, and then accept it grudgingly, indifferently, concealing her greed and pleasure. He handed her the glass of sherry and watched as she raised it to her lips. They were thin, unsmiling lips, set in a hard line, and the upper one was shadowed by dark hairs. He noticed that her hand trembled slightly these days. She took a sip, and a few drops spilled unheeded on to her chin; one or two fell on to the heavy fobs and pearls that hung around her thick neck and on the bolster of her bosom. He turned away and poured himself a glass of whisky.

Then he remembered the piece of news he had to tell her. The prospect of gaining her attention, if not her approval, brightened him as it had done as a child, when he had been

11

seeking, craving some way into her affection. There was, he had since discovered, no affection and no way in. But still, as though from a reflex, he felt impelled to try.

'I had some news today,' he said with grave importance. 'Alexander has died.' He had the satisfaction of seeing her glance sharply towards him. She waited; she would not, he knew, pursue the matter, but she was hungry for details. He must feed them to her. 'The newspaper said it was viral hepatitis. It was in Italy.'

'Italy,' muttered Mrs Montacute, transferring her morose gaze to the electric fire. 'Italy,' she repeated with contempt. 'What a fool that boy was. As big a fool as his mother.' Alice Montacute had taken satisfaction in outliving her younger sister, Alexander's mother, and now she gave a faint smile of triumph at having outlived her nephew.

'It will be a considerable estate, I imagine,' said Geoffrey His mother's glass was already empty, standing by the table lamp. He picked it up and refilled it, setting it down by his mother's elbow. She said nothing. 'I drafted his will, and am one of the trustees. I shall contact his ex-wife tomorrow to discuss it with her. The children are the sole beneficiaries, as I recall.' He tried, as he so often tried, to impress her with some sense of the importance of his work. But in the chill, dead atmosphere of this house, and in her presence, the attempt failed. She leaned her head back and closed her eyes, as though wearied by him. She was in pain, he knew, as she was much of the time. But instead of pity he felt resentment; it was as though she used her pain as a weapon against him, like a child more favoured than he was, more worthy of her attention. She used it to dismiss him, too, to put him at a remove from her when he tried to come too near.

He stood silent for a moment. Then he put down his whisky glass. 'I'm just going up to change,' he said, as though she cared.

As he mounted the staircase he slid off his jacket and slung it over his arm, and unbuttoned his waistcoat. He went into his bedroom, switched on the light, and hung both jacket and waistcoat carefully in the large mahogany wardrobe. He put on a bottle-green cardigan with leather buttons. Then he sat

12

down on the edge of his bed and unlaced his black shoes, took them off, and put on his carpet slippers. He thought, as he did all these things, about his mother. He wished, almost desperately these days, that she would betray some signs of feebleness, some grotesque manifestation of incipient senility, some gathering illness greater than the arthritis which racked her joints. A nursing home, he thought. His mother reduced, demeaned, helpess and dependent. Somewhere where she could vent her unpleasantness on others, and leave him free of her oppressive, tyrannical personality. Perhaps that time was not far away. She could not manage alone. Even now they had to have a home help who came every day and cleaned and shopped and made his mother her mid-day meal.

He sat there on the edge of his bed in his cardigan and slippers, and sighed. He had long since ceased to look for any love from her; even as a small boy he had learned that lesson. But there must be something beyond this. He tried to imagine what he would do if she was not with him any more, if he were free to live where he pleased, to go where he chose. It was a blank. He was middle-aged; the possibilities had passed him by long ago. He could imagine nothing other than this.

He made his way downstairs and into the sitting room, where his mother still sat with her eyes closed. Her sherry glass was three-quarters full. He knew that she had finished it and refilled it, secretly, while he was upstairs, as she did every evening. He did not know why she did this, instead of simply asking him for another drink. He wondered what it cost her to lever herself with frustrating slowness from her chair and make her way to the sideboard, slyly extract the bottle, and pour with trembling urgency, listening for his step on the stair. Maybe, if she would acknowledge her little weakness and let him indulge it, they could like each other better. Instead, she kept up her pretence, just as she kept up her mask of cold indifference. Perhaps it gave her excitement, pleasure, he thought, this greedy little secret deed.

'Shall I make us some supper?' he asked. 'I could make an omelette, with a little ham, perhaps?'

She merely lifted her chin slightly in distaste, keeping her eyes closed. 'You know I don't care for the way you make omelettes,' she replied. 'You always make them too runny.'

'Would you care for something else?' His voice was heavy and cold, even though he intended to coax, to propitiate; he knew, and had learned, no other way of speaking.

'Thank you, no.' She shook her head. 'I had some soup earlier.' She paused. 'When it was obvious that you were going to be late.'

He left the room and went through to the chilly kitchen. It was old-fashioned and gloomy, with no concessions to modernity beyond a Hoover washing machine and a refrigerator. A wooden rack and pulley hung above the kitchen table, with some clothes drying on it. Occasionally Montacute would look round at the shabby, cream-coloured walls and cupboards and think of painting them, but somehow he could never summon up the energy or enthusiasm when the weekend came around.

He took an apron from the hook behind the door. It was of faded cotton with blue flowers on it, and his mother had had it since he was a child. The familiar sight of it, however, did not touch him with sentimental pleasure. Sentiment and pleasure were not bonds between himself and his mother. He put the apron over his head and pulled it down, tying it somewhere between his armpits and his waist. Then he took some eggs from the fridge, some ham, and a packet of butter, and set about making his omelette.

If someone had described to Richard Ranscombe (who at that moment was making his way cheerfully to a pub in Herne Hill with his flatmate) the picture of his senior partner standing in his slippers and cardigan and blue-flowered apron, whisking eggs, he might have laughed. But if he could have been transported to that dreary kitchen in that house in Richmond, and had seen for himself the existence of its two inhabitants, it is doubtful whether he would even have smiled.

Chapter two

Paul Laing was sitting patiently in the empty hallway of his school, waiting for his mother to come and fetch him. He was a slender boy, with limp, flaxen hair and a gentle, somewhat startled manner, as though recently woken from a dream. He sat, angular and unkempt, gazing at the honours board opposite, and wondering why having a father die meant going home early, before term had ended. He supposed he could see why. He listened to the sound of boys and girls rehearsing carols in the hall for the school carol concert and wished vaguely that he were in there with them. Not that he did not want to see his mother – it was just that she could be rather unbearable at times like this.

Funny, really, how sometimes you felt fairly grown up, and then, at other times, not very different from when you were a lot younger. That was what sixteen was like. This was one of the times – feeling grown up. Or at any rate, finding that the news of his father's death did not make him cry. Not that he wasn't sad he was. Although because he only ever saw him once a year during the summer holidays, it was difficult for it to feel real, somehow. For Paul, the event existed chiefly in terms of its implications for his own future. No more holidays at the villa in Tuscany. He had enjoyed those, on and off, though it had largely depended on who was staying there at the time; that had seemed to matter more the older he got. There had, for instance, been that awful time two years ago when the woman with the red hair had been living with his father. She laughed too much, she fondled his father in public in the most awful way, she got drunk and she got his father drunk as well. Oliver Pocock, who was often there in the summer as well, hadn't liked her either.

But then, there had been other, really brilliant times, when he and his father had gone off with their paints and a basket full of chicken and bread and wine, and just stayed there all day, till the sky grew lilac at the edges and the sun began to dip behind the hills. Or evenings when they had all stayed up late, eating outside under the trellis of vines, the night air warm and fragrant and full of moths and the sound of talk and laughter. Those had been the best times. Helena, he thought, had liked it at the villa, too, though she seemed to prefer it when there were lots of people around. He had liked it when it was quieter, just them and his father and maybe Oliver. One thing both he and Helena had agreed – it was a relief to be somewhere without their mother.

All that would be gone, he told himself, looking down at the dusty toes of his shoes and trying, without success, to recall how his father had looked the last time he had seen him. Had he looked ill? He had always been thin, skinny really, and he drank an incredible amount, but Paul hadn't thought he was ill.

As he sat, trying to comprehend the reality of his father's non-existence, the door opened, and he glanced up to see his mother. She was wearing black, he noticed – whose benefit was that for? he wondered – and a look of pain crossed her face as she caught sight of him and went to embrace him. The expression, he knew, was for him.

'Darling,' she murmured, then stepped back to study his face sorrowfully. She was a small woman in her late thirties with hair as blonde as her son's, pulled back from her face in a black velvet Alice band. There was something girlish and almost old-fashioned about her; she had a pretty face that had once been beautiful but was now slightly plump, cornflower blue eyes, a small, full mouth, and a faintly restless manner.

'It's very sad, isn't it?' she murmured, still examining him with a look of pity and affected sorrow. He felt annoyed; she couldn't care less about him, he thought. She's probably glad.

'It was a bit of a shock,' he said, nodding, pushing his hair back with his hand and looking away from her gaze, determined to behave in an entirely adult fashion. 'Poor old Dad,' he muttered. For some reason, saying the word 'Dad' brought tears to his eyes for the first time. He couldn't help them, tried to stop them, especially in front of her. And oh, God, there was the headmaster's door opening. He turned away, brushed his sleeve hard across his eyes and tilted his head back, willing the tears to slip back. He felt his nose running and rummaged in his pocket for a handkerchief as he heard Mr Derwent greet his mother. Couldn't find one. He wiped his nose with the back of his hand and then turned round, blinking quickly.

He followed his mother as Mr Derwent ushered them into his study, articulating grave noises of sympathy. Paul stood there, looking at the walls and then the carpet, as his mother refused, with thanks, the offer of tea, and accepted, charmingly, Mr Derwent's condolences. He watched, with some admiration and a little contempt, the quiet artifice of restrained grief that his mother displayed. You'd think they'd been happily married for the last ten years, he thought, feeling a little happier to have had such a cynical thought.

He watched as his mother talked and Mr Derwent listened, murmuring and nodding, his eyebrows set at the correct compassionate slant. What an act, thought Paul, feeling in one of his more adult moods, grateful for the sense of superiority that allowed him to forget his brief tears in the hallway.

At last it was over and they could leave. Paul's heart felt quite light as he watched his trunk being put into the taxi; he wanted to be home, wanted to see Helena.

'When's Helena coming home?' he asked his mother, as they climbed into the taxi. Marion Laing's features were still set in their polite expression of farewell as he spoke, but as she leaned back in her seat and the taxi throbbed into life, her face relaxed and she closed her eyes.

'What?' She opened them again and glanced at her son. 'Oh, she's already at home. She came back this morning.'

She said nothing more to Paul, but tilted her head back and closed her eyes again as though exhausted. It was not in Marion's nature to extend greater sympathy to her son than she had already shown; she left him to his own feelings. The loss was far greater to him than to her, but she knew nothing of whatever relationship Paul and his father had had over the past few years. Besides, she had preoccupations of her own, preoccupations which had haunted her ever since she had

17

heard, disbelievingly, of Alexander's death. Eyes closed, she tried to compose her thoughts, to ignore the worries that nagged at her, but the small band of fear which had tightened round her heart when she first heard the news was there still. She opened her eyes impatiently and stared unseeingly out of the taxi window. Then she examined her small, white fingernails, one by one, revolving again the same thoughts in her head.

If she had known he was likely to die . . . How could she possibly have known? How typically selfish and stupid, to drink himself to death. If she had known, she would have taken a lump sum settlement after the divorce, instead of an income. That bloody lawyer. But what good would it have done? She picked savagely at a shred of skin under a cuticle. Everyone had said how lucky she had been to get the enormous income from him that she had. It had never occurred to her that it would dry up so soon. But now it had. He was dead, and everything was at an end. What was she to live on now? There would be plenty of money under his will, that much she was certain of. But she was equally certain that she would receive little or none of it. Well, she would know tomorrow when that lawyer cousin of Alexander's called to see them. At least then she would know the true extent of her plight, instead of fighting this constant anxiety of knowing nothing. She abandoned the examination of her fingernails and fished in her bag for a cigarette.

When they reached the station, they had to wait for twenty minutes for their train, and they sat in the chilly waiting room, each with their own thoughts, exchanging only occasional remarks. Marion would direct a small, warm smile at Paul from time to time, but her thoughts were clearly elsewhere. Paul gazed at his mother as she smoked and cogitated; her face looked cold and expressionless. Maybe, he thought, she was a bit sad about Dad dying. She'd said some fairly nasty things about him, but they had been married once, after all. It had to count for something, otherwise he and Helena wouldn't exist. He took his copy of *The Life of Dürer* from his pocket and began to read.

*

Helena was watching at the window of one of Roffey's two large drawing rooms when the taxi containing Paul and her mother turned in through the gates of the driveway. She was slender like Paul, taller than her mother, and her hair, though blonde, was of a darker, honey colour, hanging straight to her shoulders and cut in a fringe above her eyes. She had her father's eyes, brown and faintly oriental in shape, and her face, like Paul's, was square and delicately featured. It already had a strength and charm that did not exist in her mother's face, and the knowledge of this would have flattered her. She imagined, like many seventeen-year-olds, that she loathed her mother, although the reality was based more on faint mutual dislike and misunderstanding.

She had already expended all of her wild grief at the news of her father's death on the shoulder of her closest school-friend, Clarissa, and now it was the merest trickle. Unlike Paul, she would not harbour a quiet misery for months. She had spent one long, wakeful night piecing together every single recollection that she had of her father and their fragmented relationship, sobbing in anguish over each one, but today was a new day, and tomorrow another one. Already her mother's mention of her father's will and the visit of Geoffrey Montacute had stirred a small, excited curiosity within her.

Helena did not wish to be seen waiting for their arrival, and so she turned and went back through the house and into the kitchen, where she had been drinking tea and reading the *Radio Times*. She sat down and began flicking through the pages nonchalantly, but when her brother appeared she could not resist rising, grinning broadly, and flinging her arms around him; their pleasure at seeing one another quite eclipsed the thought of their father's death. Paul noticed that Helena barely greeted her mother, but then, the two of them had been arguing for the last two years – forever, it seemed – so that was no great surprise.

'Would you ask Anna to bring tea into the sitting room, please, Helena?' called her mother from the hallway.

'Not here,' called back Helena indistinctly, cramming a piece of cake into her mouth and picking up her own mug of tea from the kitchen table. Her mother appeared in the kitchen doorway, her face weary and irritable. 'Where is she?'

'Gone into Hindhead for some stuff,' replied Helena.

'What "stuff"?' asked Marion with a frown.

'I don't know. Shopping stuff. She says we haven't got nearly enough to last us over Christmas.'

'Oh.' Christmas, thought Marion. The cocktail parties, the dinner parties, the people she had invited over for Boxing Day lunch . . . How was she going to get through it all with this money trouble hanging over her? She sighed.

'Well, perhaps you could make me some tea then, darling,' she murmured to Helena. 'And bring it into the sitting room. I'm going in there to lie down. I'm exhausted.'

Her daughter whirled obediently round on a bare heel, her hair flying out, and went to fetch the teapot.

Montacute arrived the following day. He drove down, and Helena and Paul watched him from the window as he climbed out of the car, then bent his long body back in to draw his briefcase out from the back seat. He closed the door and stood for a moment, looking up at the handsome exterior of the house, unaware of the intent scrutiny of Alexander's children.

'I don't think much of his car,' remarked Helena. 'What's his name again?' she asked her brother, as Montacute made his way to the front door.

'Mr Montacute,' replied Paul.

'Funny name,' said Helena, picking an apple out of the fruit bowl and sinking her teeth into it. 'Funny-looking bloke,' she added, thinking how extraordinarily old-fashioned he looked, with his dark three-piece suit and his pale, haughty face – quite handsome, but in entirely the wrong sort of way.

Paul went to answer the door, while Helena ran up the stairs two at a time to tell her mother that he was here.

'The lawyer's here,' she announced, putting her head round her mother's bedroom door. Marion Laing was sitting at her dressing table. She dabbed anxiously at her face from a compact, staring into the mirror with the vacant expression that she wore when making up. Then she sat back and glanced at her daughter.

'That skirt is ridiculously short,' she said, frowning at her daughter's slender thighs. 'Go and put on something decent.'

'It's perfectly decent,' retorted Helena airily, and vanished.

With a sigh Marion got up, smoothed some imaginary wrinkles from the lap of the Ungaro dress that she had put on to reassure herself for the occasion, adjusted her face to a look of bright, charming welcome, and went downstairs to greet their guest.

Ah, I recollect you now, thought Marion, when she saw Montacute. She remembered his tall, solemn figure and his bland, supercilious gaze from the wedding. He had been an usher. As she smiled and shook hands with him, it struck her that he seemed hardly to have changed in eighteen years. He had looked pompous and ingratiating then, and he seemed even more so now. The man must have been born middle-aged.

She talked politely to him in a low voice as she led him through to the drawing room, with just the correct amount of restrained sorrow that she felt an ex-widow, or whatever she was, should display. Montacute appreciated the dainty formality of her remarks, and murmured courteous and dignified platitudes in response.

Marion offered him a drink, which he accepted, and Helena, who was swinging an idle leg beside the sideboard, watching Montacute with fascination, eagerly pre-empted her mother and mixed together a sloppy whisky and soda for their guest beneath her mother's frowning eye. She loved mixing drinks.

She handed the drink to Montacute, who thanked her and took a few sips. It was horribly weak. He saw Marion Laing take a cigarette from a box on the piano and light it, and he sensed that small talk was at an end.

'Well,' he said, with his professional smile, setting his drink down on a side table, 'shall we get down to business?' He sat down on a sofa, hitched the knees of his trousers slightly, revealing to Helena's fascinated gaze a small expanse of white shin, and drew his briefcase on to his knees. He drew out the copy of the will and the brown envelope, and cleared his throat.

'Perhaps I should explain first of all,' said Montacute, 'that there is, together with the will, a codicil which he – which Alexander executed two years ago.'

'A codicil?' asked Marion, seating herself opposite the lawyer. Maybe Alexander's attitude towards her had softened during the last few years; perhaps she had some small reason to hope . . .?

'It deals with his Italian estate – the villa in Tuscany, and so forth,' said Montacute with his cold smile. 'The will itself remains unaffected.' Marion blew out a plume of smoke and sat back, feeling depressed.

' "This is the last will and testament of me, Alexander Lyall Laing, of Roffey House, Kidham, Surrey. I hereby revoke all other wills and codicils heretofore made by me and declare this only to be my will," ' intoned Montacute. Helena listened to his serene drone; he sounded just like a minister preaching, she thought. He had the same kind of lofty, superior expression on his face. She tried to make out the sense of what Montacute was reading, but the strange language made it difficult. She understood enough, however, to be aware that most of what their father had was left to her and Paul, and certainly not to their mother. Paul didn't listen at all. He stood by the window watching a blackbird move around in the delicate tracery of the branches of the mulberry tree against the white winter sky, wondering what was for lunch.

Marion listened intently to Montacute's even tones, never moving except to tap the ash from her cigarette into the little brass ashtray at her elbow. She gathered certain things. She gathered that the children inherited everything – which she had expected – and that her own position, thankfully, did not seem as bad as she had expected. She understood, from what Montacute had read so far, that Roffey was left to her, together with an annuity of twenty thousand pounds. Twenty thousand pounds. She had been receiving from him, since the divorce, maintenance payments for herself and the children that amounted to almost two hundred thousand pounds a year. And now she was expected to live on twenty. She stubbed out her cigarette as Montacute read on, and rose to fetch another. She sat back down again. Thank God he had left her the house. At least she would be able to raise a hefty mortgage on it. As she lit her cigarette she had almost ceased to listen to what Montacute was saying; she was feverishly calculating all the luxuries that she would have to forego, now that her income was so drastically cut. Twenty thousand. What about tax? She longed to clarify matters and question Montacute, but he had now turned to the codicil and was reading through a variety of Italian bequests with relentless clarity of diction. Then he finished, folded up the documents, and smiled.

'I'm sure you largely understand the contents,' said Montacute, 'but there may be some things which I should explain to you in layman's language.'

Marion put out her cigarette. 'Perhaps we can discuss it over lunch, Geoffrey,' she said with a smile, and rose.

Montacute rose, too, and all four trooped into the dining room, where Anna had laid the table with particular formality. Montacute gazed around him as he unfolded his napkin, admiring the proportions of the room, the delicate mouldings set against the egg-shell blue of the ceiling, the light that spilled through the long windows across the oval rosewood dining table.

'This is a charming room,' he remarked. 'Indeed, the house is quite splendid. I had often heard of it, but have never visited before now.'

'Yes, it is lovely,' murmured Marion. 'I should hate to part with it. I'm afraid, though, that I shall have to raise something of a mortgage on it, in view of the size of the annuity that Alexander has left me. It is, as you can imagine,' and she smiled ruefully, prettily, at Montacute, 'a good deal less than the sum I was receiving under the divorce settlement.'

It did not occur to Montacute, at that moment, to inform Marion that it was only through his own intervention twelve years ago that Alexander had been persuaded to leave her anything at all. His attention was taken up by what she had just said. He hesitated for a moment, the vinaigrette poised in his hand.

'Ah – well, now. This is why it is so important that the terms of Alexander's will should be explained clearly to you, so that there is no misunderstanding.'

Marion glanced at him sharply. 'Misunderstanding? I can raise a mortgage on the house, can't I, if I own it? I clearly heard you say that Alexander left Roffey to me.' A little note of panic crept into her voice as it occurred to her, for the first time, that it was extraordinary that he should do such a thing as leave Roffey to her.

Montacute dropped his eyes under her demanding gaze and smiled, with some difficulty, at his plate. 'Certainly, Roffey is left to you—' he began.

'Well, then?'

'—for life. That is, the house is yours for as long as you live. You have what we call a life interest. Thereafter, the property passes to Helena and Paul. You do not own it. You cannot mortgage it.' Paul glanced at his sister, but Helena's eyes were fastened on the lawyer as she stripped an artichoke leaf of its flesh with her white, even little teeth.

Marion stared at Montacute. The information sank in. This was worse than she could have supposed. 'I see,' she said.

Montacute continued his exposition. 'As the will says, Paul and Helena are the sole beneficiaries. All of their father's estate is left on trust for them until they are twenty-four. You, Oliver Pocock and myself are the trustees.'

Trustees? She had missed that. 'I?' said Marion in some surprise.

'As you are the children's mother, I advised Alexander, at the time that the will was drawn up, that it would be appropriate.'

'Of course,' murmured Marion. Anna took their plates away and brought in a game pie.

'So,' said Helena, who had not taken her eyes from Montacute's face, 'when we're twenty-four, everything is divided equally between Paul and me?'

Montacute nodded, helping himself to a large piece of pie.

'And what happens to it in the meantime? All the money and stuff.' It had occurred to Helena that her twenty-fourth birthday was rather a long way away.

'In the meantime,' replied Montacute, 'the money is invested by the trustees – that is, ah, by me with advice from the appropriate quarters – to produce an income, and at the same time to maintain the value of the capital. That is the job of the trust – to maintain a balance between capital and income.' He smiled at Helena, but she did not smile back, merely continued to regard him with her large, luminous brown eyes.

'When do we get the income?' she asked. Alexander's daughter was certainly direct, thought Montacute.

'When you are of age,' replied Montacute. 'When you are eighteen.'

'Brilliant!' exclaimed Helena, with a long, wide smile. Marion looked balefully at her daughter; given her own financial straits, it did not seem to her appropriate that the child should be gloating over her own good fortune.

'Is it going to be a lot of money?' asked Helena, leaning forward with her chin on one hand.

'We have hardly yet begun to ascertain the extent of the assets which your late father owned,' replied Montacute. 'He was a – capricious person, and his affairs were not as well regulated as they might have been. I have to get in touch with his Italian lawyers to obtain certain information and documentation from them. There is, of course, the Italian villa and other items . . . Italian legal formalities can, I am afraid, take some time . . .'

'But it's going to be a lot?' insisted Helena.

Montacute sighed. 'A not inconsiderable amount, I should imagine.'

'What about Paul? What happens to his money till he's eighteen?' she pursued. Paul looked up idly, then turned his attention back to his pie.

'Paul's income will be accumulated for him until he attains his majority. In the meantime, the trust will be used to fund his education and so forth.'

Helena nodded, then gazed out of the window, entranced by the prospect of a private income. She would be going to art school after summer. She'd have a wonderful time, simply wonderful. She could buy all the clothes she wanted, and a car –oh God, she hoped she passed her driving test at Easter. She did not cast a thought in her mother's direction. To Helena, twenty thousand a year sounded like a load of money. And her mother had the house.

Paul regarded the thing with indifference. He couldn't quite see what was so important about having a lot of money. His dad hadn't seemed so wonderfully happy. But at least he'd be able to have all his father's paints and that brilliant easel from Italy.

Marion sat with a face like stone, thinking of the impossibility of life – even a life in Roffey; *especially* a life in Roffey – with just twenty thousand pounds a year. Something drastic would have to be done.

When lunch was over, Montacute thanked Marion and prepared to take his leave. He was aware from Marion's manner during luncheon that she had been badly disappointed by the contents of Alexander's will. He had guessed that this would be so. Twelve years ago, when the will had been made, twenty thousand pounds had been a good deal of money. Now, and in comparison to her probable recent income, it was not so very much.

He and Marion stood on the doorstep, discussing the funeral that was to be held when Alexander's ashes were returned to England. 'I understand Oliver Pocock is arranging the details,' said Montacute. 'He has been one of Alexander's closest friends over the years.'

'Yes,' said Marion, longing for him to go, so that she could begin to consider the fresh disaster of her financial position. There was enough money in the bank for the present, but nonetheless she felt a sense of urgency.

'Well, I shall be in touch shortly,' said Montacute, lingering on the doorstep, fastening the little buttons at the cuffs of his gloves. Marion nodded stiffly and said nothing. He hesitated, looking at her face. Montacute had little to do with women; indeed, he rarely came into contact with many, except for his mother, Miss Reed, the occasional client such as Lady Folgate, and the office typists, whom he scarcely regarded as female. But there was something about Marion Laing's troubled, pretty features that he found strangely appealing. He felt, as he looked at her blue-eyed blondeness, surprised that he had not remembered her from Alexander's wedding. In an uncharacteristic burst of disinterestedness, he added, 'Please do not hesitate to get in touch with me if you have any worries – or questions. I know that this is a difficult time.'

She looked up at him. As she stood, laden with dull anxiety, contemplating the economies that would now have to be made in her idle little life, there came the first stirrings of an idea. She looked at his bland, unctuous features and summoned her most trusting, charming smile.

'Geoffrey, you have been so kind. I'm sure that there are lots of things I shall need your help with. Thank you.'

When he had gone, she closed the door with a sigh of resignation, and her face became a little grimmer, a little older, as she fell to considering her future.

Chapter three

No one would have called Marion Laing a clever woman, but there were those who took the view that a combination of charm, good looks and a ruthless capacity for deceit produced its own special kind of intelligence. Certainly, when it came to looking after her own interests, Marion was capable of a concentration and single-minded dedication that would have done credit to someone possessed of three times her intellectual capacity.

The less charitable of her friends were of the opinion that, all things considered, she had done very well for herself. She came from unexceptional beginnings. Her father had been a dentist, her mother a housewife, and she had been brought up in the better, leafier part of Chislehurst. She had grown up in the late Sixties and early Seventies, when middle-class respectability was distinctly unfashionable, and had hankered after the bright, chic world that she saw reflected in the pages of *Vogue* and *Tatler*. When she left school at seventeen with the feeblest of academic qualifications, it seemed she would be fated to take the inevitable secretarial course and seek her fortune in that way. But, by sheer good fortune, her father had discovered that one of his patients required a receptionist in a small art gallery which he owned just off the Brompton Road. She merely had to look attractive, dress well, know where the various catalogues were kept, and pronounce the names of artists correctly and with a sufficient air of familiarity.

It had seemed, at first, like heaven to Marion. The gallery was small, but fashionable, and many of the people who patronised it were well-known and wealthy. They smiled at her when they visited, and some called her by her Christian name; they murmured sweetly at her in recognition when they attended the exclusive little parties held by the gallery to launch new exhibitions. She was able to observe them, to admire their clothes, imitate the modulations of their confident voices, to nibble at scraps of gossip and opinion that they dropped. She felt that she was, by association, part of their glamorous and deliciously exciting London world.

But as the months went by, Marion had begun to realise that she was not one of them, that without money or connections she was merely the most peripheral creature. And the work, once the novelty of her situation had worn off, had become very dull. She spent long hours, when scarcely anyone visited the gallery, gazing out of the window at the plane trees and the quiet street.

It was just at the beginning of her disenchantment that she had met Alexander. He was one of a group of young artists whose work the gallery was exhibiting, and she had met him at the inevitable opening party. Apart from his charm and rather gaunt good looks, it was the fact that he was not, unlike so many of the young artists she met, especially bohemian that attracted her – for traces of Chislehurst still clung at that time to Marion. He had a lazy, educated voice, easy good manners, and – as she discovered on the second occasion that they went out together – came from a wealthy family. He even had a private income. It had seemed essential to Marion that she should marry just such a man.

And so she had. It had not been difficult to persuade him to fall in love with her. She really had been very lovely at eighteen. Because he had met her at his first successful exhibition, and because she listened attentively when he talked about his work and seemed to enjoy the company of his artist friends, he felt that a sympathy, a shared world, existed between them. And because, after a delightfully virginal introduction to sex, she was the most ardent, imaginative creature in bed, he had thought her sensual and loving and passionate.

What Alexander had not realised, however – and, indeed, Marion herself was scarcely aware of it – was that Marion played roles, inhabited fantasies. She saw herself as a certain person, and became that person. She had seen herself as the chic, charming girl who worked in a trendy art gallery, moving

29

in fashionable circles, and had behaved thus, even though her life had been lonely and tedious. She had seen herself as the companion of the brilliant young artist, serious, intuitively bound to him, anxious for his career, intensely interested in his work and his friends – and she had become that. She had, as a side role, played the passionate young lover, panting, moaning, insatiable. That had been demanding, but she had been able to play it with a certain amount of honesty for a while. Neither she nor Alexander had yet discovered that Marion, after the initial and titillating novelty of sex had worn off, did not really like sex. That discovery had come later.

The first two years of their marriage had been quite successful. For Marion, they consisted of a series of tableaux in which she was called upon to play a succession of rather enjoyable roles, without time in between each for disillusion to set in.

There had been the role, first of all, with an engagement picture in *Country Life*, of the lovely young bride marrying into a wealthy family. Then there had been the rather more serious role of the wife of the rising young artist. This had required more stamina and an apparent interest in and knowledge of her husband's work. But as his work was beginning to make significant amounts of money, this interest had not been entirely assumed. After that, she had (twice) played the role of doting and beautiful young mother, cradling her newborn and/or playing with her toddler on the grass. The first time that she had played this particular part had been easier than the second, for by the time Paul was born Alexander had become a little disenchanted with his bride.

In fairness to Marion, it was not her fault that she did not like sex. It had not been her fault that she was bored and faintly disgusted by the familiarity of her husband's body, whose functions were too well known to her for it still to possess a great deal of erotic enchantment. It was, perhaps, her fault that she betrayed her disgust and impatience, for pride and sensuality were strong traits in her husband's nature. When, after the birth of Paul, she had indicated that she no longer wished to sleep with him (or not very frequently), he began the first of a series of affairs, conducted with some wildness and without any discretion.

Alexander's infidelity, while it fuelled the first of their major rows, was not, however, the only problem. He had discovered by then that she was not, as he had supposed, remotely interested in his work. She had begun to be hostile to his friends, preferring instead the company of the fashionable and rich ephemera with whom she now mixed. Alexander, while acknowledging that she had met most of them through him, regarded her new friends as useless, parasitic fools, and had deplored the amount of money that Marion spent on parties, clothes and extravagant holidays.

To give Marion her due, she had merely been throwing herself energetically into the next of the roles which it had seemed appropriate to her to play – that of sparkling socialite, renowned and inspired hostess, wife of the wealthy and brilliant Alexander Laing. She was hardly to be blamed.

The rows between them had become more acrimonious, distrust and distaste had grown – not even Roffey, so generous in its door-slamming distances, could contain their hostility. And so they had divorced, Marion citing (without difficulty – she could have named several different women) Alexander's then lover as the third party in her petition on the grounds of adultery.

Her role as the wronged wife had been a triumph. The divorce had been long and bitter, and with an energy fuelled by utter belief in her part, Marion had set about extracting as much as she could from Alexander. She gained custody of the children, she was awarded a settlement that gave her a very healthy income, and the court had ordered that she and the children, then babies, should remain in Roffey, the matrimonial home, to which Marion had made no contribution beyond spending her husband's money in decorating and furnishing it.

Sickened and wearied, Alexander had left England and taken himself off to Italy, and had never returned. His career had continued with undiminished brilliance, but as his mode of living had become increasingly dissolute, so the pace of his

31

work slackened. In the few years before his death he had produced only a handful of paintings. But by then his reputation was such that he might as well already have achieved the immortality of the dead.

And now Marion had her work to begin all over again.

In the days following Montacute's visit she devoted all thought to the problem of her newly reduced circumstances. She calculated with growing alarm the dreadful economies that would have to be made. Anna would have to go – but how was she to cope in a place such as Roffey without a cook and housekeeper? And what about clothes? The regular acquisition of expensive items of clothing had become habitual, and for Marion the effort of breaking it was unthinkable. The Corniche, too, would have to go, for she could not afford to run such a car – and, anyway, she would need every penny she could get from selling it. There would be an end, too, to her fashionable dinner parties and extravagant summer luncheon parties – who was to cook for them? The trips to Monaco and New York when the children were with their father in Italy – they were finished. Certainly there would be plenty of money from the trust fund to pay for holidays with the children, but it would hardly be the same. She would no longer be able to share the rental of the villa at Cape Fines with Sally and Hugh Howard in June.

The situation, she concluded, was impossible. She simply could not live on twenty thousand pounds a year. It was pitiful. Any other woman might simply have made a few careful economies and resigned herself to the abandonment of certain luxuries, but Marion's boneheaded refusal to do without any of the pleasures to which she had grown accustomed over the years supplied her with a determination to find some way out of her difficulties.

She did not think she could marry again. Apart from the fact that wealthy, eligible bachelors in their late thirties and early forties were scarce on the ground, she had learned from her marriage to Alexander and from subsequent affairs that the thing would never work. After the first burst of sexual novelty had expended itself, when the delicious shock of the new had worn off, Marion could not cope with the sight of hairy buttocks and slightly bandy male legs paddling off to the bathroom. She did not like to find dirty underpants in her laundry basket, shaving scum in the wash basin, or pubic hairs in the Floris soap. She knew herself too well and was aware that the delights of sex, for her, staled with habit. As she was not a person given to love –its requirement of generosity of spirit had always somehow eluded her – there was nothing to temper the ultimate indifference she felt for her lovers.

Besides, she was accustomed now to living alone; she was jealous of her time and her freedom. And she had no wish either to leave Roffey or to share it with another person. The house was the one thing in her life which she adored. It was a beautiful house, more beautiful, she thought, than any she had ever seen. She loved its spacious, light rooms, it high windows, its air of restfulness. She loved the french windows in the drawing room that opened on to the terrace and the steps down to the garden; the delight of opening those windows on a July morning to the scent of jasmine and the sound of summer birdsong never staled for her. She loved the large kitchen, its stone-flagged floor, the well-worn loveliness and practicality of old utensils and chopping boards and copper pans (which she herself rarely used). She loved the blue-and-white-tiled coolness of the dairy room, where the household laundry was now done, and the neat, pleasing abundance of the kitchen garden, where fruit trees trailed their limbs along old, sunny brick walls. She loved the long lawns and the bluebell woods, and the river that flowed nearby. Roffey was a paradise and she was its mistress.

For several days she thought of nothing but money – the lack of it, the acquisition of it, the spending of it. It seemed to her absurd, outrageous, that so much money should exist in trust for the children – not even Alexander, she calculated, would have been able to fritter away in Italy more than a fraction of his wealth in ten years – without some of it being made available to her. She needed money, and there it was, close at hand. Logic told her that there must be some method of producing money for herself, without any detriment to the children, from the wealth which Alexander had left behind him. But how?

The best thing, she decided, was to have a tentative meeting with Geoffrey Montacute. She had the matter of Paul's schooling to discuss with him anyhow. Something told her that help might be forthcoming from that quarter, unlikely though it might at first seem.

A week after Montacute's visit to Roffey to read the will, and two days after Alexander's funeral, Marion rang Montacute at the offices of De Vaut, Montacute & Strange, and arranged to have lunch with him in a smart new little French restaurant off Sloane Square. She needed his advice, she said, about certain matters. Montacute, who had been struck by how charming she had looked at the funeral, and who had never been invited to lunch by a woman in his life, accepted.

Marion dressed carefully for the occasion, in a quiet suit of grey linen. She put her hair up, and wore her pearls and some discreet but beautiful diamond earrings, and looked, she thought, extremely pretty and businesslike as she stepped from the taxi on to the cold pavements of Chelsea, twenty minutes late for lunch.

Geoffrey Montacute was not accustomed to lunching in smart little French restaurants, particularly ones where arrogant young waiters sped around in tight leather trousers. He thought the tables too small and close together, and found the spindly little wooden chairs most unaccommodating to his large frame. It seemed to him that every time he moved they threatened to skid his dignified bulk across the polished wooden floor. The clientele, too, were not of a type with which he was accustomed to mixing. They were young and fashionable and noisy, and he felt that they stared at him as he sat impatiently in his dark City suit, quite out of tune with his surroundings, waiting for Marion.

Thinking that the traffic from the City to Chelsea would be bad, he had left his office early. The taxi ride, however, had proved very quick and he had arrived ten minutes before the appointed time. He had now been waiting half an hour. He did not like to drink a great deal at lunchtime, and he had only just managed to spin out a gin and tonic – it was not to his liking, since it came in a long glass with a great deal of crushed ice, which surfed with chilly unpleasantness against his upper lip every time he drank. He was also beginning to get extremely hungry and was not in the best of tempers by the time Marion arrived.

As she came into the restaurant and caught sight of Montacute sitting at a small corner table, she instantly read the cold ill-temper on his face. He did not see her until she reached the table. To his surprise, she bent down and bestowed a light kiss upon his large, closely shaven cheek, murmuring an apology for being late. He was aware of some subtle, very pleasant fragrance, which intensified as she tucked herself into the seat opposite him. He relaxed only a little, still feeling ill at ease, as she gave him a sweet, intimate smile.

'Thank you so much for meeting me, Geoffrey,' she said. 'I know how busy you solicitors are. I just dread the City, you know. Can never find my way around. I have some errands to run in Chelsea and didn't think I'd get out before the rush-hour traffic if I had to go all the way to Lincoln's Inn—' She glanced up at the murmuring waiter who had materialised at their table. 'Oh – yes, a white wine and soda, please.' She looked across at Montacute, her lips parted in pretty enquiry. 'Geoffrey?'

Montacute nodded stiffly at the waiter. 'Another gin and tonic, please.' He didn't know why he had ordered a second drink; there was something disarming about Marion Laing that made him feel less decisive and composed than usual.

Marion's manner was immediately intimate, as though she and Montacute had been friends for years. This was not done from any particular design on her part; it had been her habit for so long to behave in a mildly seductive manner towards most men that it was by now second nature. She did not launch into her business straight away. Her conversation was animated and amusing, and she succeeded in making Montacute feel, after his second gin and tonic and his first glass of wine, that he was a little of both those things himself. He thought of his colleagues at their stuffy City lunches, and was suddenly aware of a sense of lightness and recklessness. It was a sensation entirely foreign to him. He found himself looking at the pretty woman opposite him with a new awareness. He enjoyed her soft little glances, her low, amused laughter at his ponderous pleasantries. If he was conscious of being subtly flattered, he did not mind.

As the waiter cleared their plates away, she turned to her business.

'One of the reasons that I wanted to talk to you, Geoffrey,' said Marion, reaching instinctively into her bag for a cigarette, and then changing her mind, 'was to ask your advice about Paul's education. You see, circumstances have changed somewhat, haven't they? I mean, before Alexander died, I was literally scratching around for school fees.' (Nothing could have been further from the truth, but Marion had never seen much point in laying out enormous amounts in school fees when, as she saw it, a perfectly decent education could be had relatively cheaply.) 'Alexander's views on schools – well, you can imagine,' she went on, with a dismissive little smile. 'They would have gone to the local comprehensive if he had had his way.'

'Would you care for some dessert?' Montacute asked her, as the waiter approached.

'No. No, thank you.' Marion shook her head.

'Just two coffees, please,' Montacute said with some constraint to the bulging leather crotch just below his eye level.

'I really feel that, with all the trust money that's going to be available,' continued Marion, 'it might be more useful to Paul if he went to – a better sort of school.'

'One of the large public schools, you mean?' replied Montacute, putting his elbows on the table and placing the tips of his long white fingers together. He cast his mind back to Paul as he was when he had met him at Roffey and at the funeral; a rather quiet, dreamy sort, he recalled.

'Well, yes,' said Marion, 'I suppose so.' Marion had always sought to have her children reflect well upon herself, though not at significant expense, but hesitated to lay this little snobbery bare. 'I mean,' she continued, 'the school he is at present is fairly good, in its way. They certainly let him concentrate a good deal on his art, which is very important to him. It's a very relaxed sort of school, not academically very demanding . . . But it really is rather *minor*, you know . . .' She looked at him ruefully. 'The trouble is, I know nothing

36

about boys' schools. I just know the names – Eton, Winchester, that kind of thing.'

Montacute said nothing for a moment, recalling his own school days. If anything in his recollection troubled him, his bland countenance did not betray it. He smiled his magisterial smile at Marion.

'As a trustee, I should be failing in my duty if I did not seek to assist you in securing the best possible education for Paul. One must, of course, be careful in the choice of school. But I cannot but believe that time spent at one of the major public schools could be anything but a distinct advantage to any young man. Paul is – how old?'

'Sixteen – seventeen next June,' replied Marion.

Montacute nodded. 'There are,' he went on, 'those who speak disparagingly about "the old-boy network"—' He picked out the words with heavy archness. '—and there are those who try to pretend that such a thing does not exist. But, of course, such a thing does exist, and always will. In my own profession, for example, its importance can be incalculable. Not indispensable, naturally – but extremely valuable.'

The product of Bromley Girls' High School murmured that she thought that Paul's future probably lay in art rather than law, and wondered, privately, if this was going to be a very long lecture on the advantages of the public school system.

'Quite,' agreed Montacute with a certain condescension, 'but whatever his profession, I can guarantee that such connections will not be without their usefulness.'

Marion nodded, working her way slowly round this double negative and wishing that he wouldn't use quite so many of them.

'So,' resumed Montacute, 'we must consider the choice of school carefully. Just a little, thank you,' he said to the waiter, who had advanced upon them with the coffee pot. 'Eton?' He arched his heavy eyebrows as he considered his own proposition. 'On the whole, I should be inclined to think not, from what you say of Paul. A little rigorous academically, I feel.'

'I shall be guided by you, of course,' said Marion, 'but I'd always thought it was the best. Isn't it?' She rather liked the sound of saying that she had a son at Eton.

'Oh, yes, of course. There are those who believe so,' replied Montacute, who was an Old Carthusian. 'Certainly it is the most well-known. But, you know, I don't quite see Paul as a cabinet minister, or a leading light in the diplomatic corps, do you?' He enjoyed dealing with Marion. It brought out a lightness of touch in him, he thought, which would quite have startled his mother, who was always accusing him of being slow and dull.

Marion said she supposed not. Get to the point, she thought.

'I should have thought that somewhere like—' Montacute paused reflectively. '—Ampersand, say. That might suit him very well. The headmaster is a client of mine.' Montacute thought this rather a clever choice, since it was a school of sufficient cachet to satisfy the small, snobbish appetite that he detected in Marion. 'And I know quite a few Old Ampersonions personally,' he added. 'It has an excellent reputation. I'm sure it's the kind of school which would take care to nurture his artistic talents. It's rather more . . .' He searched for the word. '. . . more *spiritual* than, say, Harrow or Winchester. Not quite so aggressive.'

Marion decided she quite liked the sound of Ampersand; it was definitely top-notch. She put on her trusting, childlike face as she looked up at Montacute.

'I'm sure that you know far more about it than I do. At least it's a name that I know.' She leaned forward and looked down as she stirred her coffee.

'I suggest that you speak to Paul about it,' said Montacute, 'and then perhaps visit the school with him. I could ring Dr Whatley personally, if you wish, and explain the circum- stances. I'm sure there would be no problem about his starting in the middle of the school year.' He smiled at Marion. Her face was quite close to his. What a charming mouth she had. He didn't normally find himself thinking of women of his acquaintance in this way. It was a mildly stirring novelty. He sat back and contemplated her.

'That sounds a very good plan,' said Marion. 'Thank you so much for helping. I know nothing about these things.'

She noticed that he was looking at her in a particular way.

Then he said, 'Now, you said that Paul was *one* of the things you wanted to talk about. What was the other?' He tried to sound unhurried, but a discreet glance at his watch as he sat back told him that it was nearly three, and he had a client at a quarter to four. He smiled encouragingly, aware that he had smiled much more in the past two hours than was customary for him. There was a faint ache in his cheek muscles.

'Oh, I don't know if it's anything I should be troubling you with . . .' And she hesitated, giving him a sad little smile. He looked at her in a kindly fashion, feeling expansive and avuncular. Her slightness, her blondeness, her charming troubled face, made him feel quite masterful. The client could wait for fifteen minutes or so.

'My dear Marion—' He had not felt quite comfortable using her Christian name before, despite the fact that she lavished 'Geoffries' upon him at every opportunity, but now he rather enjoyed the intimacy of the sensation. '—you know that I am only too happy to help you, whatever the problem might be.'

She looked up at him, her eyes very blue and large.

'The fact is, as I'm sure you know, the annuity which Alexander has left me – well, it's rather less than the money I was receiving under the divorce settlement.' Montacute nodded and took a sip of his coffee. In his role as a lawyer now, he would say nothing until she had said everything, and then not until she had put her problem directly to him; this was not calculation, merely habit. Marion found it a trifle disconcerting, used as she was to conversational triggers and signals. 'Well,' she went on, 'I know that the annuity is produced through investments.' Again Montacute merely nodded, not looking at her. 'I wondered, you know, what those investments might be. I mean, could they be made to produce more?'

This was a question, and he frowned at it, then looked up. 'Well, yes,' he replied. 'Strictly speaking, yes, they could.' Marion's heart rose slightly. 'However,' he went on, and at his tone her heart sank again, 'even if the investments used to produce your annuity were invested to greater effect, you would still only be entitled to the sum of twenty thousand pounds.'

'I see,' she said. She bit her lip and glanced shyly at him. 'I'm so bad about money, you see, and it's rather a thing, when one is used to it, to have one's income cut by so much. There's Roffey, you see. Its upkeep is far more than I can afford on so small an income.'

'Roffey,' mused Montacute. 'It is yours for life. You could always let it, if you wished, and increase your income that way. And at the same time, you would be able to find somewhere – ah – more manageable to live.'

Marion's face turned to stone. 'Leave Roffey?' she said incredulously. To do that would be to abandon everything lovely and worthwhile in her life. Where else could she go that would not seem shabby and second-rate by comparison, that would not inspire pity in her friends and imply losses far greater than she wished to acknowledge to the world? 'That is out of the question.' There was a short, cold silence.

'No, well, I do understand that you are very much attached to the house. Such a beautiful house . . .' murmured Montacute, somewhat taken aback by the curt chilliness of her response. Obviously that was not an acceptable solution to her difficulties.

'I don't suppose,' she said after a pause, trying to bring a little warmth back into her voice, 'that any additional income could be made available through the trust?'

'In what sense, do you mean?' Montacute genuinely did not understand the purport of her question.

'I mean,' she said, hoping that she was proceeding with sufficient caution under the mask of her naïvety, 'couldn't the trust be made to produce more income?'

'I understand. The answer to that is, of course, yes. We are, however, somewhat restricted in the type of investment we can make. There is a thing called the Trustee Investment Act, you see.' She nodded. 'It rather ties one's hands,' he went on. 'One can't invest in anything precarious or speculative.'

'But, without this act thing, you could make a lot more money?'

Montacute smiled tolerantly at her ingenuousness. 'Or lose a great deal more. That is why trustees are not allowed, by law, to speculate in high-risk investments. A steady level of income must be produced for the beneficiaries without risk to the capital.'

But what, Marion was thinking, if you maintained that steady level and still managed, through careful investment, to cream a little extra profit off the top? Or more than a little extra? How could that hurt anyone? But now, if ever, was not the time to suggest such a thing, and Montacute was not the man to whom to suggest it. Or was he? She looked speculatively at his large, satisfied face and the flicker of interest when his eyes met hers. With a little care and hard work, he might be. She half-smiled at the daring of her thoughts.

Montacute was draining his coffee cup and signalling to the waiter for the bill.

'There's just one other little thing,' said Marion. 'I have some investments of my own, very small . . .' This was true; the remainder of her parents' estate existed in a very small portfolio whose shares produced a negligible amount of income for Marion. Her shoe money, was how Marion had always looked at it. It could now be turned into a useful little device. 'I really do need to maximise my income after all this, and I was wondering if you could look at them and give me some advice?'

'Well, of course,' Montacute replied, taking out his wallet as the waiter brought the bill. 'I can put you in touch with a good stockbroker—'

She laid a hand on his sleeve. 'Oh, no, I'd much rather you looked at it. I'd feel *so* much happier if I thought that you were able to help me personally. You've been so kind so far,' she added, her hand gliding down his sleeve until it rested warmly, insistently, on his hand. 'Geoffrey.'

He met her candid blue gaze and felt an unknown and exquisitely pleasurable lightness of being. Outside she kissed him warmly on his cheek as he handed her into a taxi, and he made his way back to his office in something of a daze, unable to think of anything but the soft, lingering pressure on his hand, and the look in her eyes. It was a treasure he carried home with him that night, and nursed throughout his cheerless supper with his mother, and took carefully with him to bed.

41

Chapter four

When he received Geoffrey Montacute's imperious summons to lunch, Oliver Pocock was sitting in his snug, overheated little office in the suite of rooms in Hay Hill which he shared with two never-present theatrical agents. After he had put down the telephone, he rubbed the side of his nose, adjusted his glasses, and felt dejection wash over him. All contact between Geoffrey Montacute and himself invariably produced this reaction.

'Blast the man!' he muttered to himself, as he bustled his fat little body out of its chair and went over to the window to survey the rain-washed pavements of Mayfair. What a start to the New Year. Poor Alexander's death had been bad enough, but then to discover that he had made him a trustee of his will, along with Marion and Montacute . . . Oliver wondered bleakly whether this was Alexander's idea of a joke. It seemed fated that he should be thrown constantly into Montacute's society. Ghastly.

He gazed down and sideways from his window at the inverted umbrella sign of the Rififi Club, his mind wandering back to the time when he had first met Montacute. They had been studying law together at Oxford. Law. Oliver smiled to himself at the thought of himself as a lawyer. They had had the misfortune, as Oliver saw it, to share the same tutorial group, and from the very first Oliver had found something faintly repellent in his fellow student, in the way in which he managed to be both ingratiating and overbearing at the same time. Montacute's bland superciliousness had always made Oliver feel belittled and ill at ease. He had tried his best to avoid him, but Montacute's large, dark presence seemed to be everywhere, in lectures, in tutorials, in Hall and in the common room. Oliver had felt positively latched on to.

And then, at the beginning of their second year, Montacute's cousin, Alexander, had come up to Balliol. He and Oliver met at a dinner party, when Oliver was in the company of a young Jewish artist whose work he admired and whose eyes he adored. Montacute had introduced Alexander to Oliver, Oliver had introduced Alexander to the Jewish artist, and out of that evening was born a friendship between Oliver and Alexander that had lived on long after the Jewish artist had deserted Oliver, and long after Oliver had learned from Alexander that his work had not really been admirable at all. (Although his eyes remained eternally adorable.)

After he came down from Oxford, Oliver had read for the Bar and then made a dashing headlong little pitch at a criminal practice, not without some success. But his heart had not been in it. Alexander, with whom he had remained close, encouraged his interest in art, and Oliver had begun to develop a sideline in writing occasional pieces for various art magazines. The sideline had grown and he had been given a regular column in a monthly journal. He had discovered that he could keep rather more congenial company in his new sphere of work than was generally possible within the purlieus of Uxbridge Crown Court. He found, too, that his circle of homosexual acquaintance was widened, and that he felt more comfortable in their society than with his fellow members of the criminal Bar. He had begun to become known in the art world, and several young artists had come under his wing seeking encouragement and opportunity. Assisting the more successful of these had proved financially rewarding, and he had thrown himself energetically into the business of acquiring a select little coterie of rising artists, for whom he acted as agent. Of these, Alexander Laing had been one.

Montacute, meanwhile, had vanished to a Chancery practice in Lincoln's Inn, and Oliver had not imagined that their paths should ever cross again. But somehow they did. Montacute, as he had watched his cousin's rise to artistic fame, had stuck closely to him, and it was natural that Alexander should turn to his own cousin when it came to legal matters. He had not especially liked or disliked Geoffrey, but had tolerated him, and happily allowed him to advise him in matters which he found too tiresome or boring to attend to. Thus Oliver had found himself seeing Montacute more often than he would have liked, bound as they were by their mutual interest in Alexander's affairs.

Over the years they had lunched together regularly, usually at Montacute's club, and always at Montacute's behest. Oliver found that these occasions left him vaguely depressed. No matter how carefully dressed or tidy he was, he always came away from his meetings with the serene, immaculately attired Montacute with the feeling that his shirt cuffs had somehow grown grey and frayed, that he had mismanaged his treacle tart and cream, that he had made his wine glass grubby with fingermarks. Montacute was not a man to make one feel comfortable.

To his shame, Oliver had never been able to bring himself to return the hospitality. He abhorred the thought of inflicting the dreadful Montacute upon the delicate sensibilities of his friends or the waiters at the discreet little West End restaurants where he ate and talked and giggled happily over his wine and Perrier. His attitude towards Montacute was one of distaste mingled with pity. He saw him as a lonely, charmless man, living entirely upon the fruits and dignity of his profession, without friends or lovers. Oliver did not recall Montacute having any intimate acquaintance, male or female, during his time at Oxford, and he sensed that nothing had changed for the man since. The barrenness of such an existence seemed to the tender-hearted Oliver to be inexpressibly dreadful. How could he refuse the man's luncheon invitations? He knew it was weak of him to let the lawyer impose upon him in his droning way, but he allowed it, if only out of Christian kindness.

So, two days after the receipt of the summons, Oliver made his way by taxi to Pall Mall and ascended the steps of Montacute's gloomy club. He reflected, as he crossed the dining room to where Montacute sat waiting for him, that this business with Alexander's will bound them even closer together. Poor, dear Alexander. Why had he had to die in that untimely way? Now Oliver was probably cursed with Montacute for life.

Montacute greeted him with his usual heavy courtesy, and lunch proceeded. Oliver did not especially care for the food at Montacute's club – it reminded him of school food – but he did like the puddings. He tackled his lamb cutlets half-heartedly and did his best to attend while Montacute gave him a lengthy exposition of the terms of Alexander's will, and of their duties as trustees of the estate. Only once did Oliver gently remind Montacute that he, too, knew something of the law.

'I think you might find that things have moved on somewhat since you were at the Bar,' replied Montacute with lofty condescension. The waiter set a plate of apple pie and ice cream before Oliver, and Oliver did not feel disposed at that moment to take issue with Montacute. The less he had to do with the law nowadays, he felt, the better.

'So Marion is a trustee as well?' said Oliver, picking up his spoon. 'I find that curious.'

'Why?' asked Montacute, putting his elbows on the table and pressing the tips of his fingers together in the manner that was habitual with him when he was about to debate a point.

'Oh, I don't know,' replied Oliver, pausing with a spoonful of apple pie in mid-air. 'Just that he loathed her so dreadfully, I suppose. Alexander wasn't really a man to take violent dislikes, but she was definitely the exception.'

'I suppose he took the view that, as the children's mother, and since they were to be the beneficiaries under his will, the thing was only natural.'

'I suppose so,' murmured Oliver through his apple pie.

'I find her a very agreeable woman,' continued Montacute after a pause. He found himself impelled to talk about her, he did not know why. 'Quite charming. I do think that Alexander has left her in something of an awkward situation, with such a slight income and yet the responsibility of the upkeep of that house.'

'Well,' said Oliver between mouthfuls, 'I don't know her that well. See her about from time to time. Quite a socialite. But I would have thought her quite capable of looking after herself. I only hope that the children are all right – that this money thing doesn't create more problems than it solves.'

'I hardly see how that can be the case,' said Montacute. 'In

45

fact, Marion and I were discussing that over lunch just the other day.' He liked that; he liked the intimate picture that it conjured up. 'She takes the view that Paul ought to go to a better school, now that sufficient money is available. I recommended Ampersand. It's quite one of the best these days. I know the headmaster personally.'

'Ampersand!' exploded Oliver through a mouthful of ice cream. 'That's a preposterous idea! It would be a living hell for someone like Paul. He's perfectly happy where he is. Hamilton House is a decent, quiet little school, perfectly suited to him.'

'That may not be sufficient, you know, when you consider what Paul's future will be, financially, socially,' replied Montacute.

'Oh, balls!' said Oliver.

Montacute raised his eyebrows. 'I hardly think you can compare the very slight merits of his present school with the obvious advantages of a place like Ampersand. It is, after all, one of the leading public schools.'

'Exactly,' retorted Oliver. 'How could someone of Paul's temperament possibly thrive in such an atmosphere? I know the boy – you don't.' At this, Montacute merely inclined his head, rubbing some breadcrumbs across the white linen tablecloth with the tip of one finger. 'At least at his present school,' went on Oliver, 'he is allowed to go at his own pace, to develop his art – which is what his father always wanted for him. The boy has tremendous natural talent, you know. Tremendous.' Oliver dug into his apple pie again.

'At any rate,' replied Montacute, sitting back, 'I'm sure that his artistic ability will survive a first-rate education.'

'But will it?' asked Oliver excitedly. 'Can it? I wonder. I do not believe that you can thrust someone like Paul into the environment of a public school such as Ampersand and expect him to – to survive happily.'

'You did. I did,' replied Montacute, his eyes expressionless as they met Oliver's. They looked at one another for a long moment.

'What my school taught, or did not teach me, is neither here nor there,' said Oliver. 'Perhaps that is why I am so much against the idea. As for you—' But he decided not to pursue this, and resumed the eating of his pudding in a state of indignation.

'The point is,' said Montacute, 'that life may require more of Paul than mere artistic ability. He will need preparation for the slings and arrows of outrageous fortune which he will undoubtedly encounter in the coarser adult world, surely?' Montacute looked at Oliver. 'You have apple pie on your chin.'

Oliver felt that he loathed the man acutely at that moment. He loathed him when he came out with his arch little quotations, and he loathed him even more when he did it when he, Oliver, had apple pie on his chin.

'I very much doubt if the adult world is coarser than life at a public school,' he retorted, wiping his chin with his napkin.

'At any rate,' said Montacute, 'I am merely telling you what Marion has indicated her wishes to be.'

'There are Paul's views to take into account,' said Oliver. He dabbed at his chin again.

Montacute bowed his head with slow gravity. 'Naturally. He may well have his own ideas.' Both men, separately, doubted this. 'As I see it, Marion simply wishes her children to be socially equipped for the world into which the possession of any degree of wealth must necessarily bring them into contact.'

Oliver blinked at this. 'What nonsense,' he muttered. 'How does she propose to "equip" Helena? That young lady will spend her money faster than she can get it, if I know her.'

'Helena, as I understand it, goes to some art college in London after the summer. As she will be eighteen in August, she will be free thereafter to do as she pleases with her income. I cannot say I know the girl, so I have no idea of how that will turn out.'

Oliver sighed. He loved Helena, loved her exuberance, her restless spirit that hungered for pleasure in the way her father's had, her bright good looks and teasing friendliness. What could money do for her, except an infinite amount of damage? And Paul – he thought of Paul, with his shy, slow ways, trying to survive at a place such as Ampersand, and sighed.

Montacute moved his chair back with a little scraping sound and signalled to the waiter. Oliver felt powerless; if Marion thought that it was a good idea, then there was nothing he could do about it. He and Marion had never been especially friendly, and he hardly felt he was in a position to try and dissuade her. It just seemed to him such a manifestly wrong decision. He felt, however, as though he had made an unnecessary fuss over the matter, been unduly argumentative. He watched unhappily as Montacute uncapped his fountain pen and signed the account.

'I shall have some documents for you to sign in due course,' said Montacute, looking up. 'And I may have to contact you regarding certain matters before then. But, of course, the administration of the estate has only just begun.' He put his fountain pen back in his pocket and clasped his hands on the tablecloth. 'I may, if you can spare the time, ask for your assistance regarding the legatees named in Alexander's codicil. I have very little knowledge of his Italian affairs.'

Oliver smiled sadly as he thought of the villa in Tuscany, of Alexander's friends, and of the long, happy summer days he had spent there. He thought, as he had a hundred times, of Alexander's lonely death in that hospital room, and wished again that he could have known, could have been there. 'Of course,' he replied. 'You know where I am. Just pick up the phone.'

Then he thanked Montacute for lunch, and they went their separate ways.

Oliver was rather surprised when, that evening, he received a phone call from Marion Laing.

'Marion,' he said, 'I thought we might be speaking to one another before long.' He and Marion occasionally drifted in and out of the same social circles, and he quite liked her whenever he met her, feeling faintly disloyal to Alexander because of it.

'I know,' she sighed. 'This wretched will thing. I frankly didn't expect to be very mixed up in it. Still, there it is.'

'I had lunch with Geoffrey Montacute today,' said Oliver, 'taking me through it.'

'Then you'll know what kind of fix I'm in,' replied Marion mournfully. 'I suppose I'm lucky that he left me anything, but things are going to be a bit tight around here.' Oliver made a sympathetic noise. 'But the thing is, Oliver, I wondered if you could help me with something.'

'Anything,' said Oliver, watching out of the corner of his eye as Dominic, his present lover, came through from the bathroom, pulling a blue T-shirt over his head.

'You see, I've really got to raise some money from somewhere. I mean, I'm all right for a little while, but I have to look ahead. I've got these paintings, and I wondered if you'd help me sell them.'

'Paintings?' He followed Dominic with his eyes as the boy wandered over to the television and switched it on, then dropped on to the sofa.

'Some things of Alexander's, actually.'

'Really?' Oliver became more interested. 'Dominic, can you turn that down a little?' Dominic paid no attention.

'Yes, a portrait that he did of me, and one or two things from when we lived in Brittany. I don't know if they're any good . . . but then, that wouldn't really matter, would it?' Oliver sighed and gritted his teeth. 'And there's a portrait he did of Helena when she was just two. That's rather lovely. And one of Paul when he was a baby.'

'But surely you don't want to part with those?' said Oliver in astonishment. 'Not with the children's pictures, at any rate?'

'I'm afraid it's a case of "needs must",' replied Marion.

'Times must be tough,' said Oliver wryly. 'But, of course, they'll bring you a tidy little sum, I should imagine.'

'I know. I was rather pleased when I thought of them,' said Marion brightly. She did not tell Oliver that the portraits of the children belonged to Paul and Helena. The pictures had hung on her bedroom wall for years, and neither Paul nor Helena had ever shown any interest in them. She didn't really think it mattered.

'Anyway,' Marion went on, 'I thought I should get in touch with you about it – I haven't a clue how one goes about selling pictures. I have to come up to London next Friday, so perhaps I can bring them with me then.'

'If you think you can manage,' said Oliver.

'They're not very large,' said Marion. 'And I'm bringing the car up. Look, this is sweet of you. Just give me your office address, will you?'

Oliver gave her the address, said goodbye, and hung up.

'Extraordinary,' he said to Dominic. 'Alexander Laing's ex-wife is going about selling off Laing's portraits of their children.'

'So what?' said Dominic, his eyes fixed on the television screen.

'Well, they're not the sort of thing you would expect her to start hawking about,' said Oliver, detecting with misgivings the bored, sulky tone in Dominic's voice.

'Maybe she needs the money,' said Dominic. Then he glanced up at Oliver who was standing behind him, leaning on the sofa. 'Speaking of which,' he added, 'can you lend me twenty quid?'

'What for?' asked Oliver, knowing what for.

'I want to go out.'

Oliver did not ask where, or with whom. He handed Dominic the money from his wallet, and watched as the boy picked up his jacket and opened the front door of the flat. 'When will you be back?' he asked, detesting himself for his weakness.

'Don't worry,' replied Dominic, with an insolent smile. 'I shan't be late.' And he blew Oliver a kiss before closing the door behind him.

Chapter five

Looking back to the time when he and his mother first visited Ampersand, it often seemed to Paul, later, as though it had been another place, in another time and another country. They had gone early in January, when the light snow that had fallen over New Year was beginning to thaw, and the school had looked, beneath the brilliant blue sky and the cold sunshine, large and grey and beautiful. Leafless poplars stood like sentinels around the playing fields, woods and fields stretched out into the countryside around, and every tint and aspect of the place delighted his eye. Hamilton House, in his mind, seemed cramped and shabby by comparison. Term had not yet begun, and as he and his mother and the headmaster had paced solemnly round the school, their steps ringing on the wooden floors, their voices carrying through the still air of empty classrooms, the atmosphere had seemed cheerful and comforting, the smells of polish and age and ink and bunsen burners mingling with peculiar charm. He had liked it very much. It had seemed peaceful. The art rooms, right at the top of the building's east wing, were full of splendid light. His heart had risen. And his mother had been relieved.

But that, as he later thought, had been somewhere else.

When he arrived at school on the first day of term, standing in his new dormitory with his trunk and other effects, everything seemed to have changed colour. The day outside was raw and grey and blustery. All the rooms and dormitories and corridors that had seemed light and full of calm were, to his senses, now an odd shade of brown, and the clamour that rang around him utterly demolished any recollection of quiet. Feet thundered and scuffled, boys and their bodies barged and scrambled everywhere, their voices high and wild, spinning through the rooms and up against the ceilings. He felt as though he were moving in a daze. As he made his way from the dormitory in search of the lavatories, he was like a blind man stepping with panicky uncertainty through a sea of sound and movement, none of it making sense to him. When he had found his way back to the dormitory and resumed his unpacking, he became aware that he was being watched by a dark-haired boy who was leaning on the locker of the bed next to his. Paul looked up and offered him an uncertain 'hello', and the boy nodded and smiled. Paul bent back over his trunk.

'Where was your last school?' asked the boy suddenly, his eyes following Paul's face with bright curiosity. Paul straightened up, pushing his hair from his face.

'Kent,' he replied. 'Hamilton House.'

'Never heard of it,' said the boy. 'Were you expelled?'

'No,' replied Paul, startled. He paused in his unpacking to look at the boy, then put a small pile of books on top of his locker.

'I just thought it was an odd time to be starting a new school,' observed the boy. 'I'm Beasley, by the way.'

'I'm Laing,' replied Paul, wondering whether they should shake hands. It appeared not. Beasley had glanced away, his attention arrested by the photograph of Paul's sister and mother in its little leather frame, which Paul had placed on top of his locker.

'Those your people?' he asked.

Paul looked at the picture and nodded. 'It's my mother and my sister. My father's dead.'

Beasley looked thoughtfully at the picture. There was a pause, during which Paul half-hoped for more conversation, but Beasley pushed himself off the locker and sauntered off, saying, 'Catch you later.'

As he continued his unpacking, Paul recalled how still and bright this dormitory had looked when he had last seen it. He had carried the notion of it, unoccupied by anyone, around in his head. He wondered now at this absurdity. The room belonged, almost to the exclusion of himself, it seemed, to this group of sixteen- and seventeen-year-olds, all of whom seemed in familiar possession of themselves and their territory. They spoke to one another with a boisterous yet languid

52

familiarity; they had an air of collected confidence quite unlike anything he had experienced at Hamilton House. One or two glanced at him and said 'hello', but nothing more. Their urbanity intimidated him, made him feel alien and unsophisticated, almost juvenile. Their conversation was fluent and foreign to him, containing terms of reference and the names of masters and prefects whom he had yet to encounter.

He managed to spin out his unpacking until the bell rang for tea, and was still putting the last of his things away when the rest of his room-mates were jostling their way to the door. As he walked past Paul's bed, Beasley remarked to him, 'Better get a move on, Laing, or you won't get any tea.'

With vague gratefulness Paul followed him out on to the landing and down the clattering stairs, where they joined more boys all making their way to Hall. The noise of voices was tumultuous, echoing up the stairwell. At Hamilton House there had been voices, but nothing like this; here was a multitude, more boys than Paul had ever seen in one place together.

He followed Beasley into Hall and sat down next to him at one of the long wooden tables. There was a formality, a grandeur about the Hall which struck him forcibly, as he recalled the scattered groups of tables and chairs in the small dining room at Hamilton House. When the Hall was full, a hush fell and Dr Whatley rose. He paused, bowed his head, and murmured grace, which everyone followed in a sea of mumbling sound: 'Per Jesum Christum, dominum nostrum, amen.' Paul muttered hollowly to himself, the grace unknown to him. Then the rumble of voices rose again as food was served.

For Paul, tea passed largely in silence. A naturally reserved youth, he was not one to initiate conversation; anyway, most of the other boys seemed to be following an animated discussion with the prefect at the head of their table concerning the house rugby shield. Paul, as he ate his food, gazed at the portraits of ex-headmasters which lined the panelled walls. Curious, he thought, how technique and approach had altered gradually over the years; the formality and coldness of earlier portraits was quite blurred by the time they reached the Sixties, as were the very brushstrokes of the various painters down the years. He liked best, he thought, the one of some bloke whose name he couldn't make out, but whose dates were 1908–1915; a round, almost smiling face – smiling was rare amongst the earlier portraits – leaning forward in a friendly way from the shadows. Nineteen-fifteen. Paul wondered if he had died in the First World War. He supposed he must have. Like Wilfred Owen, he thought. *'So secretly, like wrongs hushed-up, they went. They were not ours: we never heard to which front these were sent . . .'*

Paul suddenly became aware that Beasley was nudging him. He looked round, startled, and there were a few suppressed smiles at the vacant, just-woken look on his face.

'Priday's speaking to you,' murmured Beasley. Paul glanced uncertainly around, and then realised that Priday was the sixth-form prefect at the end of their table.

'Sorry?' said Paul.

'I was asking your name,' said Priday, with mild exasperation.

'Paul,' replied Paul thoughtlessly. One or two of the boys near him smiled, and Paul flushed; it had been customary at his old school for the boys and girls to call one another by their Christian names. In his acute embarrassment he felt oddly stifled, suddenly, by his surroundings. The faces of the boys around him impinged like white blobs upon the edges of his vision; the walls of the Hall seemed to be leaning in upon him, ready to collapse from a great height. 'I mean Laing,' he added.

'Priday,' murmured Beasley, taking another mouthful of bread and butter.

'Oh, Laing, Priday,' said Paul again.

'Which house are you in, Laing?' asked Priday in a conversational way.

'I don't know. No one's told me,' replied Paul. 'Priday,' he added.

'Well, somebody should be showing you round for the first week, Laing. Somebody should be showing you the ropes.'

'I think it was meant to be Chalmers, Priday,' offered Beasley. 'But he's not coming back till next Tuesday.'

Priday looked round at them. 'Well, you lot, show Laing what's what. Remember what it's like to be new.'

Now that his embarrassment had passed, Paul felt vaguely humiliated by this remark, even though it was well meant, as though he were some helpless kid who couldn't find out anything for himself.

Priday's admonition, as it turned out, was scarcely heeded. Everyone seemed to have far too much to do to pay attention to Laing. As a result, Paul found his first week difficult. Neither he nor his mother had foreseen certain problems involved in starting halfway through the year. In English they were studying books and plays with which he was unfamiliar, and which the rest of the class was already halfway through. The academic pace was considerably faster, too – Paul had been accustomed to an undemanding regime, and struggled to keep up. In French they were studying irregular verbs and tenses of dizzying sophistication, and to Paul's horror the master addressed the class in French throughout the entire lesson.

As for mathematics and science, Paul sat through these lessons in a state bordering on blank incomprehension. The work of his class had reached levels that Hamilton House had not even approached, and for the first week none of the masters detected that the pale, fair boy at the back of the room did not have the faintest idea what was going on.

His first visit to the playing fields was a nightmare. Football, which they played at Hamilton House, he quite liked, even if he was not especially good at it. At Ampersand the game was rugby, and rugby played with serious, youthful, masculine dedication. Paul told the games master that he had never played rugby, and the games master stood him on the touchline, telling him to watch and try to pick it up. Paul stood there, thin and inelegant in his new maroon-and-green-striped kit, huddling and shivering in the drizzle, trying to make sense of the muddy, careering figures as they ran about, sometimes forming knots, sometimes breaking apart, never seeming to get anywhere much. The longer he watched, the less sense it made, and then, in a hellish moment, the games master suddenly blew his whistle, grasped Paul by the shoulder and propelled him on to the pitch, saying, 'Go on – you take Chisholm's place on the wing. Let's see what you've made of it.' The rest was a dreadful eternity of mud and chill and bodies, some sort of blind struggle in which voices roared 'Pass!' and other things that he did not understand. He tried to run in the same direction as the rest of his team, but as he was uncertain as to the identities of his particular team-mates, more often than not he ran in the wrong direction. He had seen enough to understand that what everyone seemed to do when they got the ball was to get rid of it, and on the one occasion on which he found it in his hands he flung it wildly away from him, not caring where it went.

The double period of art did not provide any antidote to the miserable incomprehension of the other lessons. For the first thirty minutes the class discussed a Mantegna exhibition which they had all gone to the term before, and which Paul had not seen, and for the rest of the lesson they drew a stuffed bird or an earthenware jar with paintbrushes in it, whichever happened to be most conveniently within range. It was not therapeutic, and there lingered in Paul's mind a memory of the games lesson, and the dread knowledge that next week he would be required to take to the rugby pitch again. He could not bring himself to ask anyone to explain the game to him, nor anything else for that matter.

This was the beginning of Paul's life at Ampersand, bleak, lonely and incomprehensible; his dreams were full of chaos, eternal struggles down dark corridors.

He dreamed, too, of his sister, and it was always the same dream. They were playing some intricate game of chase in the garden at Roffey. But in his dream there were seven Helenas; wherever he looked, whichever way he turned in the game, she was there, laughing and shouting and about to catch him; figure after figure, like light splintering from a prism, clutched at him as he ran. And then it would be his turn to chase, and it seemed at first impossible, for there were seven Helenas to catch and they ran in every direction. Then it began to get easier, for they were all in some way less than he, slighter, ghostly and insubstantial. He caught each one of them effortlessly, and said to himself in his dream, the last one I catch will be Helena; she will be the real Helena, solid and my sister. But he caught every last one of them, and they were all the same, each as frail and illusive as the last, fading and shrivelling at his touch.

The day's struggles were less ethereal, but were characterised by the same sense of vexed hoplessness. By the end of the second week things had improved in one way, though not in others. The advent of written prep meant that Paul's academic weaknesses came to light, and most of the masters arranged to set aside time to bring him up to scratch. Paul, however, was painfully aware of the singularity of his position. Being singled out for extra tuition meant that he was perceived, just at a stage when his personality was beginning to take shape in the consciousness of his peers, as being thick. This, coupled with his naturally withdrawn character, produced an overall impression that Laing was really something of a dead loss. Nothing wrong with the chap, just that he was a bit useless at everything. The masters could not, of course, help coming to roughly the same conclusion.

Paul was unhappy, but a mixture of pride, isolation, and the sense that this was somehow all of his own making, prevented him from betraying the extent of his misery in his first letter home.

Dear Mummy,

Thanks for sending on the sweater and the paintbrushes. I forgot to ask if you could send me some cartridge paper, too. Not A4, the next size up.

Things seem not bad so far, but I'm rather behind with a lot of subjects and am having extra prep to catch up. We're doing Jude the Obscure in English, which is only marginally worse than the Jane Austen we were doing at HH. The title is about right. But the English master, Mr Cummings, is the best of the masters.

Art lessons are pretty babyish here. Apparently the last art master was really brilliant, but he got multiple sclerosis, so now we've got this chap Lawrence. He thinks he knows a lot but he's useless.

Not much more to tell you. I'm about as bad at rugger as I was at football. I've got an exeat on February the tenth, if you want to come down that Sunday. Only you have to ring my housemaster Mr Jessop to let him know.

Tell Helena I'll write to her soon.

Love, Paul

Marion showed this letter to Geoffrey Montacute, whom she had invited to a luncheon party one Sunday, along with Oliver Pocock and others.

'He doesn't sound *too* unhappy, do you think?' Marion asked him, sipping at her sherry. 'I imagine it's quite natural for them to be a little lonely in the first weeks.'

'I'm absolutely sure that he is doing splendidly,' replied Montacute, with the hearty reassurance that was one of the many little modes of response being tested by him as a path to greater intimacy with Marion. This one worked quite well. She smiled up at him sweetly and gratefully, laying one small, white hand on his sleeve.

'I must just go and see if lunch is ready,' she said, and left him. He stood serenely on the hearth rug, his large bottom bathed in warmth from the log fire. He was glad he had come. So far she had treated him with a sort of select kindness, introducing him to her friends as though he were, in some discreet sense, a special guest. It was a novelty to Montacute to be treated by any woman with such complete and fascinated attention. It made him question himself, look at himself anew. A fresh sense of being a man that women might find attractive had caused him to pause before the bathroom mirror that morning, after shaving. That which he saw, he decided, was not unpleasing. As he had driven down to Surrey that morning several scarcely admitted little fantasies had woven themselves in his head, the conclusion of all of them being that a grateful and loving Marion Laing lay in his strong embrace. The fancies of adolescence had never had free rein before, and now he found their indulgence shamefully delightful.

As he surveyed the charms of the drawing room yet again, thinking how pleasant it would be to own such a house as Roffey, he caught sight of Oliver entering the room with Marion. Late, he thought. Typically unpunctual. If the man had taken a lift down with him, as he had suggested . . . As Marion fetched Oliver a drink, Montacute crossed the room just as Oliver stood suspended in a brief moment of social isolation.

'Hello, Oliver,' said Montacute, as Marion returned; he turned to her. 'Marion, if I can help with drinks for latecomers, please let me know. You have enough to do.' Oliver blinked and took a sip of his vodka and tonic. Bloody man.

Marion smiled and replied, 'Geoffrey, you are sweet. I'll let you know if there's the least thing you can do. Luncheon is nearly ready.'

'The least thing,' repeated Montacute, as she glided off again. He felt that he had established before Oliver that a special relationship was forming between himself and Marion.

'Well, Oliver, car let you down again?' asked Montacute solicitously.

'I got the train, actually. It was late leaving Waterloo. I had some things to read,' he added, remembering Montacute's previous offer of a lift. He tugged a little at the collar of his shirt, a new affair of coral cotton. The trouble was, if he got shirts of a larger collar size, the sleeves were always too long. Maybe Dominic was right; maybe he should get them custom made. The thought of Dominic suddenly returned to vex him. These last-minute tantrums of his were becoming too tiresome. It was just as well the train *had* been late. Did the boy really expect him to take him, uninvited, to luncheon parties? It was unthinkable. He looked up at Montacute with a frown, realising that he was talking to him.

'. . . and I have had the schedules drawn up, if you would care to step round to my offices some time to look at them. They are rather detailed, I'm afraid, and some of the transfer documents—'

'I'd much prefer to leave it all up to you,' Oliver interrupted him. The thought of endless little trips to Lincoln's Inn, dreary half hours spent in Montacute's office while he droned over documents, was more than he could bear.

'I'm afraid,' replied Montacute with a small sigh, 'that there are several things that require your signature. As a trustee you—'

'Can't you just send them round? I have rather a lot on my plate at the moment, you know.' Oliver looked round, trying to see if there was anyone else here he knew. He hoped he wouldn't have to sit too near to Montacute at lunch.

Montacute raised his eyebrows and looked into his empty

sherry glass. 'I suppose I can. Still – ah, here is our charming hostess,' he exclaimed, as Marion reappeared.

'Luncheon is ready, everyone,' she announced, and bestowed a special smile on Montacute. Oliver blinked, first at her, then at him. What was all this? Good God, surely she didn't . . . ? Woman must be mad, he concluded, tossing back the remains of his drink and proceeding through to the dining room. He could smell roast lamb. Wonderful. Dominic could never be bothered to cook anything decent on Sundays, or any other day, come to that.

It was hardly possible for Oliver to refuse Montacute's offer of a lift back to London, and by the time dusk came and the other luncheon guests had disappeared into the gathering darkness of the late afternoon, Oliver scarcely cared if he had to endure the man's company on the journey back, so happily full was he of good food and excellent wine. Perhaps he'd had just a little too much of that dessert wine. Marion came back into the drawing room, having closed the front door on the last guest, and began to switch on lamps around the room. Oliver hoisted himself up a little from the comfortable slump that he had fallen into in his armchair next to the fire, and tried to look attentive. Montacute had already arranged himself in a chair opposite, trust papers at the ready. He waited for Marion to sit down, and then began to talk about the will and the trust investments. Marion and Oliver both regarded him, initially, with expressions of polite interest, but these rapidly faded as Montacute's monotonous catalogue of companies and dividends and rights issues gathered momentum.

'Drink, Oliver?' asked Marion, rising impatiently after ten minutes. Oliver roused himself once more from the stupor into which the warmth of the fire and the drone of Montacute's voice had thrown him.

'Mmmm, please. Whisky and soda, I think.' He probably shouldn't, he knew.

Montacute had stopped talking and was looking at them both with exaggerated patience.

'I know that this may be rather dull for you, Marion and Oliver, but I'm afraid it has to be done.'

Marion pouted theatrically as she splashed soda daintily into Oliver's whisky.

'Oh, weren't we paying attention, Geoffrey? So sorry. Drink?'

'No, thank you,' replied Montacute coldly. 'I have to drive. If you will bear with me for just a little longer, I have nearly finished.'

Marion handed Oliver his drink and subsided meekly as Montacute resumed his discourse.

'The remainder of the proceeds of the sale of the Italian villa, which will, of course, be utilised in part to satisfy those bequests which Alexander made to his staff, etcetera, and which are referred to in "Schedule C" as "The Italian Bequests", will be divided into two parts . . .'

Oliver tried hard not to close his eyes; extraordinary, he thought. It was almost possible to nod off with one's eyes open. He glanced at Marion, who had curled herself up in a corner of a sofa and was watching Montacute attentively. She couldn't possibly be listening to all this rubbish, thought Oliver. He wondered what she was thinking.

His mind moved back to Paul's letter, which Marion had shown him earlier. He had said nothing at the time, but had concentrated on reading it twice through, quickly. Not much to be learned, but he suspected that the boy would sink rather than swim. He suppressed the little wave of anger that rose in him. What was done was done. He would go and visit Paul soon. That was the thing. He lay back and gazed into the firelight, waiting for Montacute to finish. What a dreadful bore the man was.

Montacute drew his discourse to a close at last. Marion looked at him with sleepy boredom as he put his papers back in his briefcase with an air of complacency.

'There we are,' he said, with as much brightness as his ponderous manner would permit. 'No more business – not until next week, at any rate,' he added archly to Marion. 'We shall need to get these documents signed promptly if the Italian lawyers are not to be allowed to drag their heels. Do you think you will be able to come to my office some time then?'

Marion stretched her plump arms above her head and

yawned, then collected herself and blinked at him. 'Of course. But it's half-term next week, and I promised to take Helena shopping. I shall bring her along, if you don't mind. Paul can stay here with Anna. Wednesday, I think, would be best.'

'Then shall we say – two-thirty?' Marion nodded and began to uncurl herself from the sofa. 'What about you, Oliver?' Montacute turned to Oliver, who gave a sleepy grunt.

'What?'

'We were arranging to sign these documents—'

'Oh, for goodness' sake, Geoffrey,' said Oliver irritably; the effects of the wine at lunchtime were beginning to wear off. 'I told you to have anything sent round to my office. I can't go trotting back and forth to Lincoln's Inn all the time.'

Marion smiled slightly at this image. Montacute gave him a stiff look. 'Very well,' he said.

Oliver and Montacute drove back to London together, and after a little dull conversation Oliver fell silent, wondering what kind of welcome awaited him at home. He hoped Dominic would have come out of his sulk. They would have a lovely making-up. The thought of this cheered and soothed him, and gradually he fell asleep.

Montacute, too, thought of home, but without any pleasure. The best that could be hoped was that his mother would already have taken herself off to bed, and that he would be spared the ritual of criticism and complaint that always ensued when she was denied her Sunday drive and his company, despite the fact that she took no pleasure in either.

As he contemplated the bleak prospect of his return to the house in Richmond, he turned to glance at Oliver's fat face in repose, the chubby little mouth hanging slackly open as he slept, the bouncing reflection of the roadside lights on his glasses. He wondered what Oliver had to return to. Whatever it was, he almost envied him.

Chapter six

Marion and Helena's shopping expedition the following Wednesday was not as pleasurable as it might have been. Usually the absorbing business of buying clothing would melt away their habitual antagonism, the fruits of their trips through Knightsbridge and Piccadilly reducing them, by lunchtime, to a state of satisfied amiability. The day, however, had begun fractiously. Although her late father's estate had not yet begun to render up the income which she anticipated as her due, Helena already regarded herself as an incipient heiress. She began by selecting the costliest items, and when her mother pointed out that she could not afford them, a squabble broke out, which had to be conducted in muted tones away from the ears of the shop assistants.

'I simply can't afford that kind of thing! I have little enough money these days as it is!' snapped Marion.

'I'm not *asking* you to spend your money!' retorted Helena, hugging to herself an Armani confection of hand-painted silk. 'I thought there was *lots* of money for Paul and me now. That's what the lawyer said.' She pouted, and glanced again at her reflection as she held the dress against herself.

'That is as may be, young lady,' said Marion, 'but you may recall that you are not entitled to that money yet. Anyway, a great deal has to be done before there *is* any money, and when there is, it shall certainly not be spent on anything as ludicrously expensive as this.'

'Oh, for God's sake, mother!' muttered Helena. 'And I wish you wouldn't call me "young lady".' She thrust the dress sulkily back on to the rack.

And so the morning continued. Helena harped on about her father's estate to such an extent that Marion determined that she must find out from Montacute if an advance could be made from the trust to buy Helena some clothes and shut her up. They finished lunch, Marion in a state of exasperation and Helena in one of petulance, and made their way to Lincoln's Inn.

The prospect of Marion's visit that afternoon made Montacute feel more than usually affable. When he encountered Richard Ranscombe in the men's washroom after lunch, where Montacute was carefully combing his hair and adjusting his tie, he even managed a stiff smile at his articled clerk.

'I am happy to see that you seem to be managing to get back from lunch on time these days, Richard.'

Richard could think of no appropriate reply, and gave a sycophantic little laugh, as though his senior partner had said something amusing. That seemed a fairly safe bet, since the old boy didn't seem in too bad a mood.

'Have you done much probate work since you joined us, Richard?' asked Mr Montacute as they left the washroom.

'No, sir,' replied Richard. 'Not yet.'

'Mmm.' Montacute paused outside his door, adjusted his cuffs, and looked appraisingly at him. 'What are you busy with just now?'

'I've just finished drafting an affidavit for Clive. Then Miss Reed asked me to get the Current Law Index up to date.'

'Well, I think the Current Law Index can wait. I'm presently dealing with the estate of Alexander Laing, the artist.' Montacute paused. 'He was a cousin of mine.'

Richard hoped his expression was suitably attentive and impressed.

'It's an estate of some interest – and considerable size,' went on Montacute. 'Probate has been granted and we are currently in the process of transferring the assets. Since you haven't done any work of this kind before, perhaps it would be useful for you to become involved in this from the outset. I have members of the family attending this afternoon to deal with one or two matters. I think you should join us.' He glanced at his watch. 'Come to my room in fifteen minutes and I will let you go through some of the documents.'

The prospect of working closely with Montacute on any business did not especially inspire Richard, who found that the senior partner's methodical manner often made him itch with impatience, but the notion of dealing with an important case, instead of being tossed dull little scraps of work that Clive Fry couldn't be bothered to do, pleased him. Alexander Laing, he mused as he made his way back to his room. Very big stuff. Not that he was into art in a big way, but even he had heard the name. Probably worth a fortune.

He went back to Montacute's room at two-fifteen, jacket on, armed with a pen and a counsel's notebook, ready for the fray. He had taken some satisfaction in telling Clive where he was going and what he would be doing. Clive was a little galled; Montacute usually asked him to assist in the administration of the larger estates.

'Don't worry,' he said to Richard, 'I shouldn't think he'll want you to be anything much more than a spectator.'

Montacute gave Richard the will and codicil to read, and explained to him the procedure for obtaining probate of the will. Richard had actually learned about this for his solicitor's exams, but he didn't remind Montacute of that.

'You will see that I am executor and shall be attending to the day-to-day administration of the trust. I am also a trustee, along with Laing's agent, Oliver Pocock, and his ex-wife, Marion Laing. You will meet Mrs Laing and her daughter this afternoon. In fact,' said Montacute, as his intercom buzzed, 'I imagine that that will be them now.'

Richard thought that Montacute really looked quite animated as he rose and prepared to meet his clients; then again, they were pretty important.

When he remembered the afternoon later, he supposed he must have been introduced to Helena's mother, but he couldn't recall it. All he had been aware of was that there was some woman, and with her, the most fantastic girl he had ever seen.

Helena was, in fact, still indulging in her shopping-expedition sulk when she entered Montacute's room, and was not inclined to respond to Montacute's avuncular smile. Richard looked at her square face, its long mouth drawn into a pout, the expression in her slanting eyes cross and cold, and fell instantly in love. When he was introduced to her and his eyes met hers he lost, there and then, the ability to concentrate on anything that was said regarding Alexander Laing's will for the rest of the afternoon. He stepped back after shaking her hand, and sat down, unable to take his eyes off her. She was wearing a short pink skirt, and the sight of her long thighs encased in black tights sent a sensation through him that he was unaccustomed to feeling at two-thirty in the afternoon. He drew his counsel's notebook on to his lap and coughed slightly.

Helena did not notice him at first. He was Mr Montacute's articled clerk, that was all. But he was a young man and her natural tendency, as a seventeen-year-old, was to take a passing interest in any young man. So she looked at him from time to time – although she found this difficult, since every time she glanced appraisingly in his direction, he was staring at her.

This was the beginning of an interesting game. Anything, she thought, to while away the tedium of listening to Mr Montacute going on and on about the trust and formalities and shares and other boring things. After a couple of cold, cautious little glances in his direction, she let her eyes meet his. They were blue eyes, nice eyes, and they were looking at her with more than a little admiration. She felt a flicker of pleasure, and suppressed a small smile by looking haughtily away. She pretended to attend to what Mr Montacute was saying, and indeed, insofar as he was assuring her mother that some advance could be made from the estate in respect of the children, she did actually pay attention for a while. Then her glance strayed back to Richard, but at that moment he, too, was listening to what Montacute was saying. She felt faintly annoyed.

The next time her eyes caught his she actually let her gaze remain fastened to his, and this had an extraordinarily profound effect on both of them, so much so that Helena found herself blushing, and Richard, as he looked away, felt his heart pounding.

'. . . and I think that since Helena is hardly a child, after all,' Mr Montacute was saying with a patronising smile, 'she might be interested to see the nature of the assets so far.' Helena looked at him blankly. She didn't in the least care to see. 'Richard,' said Montacute from behind his magnificent desk, 'if you would pass Miss Laing a copy of the schedule?'

Helena watched as Richard rose from his chair and took a piece of paper from Mr Montacute. He brought it over and handed it to her, bending over to point out something.

'These are the investments which your father held,' he said, 'and these are the recent acquisitions.' She looked up at his face, very close to hers, as he spoke, but he did not meet her eyes. As he traced the list of investments down the page, his fingers accidentally brushed against hers, and the effect on both of them was electric. Mr Montacute and her mother were at that moment murmuring to one another about something else, and the rapid, astonished glance that Helena and Richard exchanged told each other everything they needed to know. Helena felt as though something had been uttered that should not have been, and glanced around herself for a second in embarrassment.

Richard sat back down and looked at the floor. He did not think that this kind of thing happened to people. When he looked up, she was staring straight ahead of her. She did not look at him again. She felt she did not dare.

Richard did manage to concentrate for the last fifteen minutes or so of the interview and was at least able to take down some fairly intelligible notes. Then everyone stood up and Montacute and Mrs Laing began to make polite noises preparatory to their departure. They all moved towards the door, which Richard was about to open, when Marion Laing said, 'Oh, Geoffrey, do you mind if I take an extra copy of that schedule?'

Montacute murmured, 'Not at all,' and moved back to the desk with her. Richard was left standing next to Helena, his hand on the doorknob. He looked at her, but she was standing stiffly, her handbag clutched in front of her coat with both hands. He knew, however, that she was aware of his gaze. He turned the knob and opened the door, glancing back at the figures of Marion Laing and Montacute bent over the papers on the desk, looking for a copy of the schedule. He held the door open and Helena had no alternative but to walk through. They went only a little way outside the door.

'I know – I know this is a bit of a cheek,' said Richard in a low voice, 'but would you like to go out with me some time?' He didn't know what else to say in the space of time available; it was what he customarily said to girls he liked.

Helena looked at him, slightly startled. At seventeen, she was unused to intense sexual attraction and was feeling a little wary of the sensation and, therefore, of Richard himself. Her experience of boys was limited to those of her own age, gauche and unthreatening, and Richard was not like them. He was decidedly grown up.

'What do you mean?' she asked, looking at his face. She liked his face very much; it did not occur to her to think whether it was handsome or not. She liked his smile, which was lopsided and funny, and his blue eyes. She saw him glance anxiously back into the room, then he looked at her again, shrugged his shoulders and spread his hands.

'I mean—' he began; he couldn't think what else to say.

She smiled at him awkwardly and dropped her eyes. When he did that thing with his shoulders she felt the funny feeling in the pit of her stomach that she'd felt when he had touched her hand in the room. She thought she should say something – it did not occur to her that she could say 'yes', since he seemed so much older than she was – but at that moment her mother and Mr Montacute reached the door. Richard and Helena merely looked at one another like children, and then Montacute shook Helena's hand and said goodbye to her. Richard, too, held out his hand and she took it, acutely aware of the warmth and firmness of it. Her hands and face felt as though they were tingling afterwards.

When Helena and her mother had left, Richard and Montacute went back into the room.

'So,' said Mr Montacute, who seemed quite pleased with the afternoon's events, 'you can see that the next few weeks are simply to be taken up with the transfer of assets into my name as executor. That is something which Clive has been doing so far, but I do not see why I should not entrust the task to you now –although I shall ask Clive to keep an eye on things. I shall also give you the file to go through the correspondence to date, so that you can see the form of the letters which we write to the company registrars. I shall expect Clive to see every letter that goes out.'

That's one for you, Clive, thought Richard. This meant that he would be dealing with the day-to-day administration of the estate which, dry stuff though it was, brought him a little bit nearer to the girl he had just met.

'Some of my late cousin's investments,' remarked Montacute as they sorted through the documents, 'will be maintained by the trust – I suggest you keep all these certificates in one folder. This is a little flimsy; ask Miss Reed for one of the stronger ones. The bulk of them, however, we have been selling and reinvesting. Although the daughter is eighteen later this year, the boy will not attain his majority for eighteen months or so. A balance has to be struck between maintaining a sound capital and producing a sufficient income – some of the investments are too speculative and quite unsuitable.' Always a gambler, a spend-thrift, thought Montacute, contemplating some of his late cousin's wilder speculations.

Richard was astonished. Seventeen! He had thought she was twenty – nineteen at the outside. His heart dropped slightly. A schoolgirl. No wonder she had just stared at him like a child when he'd asked her out. As he thought of it, the recollection touched him. He was a tender-hearted young man, regularly disappointed by the brittle self-centredness of most of his girlfriends, wanting only to expend his affection on some gentle, responsive creature. She did not seem to exist. Or not, he thought, until he had seen Helena. But seventeen . . . And that mother hadn't looked too easy-going, for all her smiles.

He took the file and the various folders back to his room. Clive wasn't there. Good. He sat in his chair and stared at his hands. The electricity, the sensuality of the encounter was beginning to fade, and the more pragmatic side of his nature was taking over. You didn't start messing around with seventeen-year-olds, he told himself. Not at twenty-four. That was just a recipe for disaster. Anyway, what would they have in common? She was still at school. He thought of her long, dusty-blonde hair, those brown eyes, the sulky mouth, and the bold uncertainty of her stare as she had looked into his eyes, as though trying to fathom something. She was fabulous, that was undeniable. But seventeen. It was ludicrous. He tried to remember himself at seventeen – it was like being in another world at that age. He sighed and dismissed her from his mind, turning his attention instead to the assets in the estate of the late Alexander Laing.

Helena's reaction to the encounter went rather in reverse. The faint alarm and sense of confusion that had been aroused in her by Richard now dwindled as she and her mother made their way home. In its place there grew a new recollection of events, one in which she had been coolly aware of Richard's interest in her, but had merely been flattered and amused by it. This was entirely in keeping with her idea of herself as a self-possessed young woman, someone who was no longer a child. The chemistry of the moment between Richard and herself was forgotten, for she was now preoccupied by the romantic aspect of the encounter. She enjoyed recalling the look of evident admiration on his face when he had looked at her, and took a novel pleasure in the idea that someone as old as he was should regard her in adult terms. That must have been what he meant when he asked her out, mustn't it? Oh, if only . . . she thought, glancing at her mother and then casting her eyes over the passing traffic. Just think – a boyfriend of twenty-three, or even twenty-four. How utterly sophisticated. She thought of her schoolfriends and of the envy such an acquisition would arouse. By this time, she was no longer thinking of Richard Ranscombe, but of herself, elevated by the possession of an older boyfriend to a level where she did not have to bother with the clumsy attentions of seventeen- and eighteen-year-old males. If she was naïve, she was nonetheless true to her age. Her fear had turned to self-flattery; there could be no danger in her daydreams. The sensual shock that had shaken her in Mr Montacute's office was entirely beyond recall.

Chapter seven

'When?'

'Last August. Apparently she's been sleeping with her brother for years. He's French. Well, sort of a half-brother, really.'

Marion, twenty minutes into one of her regular telephone conversations with Sally Howard, her closest confidante, flipped up the lid of the packet of Benson & Hedges that lay by the telephone on her dressing table and scrabbled unseeingly in it for a moment, her gaze fixed absently on its own reflection in the mirror, before realising that it was empty. Her only other packet was in her handbag downstairs. Sally was still talking. She picked up the thread of Sally's drawl of scandal and tried to concentrate.

'. . . which *someone* said – I think it was Lucia – was in return for her fixing him up with some Venezuelan girl who was staying with her in Capri. Can't have been more than a child. But then, you know these polo players . . .'

'Mmm.' Marion drew the silver foil paper out of the empty packet and creased it neatly and exactly across the middle, drawing one white fingernail down the edge.

'I must say, darling,' said Sally after an unfilled pause, 'you do sound very blank today. How is everything going with Alexander's will? Is it very tiresome?'

Marion's shoulders drooped slightly as she turned away from her reflection. 'Sally, it's just dreadful.' She had told no one, as yet, the full extent of her financial worries; she certainly didn't want to be on the receiving end of the delighted pity of her friends. But Sally's sympathetic voice had brought to the surface a bright bubble of self-pity, and now it burst.

'God knows, I didn't expect anything when he died – I didn't even expect him to die!' she moaned, pleating the little piece of silver foil. 'But the fact is, I'm worse off now than I was after the divorce.'

'You won't have to leave Roffey, will you?'

'Oh, no,' replied Marion with a sigh. 'That's something. I have the house. And an annuity. Not a bad one, by some people's lights. But, Sally, it won't be enough. I'm going to have to make all kinds of sacrifices to make ends meet. It's too awful.'

'Well, darling, it can't be that bad,' coaxed Sally kindly. 'What about the children?'

'Oh, the children are no problem – he left everything to them. It's all theirs when they reach twenty-four. The money is all in trust in the meantime. At least there's tons of money to spend on *them*. Paul can afford to be decently educated, which is one thing – Alexander frankly didn't give a damn about that. They would have gone to state schools, if he had had any say in it. Imagine.'

'Well, quite,' responded Sally, waiting for more details of Marion's plight.

'Helena's off to art school after summer – at least I shan't have her upkeep to worry about. She has her own income after her birthday in August.' At that moment Marion caught sight of Helena from her bedroom window; her daughter was sauntering down the driveway, presumably towards the village. She wondered vaguely what Helena did all day to keep herself amused during the Easter holidays.

'Lucky child,' said Sally. Lucky indeed, thought Marion; Helena's income would probably be three times that of her own.

'Paul's at Ampersand now,' added Marion. 'He started last term. Of course, he's home for the holidays.'

'Ampersand? *Very* good,' murmured Sally. 'I think Gervaise and Kathy Hamilton's boys are there.' Sally sounded gratifyingly impressed, enough to make Marion feel that she'd made the right choice for Paul, after all. He seemed so – so non-committal about the place. But then, he was non-committal about most things. Everyone said it was a wonderful school.

'I believe it will be good for him,' said Marion; she unpleated

72

the little piece of silver foil and flattened its creases out with her thumb.

'But what about you, dear? Things can't be so very dreadful,' pursued Sally encouragingly.

Marion's mind reverted instantly to her own plight. 'Can't they?' she said. 'I'm having to let Anna go.'

'Oh, how awful for you. She's such a fabulous cook – those dinner parties of yours. Just amazing.'

'I know,' said Marion. 'And I can't cook to save my life, you know that. I'll be living on baked beans. There may be a little money from somewhere—' She thought of the paintings which were now in Oliver Pocock's keeping. '—for another cook, but only on a temporary sort of basis, and certainly not someone who could housekeep as well.'

Sally murmured sympathetically and mentioned the name of a good agency. Marion thanked her and continued her tale of woe, which was unstoppable now.

'And I've sold the Corniche. I loved that car. But I need the money.' She sighed again and refolded the piece of foil into a thin band, which she then rolled up into a little ball. 'Couldn't possibly afford to run something like that now. I've got myself a BMW. They're rather smart, don't you think?' She certainly did not intend to tell Sally that it was second-hand. Anyway, it was a very new second-hand, so it hardly counted.

'Very zippy,' said Sally. She was still listening patiently, hopefully, but she was, frankly, a little disappointed. This didn't sound like the kind of rack and ruin one could complain about. Marion still had the house, she still had a car, she was even talking about getting another cook – good heavens, what was the woman going on about?

'And the gardener is only going to be coming in once a fortnight now,' went on Marion plaintively. 'I can't afford to have him more often.'

'Well, it's dreadful, of course, darling, but I have to say that it doesn't sound *too* bad. I mean, you're not exactly going to have to go out and get a job, are you?'

'My God, don't even *talk* about such a thing. Still, there's this very good lawyer – Alexander's cousin, actually – in London who's tidying up my investments for me and helping me with things. Trying to maximise the little I have left.' Another sigh, as she unrolled the little ball of foil. It was becoming frayed now, she noticed, as she unpleated its creases for a second time.

'Attractive?' asked Sally; Marion could tell from her muffled voice as she said this that she was lighting a cigarette. She heard the click of a lighter, and her own mouth watered with longing.

'Well, I suppose so . . .' She thought for a second. 'You could say so, in a sort of dark, heavy way. Very old-fashioned, positively pre-war, to look at his clothes. I don't know, though. There's something rather – off-putting about him. I don't know what it is . . .' Her voice tailed away; she crumpled up the piece of foil and flicked it into the ashtray, then turned to examine her reflection again.

'Single?' asked Sally.

'Yes. Yes, he is.' Marion paused again, then giggled. 'Do you know!' she exclaimed, as light dawned. 'I've just realised what it is! I think he's a virgin!' She laughed again.

'No! How old is he, for heaven's sake?'

'Mid-forties, I suppose.'

'Then he can't possibly be!' Sally replied. 'Not if he's remotely attractive. No man could reach that age and still be – well, inexperienced.' She mined the possibility with awe and delight. Marion suddenly considered the new angle that this put on the tentative attempts she had made so far at manipulation of him.

'How can you tell?' asked Sally.

'I don't know. It's just – just the way he behaves. Behaves to me, I mean . . .' She smoothed one fair eyebrow with her finger, still gazing raptly at the mirror, considering the new possibilities that her discovery opened up '. . . but it's just – well, something I can't put my finger on. He reminds one of a sweaty adolescent. Not *him*, I mean,' she added, remembering Montacute's faultlessly dressed dignity, 'but the look in his eyes.'

'You're sure he isn't gay?' suggested Sally.

'Heavens, no,' replied Marion.

'Well, what fun!' said Sally. 'I mean, what a novelty.'

74

She sounded positively salacious, thought Marion with faint distaste.

'If one cares for that sort of thing,' she replied, thinking that it was probably about time that she brought this conversation to a close and went in search of a cigarette. She was absolutely gasping for one.

'Oh, but I do!' said Sally. 'Just imagine! All that divine adolescent groping and excited fumbling! Just like being a teenager again! What's his name, this virgin lawyer?'

Marion could hardly make an evasive answer. 'Geoffrey Montacute,' she replied shortly. 'Look, Sally, I think I'm going to have to make a dash – I have a hair appointment at two—'

'Of course, darling,' replied Sally, who knew her cue when she heard it. 'It's been lovely chatting. Look, before you go – Linda and I were thinking of popping over to Paris in a few weeks' time to have a look at the collections and pick up some things. The week of the fifteenth, we thought. You free?'

Marion turned away from the mirror. 'I'd love to,' she said with an effort, real regret in her heart. 'But I think I've promised to see some people in Norfolk that week. What a pity. I should have loved to come.'

'Not to worry,' said Sally brightly. 'Another time, perhaps. I know how you love those little trips. Speak soon. Bye, now.'

Marion said goodbye. Misery and envy lay heavy in her heart as she replaced the receiver. Not even enough money for a trip to Paris with her friends. How desperate could one get? She wished Oliver would get a move on and do something with those paintings. She didn't want to have to tell Sally that she wouldn't be able to afford the villa at Nice in June.

As she made her way downstairs for her cigarettes, she pondered her plight. Of course, she could afford the flight to Paris. That wasn't the problem. It was all that the trip would entail – the Georges Cinq, for a start. She could hardly suggest to Sally and Linda that they stay somewhere cheaper; why should they, when they could afford the best? And then, clothes; the unbearable thought of seeing all those divine new things and being unable to buy even just one. Oh, what a difference that lost income was going to make to life! She was faced, as she saw it, with a cheese-paring existence. Bespoke clothing, a second-rate cook (possibly none at all), a second-hand car. And yet the children were rich.

. She fished her cigarettes out of her handbag and lit one. Any little expense of the children's – well, that would just come out of the trust fund. Anything. Within bounds. As she reflected upon this, an idea – one of which she was not even half-ashamed – occurred to her. She pondered it. It would take, of course, a certain delicacy of handling, but where Geoffrey Montacute was concerned, she was beginning to think she could manage that.

That evening, while Helena was idling away her time with a Simply Red tape and a copy of *Slaves of New York*, Richard Ranscombe rang her. In fact, it was Marion who answered the phone and Richard thought of ringing off, but that seemed unnecessarily evasive, so he asked to speak to Helena and gave Marion his name.

It meant nothing at all to Marion; various young men with various names, some familiar and some unfamiliar, regularly rang for Helena during the holidays. She took the telephone out into the hall and called up to her daughter. Helena padded out of her room and halfway down the stairs, and took the phone from her mother over the banister.

'Someone called Richard Ranscombe,' said her mother absently.

The name meant nothing to Helena either. 'Hello?' she said cautiously, making her way back upstairs.

'Hello – is that Helena?'

'Yes.'

'Hi. This is Richard Ranscombe.' He paused. Of course, she probably didn't remember him; why should she? 'From the lawyer's office. We met when you came with your mother to see Mr Montacute.'

'Oh. Oh, yes, I remember.' She felt a sudden little surge of blood to her face. She had thought of him quite often since then, embroidering the memory with certain romantic little fictions, and had the fleeting, embarrassing sensation that he had somehow been able to read these thoughts.

'I got your telephone number from the file,' said Richard. 'I thought you'd be home for the Easter holidays.'

'Yes, we broke up a week ago.'

There was a long pause. Helena wished she could think of something bright and witty to say – of *anything* to say. Richard was wondering why he was doing this at all. Then he thought how she must look at that moment, holding the phone, her mouth as she spoke, and remembered why. He had to stop himself from asking her what she was wearing.

'So – what are you doing with yourself in the holidays?' he asked instead. No, no, he thought – don't make a big thing of her still being at school.

Helena settled herself against the pillows on her bed and stretched out her legs. 'Oh, nothing much. Riding a bit. Reading. You know. Arguing with my brother.' God, she was sounding boring, she thought.

He laughed. 'Yeah – I used to fight a lot with my brother in the holidays. I mean, I still do. When I see him.' He coughed, and then the cough turned into the kind you couldn't stop. 'Sorry,' he said, when it had finished. 'I played rugby on Sunday in the rain. I think I caught a cold, or something.'

'I thought people always played rugby in the rain,' said Helena. God, what a dumb thing to say. 'I mean, they always seem to be covered in mud when you see it on television.'

'They usually are,' he said. Why were they talking about rugby? He still wanted to know what she was wearing, where she was sitting . . . He used to ask Lisa that; God, he used to love the answers she gave. But she had been twenty-five. This was Helena, and she was seventeen, and home for the school holidays. 'So listen,' he said, getting to the point, 'do you ever get up to London these days?'

'Only when mother goes up.' That sounded pathetic, as though she had to go everywhere with her mother, so she added, 'I've got some friends who live in London. I stay with them sometimes.'

'Oh, do you?' said Richard. 'Because I was wondering you know, if ever you do come up, whether we could meet up, or something.'

Helena thought about this, winding her hair round and round her fingers. 'I suppose so. The thing is, if I go to stay with friends their mothers expect us to go out together. I mean, that's the problem.'

To Richard, having friends in London meant having friends at whose flat you could stay for the night; to Helena, it meant having friends at whose parents' house you could stay, and whose rules you obeyed.

Richard pondered this. In the pause Helena suddenly said, 'Why do you want to see me?' She said it in a tone of genuine, childish curiosity. It was a tone that Richard was not used to. With most girls, everything was much more glib, almost coded.

He opened his mouth – then hesitated. Then he said, 'Because I really like you.'

There was a longer pause. Helena felt a warm glow of pleasure when he said it; she knew it, but she had wanted to hear it. 'Do you?' she asked, smiling to herself. She unwound her hair from her fingers.

'Yes,' replied Richard, and flipped the beer mat that someone had left on the coffee table. 'And you really like me.' It was as though some sudden charge of intimacy had connected them; neither spoke for a moment. 'Look,' said Richard, breaking the spell, 'I tell you what. Give me a call when you're going to be in London again. Yes?'

'All right.' And he gave her his number. 'I'll probably be up with Mummy before the end of the holidays,' she added.

'Good,' he said. 'We can go out somewhere.'

'All right.'

There was a pause.

'Right, then. Goodnight,' said Richard.

' 'Night.'

'Sleep tight,' he added. He wished he knew what her bedroom was like, what she wore when she went to bed. He put the phone down. Why was he doing this? Seventeen. He must be bonkers.

Helena clicked off the portable phone and lay back on her bed, smiling to herself.

Chapter eight

The idea that had occurred to Marion after her telephone conversation with Sally was nursed carefully for a week or so, during which time she consulted the Ampersand prospectus and made certain calculations. Then, when the idea was healthily developed, she called Geoffrey Montacute at his office.

Montacute was surprised to feel a distinct tightening of his heart when Miss Reed told him who was on the line; he even felt somewhat nervous as she was put through to him. Nonetheless, his suave self-possession, by now second nature, asserted itself when he spoke. 'Marion,' he said with real pleasure, 'what a delightful surprise. I have thought of you more than once during the past week.' This was true, since he had certain matters to discuss with her concerning the estate, but he was struck now by the pleasant appropriateness of his words.

She laughed prettily in response, then paused, wondering how to approach the matter. Best to be direct. 'I felt I should ring you, Geoffrey, because some small matters concerning Paul's schooling have arisen. I find that, on top of the fees, there are some extras which are only just beginning to come to light – extra kit, oboe lessons, not to mention the oboe itself . . . oh, and some foreign trip they take this term. I shan't bore you with the details, but I find that it all rather adds up.' She paused for breath. 'I realise, of course, that all this should come out of the trust, shouldn't it? So I thought I should apply to you. Don't think me mean, but you know my own financial position is somewhat tight, and—'

'Of course,' interrupted Montacute. 'You're perfectly right to come to me. Any such expenditure in the course of the children's schooling will be dealt with as part of the trust.'

'Oh, good,' said Marion. 'It's just that these things do rather mount up. Of course, Helena's had to have rather a lot of new things. You know what girls are.'

Montacute did not know, but he gave a ponderous little chuckle. 'And she's taking a small trip to France with a friend after her exams – there will be air fares, the hotel, heaven knows what else—'

'Marion, Marion,' interrupted Montacute again, very much enjoying his sense of gentle mastery. 'Please put it all down on paper and out of your head. Just let me have a clear note of all the expenses and I shall ensure that the trust reimburses you. Or rather, that you reimburse yourself – as a trustee, that is. Ha, ha!'

She laughed, too. Reimburse. What a beautiful word, so full of promise.

'And let me have copies of receipts – from the schools, and so forth.'

'Receipts?'

'Yes, for the trust accounts.'

'Oh. Oh, yes. I'll see what I can do.' Her voice sounded a little distant. 'I'm so hopeless about money, you know . . .'

Montacute smiled to himself. There was a longish pause. Why not? he thought. There was something about Marion that made him feel positively boyish. 'I'm rather glad you called, in fact,' he said daringly, 'because it gives me the chance to ask if I might invite you to dinner.'

'To dinner?' She was still thinking about the problem of the receipts.

'Yes – some time this week, perhaps. Friday? I have some things to discuss concerning the estate, and of course they could be dealt with on the telephone—' He paused. 'But it would be so much pleasanter to see you in person.'

She collected herself, and smiled an unnecessarily charming smile at the receiver, watching her reflection in the mirror above the drawing-room mantelpiece as she did so. 'Geoffrey, what a delightful idea. Of course, I should love to dine with you.'

After they had made their arrangements, Montacute put the phone down in a most satisfied frame of mind. Marion felt less complacent. She had no particular desire to have dinner with Geoffrey Montacute, but the card she had played was a strong one – he seemed to respond rather well to the hopeless little woman tactic – and had to be followed up. This receipt business was going to be rather a nuisance, but she would find a way round it.

After a little more work with figures on paper Marion felt more cheerful. So much so, that she rang Sally Howard and told her that she wasn't going to Norfolk after all, and would love to go to Paris with Linda and her on the fifteenth.

When Marion told Helena the next day that she was going up to London on Friday, and would return on the Saturday, Helena leapt at her chance.

'Look, can I come with you, Mummy? I really want to see Fiona.'

'You'll be seeing her next term, won't you?'

'I know, but it's not the same as during the holidays. We could go out in the evening – we can't do that at school.'

'I don't see why not,' replied Marion. Helena's hotel bill could be added to the other bits and pieces the trust was paying for, and she might be able to slip her own in as well. 'I'll have to see if Paul can stay the night at Tony's, though. I don't want to leave him here on his own.'

When the thing was settled with Tony's mother, Marion told Helena that she could come up to London with her. Filled with delight and anticipation, Helena went down to the phone box in the village and called Richard's office.

Helena's call came as something of a surprise to Richard. He had not seriously expected to hear from her. When he had rung her, he had been feeling lonely and bored, and the memory of her face had been haunting his mind somewhat persistently. He had not thought anything would come of it.

'Mummy's coming up to town on Friday and I'm coming with her. We're staying at some hotel in Knightsbridge. I know she's going out in the evening. I've said I'm going to see a school-friend.' She sounded quite excited, he thought. Very girlish. He smiled.

'Wonderful,' he said. 'I could pick you up at your hotel and we could maybe go – well, wherever you like. The pictures.

Anything.' He paused. At the other end, she felt slightly disappointed; she had hoped for something a little more grown up. Dinner at some expensive restaurant, perhaps. But the pictures – that was where any boy might take her. Then he added, 'Don't you think it would be better if you told your mother what you're really doing? I mean, it's not that dreadful. I could meet her when I come to pick you up. It might be more sensible.'

But Helena was not sure that she wanted to be sensible.

'Oh, no!' she said quickly. 'That's not a good idea. I mean, she might not like me going out with someone – well, so much older than I am.' It felt ridiculous having to say it; it made her sound like she was a child. 'Anyway, I've already told her. It would sound a bit odd if I suddenly said I was going out with you instead.'

It occurred at that point to Richard that it might not be a good thing to become entangled in a web of deceit, however small – especially one that involved the daughter of one of Mr Montacute's more favoured clients. He hesitated. Still, what harm could it do? It was only one evening.

'If you say so,' he replied.

'Great,' she said. 'My money's nearly run out. Hang on while I find another ten pence.' She fed some more money in, and the realisation that she was calling from a call box, instead of from her own home, renewed his doubts. 'You still there?' she asked. 'Good. Well, look, I don't really like going to the pictures that much. Why don't we go out to – to dinner? I could meet you somewhere.'

This was all getting a little too clandestine, he thought. Still. 'Well, that's fine with me. Do you know Grunts in Maiden Lane?'

'The pizza place?' said Helena, a little crestfallen.

'That's right. I could see you there at half-seven. How does that sound?'

'Yes. Fine. OK. Great.'

She hung up. Well, maybe when he got to know her a bit better and realised she wasn't completely unsophisticated, he would take her somewhere better. And Richard, in his office, hoped that she didn't mind just going for a pizza. Being an articled clerk, he didn't have that much money. Anyway, he told himself, going for a pizza was what seventeen-year-olds did. So that was all right.

On Friday morning, as he shaved and dressed himself with special care, Montacute felt buoyant at the prospect of his evening with Marion. It was nineteen years since he had taken someone out to dinner. He reflected briefly on that former, distant failure. Bernice, her name had been, the daughter of a woman with whom his mother had played bridge. It had largely been arranged by their respective mothers. He had not even liked the girl much. They had sat through a painfully dull evening, he groping for conversation while she eyed him with cold impatience. The incident had merely reinforced the conviction, planted in him from an early age by his mother, that the opposite sex had no use for him. He had left them alone ever since. He remembered the peculiar satisfaction his mother had taken in hearing, in reply to her endless enquiries, that he was not going to see Bernice again. She had regarded his failure as her own triumph, a testimony to the correctness of her view of him. 'Of course,' she had told him, 'you are quite as charmless as your father. I might have known.'

He thought bitterly now of what she had said. Well, this was different. For the first time in his life a woman had smiled upon him with kindness and affection, and he was to take that woman to dinner. It had nothing to do with his mother. She would not even be allowed to know of the arrangement. He thought of all the ways in which she might seek to pollute this friendship and resolved, as he tied his tie, that for once in his life he would prove his mother wrong. Just because she did not love him did not mean that others might not. Montacute almost felt that he could be reborn as a new person, as he admired his tall, darkly dignified figure in the wardrobe mirror.

The April day was mild and cheerful, and Montacute felt its influence. He found his mother sitting downstairs in her armchair, reading the paper, her cup of tea on the little table at her elbow.

'How did you sleep?' he asked, almost pleasantly.

She did not look up. 'I had the most wretched night. I hardly slept at all,' she replied. 'My shoulder gives me the most intolerable pain. I don't know why you bother to ask me, since you know the perpetual pain I suffer. Perhaps you do it just to remind me of how wretched I feel.'

He went quickly to the kitchen and poured himself a cup of tea from the pot on the table. Then he made himself some toast and buttered and ate it, gazing from the kitchen window at the unkempt back garden, noticing the blossom on their neighbour's pear tree. He went back through to his mother.

'It seems such a pleasant day,' he remarked, 'that you might care to have the french windows open. Shall I do that for you?'

'Don't be ridiculous,' she snapped, glancing at him. 'Do you want to me to catch a chill, and end up in hospital with pneumonia? Come to think of it, you probably do. No, I do not wish to have the french windows open. I don't suppose it occurred to you to make me any toast while you were through there?'

'I thought perhaps you had had your breakfast,' he replied mildly, glancing at his watch, and went through to make his mother some toast. He took it back through to her, who accepted it without a word. 'By the way,' he said, 'I shall be back rather late tonight. I shan't want any supper.'

She chewed for a few seconds, eyeing him, then sat back in her chair. 'Spending the evening with some woman, are you?' Montacute felt a shock of dismay. 'That piece of rubbish that Alexander was fool enough to marry, I suppose.' He stared at her. She smiled at the expression on his long face. 'Don't look so surprised. Do you think I don't know you? I've been watching you.' She nodded cleverly, taking another bite of toast. Little crumbs clung to the hairs of the moustache on her upper lip. Her eyes fixed his with bright malevolence. 'You've been going around with that self-satisfied smile, thinking that you have a secret that I can't guess. Pah!' She looked away dismissively. 'I know all about you. I know every look on your face. You are a mere child to me.'

Montacute stood, saying nothing, aware of a sense of detestation mounting in him, poisoning his pleasure in the day. He felt that if he were to raise his hand to the heavy black marble clock on the mantel, and bring it down on her skull, he would be doing no more than ridding the world of a witch. How could she have guessed? He had mentioned Marion a few times, but only in connection with Alexander's estate. He thought he had betrayed nothing, although he had told himself once or twice that it might be better never to mention her. But he could not help it. Something compelled him to speak of her, even to his disdainful, unresponsive mother.

'You are utterly wrong,' he said at last, his voice and face assuming their customary stiffness. 'I do not know how you come to conjure up such ideas.'

At this, she laughed outright. 'You are such a fool, Geoffrey – so transparent! Of course I am right. You've spoken of her too many times these past weeks for me to be wrong. When do you ever talk about any woman?' She was consumed with triumph. Now she darted another look at him as she chewed the last morsel of her toast. 'Look at yourself. The very image of a successful man – that's how you see yourself, isn't it? You think she likes you, admires you—'

'Mother, I think you have said enough,' interrupted Montacute coldly. 'I have to go or I shall be late. Don't forget to give Mrs Carmichael the money to pay the milkman.'

But his mother was unstoppable now, leaning forward in her armchair to spit out her vituperation. '—You are nothing but a pathetic fabrication of a man. You couldn't make any woman look at you, let alone like you! She probably pities you—'

Montacute had reached the door of the living room. Now he turned, paused for a second, then strode heavily past his mother's chair to the french windows. He bent down and worked at the heavy bolt that held them in place, eventually wrenching it free. The windows had not been opened since the previous summer and the wooden frames were warped; Montacute had to push them hard with his shoulder before they flew open, letting in a sudden gust of April air.

'There you are, mother,' said Montacute calmly, dusting his fingers and adjusting his tie. 'I think the fresh air is just what you need. You may find it a little difficult to close them yourself –perhaps Mrs Carmichael will help you when she comes later. Goodbye.'

He left the house, thinking to himself that it was a pleasant and novel sensation to use his masculine strength against her feebleness. It was a weapon he had not thought of using before. Perhaps he should do it more often. Perhaps he should have taken her walking stick and flung it out of her reach.

Working steadily through the day, Montacute managed to obliterate the unpleasantness of that morning's scene with his mother. Although he had been disturbed by the ingenuity of her guess as to his doings that evening, he resolved that it should not worry him. What if she did know? There was nothing she could do. She was utterly dependent upon himself and others. He pictured her, feebly tugging at the stiff windows to close them, unable to, forced to return to her bedroom to fend off any chill. And in the evening, stumping stiffly, slowly, to the sideboard; she could drink as much sherry as she wished, but she would be denied the furtive pleasure of her imagined deceit of him, denied the sole excitement of the day.

By the time eight o'clock came he put her from his mind, unable to think of anything but Marion Laing and the coming evening.

For their rendezvous he had chosen an expensive, red-plush little nest of a restaurant, French, of which he had heard one of his wealthier clients speak. It had not disappointed him. Their table was in a small booth, curtained off with a looped-back swag of red velvet, and Montacute felt the atmosphere to be both intimate and faintly dangerous. It spoke to him of illicit lovers, of men and their mistresses. Thoughts such as these, which he had always thrust from his mind before, since they involved pleasures which were not to be of his tasting, had come crowding and stumbling into his mind in recent weeks. At the recollection of Marion's sweet, confiding manner, he felt a surge of possibilities, sexual and romantic.

Marion found the restaurant stuffy, and the sight of red plush made her want to sneeze; nonetheless, she knew that the low, pink lighting showed her complexion to its best advantage, and she tried to look pleased and animated as they sat down opposite one another.

Montacute discussed business matters with his usual gravitas, but as the meal progressed and business was gradually dispensed with, a certain boyish animation took over. He had, she noticed, drunk a good deal of wine.

'May I say, Marion,' said Montacute, after dessert had been cleared away and he was feeling reckless with wine and admiration, 'how utterly charming you look? That dress is most becoming.'

It was a black, low-cut Gaultier dress, one which she knew showed a tantalising amount of cleavage and set off her round, smooth shoulders. It amused her to hear it called 'becoming'.

'Thank you. I bought it just last week. I couldn't afford it, of course, but I did want to wear something special tonight and I found this quite irresistible.' She smiled her soft, curving smile.

'Quite irresistible,' repeated Montacute with fervour, dazed by the idea that she had wanted to look lovely for him.

'Oh, by the way,' said Marion, feeling it was time for a slight change of mood and subject, 'I made a list of all those expenses that I mentioned to you on the telephone. Now, where did I put it?' She rummaged with charming impatience in her bag – it seemed charming, at any rate, to Montacute. He found her utterly feminine, embodying all those endearing qualities which he had always imagined in the perfect woman, but which he had found in none. She was helpless and a little hopeless, of course – women naturally were. She was forgetful and vague and lovely – as women naturally should be. She brought out, he thought, the very best of his chivalrous and protective instincts. All this he was thinking, fondly and tipsily, as she produced a folded piece of paper.

'Look, I've set them all out for you.' She leaned over the table to show him the list; a subtly exotic fragrance assailed his nostrils, and he had a tantalising glimpse of the curve of her breasts as the fabric of her dress fell slightly away. 'I've added it all up,' she said, biting her lower lip and frowning like a six-year-old, 'but my arithmetic isn't very good.' She relaxed her frown and smiled up into his eyes. 'Children are terrifically expensive,' she added.

Montacute felt exquisitely disturbing passions seethe in his breast as he returned her gaze. Then he turned his eyes to the list. Quite a lot of things. Well over two thousand pounds. Still, as Marion said, children were expensive things, and Ampersand was an expensive school. Clearly teenage daughters were expensive things to run, too. At the touch, the briefest touch of her hand on his, his mind toppled from its perch of legal calculation and back into the soft sphere of love.

'I know you'll think me incredibly stupid, Geoffrey,' she went on; he loved to hear his name on her lips, he thought. 'I did put together as many of those receipts as you asked me to, but when I was looking for them this morning in my desk, I couldn't find them anywhere. I rather think that the new cleaning woman may have thrown them out. I hope they're not dreadfully important. I could have another thorough search, if you like, or even write off to Paul's school—' She broke off, hoping for a reassuring interruption; no, he was just looking at her with cow-like devotion; well, press on. 'The thing is, all that will take *such* a time, and I'm short of funds as it is. Aren't I hopeless?'

'Hopeless,' he repeated adoringly, and laid his large hand over hers. It felt damp, she thought, just like an eager boy's. 'Of course it doesn't matter,' he said, as she gently disengaged her hand to fold up the paper again and lay it by his plate. 'I'm sure we can make up the trust accounts with this.' He smiled benevolently, and she felt relief wash over her. Time, she thought, to play another, smaller card.

'I've just remembered,' she said, and dipped into her bag again. 'I do have a couple of things – receipts from Harrods for some of Helena's things, dresses and so on. Oh, no, one of them doesn't seem to be here. There's the other. Still,' she said with childlike pleasure at her small success, 'it shows I'm not entirely clueless, doesn't it?'

She handed him the receipt and he put it carefully in his pocket with the list. He did not in the least care about the expenses. He would pay her three times the amount, if he had to. This was, he thought, the most perfect evening of his life. He felt loving, protective, as though he could do anything for this woman.

Marion played her part and responded perfectly to his

ponderous compliments and evident ardour; she wished, though, that he would not keep taking her hand in his and pressing it. The sensation was uncomfortably moist. When she allowed him to kiss her on the way back to Knightsbridge it was, she thought, just like being kissed by a large, over-eager schoolboy who'd never kissed anyone in his life before; he even kept his mouth closed, which would have amused Sally.

But for Montacute, who had hitherto never known the faintest pleasure of physical affection bestowed and received, that kiss was heaven. And when Marion, gently and chastely withdrawing herself from his warm embrace, murmured that it really would be so useful if she had a little flat in London – nowhere too expensive, the West End perhaps, much better than hotels – he could not help but agree.

As the taxi carried Montacute back through the night to a convenient station (Montacute had never taken a taxi all the way back to Richmond before, and did not intend to commence the indulgence even on this night of nights), Richard and Helena were making their way slowly along Maiden Lane. She was still talking. The whole evening had been like that. She had asked him a few questions about himself, listened while he told her of his couple of years spent on building sites after university, and about the flat he shared with his friend, Pete, but the conversation had largely concerned her, her life history, her friends, her likes and dislikes – a ceaseless flow of information, bright, animated and utterly self-centred. Richard did not mind. He found her entirely lovely; her chatter was something of a change from the precocious sophistication and affected boredom of many girls of his own age.

What puzzled him was that, pleasant though the evening was, the peculiar current of sexual energy that he recalled from their first meeting seemed to have disappeared.

They sauntered idly through Covent Garden. He did not even take her hand. As they passed the Market Tavern Richard suggested a drink. Then he said, 'I forgot – you're under age.' Then he wished he hadn't said that.

Helena flicked her silky hair back over her shoulders and

lifted her chin slightly. 'I can still go into pubs, you know,' she said scornfully.

'I know, I know,' he said. 'Sorry. Come on.'

They went in. The pub was very full and smoky, and all the tables were taken. They stood uncertainly.

'What would you like?' asked Richard.

'I'll have a lager, please,' she replied, glancing around.

'You're under age,' he said. She looked at him with curious derision, her brown eyes wide.

'Don't be such a prat,' she said sweetly. He smiled his crooked smile, and she could not help returning it.

'Only joking,' he murmured, thinking what a child she was. And then he bent his head slightly and, on affectionate impulse, kissed her lightly on the cheek just beside her ear. Suddenly the sensation that he had experienced on first touching her hand in the office returned. Perhaps the smell of her skin, or the nearness of her mouth – whatever it was, he felt an intense physical longing for her. She glanced up at him, startled, and he went quickly to the bar. He ordered their drinks and paid for them, scarcely paying attention to what he was doing. He gave her her drink and they stood together, exchanging only a few remarks. To outside eyes, they looked like two people who felt uncomfortable in each other's company. Helena's bright flow of conversation had dried up.

Richard finished his drink; he had hardly tasted it, his throat seemingly constricted by his intense consciousness of her physical proximity. Helena's glass was still half-full.

'I can't finish this,' she said. 'I don't really like it.' She smiled and held it out to him, and he put both glasses on the bar. She walked ahead of him as they left, pushing the door open and breathing in the fresh night air in relief.

They walked for a little way over the cobbled piazza until they reached the shadows of the market pillars. He stopped her and turned her gently towards him. They stood looking at one another, neither of them smiling, examining each other's face. They were standing a little apart. He put out both hands and rested them lightly on her shoulders, then drew them softly down her arms until their hands touched. Still they did not take their eyes off one another. She shivered slightly, and he lifted her hands in his and kissed the knuckles of each hand gently, thoughtfully, his eyes still on hers.

'What are you thinking?' whispered Helena, wondering why he did not kiss her. She was aware of a warm current that spread through her as his lips grazed her knuckles.

'I don't really know,' he murmured, kissing her hands again. He looked at her reflectively. Then he said, 'That's actually not true. I was thinking how beautiful you are.' He stroked her hair with his hand, and she smiled. 'Amazingly beautiful. And,' he sighed slightly, 'I was thinking that if I kiss you, I might have a real problem.'

'What problem?' She scarcely breathed the words, moving a little closer to him.

His eyes were on her mouth as she moved towards him. Oh dear, he thought. 'Well—' and his lips brushed hers lightly; he closed his eyes, quite dizzied by the sensation of touching her mouth with his. 'I don't think I shall want to stop.'

'No?' She moved her mouth against his, loving the way he closed his eyes.

'No,' he murmured. 'Not ever.' He pulled her closely to him and they kissed for what seemed like a long, long time, while the night seemed to dissolve around them.

Chapter nine

For the remainder of the Easter holidays Helena lived in a state of intense romantic speculation. So far as she was concerned, anything that made her feel as she had felt when being kissed by Richard had to be love. She had never been kissed in such a way before, without heavy-breathing urgency or the demanding ardour customary in boys of her own age. This, she told herself, was what love was like. The intensity of her feeling was, of course, heightened by the fact that she would not be able to see Richard again until the summer holidays, and therefore had an entire term in which to recreate all her romantic fantasies. He was, when taken together with the recollection of that utterly wonderful kiss, the perfect emotional indulgence.

Richard saw things rather differently. When he left her that night and made his solitary way back to Herne Hill, he told himself that things had to be taken very carefully indeed. Of course, she was wonderful to kiss – how could she not be? There had then followed a five-minute reminiscence on the platform of Waterloo Station. But he was perfectly well aware where feelings such as those he felt for Helena were bound to lead. You could not go around kissing girls in that way, on a regular basis, without finishing up in bed with them. One thing led to another. Or, at least, in his experience it did. He pondered this. Richard was a scrupulous young man and it was not in his moral code to lure seventeen-year-old girls into bed, however much he might want to. He knew himself quite well, however, and was aware that his good intentions in that direction were very likely to be ruined by many more encounters such as the one under the pillars of the Covent Garden piazza. The solution, he told himself despondently, was to stay away from her. He felt wretched at the thought. He knew that he was half in love with her, that he found her more intensely desirable than any girl he had ever met, but he had more than an inkling of the complications that a relationship with Helena Laing might cause. In any event, he told himself, they weren't even going to see one another for the next three months. If three months could pass by, then so could six. So could a whole year.

It was perhaps just as well that Helena knew nothing of his state of mind as she returned to school for the summer term, having resolved to write to her new love at the end of the first week.

For Marion, the end of the Easter holidays meant simply a relief from the presence of the children, especially Helena, and the welcome approach of her trip to France. Montacute, true to his word, had been prompt in his reimbursement of the expenses, and Marion felt that she would be able to pass a very pleasant week in Paris without having to be unduly close-handed.

Only Paul viewed the coming summer with something less than equanimity. His return to Ampersand was shadowed with dread, and it was with a heart full of mutely suppressed misery that he settled back into the same dull pattern as before. He struggled with his work, feeling the relentless academic pace to be overwhelming him. He knew his results were wretched, and the growing impatience of even the most forbearing and helpful of the masters ate at his self-confidence. The prospect of the summer exams unnerved him utterly, even though he was aware that he was not generally expected to achieve anything.

He had grown nervous, and was entirely without the former solace of his painting, which he had been able to pursue in quiet hours at his last school; here, however, everything seemed, outside the classroom, to be noise and tumult, people doing things, pushing in on him, ordering him around. It was not a school well-suited to the individual; it prided itself on bringing out the team spirit in boys, and the boys themselves were correspondingly boisterous and energetic in their pluralist activities. No one, it seemed to Paul, was allowed to be on his own for long. Even Matron, when she found him one warm May afternoon in the dormitory, peacefully reading, said to him, 'Come along! This is no way to spend your free time on a lovely afternoon like this! You ought to get out there and get some fresh air. You look so pale. Plenty of time for this sort of stuff in the classroom.' And she hustled him out.

He wandered aimlessly over to the cricket nets, thinking with longing of the art room at Hamilton House, with its pale wooden floors and peaceful light. He had been able to go there in his free time, whenever it wasn't being used, and get on with his work. No chance of that here. Everything was a means to an end at Ampersand, work that must produce a result. He thought with loathing of the 'project' that his art class was currently engaged in. God, it was pathetic. He stood by the nets, absently watching the bowlers, conjuring up in his mind the delicious smell and texture of oil paints and thick brushes.

Wherever he went now he subconsciously, longingly, painted in his mind everything that he saw. It was sketched out in his eye in a minute, then his overworked brain would add colour and light and texture in unstoppable strokes, over and over in his head. He gazed at one of the upper-sixth-formers bowling, a tall youth with dark blond hair, and brushed charcoal lightly on to the blank surface of his mind as he watched the way the boy's sinews slid and twisted beneath the skin as he threw his arm back; two more strokes caught the creases in his white trousers as his thigh muscles flexed in the run-up. And then, as though his mind had suddenly woken up, he realised what he was doing. Well, if he was going to have it going on in his head, he might as well do it properly.

He felt elated as he hurried back to the dormitory and pulled out from under his bed his block of cartridge paper and a couple of sticks of charcoal from his tin. As he made his way quickly back downstairs he hoped that the same boy was still bowling. Oakshott, that was his name. He was one of the prefects. Oakshott.

And, indeed, Oakshott was still bowling in his calm, unhurried way as Paul settled himself down on the warm grass, his back against a tree trunk, and began to sketch.

He sketched Oakshott over and over again, with deft, strong strokes, in all kinds of different attitudes. Running, his hands still low down at his waist as he held the ball and prepared to draw his arm up over his head. Bringing his arm up, at the very top of his swing, his trunk and arm and fingers all following one long, sinewy curve up to the ball. Bowling, all the muscles of his back and throwing arm extended to one point of force as the ball left his hand. And walking, relaxed, his head down and his blond hair falling over one eye, back to his mark.

Oakshott was as happy to bowl as Paul was to sketch. He was vain about his cricket, and his bowling in particular. He was a good bowler, the best in the first eleven, and the satisfaction he took in his own strength and collected grace as he ran and bowled never failed him. But he and Sedley, who was batting, began to tire eventually, and it was as his concentration slackened in the last over that he noticed the fifth-former sitting under a tree not far away, glancing up occasionally as he busied himself with his sketch pad.

Oakshott bowled his last ball, and then walked over to Paul with a mixture of interest and vanity. Paul glanced up and stopped sketching as he watched Oakshott walking towards him.

'You drawing me?' asked Oakshott with his customary directness. He asked it with a smile, and Paul nodded.

There was a pause while Paul looked up at the older boy, his mind already busy with the crooked length of his nose, his angular smile, and the smudge of shadow across his eyes from the overhanging tree branch, and then Oakshott said, 'Let's have a look-see, then.' He held out a friendly hand, a brown, sinewy arm lightly dusted with blond hairs, the cotton sleeve of his shirt rolled up to the elbow, the tips of his slender fingers grey with dirt. Paul looked down at his sketch pad, then handed it up to the older boy. Oakshott stood turning the pages, scrutinising the different images of himself with attentive pleasure. Paul felt uncomfortable sitting on the ground at his feet, and scrambled awkwardly up, dusting down his grey trousers and flicking his limp hair away from his brow with nervous fingers.

'Not bad,' said Oakshott, pleased with the grace and muscularity with which Paul had depicted him. He looked closely at a rough sketch of his own face, half-turned away from the artist, which Paul had done. 'Looks more like you than me,' he said.

Mildly surprised, Paul glanced at the picture. He was right. 'Well,' said Paul, 'I suppose it's because we look a bit the same.'

Oakshott looked up at Paul. 'Hardly,' he said, his eyes scanning Paul's features critically. Paul felt awkward.

'Superficially, I meant,' he replied.

'Well, yes,' conceded Oakshott, looking back at the picture. 'You could say so.' He flipped back through the pages. 'I still think they're ruddy good. You're a bit of an artist, aren't you?'

Some people knew nothing, thought Paul with faint contempt. 'Thank you,' was all he murmured.

'Ruddy good,' said Oakshott again, more delighted with so many attractive versions of himself than with Paul's talent. 'Sedley, come and look at this,' he called to Sedley, who was unbuckling his pads. Sedley chucked down his pads and ambled over, a thin, dark-haired youth with a tapering chin and very thick eyebrows. He looked at the sketches.

'They're very good,' he said, glancing from the pictures to Paul and back again. 'You should get him to sit for a portrait.' It was a joke, but Oakshott, when it came to himself, did not recognise such jokes.

'That's an idea!' he exclaimed. 'Why don't you paint my picture?' Sedley smiled and turned away, while Paul gazed at Oakshott in surprise.

'Don't be daft!' said Sedley. 'Who'd want a picture of you?'

'I would,' replied Oakshott, not even mildly offended. 'My mother would.' He turned back to Paul.

'I – I don't mind,' said Paul. At least it would be an opportunity to do some real work, instead of still lives of bits of fruit and dead birds. 'But when would I do it?'

'Come to my study in the evenings,' said Oakshott, handing the pad back to Paul, oblivious of the smirks and raised eyebrows of Sedley. 'You can come after prep. Good practice for you.' He smiled and walked away. Paul watched him go, mildly amazed at the perfection of his conceit. Sedley laughed at the expression on Paul's face, thought of saying something, and then changed his mind.

It did not occur to Paul to go that very same evening. He left it until the next day and went to Oakshott's study after prep. He stood outside for a moment, hearing voices within, and was half-minded to go away again. It had probably been a joke, something devised to humiliate him. But he hesitated for a second, and then knocked.

'Come!' called Oakshott with all of his sixth-former's arrogance. Paul went in. Oakshott was lounging in a chair at a table by the window of his narrow study, one foot on the table and the other hooked over the arm of the chair. Another upper-sixth-former, Carter, was leaning against a locker. He stared at Paul.

'There you are,' said Oakshott, without surprise. 'I was expecting you last night. Still.' He swung his leg for a moment. 'Going to paint my portrait,' he remarked to Carter.

'Your what?'

'My portrait,' repeated Oakshott, smiling faintly with pleasure and looking at Paul again. 'Aren't you?'

'I'm not quite sure what with,' replied Paul, annoyance at the absurdity of all this overcoming his nervousness. Oakshott's face went blank.

'Oh, that's a point,' he said.

'I have my own paints,' said Paul. 'They're only water-colours, though, and not quite suitable.'

'No?' said Oakshott, and frowned. 'Well, we want to do this right. Look,' he said to Carter, 'you still use the art rooms sometimes, don't you?'

'Now and then,' said Carter cautiously. Oakshott was always talking him into doing things. 'Just for the odd bit of pottery.'

'Well, look, now,' said Oakshott easily, 'you go to Webster and tell him you've got to go up to the art rooms to get some – well, whatever you use up there, or – say you've left something there—'

'Oakshott—' began Carter.

'No, no, listen. It's all right. Then when you've got the keys, you and—' He paused and looked at Paul. 'Here. I don't know your name.'

'Laing,' said Paul.

'OK. You and Laing go up and get whatever Laing needs.'

Carter sighed. To refuse would involve long and tedious argument. 'OK,' he said. 'If you lend me your Happy Mondays CD.'

Oakshott raised an elegant finger and smiled. 'It's yours.'

By the time Paul and Carter had sneaked an easel and an assortment of oil paints and brushes out of the art rooms it was nearly nine o'clock. They hurried the stuff back to Oakshott's study, where Oakshott sat reading and eating an apple.

'Well done,' he said. 'Here.' And he handed Carter the compact disc. 'Don't mess it up.' Carter took it and left. Paul looked at Oakshott, watching him finish his apple.

'I can't start tonight,' he said. 'It's too late. I have to be in the dorm at nine-thirty.'

Oakshott nodded. 'OK, then,' he said, chucking his apple core into the bin. 'Come back tomorrow evening.' He turned back to his book.

Paul felt strangely exasperated; he wondered suddenly why on earth he was doing this. Why he and Carter had taken such a risk sneaking stuff out of the art rooms. Detection in that crime could have serious repercussions. Perhaps people just did what Oakshott wanted; Oakshott certainly seemed to expect it.

'What about all this stuff?' asked Paul. Oakshott glanced up.

'Don't worry. I'll stash it somewhere. It won't be found.' And he smiled at Paul. 'Off you go.'

And off Paul went.

Paul returned the following day after prep. Oakshott had already set up the easel and the board, and Paul got the rest of his things ready and stood uneasily in front of the canvas.

'Where d'you want me?' asked Oakshott, and he sat down in his chair by the table at the window and leaned back. 'This do?'

Paul looked at him for a moment, marvelling at the ease of his conceit, the perfect way in which he took his own charm for granted. He was certainly handsome, a good subject for a portrait, with his long, lean face and dark blond hair.

'Turn your head a bit – no, as though you were looking slightly out of the window,' said Paul. Oakshott adjusted his head, lifting his chin a little. The miracle of his vanity was that he himself seemed quite unaware of it.

Paul drew up a chair and adjusted the height of the easel. He picked up a short stick of charcoal, gazed at Oakshott, lowered his arm, and sat back. After two minutes of this Oakshott said, 'Well? Aren't you going to start?'

'I will in a moment,' said Paul.

'Well, hurry up. My neck's getting stiff.'

'I'd rather you didn't talk right now. Anyway,' Paul added with a sigh, 'there's not much point in your sitting in a position you don't feel relaxed in. Lower your head a bit and turn it slightly more towards me. Right.'

'Bossy little bugger, aren't you?' said Oakshott.

Paul picked up the charcoal again and made a few basic strokes on the white canvas. He looked at Oakshott. The very first glimmer of the day's end touched the sky behind the cricket pavilion, and the glow of light cast strong shadows across Oakshott's face and neck. It was perfect, he thought; but the light would not last very long like that. If only he could paint him thus . . . Having paused and calculated, he made his decision, put down the charcoal, and began to paint immediately, as fast as he could. There was only an eighth of an inch of linseed oil in the bottle that Carter had taken, and the palette had a narrow crack in it, which was messy, but for the time being he was satisfied. He worked for a steady thirty minutes and felt, when he laid down his brushes, that he had got good groundwork done.

'That it?' said Oakshott, who had actually, Paul thought, been an extremely patient and good model. The novelty would wear off, he supposed.

'The light's going,' said Paul.

Oakshott looked at Paul's hands and at the newspapers they had laid on the floor below the easel. 'Messy business,' he said.

Paul found it difficult, within the confines of Oakshott's study, to clean his brushes and hands satisfactorily, but he managed somehow. He had begun to paint with such haste that he had not rolled his cuffs back, and they carried one or two smears of paint.

'I'll need to have some sort of overall,' he said, looking down and noticing another smudge of paint on his trouser leg.

'I'll fish out one of my old rugger shirts for you,' said Oakshott as he helped Paul to lift the canvas from the easel and stand it behind the locker. Paul dismantled the easel as Oakshott stuffed the rags and brushes into a carrier bag and tucked them at the bottom of his wardrobe.

'Well,' said Paul, standing uncertainly in the middle of the room. They looked at one another for a moment; the light had deepened to the point where the far corners of the room lay almost in darkness. They smiled at one another.

'See you tomorrow,' said Oakshott.

'OK,' said Paul, and off he went, lighter in his heart than he had been since he first came to Ampersand. He had spent forty minutes or so in Oakshott's company, doing the thing he loved best, and although they had been passed largely in silence, those forty minutes had been companionable.

The next evening he carried on, this time arrayed in one of Oakshott's old rugby shirts, put on back to front. He had managed to get some more linseed oil and some essence of turps, and he painted steadily and confidently. It had only occurred to him that day that he had begun painting in a light which could not be guaranteed every evening, but the sky was clear again tonight.

As he had predicted, Oakshott was more disposed to conversation this evening; the pose that he had struck for the painting meant that he kept his head slightly turned away from Paul, and so his pronouncements had something of a wistful air about them and less conceit. Paul was aware of this and rather liked it, but eventually he was constrained to say, 'I'm not doing your face at the moment, so you can look at me when you talk, if you want. Just don't move your shoulders.'

Oakshott turned his head carefully and looked at Paul. They

100

smiled at one another. He wasn't a bad bloke, Paul supposed, looking back at his canvas; if you looked like that and were in both the first eleven and the first fifteen, you were probably entitled to be as vain as you liked.

'I've never done this before, you know,' said Paul.

'What? Painted someone's picture?'

Paul shook his head. 'I've never done any portrait painting,' he said, and sighed. 'So it may be completely useless.' But, in fact, he thought it was going rather well.

Partly because of his loneliness and natural introspection, and partly because of the fact that no one paid much attention to him, Paul's disappearance every evening after prep went unnoticed. There was struggling within Paul a raging sense of unfairness, the product of his own special vanity. At Hamilton House he had been regarded as someone special; his talent was known and admired. Here at Ampersand he was just another boy, not especially good at anything, so far as anyone could see. The art master saw that he had ability, that he could produce better than average likenesses of the subjects the class was asked to draw, but within the limitations of the subject matter and the materials that these classes encompassed, he was not recognised as having any peculiar talent. In fact, Paul dawdled his way rather aimlessly through his art lessons, nursing a vague contempt.

Now, in luxuriant possession of his own time and his own subject, with a medium that delighted his senses, he threw himself into the portrait of Oakshott with a kind of avenging fury.

The serene days of May endured, and the evening light continued to bless his endeavours. He ate, worked and slept with the image of Oakshott, sitting loose and untidy in his chair against the pale first glimmer of dusk, ever before him; in his mind, colour and form ebbed and flowed. By the time prep came, he was longing to be back at his easel.

Occasionally, in the first week or so, Oakshott's friends would poke amused heads round the study door. Oakshott's vanity was legendary, and the portrait was something of a joke among them. But their presence had no effect on Paul. He had ceased to care for them, for the school, or for anything else; this was important. This, and this alone. Gradually Oakshott's friends found it less of a novelty and ceased their visits.

'You don't use many of those tubes of paint, do you?' asked Oakshott one evening. He had ceased to call Paul by his surname after the first week, but still did not call him anything else. The peculiarity of their positions as artist and subject had produced a kind of informality between them that blurred the otherwise sharp edges of distinction between upper-sixth-former and fifth-former.

'I only need four,' replied Paul. 'Yellow, madder lake, blue and white.' Paul was not confident about this and doubted the sufficiency of his experience to carry it off, but nonetheless he found the experiment exciting. 'Rubens only painted with four colours,' he added. 'Sometimes five. Titian said it was possible to be a great painter using only three colours.'

'Oh?' said Oakshott. He yawned and looked at Paul. 'You need a haircut, you know. You really look a bit of a girl with that thing on back to front.'

Paul said nothing and carried on painting.

'You know any girls?' asked Oakshott.

'Not really – not well. Only my sister,' replied Paul, 'and my cousin. There were girls at my old school.' He felt on uncomfortable territory here. He was aware that he did not know anything about girls – certainly not as much as he should do, according to the general tenor of the dormitory talk after lights-out. He was also aware that he did not feel himself to be possessed of the same curiosity as his fellows concerning his body and its relationship to the opposite sex. Perhaps there was something wrong with him.

'Does she look like you, your sister?' asked Oakshott.

'Not really. Well, sort of, I suppose.' Paul picked up a rag and rubbed at the canvas. 'She's blonde, like me, but a bit darker. She's nice.' He stopped then and looked at Oakshott, who was moving his head in small circular motions to relax his neck.

'Sorry,' said Oakshott, and resumed his distant gaze at the trees, behind which the clear sky was beginning to take on a faint roseate tinge.

Paul worked on longer than usual, anxious to finish a troublesome detail around the line of Oakshott's shoulder. Oakshott appeared to lounge in the same position every day, but there always seemed to be something different about the angle of his right shoulder. As he worked, Paul was aware that Oakshott was still talking about girls, was telling him about some girl he'd met over the Easter holidays. As he described what he'd done with her, Paul tried to blot out the more explicit details and concentrate. He even told Oakshott to stop talking at one point, but Oakshott held his peace only for a minute or so, and then carried on, reliving his conquest in the recounting of it.

When Paul finished at last and stood back, wiping his brush on a rag, Oakshott did not get up, as he usually did, to start putting things away. He sat where he was, his face half in shadow, looking at Paul.

'You really do look like a girl,' he said; Paul pushed his hair away from his forehead with his fingers, a customary gesture when embarrassed. 'You've got paint on your forehead,' said Oakshott. 'Come here.'

Paul approached him, and Oakshott dipped the end of the rugby shirt that was serving as Paul's overall into the pot of white spirit that stood by the easel, and gently wiped Paul's forehead. The sun outside had dropped behind the trees and the study was full of brown and crimson colour. Burnt sienna and dark madder lake was always to be Paul's memory of that evening. Oakshott still held the corner of the rugby shirt. 'Is your sister as pretty as you?' he said, his voice a little thick, pulling Paul's hand towards him.

Paul closed his eyes, and then opened them. He could see only one side of Oakshott's face, the face that he lived with day and night, awake and in his dreams. Oakshott had placed Paul's hand against the waistband of his trousers. 'Is she?' he repeated with urgency. Paul could say nothing. 'We like each other, don't we, Laing?' Then he said, still looking intently at Paul's face, 'No, I shouldn't call you that, should I?' Just as Paul was thinking, no, don't call me that. 'We do, don't we?' said Oakshott again.

Paul nodded. Oakshott murmured something, his voice not his own.

Outside, the shadows deepened, and the shouts of boys coming back from the tennis courts echoed faintly in the air.

The next evening Paul went to the study as usual. Oakshott was there, and the painting was resumed. But the atmosphere was different, and highly charged.

'I didn't think you would come this evening,' said Oakshott after a while. His voice sounded studiedly careless.

'Why not?' asked Paul, blending the flesh tones of Oakshott's face with his middle finger. His voice was even. 'Because of last night?' he said, when Oakshott made no response.

Oakshott turned to look at him. 'Anyway,' he said, 'why did you come?'

'Because I wanted to. Because I like to,' replied Paul. And he smiled at Oakshott, who looked at him for a moment and then returned a thin, cautious smile.

Again, Paul stayed until the shadows fell, and beyond.

And every evening after that Paul would paint until the first clear streaks of red touched the sky, and then put down his brush and go to Oakshott.

Chapter ten

There was love, too, in the May air around Lincoln's Inn. Montacute, as he made his way through Bell Yard to the Strand, was full of it. But love did not have the same effect upon Montacute that it might have on most people. It had not tempered him, had not brought a smile to his lips nor a softness to his demeanour. It simply seemed to have enlarged him, to have given him an even greater sense of personal magnificence, and the coldness of his eye and the stateliness of his step betrayed nothing of the lightness of his heart.

He passed from the brilliant sunshine of the Strand into the chill grey air of the law courts, pausing loftily at the security check, his heart brimming with love. He carried his love with him as he made his way across the echoing black and white flagstones, up the grim, winding staircase, and along the gloomy corridors to number seven court, where the case of *Edelmann und Gützweig Montage GmbH v Reckitt and Others* had reached its tenth wearisome day. He made his brief, grave bow in the direction of the bench and slid into a pew next to Clive, who was sitting flicking through a large pile of documents. In front of them stood the portly figure of Henry Gilbert, QC, swaying slightly to the rhythm of his own oration while the rest of the court, from the judge down to the usher, sat mute with boredom. The tedium was almost hypnotic.

'. . . and I would respectfully remind your Lordship that no point has ever yet been taken on the question of whether or not the fax messages purportedly sent from Bremen ever in fact reached the bank. If that *is* to be brought into question, then it is only right that I should direct your Lordship's attention to the content of those fax messages, and in particular the one dated 7 July 1984. I believe your Lordship will find these in Bundle B . . .'

Mr Justice Sloman, with a weary and depressed air, reached out for his bundle and began to turn the pages. Never were pages so slowly turned. Clive dutifully turned his, suppressing a yawn. He glanced at Montacute, faintly surprised to see him there. Important though the case was, it had been trundling along without his presence since the third day, and Clive could think of no reason why he should turn up now. The truth was that Montacute had been sitting in his office, acutely aware of the summer sunshine in the streets and the unaccustomed happiness in his heart, and had been unable to fix his mind on anything. He had wanted to be out walking somewhere, thinking of Marion, and so on impulse he left the office, using this case as an excuse.

Now he sat, his eyes scanning the contents of the fax message of 7 July with apparent gravity, his thoughts entirely elsewhere. He was pondering his last meeting with Marion, their discreet little supper the previous week. He was beginning to regard these meals as merely the prelude to the altogether more delightful business of being allowed to kiss her – with a passion that seemed to grow more intense each time he saw her. It was little enough for a man of forty-seven, but for one to whom physical intimacy was an unexplored realm, it was paradise. Montacute believed in his heart that he possessed a genuine love for Marion, for her company and conversation. But above all he was physically entranced, burning with all the suppressed urges of his bleak, middle-aged existence. The sensations and longings which he had only ever secretly and ashamedly indulged, he now tethered to the image of her in all his fantasies. He relived those kisses countless times. He had no understanding of the pathos of his position, for he was unaware that the limitations of his romantic and sexual experience might make him faintly ridiculous in Marion's eyes. He only knew, as he sat there in number seven court, recalling the sensation of her small body pressed close to his own large one, that there must be more, that he must – if he were to be the man his mother claimed he never could be – consummate this love, the one love of his life. He felt his heart contract at the thought.

He would see her again this evening, going with her to look

106

at a flat which was to be purchased with the trust funds, and then taking her to the opera. He was a happy man. He considered again the matter of the flat, running the thing briskly through his mind as if to reassure himself of the soundness of the scheme. It was true that Helena obviously required somewhere to live when she came to London to commence her studies at art school in the autumn. Now was a very good time to buy. The fact that Marion might also be able to use the flat, and so spend rather more time in London, was purely incidental. Nonetheless, it was a distinct advantage; it presented him with opportunities which the far reaches of Surrey did not. He was pondering these opportunities and the fruit they might bear when the voice of Mr Justice Sloman interrupted his musings.

'That is all very well, Mr Gilbert,' the judge was saying in a tired, reedy voice, 'but it is Mr Henderson's contention, unless I have misunderstood him, that if the other facsimile messages were not duplicated to the sister bank, then the contents of those subsequent telexes must be irrelevant. That is your point, Mr Henderson?' He cast a mournful eye at Mr Gilbert's learned opponent. The learned opponent rose gracefully halfway from his seat, murmured that his Lordship had put the point most succinctly, and subsided. Mr Gilbert smiled acidly, paused for a moment and picked up his notes again.

'Well, my Lord,' he said, shifting his weight forward at the same moment that Mr Justice Sloman settled wearily back, 'with respect to my learned friend, such an argument fails to take into account the initial letter sent in respect of the proposed sale of the shares. When that issue first arose . . .'

Montacute's mind slipped away. Gilbert should make the best of a bad job and shut up shop now. He was getting nowhere. Sloman had made that clear to him, as clear as he could. But Gilbert had this tendency to persist beyond the point of hopelessness. Montacute wondered what the flat was like. He recalled the occasion when Marion had brought to his offices a sheaf of particulars for properties in Belgravia, and he had been forced to dampen her enthusiasm, pointing out that young art students, even the daughters of wealthy and deceased artists, did not normally require establishments in

Belgravia. She had looked at him wide-eyed, hopelessly lovely, and had said something about making the best possible investment. Grudgingly she had confined herself to the Sloane Square end of Chelsea; a sum had been discussed, and that sum was not to be exceeded. Clearly Marion had extravagant tendencies which required a careful rein.

He would tell Oliver about the flat when he saw him at lunchtime. He passed a hand over his face. It really was remarkably stuffy in this courtroom. He blinked and gazed ahead of him, thinking again of Marion, of undressing her. He did not allow his fantasy to be marred by the knowledge that such an operation would terrify him. He dwelt only on her body, on the unseen, half-felt softness of it. In these fantasies Montacute did not allow his own unclad body to appear. That thought frightened him, too. He supposed that these things could, should, be done in the dark. But in his daydreams Marion's body and his own hands upon it were clearly visible. And her mouth. Her mouth . . . Then suddenly, horribly, the thought of his mother sprang into his mind. It happened often. He did not know why. He only knew that the image of her sour, heavy countenance would loom up in the sensual trance of his fantasies like a reproach; indeed, a faint flush of guilt and resentment coloured every thought that connected the two women. He clenched his white hands and unclenched them. A light film of sweat stood on his palms.

'I think we must consult the record, Mr Gilbert, for if the point was not taken in examination-in-chief—' said Mr Justice Sloman.

'My Lord, to the best of my recollection—' began Henry Gilbert. But the judge's attention was now diverted by his own discomfort.

'I must say that I find the heat in this courtroom quite intolerable. Is there something the matter with the air-conditioning?' he muttered, and called over to the usher. During the murmured discussion concerning the ventilation and whether anything could be done about it, Henry Gilbert sat down with a sigh, then propped his arm on the back of his seat. He caught sight of Montacute and turned to nod in recognition. Then he thought for a moment, turned, and remarked in a low voice that it was a pity that Mr Reckitt could not have been more specific in his affidavit. At that moment, Montacute did not care one way or the other about Mr Reckitt's affidavit, and merely murmured in reply that it was not always possible to arrange the contents of witness statements entirely to counsel's convenience. Gilbert looked at him, stung. Even for Montacute, that was unnecessarily unpleasant.

Montacute looked at his watch. If he stayed here much longer, Gilbert would start discussing points with him in his round undertone. The normally diligent and attentive Montacute suddenly had no wish for any such discussion. But the matter of the heat in the courtroom seemed to have been taken in hand, for the usher drifted out of the courtroom and Mr Justice Sloman straightened up, apologised to Mr Gilbert for the interruption, and the proceedings continued.

Montacute fell back into his reverie. The problem of his mother had been preying on him for some weeks now. In the plans that he was constructing, she could have no place. Montacute had never been in love before. Indeed, he had never properly loved. He had been taught throughout his life that his was not a personality which inspired affection, and so he had neither offered nor received any. He had witnessed love, understood its processes and results, but its real, warm heart had been a mystery to him. Now, with Marion, he felt he knew. For him, the logic of his passion was not merely to have Marion Laing, but to keep her. It did not occur to him that marriage was anything but an inevitable conclusion to the emotions that he now felt.

But would she have him? He felt that his ardour was returned with a sufficiency that entitled him to hope – under favourable circumstances – that she would allow herself to be made to love to. Beyond that, however, he had only a dim understanding of the machinations of love affairs and their results. Inexperienced and infatuated as he was, Montacute could not conceive of a time when he might want her less, or grow tired of her company. He was in love, he told himself, as he gazed sightlessly at Mr Justice Sloman's long, thin features. He was in love, and he wanted to marry her if he could. Although he did not admit it openly to himself, there lived in the farthest reaches of his mind a picture, one in which he and Marion lived together in contentment at Roffey, loving and envied. There was that advantage. Though well-to-do, Montacute could never have aspired to a Surrey mansion, especially one as charming as Roffey.

But in these dreams there was no place for his mother. He thought of their life together as though contemplating a distant picture. She had lived in his company in dull hostility for so many years, chafing at his remarks, impatient of his presence, scornful of his abilities – yet indissolubly bound to him, unable to cope without him. And he – what was he? He might as well be a faceless provider, a one-man institution facilitating the continuance of her existence. She needed, wanted, nothing from him beyond the physical necessities of life which his earnings provided for both of them. Although he was her son, she took no spiritual, familial sustenance from him. I am a cipher, he thought. She would be as well off in a home. And that is where she would have to go, if . . .

'It seems to me, Mr Gilbert,' Mr Justice Sloman was saying, 'that that might be a convenient place for us to stop. We shall resume at, say—' He glanced at his watch. '—two-fifteen? Thank you.'

The court rose with a general air of relief. Montacute sat for a moment, vaguely aware of Clive gathering up papers next to him, and of Henry Gilbert murmuring to his junior. Any minute now, thought Montacute, he will turn and start to talk to me about this case. He will carry on talking about it as we make our way out, talk and talk in that self-satisfied voice. And I do not care to hear a thing he has to say. Why was this? he wondered. A month ago this case had been absorbing him, night and day. He passionately wanted his clients to win. He had taken telephone calls from New York in the middle of the night without any irritation. He had spent long hours drafting and redrafting statements, occupying whole weekends, during which his mother grumbled and sighed, dragging her impatience from room to room. She hated his work, as she hated anything which distracted his attention from her, even though she did not seem to want that attention. And now the thought of his clients, their greedy, time-consuming anxieties, bored him unutterably. He wanted only to be with Marion, or to think of her. He suddenly felt a faint sense of alarm. It was as though something was decaying, some green, thriving, industrious part of him.

A hand on his arm woke him from his reverie. 'I'm glad you came down, Geoffrey. This business of the sale of the shares is beginning to become a bit of a stumbling block, particularly in view of what Reckitt said in his affidavit. I thought we might have a chat about it over lunch.'

Montacute looked up into Gilbert's large, round face. Then he rose and said, 'I'm sorry, Henry, but I have an engagement. Perhaps Clive can go through it with you.'

'Yes, but—'

Montacute raised his hand and made his way out and along the corridor. He was to meet Oliver at one, and it was only twenty to, but he did not wish even the briefest of conversations with Henry. Oh, no doubt it was just that he had been working on the case for too long, and it was going stale on him. That was only natural. He put it from his mind, and began to think again of Marion.

As he made his way along Fleet Street to the wine bar where he was to meet Montacute, Oliver felt mild with happiness, benevolently disposed to all the world, even to Montacute. He had sold all of the paintings which Marion had given him – with the exception of one Brittany watercolour – for a total of a hundred and seventy-four thousand pounds. Far more than he would have expected nine months ago – but then, an artist's value always naturally increased after his death. The scarcity point, reflected Oliver, jabbing a fat finger at the button of the Pelican crossing, the sunlight catching the glasses of his spectacles as he looked up at the blue sky. All that Alexander's talent could do had been done, his gifts expended. His pictures would eddy in circles down the years, moving from collection to collection, staying a while in galleries, passing to auction, into loving hands and out of them, into careless, wealthy hands, then out again. At least, thought Oliver, crossing over when the lights changed, Alexander's pictures were good, brilliant even. He thought without guilt of the

111

modern work he disposed of sometimes, of the fantastic sums paid for rubbish and the tidy commissions which he blithely pocketed. If people were such fools as to pay for those jokes – though some of the jokes were rather good, in a throwaway fashion – they were welcome to, thought Oliver, as he pushed open a small door and went down the dim steps to the cool depths of the wine bar.

He found Montacute already there, sitting with a glass of wine before him, gazing into space; he did not notice Oliver until he tapped his arm. Oliver greeted him and glanced at the untouched glass of wine. Why could the man never buy a bottle?

'Let's see,' said Oliver, sitting on the stool opposite the lawyer and scanning the blackboard. 'Tuna, roast beef, smoked salmon . . . How about a round of smoked salmon and a round of beef with horseradish?'

'Yes. Whatever you like,' replied Montacute.

Oliver bustled over to the bar and stood, waiting his turn. As he waited he turned to look at Montacute, who had resumed his distant gaze. There was something odd about him, thought Oliver. As though he were in some way – lessened. He noticed that Montacute's features lacked their usual possessed, self-important awareness. Maybe the heat, thought Oliver. He ordered the sandwiches and a bottle of Chardonnay, and made his way back to the table with the bottle and a glass.

Montacute appeared to have recovered himself somewhat and remarked, as Oliver sat down, on the intensity of the heat for late May and the discomfort of the courts. Oliver murmured something in reply, took off his new, straw-coloured blazer, of which he was rather proud, and poured himself a glass of wine. He thought briefly, happily, of the couple of bottles of Tattinger that he might pop into the fridge at home later that afternoon, so that he and Dominic might toast the sale of the pictures and the commission that it had earned Oliver. He thought Dominic had seemed a bit better the last couple of weeks. Less moody. More settled.

'Well,' said Oliver, setting down his glass and taking out a large green snuff handkerchief to wipe his brow, 'what did you want to talk to me about?'

'Ah, yes,' replied Montacute, lifting his chin vaguely, 'I just thought you should know that the trust is buying a piece of property. A flat.' He rubbed his chin. 'Something for the children – well, for Helena mainly, when she commences her studies. You must, of course, as a trustee, be kept abreast of what is going on.' He stared down at his wine as though seeing it for the first time.

'Whereabouts?' asked Oliver.

'Well, nothing is settled, as yet, but it seems that Marion is looking in the Chelsea area. It is an excellent time to buy.'

At that moment the sandwiches arrived, and Oliver's mind jumped to another topic. 'Look here,' he said, squeezing lemon on to the interior of a smoked salmon sandwich, 'I went to visit Paul at his new school the other week.'

'Oh?' said Montacute.

'I took him out to tea on Sunday afternoon,' went on Oliver, 'and if you ask me, all is not right with the boy.'

'He has only been there for two terms,' replied Montacute, selecting a roast beef sandwich and picking a scattering of cress from it with his finger and thumb. 'And it is something of a change from his last school. All for the better, I believe.'

'I don't think he's going to cope,' sighed Oliver, taking a moody swig of his wine and wondering why he was bothering to talk to Montacute about this.

'Of course he will cope,' said Montacute impatiently. 'It is an excellent school, with every facility. He is not overworked or underfed, is he? I cannot recall that my own schooldays were especially enjoyable,' he went on, 'but then, school is not supposed to be. It is a discipline. A training.'

'He's withdrawn,' said Oliver, gazing into the depths of his wine. 'He's not communicative. He was never an extrovert child, but with me he was always lively and pleasant. He doesn't even appear to enjoy his art lessons. And I have the impression that he hasn't made many friends. He has exams next month.'

'Well, perhaps he's worried about them. All boys fret about examinations. Besides,' added Montacute, 'Marion seems perfectly satisfied. He was with her for the entire Easter holidays, after all, and as his mother I'm sure she would have noticed if anything seemed amiss.'

Oliver reflected that Marion did not seem to pay particular attention to anyone or anything besides herself, but he did not say so to Montacute. He thought again of Paul, sitting uneasily in the tea room, pushing back his blond hair with his hand each time he answered one of Oliver's gentle questions. The boy had seemed distant, as though retreating from the world into his own mind. He had shown only one brief flicker of enthusiasm, when talking about a picture he was painting, something to do with an older boy. But then he had subsided, his glance trickling away across the window of the tea room and out beyond.

He had asked Paul if he had made any friends. And Paul had said, remotely, 'I have one friend. Sort of a friend.' Then he changed the subject, and Oliver did not pursue it, knowing that it would not help to lay the boy's loneliness bare.

Perhaps he should mention it to Marion . . . No, that might not be wise. At the thought of her he remarked to Montacute, 'I have some good news for Marion. I've sold a couple of Alexander's early paintings for her. Got a very good sum.'

'She will be delighted,' said Montacute, looking a little more animated and pouring them both some more wine. 'I shall tell her when I see her this evening, if I may.' He could not resist this; he was burning with the lover's desire to share his treasure with the world, even with Oliver Pocock.

So Montacute was seeing Marion, was he? Oliver said nothing for a moment, took another sandwich from the plate, and murmured, 'Yes. Yes, do tell her. I'll be calling her tomorrow, anyway.'

They finished their sandwiches, left a third of the wine, and parted, each thinking that it had perhaps scarcely been worth bothering to meet for lunch.

Montacute went back to his office and fell to considering which of the trust assets might most prudently be disposed of to provide the purchase money for the flat. He thought of the money from the paintings which Oliver had sold; she would be delighted, grateful. But her delight and her gratefulness would all be for Oliver. If he, Montacute, could only do something to make her as pleased and thankful. He took out the piece of paper that listed the investments which produced

Marion's annuity. Safe, dependable Treasury Stock. He gazed at it. Judicious investment in some more adventurous area of the market might produce a much greater sum. And how pleased Marion would be. She was always bewailing her lack of money, the difficulty of keeping Roffey going. And it need not affect the rest of the trust. There need be no particular risk. He could get sound advice from any number of contacts; even a little insider information. The City lived on that.

Montacute sat thinking for a little longer, then picked up the telephone.

That evening, as Montacute and Marion were having a drink before the opera, Oliver sat in the living room of his Pimlico flat, gazing around him. One by one, his eye lit on the spaces where certain objects had stood: here a Chinese ceramic bowl of great loveliness and some value; there a silver trinket of a paper knife; and there a mahogany box, his father's, which had contained oval Turkish cigarettes – of no great worth, but something he had loved. He knew, without looking further, the kinds of things he would find missing. He had known since he first came back from Mayfair to put the champagne in the fridge, and found Dominic's wardrobe open and empty, and his own drawers gaping and spilling belongings. There was silence all around him, a terrible silence; the silence of desertion and theft. He sighed, rubbed his chubby face with his hands, and rose as something occurred to him. He went into his little study. The drawer of his desk was open, but there had been nothing of value in it. There, still hanging on the walls, were his Laing water-colours, early works. At least those were still there; but then, Dominic had had, for all his posturing, very little under-standing of or regard for art.

He would not call the police, he reflected, as he closed the study door and went back into the living room. Where was the point? The feeling which overwhelmed him as he went to his drinks cupboard to pour himself a drink – if the whisky hadn't been taken, that was – was one of shame. Shame at having been used and betrayed, and at having closed his own silly eyes to it. And then, spilling up and over the shame, came misery. He sat with his glass of whisky and permitted himself the luxury of a few tears.

Chapter eleven

Richard had, on and off, been feeling guilty about Helena for two months. She had written to him twice – long, chatty, inconsequential letters – and he had replied only once, to the first of them. His reply had been short (he felt bad about this, but he was not given to correspondence) and consisted mainly of a description of an injury to his ligament received during a cricket match. He tried to keep it friendly, but impersonal. In truth, he was still trying to maintain his resolution of the Easter holidays. There was no reason, he told himself as he laboured over his letter, why they shouldn't remain friends, on a sort of big-brother, little-sister level, but that was really as far as it should go. If he was troubled by any recollection of her wonderfully soft mouth, the smell of her skin, and the feel of her small breasts against his body (and he often was, especially at night), he managed to blot it out by going out with a remarkably randy veterinary nurse whom he had met at a party. It was not an intellectually distinguished liaison, but it suited Richard's purposes on a purely carnal level.

He was sitting in his room one lunchtime in late June with a cheese and tomato sandwich, a can of 7-Up, a jam doughnut, and the sporting section of Clive's copy of *The Times* spread out on the desk before him, when Miss Reed, who was manning the outer office during the quiet of the lunch hour, knocked on his door.

'There is a young lady in reception to see you,' she told him coldly. Richard took a hasty bite of his sandwich, and got up and followed Miss Reed out into the corridor. Why hadn't she just rung and told him there was someone to see him?

'I thought it best to come and inform you personally,' Miss Reed said, stopping to look at him, 'because I felt I should also tell you that Mr Montacute would not approve of your girlfriends calling at the office. I think you would do well to discourage it.' She marched on ahead. They reached the door to the outer office and Richard held it open for Miss Reed with a smile and a flourish.

'Miss Reed,' he said, 'the summer weather brings out the best in you. You look quite charming today.' Nothing, he thought, as she passed through the doorway with a wordless glare, could be farther from the truth; even her floral dress, which in the Fifties might have been a gay, juvenile thing, looked grim, particularly when teamed with thick, pale stockings and a variety of sandals that might have been made by Doc Marten. Still, he thought, this was Miss Reed's concession in her own female heart to summer and, blessed as he was with an affection for most of mankind, Richard could not help liking her for it.

He was not quite sure whom he expected to find waiting for him. He had a variety of female friends, any one of whom might drop in to see him during his lunch hour on a bright summer's day (although they never did), but he had not expected to see Helena. She stood, smiling uncertainly, between the photocopier and the water cooler, and he felt his heart leap with surprise and pleasure at the sight of her. She was wearing a short, apricot-coloured dress and her skin was tanned. She had had her hair cut, too – it swung, soft and slightly sun-bleached, just above her shoulders. He barely had time to greet her when she stepped forward and put her arms round his neck to kiss him (Miss Reed was standing rigid with disapproval by the switchboard, uncertain whether she should say something or not) and he could feel her body fluttering with joy and excitement at seeing him, holding him again. His heart quite melted with love of her, her youth and impetuosity. But he was acutely aware of his surroundings, and gently disengaged himself from her embrace, saying something in a murmur about getting out and going for a walk.

As he pushed Helena out ahead of him, she fluttered her fingers merrily at Miss Reed in farewell, and they went down the stairs and out into the heat of the London day, laden with traffic fumes and noise and brightness. He said nothing as he steered her across the street towards the trees and grass of Lincoln's Inn Fields, but she had slipped her hand into his and was twining her fingers between his, gripping them from time to time. When they reached the grass he turned to her and smiled, and said, 'What on earth are you doing in London in June? I thought you were still at school?'

She swung his arm happily and replied, 'I am. I've got a break between exams. I've done my art and technical drawing stuff, and history, and now there's just English left. That's two weeks away and it's dead easy, anyway. We're in London because Mummy – well, the trust, that is – is buying a flat. It's for Paul and me both, actually, but I'll be using it after summer, when I start art school. It's utterly brilliant – you should see it—' She stopped talking as he dropped down on to the grass and pulled her down beside him. Then she smiled at him, radiantly. 'Aren't you pleased to see me?' she asked after a pause; he was gazing at her, grinning his funny grin.

'I am,' he said. And he was; pleased, enchanted, amazed, delighted – there were too few superlatives for how he felt. All his thoughts of her, he realised, had been like faded photographs, shabby little images totally lacking the warmth, the vividness of her face and her charm. He stroked a few strands of her fringe with his fingers. 'I think I must be in love with you,' he said simply, belying everything he had told himself over the last two months. He could not resist saying it. There she was before him, sitting on the grass in the sunshine, smiling at him, the girl of his dreams. Of course he had to say it.

She laughed and laid her arms gently on his shoulders, clasping her hands behind his neck. 'Good,' she said.

He kissed her as gently, as lovingly, and as happily as was possible, oblivious of the people around them, the City workers with their sandwiches, the secretaries stretched out on the grass, the little idling gangs of clerks with their cheap suits, white socks and raucous chatter.

When they stopped kissing, he leaned back on the grass on one elbow, watching the dappled sunlight through the leaves playing on her face. 'How come you're so suntanned?' he asked, and stroked the soft skin of her bare thigh, tracing a line from the hem of her dress to her knee.

119

'Revision,' she replied, lying down beside him and gazing up at him, shading her eyes from the shafts of sun.

'Revision?'

'Lying out in the school garden, reading my notes. You should see my back.'

'I should indeed,' he murmured, and bent to kiss her again.

'And playing tennis,' she added indistinctly, through the beginnings of his kiss. They lay for a long time on the grass, kissing and talking, more and more acutely conscious of one another's bodies and the growing languor of desire.

I should not be doing this, thought Richard. Anyone might come past. One of the partners, perhaps. That would look just great, wouldn't it? This thought and the awareness of how randy he was becoming at the wrong time of day made him uncomfortable. He sat up.

'I'd best be getting back,' he said ruefully. She still lay there, looking up at him.

'It's only ten to two,' she said.

'I know. But I have to be back on the dot. Mr Montacute is very hot on punctuality.'

'Mr Montacute?' She laughed and sat up. 'He's too soft for words! You should see him around my mother. If it wasn't so pathetic it would be funny,' she added, with all youth's pitilessness for middle age.

'Your mother?'

'I'll say. He's always taking her out to dinner, or the theatre, or wherever, apparently. I can't make out if she likes him or not.'

'I suppose she must,' said Richard, 'if she goes out with him.' He tried to remember what Helena's mother was like, but couldn't remember a great deal. Youngish, blonde – that was as much as he recalled. Then he tried to think of Montacute with a woman, and found it almost impossible.

'You don't know my mother,' said Helena wryly. 'You never know what ulterior motives she might have. She's very devious.' Helena plucked little bits of grass and rubbed them on her knee. Richard looked at her knee as she did this, then at the shadows tapering up along her soft thigh into her skirt. He swallowed, and looked up into the trees.

'I've got to go,' he sighed.

They stood up together and strolled back towards his office.

'What are you doing tomorrow?' he asked, as they reached the steps.

'Buying stuff for the flat. Oh, Richard, it's *so* brilliant! I've never had a place of my own. It's got two bedrooms, so I think I might see if I can find someone to share with me once I get to art school. I haven't mentioned that to Mummy, though.' She ran a finger down the line of his chest, beneath his tie, to his stomach and was about to slide her hands around his body when he stopped her.

'Don't,' he laughed. 'It's not good for my image.'

'OK.' There was a pause. 'D'you want to come and see the flat? Say, tomorrow – after work?'

Uh, oh, thought Richard. He had cricket practice on Thursday nights, which was a good enough excuse, but caution failed to get the better of him, as he had known it would.

'All right,' he said. 'I finish at five-thirty. I'll see you . . .' He thought for a minute. A wine bar or a pub, that was no good – or was he being too conservative? Probably. 'Here,' he said. 'In Lincoln's Inn Fields, just where we were.'

'OK,' she nodded, happiness spilling out of her. He went back to work with a sense of well-being such as he had never felt in his life. The veterinary nurse was consigned to oblivion.

Equipping the flat in Caversham Place, Chelsea, was not the pleasurable affair it might have been; Helena and her mother did not see eye to eye on many matters, and there was a certain conflict of interest. While Helena's taste tended to bohemian starkness, Marion was anxious that the place should possess rather more comfort and sophistication.

'But Mummy!' wailed Helena, as they fished through reams of expensive curtain fabric, 'I want it to be *my* place! I don't want it to look as though it's been put together by some sort of parents' co-operative. Look at this stuff. All these flowers and rubbish! It's ghastly! Why can't we go to Habitat?'

'Because Habitat furnishings are cheap and nasty. You won't get fabric of this quality there.'

'I don't want fabric of *any* boring quality. I just want it all to look plain and simple – white walls, a few rugs, some really basic furniture. Then I can build it up as I go along, with pictures and jugs and stuff. Not this shit.' She flicked her fingers crossly at a bolt of tasteful chintz, a subtle but ornate pattern of blue and grey peacocks and leaves.

'Helena! I will not have that kind of language! Besides, this is beautiful and will look perfect in the drawing room. You're a very lucky girl, having a trust fund that can afford this kind of thing,' added Marion with satisfaction, glancing around in search of an assistant.

'It's not a drawing room! It's a living room, somewhere I can have friends and listen to music and stuff – I don't want big, fat, flowery sofas and revolting curtains! I wanted wooden blinds, those beautiful ones with slats like Venetian blinds—' Helena was nearly in tears of frustration and impotence, hating herself for behaving as she had promised she would not. She intended to be cool, firm, practical, persuasive . . .

'Credit me with a little more taste than fat, flowery sofas, darling,' said Marion. 'Anyway, wooden Venetian blinds are dreadfully expensive and quite unsuitable for the kind of windows at the flat. Remember, I have furnished rather more houses than you have,' she added.

'Then it should be *my* turn!' burst out Helena, tears not far away. 'I *hate* the stuff you're buying, it's revolting and my friends will laugh at it—'

'Helena,' said Marion, turning upon her the disdainful, half-smiling look that Helena hated most, 'if you are going to carry on like a child, then I shall have to do this without you and ask you to go back to school. I cannot have scenes in public.'

'But it's not your flat!' muttered Helena. 'Why can't *I* say what we have in it? *You're* not going to live in it, are you?'

'I may spend some time there occasionally, when I am in London. I am your mother, after all.'

'Exactly,' said Helena, folding her arms as a smiling assistant with a tape-measure round her neck hurried over, apologising for keeping them waiting. One of those peculiar flat calms of feeling hit Helena, as little recollections of Richard and other pleasurable things in her life nibbled away at the edge of her bad temper. She said to her mother, 'Look, why can't we compromise? You can use that for the second bedroom, only let's choose something else for the living room.' She was about to add her customary childish *'Pleeease!'*, but managed not to. As a result the proposal, particularly when made within the hearing of the smiling shop assistant, sounded very reasonable. Marion hesitated.

'I suppose we could,' she murmured. 'Very well.' She fished in her handbag for the measurements of the second bedroom windows, the one which she proposed to use on visits, and went into earnest consultation with the assistant. Helena leaned back against the bolts of cloth and sighed. Surely now she would be able to have something of her own way with the living-room furnishings. But she must remember – though it was difficult when your mother was such a know-all – not to get upset. If only she could think of a calm, rational way of dissuading her mother from bringing up the second Spode dinner service and several tons of silver and crystal from Roffey. The place would look like the V & A, otherwise.

That evening Helena watched Richard walk over the grass towards her, his jacket slung over his shoulder, and felt a little knot of wonder and fear in her stomach. How could anyone look so perfect? To have such a wonderful smile and such beautiful eyes and be just absolutely – right. He said hello and bent to kiss her, and the smell of his warm skin was quite entrancing. It will always be like this, she thought, smiling at him. I will absolutely love him forever.

They walked down to the Strand and waited at the top of Middle Temple Lane for a number eleven bus. The air was warm and sticky, and there was an atmosphere of weariness in the streets. Lawyers and bankers and office workers and secretaries waited for taxis and buses, and milled to and from stations. The siren call of the suburbs, of lawn sprinklers and cool drinks on patios and the sound of evening lawnmowers, was in the air around them.

'I don't know how you bear to work in the City,' said Helena, as she eyed the tired, impatient faces around her, the sullen eyes of commuters scanning the horizon for their long-awaited bus.

'I don't know. It's not that bad,' said Richard, happy to feel her hand clasped trustingly in his. 'It's really quite exciting, in a way. It's just the heat gets everyone down.' His eyes were scanning the distance with the rest of the queue. 'Ah, here's one now.'

They got on to the bus and found a seat upstairs. They did not talk much as the bus made its slow way through Victoria and Pimlico, to Sloane Square and then down the King's Road. They were content just to be together, happily conscious of one another's proximity.

Helena was proud and excited as she led him into the airy hallway of the flat. 'We've got the whole ground floor,' she said to him over her shoulder as she led him through, 'with a sort of conservatory thing at the back. A garden flat, the estate agent called it.'

Richard looked around admiringly as they passed down the hallway into a long room with french windows at one end, leading down on to a patio and a small pretty garden. 'The conservatory bit is off the kitchen,' she said. 'I'll show you that in a minute, we haven't got much furniture yet . . . Mummy is threatening to bring a load of stuff from Roffey—'

He caught her round the waist and buried his face in the hair at the nape of her neck. Then he lifted his head, pushed her hair aside and kissed her neck, his hands moving upwards over her breasts. This, he thought, is exactly what I meant not to do, as he pressed against her. She gave a little gasping, uncertain laugh and wriggled, trying to turn around.

'Don't,' he whispered. 'Don't turn round.' And she relaxed against him, conscious of his hardness against her buttocks, of his hands unbuttoning the top of her dress and sliding, cool and soft, lightly over her breasts. Her stomach dissolved with pleasure. The desire to kiss him was too much, and she struggled round in his embrace, bringing his mouth to hers. Then, as she kissed him, he pulled suddenly away and lifted his head, gazing upwards at the bare ceiling; she could feel him shaking slightly.

'I'm sorry,' he said, and coughed. 'This wasn't a good idea.'

He looked back at her, then began to button up the front of her dress. She gazed at him, her arms at her sides, her face a mixture of puzzlement and petulance, the features still blurred with desire.

'Why not? What's wrong?' She put her hands up to the sides of his face, troubled.

'Nothing's wrong,' he said, clasping her wrists gently. He thought briefly of trying to explain his feelings, his sense of guilt at the thought of making love to her, but he knew that anything which brought the disparity in their ages into it would only result in an argument about how she wasn't a child and so forth . . . But she was a child, he thought, as he looked at the large brown eyes and the sheen of her skin, like that of an infant. She was a child and it would be all too easy . . .

'I think,' he said, 'that we should go out somewhere noisy and friendly and have a drink, and then find something to eat.' The flat felt very still and dangerous; he wondered, without wanting to, whether there were any beds in it yet. 'Come on,' he said, giving her his most winning smile and dragging her towards the door to the hall, before she could do or say anything to dissuade him.

While Helena and Richard sat in the bliss of one another's company in a pub at the World's End, Marion sat stifling one small yawn after another in the company of Geoffrey Montacute in a restaurant in Mayfair. His talent for finding fashionable places to eat was quite prodigious, thought Marion, but she wasn't sure if she could stand much more of being wined and dined by him. The business of the purchase of the flat, with all the bothersome legal details, had afforded him innumerable excuses to seek her out over the past month, and it had been more than a relief to get away to the villa in France with Sally and Hugh. But no sooner had she got back than he had pounced on her again, as it were.

She sat regarding him as he droned on about some case he was involved in. What else did he ever talk about, except law, politics, and the City? And what use was he, anyway? It had seemed quite a promising idea at first, a little sexual manipulation that might produce some more money for her from the

125

trust fund. But what had it yielded so far? A couple of trifling thousand pounds in the guise of expenses for the children. She now doubted if there was anything more to be gained. Such an upright man, she thought as she surveyed his dark, heavy face, with its bland smile and rather hooded, slow eyes. Too upright by half. She fished a cigarette from her bag and smiled sweetly at him as he lit it for her. Anyway, the price of pushing him beyond his own corruptibility was, if not too high, fraught with too many awkward consequences. She did not mind sleeping with him if she had to – in fact, there was something rather novel, if a little tiresome, about seducing someone both morally and physically. She smiled to herself at the thought. Montacute took it as an encouragement to his discourse and talked on, allowing her further reflection. No, she didn't mind that, since he was not unattractive in a cumbersome, ardent way – but what then? What would he expect thereafter? The thing really had to be carefully balanced between two sets of expectations – her own and Montacute's. Still, it was quite a challenge, really, to corrupt that untainted, that unassailable integrity. To what might she not bring him by manipulating him to the brink of gratification?

There was much he would do for her already, she knew. He had agreed instantly to the provision of funds for a long holiday for herself and the children in Greece this summer. It was a short step, surely, to persuading him to take a few risks with the trust fund – only ever so slightly beyond the strict letter of the law – to make her some more money. To encourage him to that step would be quite a feat of emotional engineering – what was it that he was always talking about? Checks and balances. But would it be worth it? After all, she had the money that Oliver had made for her on those paintings, clever little man. Less his commission, that had left not a bad sum, enough to invest some and live off the rest for a few months . . . And was there any real correlation between Montacute's head and his heart? She had often observed the lawyer in him, and it was a cold, steadfast face he showed to the world. She might simply finish up with a demanding lover of whom she would quickly sicken – with nothing to show for it.

That thought brought her back to reality and the present. Really, she felt dreadfully tired. She put out her cigarette and drained her coffee cup. He had stopped talking and now stretched out his hand to cover hers, his invariable gesture at the end of an evening. It was always the prelude to the journey home, to being kissed feverishly in the taxi on the way to her hotel. Only now it was the flat. Greater scope for his advances. Well, that had always been an unspoken understanding, she thought wearily, and she had encouraged it.

'Are you very tired, my dear?' he asked solicitously.

'I am rather,' she replied with a wan smile. 'Such a lovely holiday, but a dreadful trip back. I could hardly sleep a wink last night.' She yawned discreetly.

'I'll get a taxi.' He smiled; the next part of the evening was his reward. 'Will you excuse me?' And he slid from his seat.

As he combed his hair and regarded himself in the washroom mirror, tilting his head up as he did so, Montacute felt that tonight must bring him one step closer, surely. She was staying at the flat now. She would ask him in for a drink, or coffee. But what about her daughter? He glanced at his watch. It was only ten o'clock. Young people never got home until after midnight, so far as he understood. He smiled complacently at his reflection.

At that same moment, Helena should have been wondering what time her mother would get back. But she wasn't. Her mind was elsewhere. She stood with Richard in the half-shadows of the living room of the Chelsea flat, her mind intent only on kissing him, and on the small, shocking waves of pleasure that she felt as he ran his fingers over and over her nipples.

That damned dress of hers, he was thinking. He couldn't even remember undoing the buttons. She felt utterly liquid in his arms, and was making tiny noises of longing in the back of her throat. He felt as though he were drugged. His mind was running on the thought that they should not have come back here, that he should not be doing this, but his body, his hands, took utterly no notice. She pulled herself away from him and took his hand, leading him to the doorway. She kissed him at every second step, and each kiss blotted out any clear space in his brain. They were in her bedroom, or someone's bedroom. The walls were dappled with pale, shifting patterns of light from the street light shining through the leaves of the summer trees outside. She dropped down on to the bed and pulled him towards her, her arms round his waist.

'Please, please . . .' she whispered, pressing her face against him. He put his hands on her shoulders and then sat down next to her. As she lay back he followed her, his mouth still on hers, something at the back of his mind telling him that this should not be happening. He managed to say so, his voice no more than a half-whisper.

'I don't care,' she said. 'I don't care,' pulling at the rest of the buttons on her dress and placing his hands on her stomach.

'But we haven't . . .' Oh, well, who cared?

'I don't care,' she said again. 'I want it to be you. I love you. I want it to be you.'

She began to tug at the button of his trousers and he thought, with what mind he had left, oh dear God. And then he gave himself up to the moment.

The moment, however, was unexpectedly brought to a halt. Helena suddenly sat up. 'Oh, my God!' she whispered.

'What?' muttered Ricard in alarm, his body still in another world.

'It's a taxi!' she kissed. Sure enough, the unmistakable running purr of a stationary taxi could be heard outside in the street. 'It's my mother!'

'Oh, Christ!' exclaimed Richard. With a swiftness born of experience, he pulled her off the bed and said, 'Do up your buttons, get into the kitchen and switch on the light. Quick! And put the kettle on! Where's the bathroom?'

'Next door!' she hissed frantically and sped to the kitchen. Richard went into the bathroom, switched on the light and stood for a moment, listening. His heartbeat began to slow. He could hear voices, Helena's and her mother's. All serene. He flushed the lavatory, walked in a small circle on the bath mat, and then stepped out into the hallway with what he hoped was a cheerful and innocent countenance. There was a faint ache in his groin.

Helena smiled at him as he came into the kitchen. 'Oh, Mummy, this is Richard Ranscombe. He brought me home. I'm just making us both a cup of tea.' She was utterly composed and cheerful as she pulled some mugs out of the cupboard.

Richard held out his hand to shake Mrs Laing's and said with his best boyish candour, 'How do you do, Mrs Laing?' He didn't imagine she would remember him, and she didn't.

She took his hand with enthusiasm and looked surprisingly glad to see him. 'How do you do, Richard? I'm sure I've heard Helena mention your name. How nice. We can all have tea together.' God bless you, Richard Ranscombe, she was thinking, you have saved me from being mauled on our new Heal's sofa. She didn't think she could take that tonight. Helena poured boiling water into the teapot and put milk and sugar next to it on a tray.

'Now, if you'll just take that through, Richard . . .' And he dutifully picked up the tray and carried it through to the living room.

Montacute was sitting on one of two new armchairs, still in their protective plastic wrappings. His expression of astonishment at the sight of his articled clerk rapidly turned sour. He recovered himself sufficiently to say in tones of the deepest disapproval, 'Good evening, Richard.'

'Oh,' said Marion brightly, as Helena followed through with a packet of digestive biscuits, 'do you two know each other? Well, that *is* nice.'

Chapter twelve

Alice Montacute lay in the darkness in her bedroom and heard her son put his key in the front door, enter, and then close it gently behind him. The relief that flooded her heart was quickly followed by the habitual fret of anger. At least he had come home. The anger that she felt barely concealed her fear. One night, she knew, he might not come home, and then the change would begin in earnest. She feared the enemy, this woman whom her son was seeing, because the enemy was faceless and unknown. If only she had something to fasten on to, some idea of the person with whom she was grappling for the security of her life. That, for her, was the hardest part – to have to acknowledge that she needed her son, that she was afraid, not of losing his affection, for such things did not exist between them, but of losing a grip on the one being whose domination gave her satisfaction in life. At least in the exercise of such feelings as she had for him, at least in the expression of her contempt and dissatisfied impatience, she could feel some power, gauge herself as an individual whose thoughts and actions still possessed effect.

She waited until she heard her son close his bedroom door, then she fumbled for the switch of the little fringed lamp which stood on her bedside table. By its dim light she read the hands of her clock. Eleven-thirty. It was an old clock, a worn but handsome little thing of ornate silver with a black face that her father had given to her on her seventeenth birthday. She did not think of such things, such dead days, now. Had there once been some young spring of affection within her, some welling fount of cheerfulness, of optimism, in her girlhood? If so, it had been quenched long ago, dried to a trickle, then parched by lovelessness to a barren hardness. Her marriage had been a brutal disappointment – that event and the succeeding years had worn away her youth and her smiles. She never thought now of the death of her infant daughter, that dearly wished-for daughter in whose life she had subconsciously hoped to find again the spent hope and happiness of her own existence. The subsequent birth of a boy, Geoffrey, had only fuelled a resentment that lay brooding in her depression and despair. She could not love him; she could not even bring herself to name him. Her husband had done that. If it had been her own failure to love and nurture her son which had, in its turn, made him the repressed, unlovable child that he had become, she had never acknowledged it. There had not been a time, within her recollection, when her feelings towards her son had been anything but dismissive and cold. There had been nothing in him, no charm or bright responsiveness, that might have softened or interested her. That that was her fault did not occur to her. She had not wanted any such softening or interest. The focus of her life was her own discontent, the object of her displeasure, after the death of her husband, her own son, a symbol of the sex which she had grown, through her marriage, to mistrust and despise.

And now he might be taken from her, and she might be consigned to a nursing home, a mumbling world full of people who cared nothing for her or about her, where she would no longer reign in importance but would be treated with patronising and energetic cheerfulness by nurses who would simply be waiting for her to die.

The thought made her heart beat faster with a painful horror. She reached for her little canister of pills and shook one out. She put it under her tongue with a trembling hand and lay back heavily on her pillows, trying to thrust away from her mind the contemplation of loneliness. Stark, utter, unrelieved loneliness. What solace could she look for in such an existence? She had no resources, no pastimes, no friends, no pleasant recollections or little associations to brighten her days. Only her son, and her continued influence over him, his doings and his life – that was all her life, and now there was someone, some woman out there, who threatened to take it from her. The phantoms evoked by her thoughts chased themselves around her head, and it was a long, fearful hour before sleep finally dispelled them.

In the morning, in the brightness of the summer sunlight and against the background of Mrs Carmichael's energetic hoovering, her fears of the previous night seemed somewhat fanciful. Of course, he would not desert her. He would not simply consign her to a nursing home in order to start a new life with this woman. Besides, what woman – particularly the former wife of a wealthy, lionised artist – would care to marry Geoffrey? Alice Montacute truly believed her son to be unattractive, unlikeable, a creature no better than his father. The thing, she told herself, was not worth worrying about. If it came to the sticking point – well, she would find some way of resolving matters.

She eased herself up from her chair, reaching for her stick with shaking hands, intent on finding *The Times* – no doubt left thoughtlessly in the kitchen by Geoffrey. She leaned painfully on the arm of her chair, her bulk feeling more sluggish than usual, and the stick fell away from her groping hand, clattering to the floor. She gave a little groan and Mrs Carmichael, who had finished hoovering the hallway, saw her plight and trotted in to help.

' 'Ere you go,' she said, supporting Mrs Montacute with one wiry little arm and handing her the stick with the other. Mrs Montacute nodded dismissively and stood, leaning on her stick, gazing at the doorway like a wounded animal. Then she began to move slowly forward; it seemed, for some reason, so much more difficult today. If only that wretched woman would not stand watching her like that.

'You sure you're a'right, dear?' asked Mrs Carmichael doubtfully, sucking on a tooth and watching the old lady's slow progress to the door. 'You only 'as to ask and I'll fetch things for you, you know. That's wot I'm 'ere for,' she added in her coaxing cockney chirrup.

'I can manage perfectly well, thank you, Mrs Carmichael,' said Mrs Montacute grimly, making her way through to the kitchen. 'I am not a complete invalid.'

'No, well,' continued Mrs Carmichael, trotting behind her and lifting the flex of the hoover out of the way, coiling it up with swift dexterity like a sailor, 'you can't be too careful with legs. My aunt, the one in Tulse 'ill, she 'ad a neighbour – lovely old gel, dead now, Gawd rest 'er – who suffered wiv 'er legs, and one day she 'ad a fall, a *reelly* nasty one it was, right down a flight of stairs. They didn't find 'er for a whole day. Not till late evenin'. Terrible state she was in. That was the beginnin', of course. Of 'er dyin'. So you can't be too careful. You let me do for you.'

Alice Montacute had by now reached the kitchen table, where the newspaper lay, and sat down, shakily and slowly, in one of the kitchen chairs. Perhaps she was right. Perhaps she should let Mrs Carmichael fetch and carry for her. But her spirit of independence railed at the thought. Really, she told herself, it was just the heat and the bad night she had passed. Normally she got about perfectly well. She was breathing, she realised, slow, shallow breaths. Mrs Carmichael looked at her briefly with sideways concern, then clapped a birdlike hand to her flat, nylon-housecoated breast, and said, 'Right, now we're in 'ere I'll fix us a nice cuppa. I'm about parched.' She bustled about with the kettle, imparting, Mrs Montacute noticed, that strange cleaning-woman fragrance, a blend of deodorised sweat, Harpic and Mr Sheen. 'I've got a luvvly bit of lamb for your lunch,' she went on, 'which'll do just beautiful wiv a bit of gravy and some nice creamed veg. Would you like that?' She put her head on one side and smiled at Alice Montacute as though at a surly child.

This is what it would be like, thought Mrs Montacute. Smirking, patronising coaxings to eat mashed potato and rice pudding and other pap. Surrounded by women smelling like Mrs Carmichael, bright, busy, chattering things with all the vitality of middle age, while she grew stiffer, heavier, decaying and ancient.

'. . . never could fancy saddle of lamb, meself,' Mrs Carmichael was saying. 'Not to eat. But you show my Ron a bit of lamb – chops, leg, bit of best end – 'e'd murder for lamb. Can't see it, meself. Now a bit of beef, a reelly nice bit of topside, that's wot I go for. Scotch is best, they say . . .'

Mrs Montacute levered herself slowly from the hard chair, tucking the paper under one arm and leaning on her stick. 'I think, if you don't mind, Mrs Carmichael,' she said coldly, 'that I shall take my paper into the drawing room. I do not feel disposed to conversation.'

'No. Well,' murmured Mrs Carmichael, briefly dashed, 'I'll bring your tea through to you, then get on in 'ere.' She watched anxiously as Mrs Montacute made her way stiffly to the door. 'You know wot you want?' observed Mrs Carmichael with sudden brightness, Mrs Montacute's little snub forgotten. 'You want one of them electrified chairs. That's wot you want. I've seen that old gel that Shirl used to do for – you know, the one 'ose boy lost 'is arm in that accident on the roundabout. She's all over the place on 'ers! Up and down the 'igh Street, buzzin' about. You should see 'er.' She chuckled and shook her head.

Mrs Montacute paused in the doorway. 'I cannot quite see myself riding on one of those things, Mrs Carmichael. Anyway, if I chose to, I could manage the walk to the shops perfectly well.' She pictured herself suddenly, leaning on her stick by the pillar box, halfway through a twenty-five-minute walk that Mrs Carmichael would probably do in ten. 'I told you – I am not disabled.' Not now, she thought, not yet.

'No, well, p'raps not quite your style. Still, they're ever so good. Got a basket for the shoppin' an' everythin'.' She had turned her attention to the boiling kettle, but her voice chattered on. 'Wot's *reely* useful, now – an' I've seen 'em advertised in the *Sunday People* magazine – is them stair lifts. They're the thing. I don't know, mind you, 'ow much they cost to put in . . .'

Mrs Montacute sighed and stumped out of earshot. Not only would she be surrounded by Mrs Carmichaels in a home, but there would be the constant, invasive babbling of other inmates. Pictures of grandchildren, stories of families . . . The thought was dreadful.

But, dreadful as it was, it must hang over her now, with the awful, unscratchable itch of uncertainty. She could speak to no one about it, least of all Geoffrey. She could never betray her dread to him, never broach her worst fears. All she could do was to wait, every long, lonely evening that he stayed out late, for the sound of his key in the door.

After the anti-climactic night when he had met his senior partner at Helena's flat, Richard did not see Helena again that term. She went back to school to finish her exams and he was left with a bad case of frustrated longing, not to mention love. Perhaps it had been as well, the rational, reasonable part of his mind told him, that he and Helena had been rudely interrupted that evening. Apart from anything else (and this included the dubious wisdom of a liaison which might bring him into embarrassing proximity, on a social level, with Mr Montacute), Helena almost certainly wasn't on the Pill, and it hadn't occurred to him to take any precautions. The part of him which was not rational and reasonable, however – the part which had lain panting with disbelief on Helena's bed as she had hissed the imminence of her mother's arrival – was not so sure that the interruption had been a good thing. Still, he told himself, there would be another time. Of that he was quite sure. As for his previous doubts about the wisdom of making love to a seventeen-year-old schoolgirl, he now realised that seventeen-year-old schoolgirls had minds of their own in these things. And who was he to stand in their way?

He contented himself with reliving the evening with Helena in idle moments by the photocopier, and supplying it with a more satisfactory conclusion. He had, he decided, nothing to fear where Mr Montacute was concerned. Any objection that his senior partner might have had to Richard taking out a client of the firm was rather scotched by the fact that he was doing exactly the same thing himself, and Richard knew it. Had old Montacute been hoping to get his leg over that evening, too? Richard wondered. If so, Helena's mother had rotten taste.

Montacute was, at first, less phlegmatic than Richard regarding their chance encounter in Chelsea. He felt that it compromised his dignity to be found in a situation of some intimacy with a client by his articled clerk. He felt, too, that it was not fitting that he and one of the most junior members of his staff – a clerk, no less – should sit making easy social chit-chat in Chelsea as though they were on the same social level. Montacute possessed an archaic and unbending view of the fitness of things, and he had been stiff and ill at ease as he had sat drinking his tea, longing to get away. Above all, he had felt that to be found with Marion Laing in a domestic setting where he had clearly expected to be alone with her in some way betrayed his intentions. He eyed Richard askance each time they passed one another in the office; on occasions he thought of saying something to him regarding the undesirability of Richard's friendship with Helena, but realised that this was impossible.

Eventually the matter passed from his mind, for he had other things to occupy him. A month before, he had sold and reinvested the Treasury Stock which produced Marion's annuity, and was anxiously following the progress of the company, Twentyfirst Holdings, each day. So far the stock was doing excellently. He had bought at 142 and the price, in early July, stood at 353. His friend at Overly Other had been quite correct in his information.

Montacute sold, setting aside the profit in a separately designated account as part of the trust investment programme, and did it again. He was interested to discover that he found the hazards of the marketplace exhilarating, and felt a vague flutter of excitement as he studied the financial pages each day and watched the stock climbing steadily. In a few weeks he should have accumulated enough to present Marion with a very handsome cheque, for which she would be very grateful. She would think him rather clever. He was, she would see, quite man enough to take a little hazard on her behalf.

Helena spent the rest of the summer term – what was left of it after her English exam – thinking about Richard and discussing both him and various forms of contraception with Camilla, her best friend.

'I think, all in all, the Pill,' sighed Helena, chewing on a grass stalk and rolling over on to her back. They were lying out behind the science labs in the sunshine. 'That coil thing that your friend's sister had sounds quite horrible.'

'They had to dig it out in the end . . .' murmured Camilla, flipping the pages of her Jackie Collins novel. 'Do you want a fag?' She rummaged in her bag, which contained three tennis balls, an applied mathematics crib, a Lillet and a tube of leaking factor-eight suncream. 'I confiscated these from some third-former. Camels. She gets them duty free.'

'No, thanks,' said Helena, and rolled back on to her stomach. 'I won't see him for simply ages, Milly. At the end of term we're going on holiday to bloody Greece. I don't even *want* to go, and certainly not with my mother. What if he meets someone else in the meantime?'

'He won't,' murmured Camilla, her eyes drifting back to her book.

'He might,' said Helena, smiling to herself, utterly certain that he would not. She closed her eyes. What bliss, just to lie on the warm grass, no more exams, playing tennis every day, freedom in sight. She thought of the flat in London, of art school, of how life might be and how it might not be. It was difficult to imagine. Even Greece wasn't that bad a prospect, she admitted to herself – she would make sure that she got a suntan on every single scrap of her body, then ask Richard to try to find any pale bits. So far, the months that stretched ahead of her looked like perfection.

For Paul there could be no perfection that summer. It was, he knew, Oakshott's last term at Ampersand, and beyond that the future at school stretched out for him in unimaginable emptiness. His adoration of Oakshott was mute, unrequited. The portrait was almost finished by the end of June, Oakshott already growing bored with it, less prepared to spend evenings in its completion, and the brief sexual coalescence had melted away. It had mattered little to Oakshott, had been no more than his feverish gropings with that girl at Easter, and was finally just a faint embarrassment. Lots of the chaps did it; it was just a way of getting something out of your system, there being no girls around.

But for Paul it was undoubtedly, and hopelessly, love. Love born, perhaps, out of loneliness, and out of closeness with the one person who had shared with him some tenderness, some intimacy, but love it was. He knew every tone and colour of the older boy's face, every cadence of his voice and every trick of his body as he lounged restlessly in his chair while Paul painted. He carried the thought of him everywhere.

Oakshott had been kind to him in his rough, conceited fashion, and that kindness was indissolubly bound in Paul's heart to the rediscovered solace of his painting. Oakshott was his god and his deliverance.

The blighting of his love came in that last week in June. He went to Oakshott's study, and Oakshott was there with Carter and Priday. He looked up in irritation at Paul.

'Not tonight, Laing,' he said. 'I can't be bothered with the thing.' And Paul left, closing the door as Carter's voice murmured, laughingly, 'Not tonight, Josephine.'

He stopped Oakshott the next day, touched him on the sleeve on his way out of Hall after lunch; dismay snatched at his heart as he saw the expression on the older boy's face, and he hastened, despite the pain it gave him, to reassure his beloved.

'I just wanted to say – about the painting—'

'Well, what about it? I'm getting a bit sick of the thing, honestly.'

'No, no – I know. I just wanted to say that I've more or less finished it. That is to say, it just needs a few touches and I don't need you for those. I can take it away, if you like.'

The relief on Oakshott's face was unmistakable, but it was blended with an expression that was both furtive and super-cilious. 'Where are you going to take it? You can't exactly take it to your dormitory or the art rooms, can you?'

Paul muttered something. The destruction of his bond with Oakshott was imminent. Indeed, it had occurred already.

'Look,' said Oakshott, glancing impatiently down the corridor, 'you can come to my study this evening and finish whatever it is you've got to finish. I'll be down at the nets, anyway. Then we'll get rid of all that rubbish. It's beginning to clutter up the place.'

That evening, when Paul went to Oakshott's room, he knocked cautiously, half-hoping to hear Oakshott's indolent voice call out in reply. But there was, as he had known there would be, no answering voice. He went in, closed the door, and stood in the empty room. It was very quiet. Only the sound of someone's footsteps on the stairs going up to the library, and voices from the tennis courts. He looked around at the familiar objects, at the clothes which Oakshott had flung on to the bed in changing. Paul walked over and picked up Oakshott's shirt, then held it to his face for a moment, closing his eyes. He knew himself now. He had found himself out. When? Or was it Oakshott who had found him out? Would he have been thus without Oakshott? But he knew there had been no moment of discovery. It had always been there, the truth about himself, just waiting to be discovered. No, he could not blame Oakshott. He could not blame himself. He did not care. He did not care if he was vile and horrible and different. He only cared that the one person whom he loved had no time for him now, gave him not one thought. Why should he care about anything else?

He pulled out the canvas from behind the locker, then got out the easel and the rest of his equipment. He stared for a long time at the portrait, but gradually his gaze melted from a sad contemplation to a meticulous scrutiny of the unfinished aspects of his work. For half an hour he added and touched, drawing back, and then advancing to retouch; he stopped at last, knowing that there was nothing more to be done. It was good, he knew; it was the first important thing of its kind that he had done. He wanted it, wanted to keep it. It was his work, after all. Oakshott didn't care about it, he thought savagely, pulling it off the easel and resting it against the locker. He put the paints and the easel away, rolled up the paint-smeared rugby shirt and stuffed it into a bag next to them. Then he picked up the painting – it was not large, only twelve by eight –and opened the door. About to leave, he hesitated. He went back to Oakshott's wardrobe, pulled the rugby shirt out of the bag, and left with it tucked under his arm, the painting in his other hand.

The landing by his dormitory was deserted, and he could hear faint sounds coming from the television in the common room below. Very quietly, he opened the large cupboard where their trunks were kept. He recognised his own at once, new and maroon, right at the bottom of a stack of three. He hauled it out, holding his breath at the bumping. If anyone came, he could say he was looking for something he thought he'd left in it. He slipped the painting and the shirt inside and closed the lid, then lifted the trunk back on top of the other two, and shut the door gently.

He did not speak to Oakshott again until the end of term, though at every cricket match he watched with fervent attention as Oakshott bowled or batted, following his easy figure, his dark-blond head, with hungry eyes. As he watched the final of the inter-house cup match, only days before the end of term, he reflected that it might be the last time he would ever see Oakshott.

In fact, he saw him for the last time two evenings later. Paul was packing his trunk in the dormitory, ready to leave the next day, when Oakshott sauntered in with Carter and Sedley. He was smiling and in good spirits, exchanging banter with Beasley and his cronies. It gave Paul a faint shock to see him so close, so suddenly. His love had been glimpsed only from a distance over the past few weeks. Oakshott caught sight of Paul and smiled, and Paul's heart soared. He straightened up, smiling back, brushing the hair from his eyes.

'Hey,' called Oakshott, strolling up between the beds, 'where's my picture, then?' He was amiable, supremely arrogant in the imminence of his departure from school into the adult world.

For a moment Paul was lost for words. He stood looking stupidly at Oakshott, who thrust his hands in his trouser pockets and glanced down at Paul's trunk.

'My picture,' repeated Oakshott, still smiling. 'My portrait. Can't go home without that.'

Paul bent down and pulled the picture out from below the few possessions that he had already packed. 'I didn't think you'd want it,' he said, handing it to Oakshott. But of course you want it, he thought, watching as Oakshott examined it with evident satisfaction. It's a picture of you. You don't care who painted it.

Oakshott turned and called out to Sedley and Carter, still chatting to Beasley, 'Come and look at this.' They came. Oakshott held out the canvas and his friends studied it admiringly. 'Bloody good, isn't it?' said Oakshott, examining it again. He was admiring himself, not the work. Paul saw all this. Oakshott looked up. 'Anyway, thanks, Laing. It's bloody good. See you.' And he turned and sauntered out of the dormitory, the painting held idly in his hand.

In years to come, whenever he came across Oakshott's paint-smeared rugby shirt, Paul was to wonder what happened to the picture. Or to Oakshott, come to that.

Chapter thirteen

'*Neuesachlichkeit*,' said Charlie Vereker, putting the picture back against the wall. 'Very exciting. Not much of a market yet, but you wait.' He wandered up the gallery, Oliver idling in his wake.

'Thank God for the strange tastes of Hitler,' murmured Oliver, glancing back at the painting. 'Poor old Dix.'

'Now this,' said Charlie, stooping to pick up another picture, 'is the kind of thing I want to be going in for here.' He held the picture up between two large, knobbly hands at shoulder height for Oliver to look at.

'Seurat,' said Oliver with a smile. Charlie watched his face, enjoying and sharing Oliver's expression of pleasure and admiration.

'Isn't it fabulous?' said Charlie, looking back to the picture. 'Such density – one might almost be tempted to say that the charcoal was excessive. But of course, it's not. It's perfect. Perfect.' He laid the picture gently back and turned his long neck up to look at the carefully positioned ceiling lighting. The place smelled of newness, clean and bright. This was sixty-year-old Charlie's proud achievement, his fondest dream made reality. A gallery in Cork Street. He breathed deeply as he surveyed the proportions of the long room.

'It's wonderful, Charlie,' said Oliver, gazing around him. 'You should do very well. You deserve to.' He had to look up when addressing Charlie, who was six feet two, with crinkly grey hair and an angular face and body.

'Come back to my den,' smiled Charlie, 'and we'll have a little drink. A celebration is in order.' He led the way. Charlie, for all his rugged angularity, had a long, swaying way of walking, like a dancer in slow progress.

'I still haven't told you about the Fantin-Latour that George has,' said Oliver, following Charlie back into his office at the end of the gallery. 'I would say, not bad for twenty-seven thousand. Not one of his best, but still . . .'

Charlie took a bottle of champagne from a small fridge and fussed around in search of a cloth. He sighed. 'Well, my dear, I have to say that I was never very keen on those flower studies. Exquisite, of course – ah, this will do – but not my thing at all.' Pulling off the foil, he wrapped a length of kitchen roll round the neck of the bottle and eased at the cork with long thumbs. 'Too collected,' he added, as the cork popped, trailing a little wisp of smoke. He poured out two glasses. 'Cheers, dears!' he said with a large smile, and raised his glass.

'Cheers,' said Oliver. 'To the Vereker Gallery, South West One.' He sipped. 'No, I agree. They're rather—' Oliver broke off as Charlie looked up in alarm at the sound of footsteps making their way up the gallery.

'Well, now, that simply shouldn't be happening!' he said, putting his glass down. 'The thing's supposed to buzz and shouldn't open unless I press a button. Those bloody alarm people. You simply can't get a *thing* done properly these days . . .' He was heading towards the office door when it opened, and a head looked round.

'Oh, Teddy!' exclaimed Charlie, thumping the flat of his hand against his chest in relief. 'You gave me the most dreadful start! That door's not meant to open, you know, the front one. It's meant to buzz.'

'Yeah? Well, it was open,' said the young man nonchalantly, coming into the room, and glancing at Oliver and smiling.

'Open!' yelped Charlie. He shot out and down the gallery, moaning something about his Seurat.

'Hi,' said the young man to Oliver, holding out a friendly hand. 'I'm Teddy Royle.' His accent was American.

'Oliver Pocock,' said Oliver, taking his hand. Teddy's clasp was dry and firm, and he smiled at Oliver with white, even teeth. He had a delicately featured face, lightly tanned, and soft, dark hair, worn long and tied back. Poor, susceptible Oliver thought him heart-stoppingly handsome.

'Wow, yeah – Oliver Pocock,' said the young man. 'Gee, you're big stuff!' Oliver laughed with nervous self-

143

deprecation. At times like this he wished he were an object worthy of desire, tall and handsome, instead of having a roly-poly body and a fat little face. 'I wish you were *my* agent,' murmured Teddy, shaking his head.

At that moment Charlie came back, breathing deeply, rolling his eyes. 'Oh, my dears! Just think, if it hadn't been Theodore! I'll have to speak to those wretched carpenters. The thing doesn't swing tight shut of its own accord. Would you believe it? Must be the spring. Oh, my goodness . . .' He went to fetch a glass for Teddy.

'Now, Theodore – oh, have you introduced yourselves? Yes? Good. Theodore is a perfect example of the other direction that I want the gallery to take from time to time,' said Charlie, pouring out more champagne. 'He's a waif and stray from New York – aren't you, darling?' Charlie beamed a great, crinkled smile at Teddy. 'And he's been in Madrid for a year, and now he's come to swinging London to further his career. When he's *very* good I might exhibit him. Not yet, though.'

'You paint, do you?' asked Oliver, turning to Teddy with interest.

'Yeah,' replied Teddy with a lopsided smile. 'I'm working on it. Actually, I'm basically commercial. I'm trying to find some freelance work with advertising agencies and stuff, but . . .' He spread his hands in a despairing gesture.

'No luck?'

'Not yet. And in the meantime, I'm trying to sell some of my work. Nothin' classy, you know, like old Charlie's floggin' here—' Charlie winked, grinned and raised his glass. '—but, y'know, kind of genre stuff?'

Oliver wondered what genre stuff might be, but thought he could guess. Still, what did that matter? he thought, gazing at Teddy's bright brown eyes.

'Anyway,' Teddy went on, 'Charlie here's got me humpin' stuff around London for him, doin' bits and pieces around the gallery— That reminds me.' He bent down and unzipped the portfolio he had brought with him. 'I got those catalogues from Sotheby's and handed that stuff in at the press office.' He handed Charlie a pile of catalogues.

'Oh! the Press – I didn't tell you, Oliver,' said Charlie, laying a delighted hand on Oliver's arm, 'we'll be in *Harper's & Queen*, and the *Tatler* is doing a special piece on the gallery's opening. I'm to be photographed here tomorrow before the launch party. You know—' he lifted his chin and set his craggy face at a haughty, theatrical angle. '—something *terribly* dramatic in black and white. Atmospheric.' He sighed and dropped his head. 'And so many of my dear old friends are no longer here to see any of it.'

Alarmed that Charlie might be about to get maudlin, Oliver changed the subject. 'You know,' he said, 'I have a young friend—'

'My dear!' said Charlie.

'No, no,' said Oliver hastily, 'he's Alexander Laing's son. I'm sort of – a guardian of his.'

'Oh,' said Charlie, pouring more champagne. He had rather hoped that Oliver had found someone new after that appalling Dominic. He liked people to be happy.

'I'd like to bring him to the opening, if I may. He's mad keen on art – and a very talented painter, too. I thought maybe you could even find him a few things to do around the gallery. He's just got back from Greece with his family and he's rather at a loose end.'

'Darling, do it,' said Charlie. 'Just so long as he doesn't expect to be paid. Teddy is all I can afford.'

Oliver glanced at Teddy and wondered if he and Charlie . . . No. Charlie had been with Rex too long and loved him too dearly. But he looked speculatively at Teddy all the same. Then he glanced at his watch.

'Charlie, I have to dash. Some things to do in Chelsea.'

'Yeah, I have to be shootin', too, Drew asked me to do a load of shopping and stuff for him and Errol. That OK?'

'Of course, sweetheart,' said Charlie, taking the glasses through to his little kitchen to rinse them. 'Theodore is staying with Drew and Errol for the duration,' said Charlie over his shoulder to Oliver. 'Until he finds his feet.'

'Somethin' like that,' murmured Teddy with a shy grin.

Ah, thought Oliver, a friend of Drew and Errol's. But still far too lovely, far too young for him to hope . . . Oh, what the hell – nothing ventured . . .

145

'They're over in Battersea, aren't they?' he said to Teddy. 'I'll give you a lift, if you like – it's in my direction.'

'Yeah, great. Thanks,' said Teddy, nodding.

Charlie walked down the gallery to the doorway with them. 'Now, Theodore, try to be here before two tomorrow, because the caterers are coming at four and there's lots to do before then. Oh! My nerves are in tatters already!' He passed a hand over his shaggy grey head.

'I'll see you tomorrow evening,' said Oliver.

'Goodbye, darlings!' he called, as he watched Oliver and Teddy crossing Cork Street. Oliver raised a chubby hand in farewell, without turning round. Dear Oliver, thought Charlie, smiling to himself as he closed the door. Poor, dear Oliver. Always searching, searching. Charlie bent down to examine the door mechanism. Some extra security might not come amiss, he thought. The Seurat might be insured, but one still couldn't be too careful, especially in Mayfair.

Teddy and Oliver chatted idly, pleasantly, as they drove through the Kensington traffic, each thinking his separate thoughts, Oliver wondering if this beautiful young American might be interested in him, even just as a friend. He had felt very lonely since Dominic left, his ego bruised enough for him to expect no more than company and conversation. Teddy was wondering if this guy was gay – he had to be – and whether he might have a little influence in the right places.

'Where can I drop you?' asked Oliver, as they headed over Battersea Bridge.

'Just there on the left – Westbridge Road,' said Teddy. 'That's real kind of you. Hope I haven't taken you too far out of your way.'

Oliver gazed at the brown skin of the young man's neck as he stretched over the back of the seat for his portfolio. Ah, well. 'Not at all,' said Oliver with a smile, as he drew up at the kerb. 'Good luck with finding work,' he added, as Teddy opened the door. If only.

Teddy hesitated, still in his seat, one foot on the pavement. He looked at Oliver. 'I don't suppose you know of anyone . . . ?' His brown eyes looked directly into Oliver's.

With an effort Oliver replied, 'If you're really desperate, I suppose there's some possibility – some book-jacket work, that kind of thing.' He paused. 'What about your paintings?'

Teddy shrugged and smiled. 'I don't know how hot they are, to be honest. I gotta work on them, I guess.'

'Why don't you bring your portfolio around and I'll have a look at it,' said Oliver. 'This evening, perhaps?'

Teddy hoped he looked sufficiently surprised as he widened his eyes and said, 'Hey, would you? Look, I'd be really grateful.'

'I could cook us a spot of supper,' added Oliver joyfully. He gave Teddy his address and drove happily back to Chelsea. Teddy made his way up Westbridge Road. The things you do, he thought.

Marion lay stretched out in the sun on a lounger on the terrace at Roffey, her eyes closed, the cordless phone and a glass of vodka and lime juice on the ground at her side. The best thing about holidays, she thought, was getting back home to Roffey. Though one could hardly say that about the holiday they'd just had. It had been perfect. The villa they had taken in Zakynthos had been a dream – spacious, cool, with white walls and marble floors, elegant furniture, a swimming pool, a cook, a maid and a gardener. Even the children, once Paul stopped moping and Helena stopped grumbling, had enjoyed it. Helena, when she wasn't perfecting her tan, had gone riding and swimming with a girl and boy from a neighbouring villa, and she and Paul had gone with them in the evenings to the disco down at the marina. She had been relieved to see Paul spend some time with other teenagers; for the first few days he had just sketched and gone for walks by himself, and she had, in a vague way, worried about him. But that was Paul's way. Perhaps he still wasn't settled at Ampersand. She must talk to him about that, she thought, taking a sip of her drink and listening to the cool plaint of the pigeons in the beech wood.

Oh, but what a marvellous holiday. Really, she had expected the presence of the children to make her feel quite geriatric. It had been some time since she had spent a summer holiday with them. But when the Hope-Murrays' yacht had cruised into Megalanthis Bay, it had all suddenly become much less of a children's party. Liz Hope-Murray had been most impressed by the villa and by the delicious food concocted by Ionna, the cook. She recalled, with a smile, the faint raising of Liz Hope-Murray's eyebrows as she had settled back in her chair on the terrace under the vine leaves, taking in the grand sweep of Megalanthis Bay and the villa's terraces and gardens dropping away to the olive groves, and could still hear her saying, 'My dear Marion, I'd heard that Alexander had left you positively penniless. Someone certainly got their gossip wrong.' Then that drawling laugh, a thin, freckled, be-ringed hand laid on her arm, and her rich, pampered voice murmuring, 'You must come over to the yacht tomorrow evening. We always have such divine parties when we come to Megalanthis. I honestly feel like poaching your wonderful cook . . .'

Oh, and what parties. Marion wriggled her painted toes and wondered, for the hundredth time, whether Arios Vourlides would call her when he came to London. His wife was a bit of a problem – but in other ways quite a help. No tiresome commitments, no threat of marriage. Just lots of lovely presents, divine company – and possibly some sex that might stay on the boil for a bit longer if it was intermittent enough not to become predictable. The man was positively dripping with money – anyone who owned so many cruise ships had to be. And he had certainly seemed more than a little interested in her.

Such a holiday, she sighed to herself. So much nicer when the children were contented and getting more civilised as they grew older. And the trust had paid for it all. Of course, the trust was not going to fund her holidays without the children – and they were growing up. Still, she would cross that bridge when she came to it . . .

The telephone buzzed by her chair. Don't be absurd, she told herself, Arios isn't going to be in England until September. Probably one of Helena's friends. But no, it was Geoffrey Montacute. My God, thought Marion, how did he do it? They'd only got back the day before. He must have been counting the days.

'Geoffrey, how are you? Sweet of you to ring. Yes, we got back yesterday. Absolutely tremendous. The children adored the villa and had a wonderful time. We all did.' Now that was out of the way, what was he after? 'Well, I hadn't planned on being in town for the next week or so, though I might pop up with Helena with some things for the flat . . .' Oh, he didn't honestly expect her to troop all the way to London just to have dinner with him, did he? 'Oh, have you?' She laughed. 'What kind of a surprise? Oh, you are mean!' What on earth kind of surprise could the man possibly have for her? He must know that the only thing she could be remotely interested in was some more money. 'Well, I think it's rotten of you not to tell me.' Her mouth stretched in a girlish smile. It might be something utterly tiresome – but on the other hand . . . 'Well, now look. Why don't you pop down to Roffey for a couple of days next week instead? It's so peaceful here, and you stuffy old lawyers need a bit of country air. Then you can tell me what my surprise is.' A pause. 'Yes, why not? Next Thursday and Friday. Wonderful. Bye, bye.'

Marion lay back with a sigh. Was it really going to be worth going the distance with Geoffrey Montacute when there might be more attractive propositions on the horizon, such as Arios Vourlides? Oh, well, she would see what she would see. She was curious to know what the surprise was.

As she closed her eyes the telephone rang again. This time it was Oliver.

'Oh, Oliver, I've just had our deeply earnest co-trustee on the phone,' murmured Marion with a yawn.

'Try not to sound too enthusiastic,' said Oliver. 'I thought you were rather special friends these days?'

'Hmm, that's a sweet way of putting it.'

'Anyway, did you have a good holiday?'

'Seriously marvellous, as Helena would say. Actually we met some people you know – the Vourlides.'

'Oh, Lord, that ship man who likes Jackson Pollocks? He buys quite a lot of stuff from Derwent. His boardroom is a positive shrine to modern art, I believe, poor deluded creature. Anyway, look, Paul rang me this morning.'

'Did he? He didn't mention it to me.'

149

'Well – you know. He wants to come up and spend a little time in London. So I asked Charlie Vereker if Paul could help out around his new gallery. It's having its opening tonight, and I thought Paul might like to come. Charlie can't pay him anything, mind.'

'Oh, Paul's money worries are all over,' said Marion airily. 'He gets an allowance from the trust. Yes, I don't see why he shouldn't come up.'

'He could have the spare room at my place,' said Oliver.

'That's a good idea. Hang on, you can speak to him yourself.'

Marion got up and took the phone into the kitchen, where Paul and Helena were hulling strawberries. She handed the phone to Paul, telling him what it was about, and he took it with a soft smile of pleasure. Helena looked up quickly from the dish of strawberries, and said, 'I could go up with him. I've still got to do all my enrolment stuff for art school and I could take some things up for the flat.' She was practising a calm, casual way of speaking to her mother, since she had discovered that this seemed to produce better results than wheedling or sulking.

Marion glanced at her, remembering Richard Ranscombe. Well, she thought, after September she's going to be there all the time, anyway. Then it occurred to her that Paul could stay at the flat, too, which would at least provide some sort of chaperon.

'All right,' she said, 'just for a couple of days. Oliver said Paul could stay with him, but perhaps you should keep an eye on him.'

'Sure, Mummy,' replied Helena with a smile, popping a strawberry into her mouth. She had not the slightest intention of having anything to do with Paul while she was up there.

It was largely because Paul found the idea of Ampersand without Oakshott unthinkable that he was able, for long stretches, to blot it from his mind. He would not, could not, think beyond the end of summer. In Greece he had deliberately shut all thought of school and the past two terms out of his consciousness, and had concentrated on his sketching and his watercolours. He found the limpid, resonant colours of the melon fields and olive groves around the villa an arresting change from the hazy, dense hues of the meadows and woods around Roffey. He had swum a great deal, floating on his back in the salt water with his eyes closed, his mind a blank up to and beyond the immediate moment.

Perhaps the most important discovery that he made was that the self-acknowledged truth about his sexuality, which he perceived as some dark secret, made no difference to his external world. He was still the same person, he was accepted by the other young people whom he and Helena met on holiday, and with whom they sat chatting and drinking Pepsi in the tavernas and the marina disco each night. It was as though he had imagined that some strange, impenetrable veil might have fallen over him, that he would never be the same again. But, of course, he was just the same. I am just Paul, he thought; that is how they see me. No one need know. If I can keep my secret, then nothing will change.

Oliver's invitation to stay with him had been a godsend. He had known once he rang Oliver that he would fix it somehow. At Roffey he would have been kicking his heels, wishing Dad were still alive and in Italy, then getting bored, with too much dread time in which to be haunted by the looming prospect of the autumn school term.

Helena and Paul went up to London by train that afternoon, and Oliver came to Caversham Place to pick up Paul and take him to Charlie's gallery early in the evening. Oliver told Helena that Charlie would probably love to see her, too, but Helena just gave him her sweet, casual smile and said that she was going out with a friend, thanks. Normally an event such as the opening of a fashionable Mayfair gallery would have found Helena hunting feverishly through her wardrobe for something wonderful to wear, but that evening her vague smile concealed only a heart thumping with panic and excitement at the thought of seeing Richard.

When Oliver and Paul arrived at the gallery it was six-thirty and already the place was thronged. Charlie, despite the presence of three exquisite young men whose job it was to dispense champagne, canapés and cold-faced hauteur to the multitude, was at the end of the room, looming above the crowd, and filling glasses with champagne. He crashed daintily through the throng towards Oliver.

'Darling!' he cried, kissing him and then pumping Paul's hand as they were introduced. 'I knew your father well when he was young,' he said to Paul. 'Oh, how I wish there were still artists of his calibre around. Sadly, there is too little nowadays that is worth the wall space.'

Oliver smiled. 'Maybe you'll be exhibiting Paul's work one of these days.'

'Now, that's an exciting idea!' beamed Charlie, taking two glasses of champagne from the tray of a passing waiter and handing them to Paul and Oliver. 'You'll never guess who's here!' he hissed. 'Jennifer's Diary! Isn't it utterly tremendous? Now, find yourselves some food and have a look round, Paul. I'll see you both later.' And he wove off through the crowd of smiling, murmuring guests, exhilaration and triumph in his eyes.

'I think this must be the happiest day of his life,' said Oliver wistfully, as Charlie paused in his tracks to embrace Rex, his partner of twenty-two years, before moving off through the room.

Paul loved it. He loved the slightly warm champagne that made his head feel as though it were expanding with lightness, he loved the people, restless and excessive and beautifully dressed, he loved the pictures, the eclectic mixture of old and modern that was typical of Charlie's catholic, unhesitating taste.

'But where is the *quiddity*?' someone was saying to someone else. 'Where is the deductible logic of a collection like this?'

'It hardly matters,' Paul heard someone else reply. 'They'll all sell. That's all the quiddity Charlie needs.'

Paul told Oliver of this exchange. Oliver smiled and pushed his glasses further up his nose. 'There are some people, Paul, who want art to be something esoteric, a mystery only for the initiated. Which is why one sees the desperate hyping of rubbish that scarcely deserves the name of art. Modernism is, by and large, such desperate trash, you know. Charlie, on the other hand, believes only in the good and valuable. No

152

emperor's new clothes for him. He sees what is worthwhile, and what is worthless, and is not afraid to say so. He is,' sighed Oliver, 'one of a rare and fast-disappearing breed. If you listen to Charlie, you'll learn all you ever need to know about art.' He took a drink of champagne and glanced around; then his face lit up with pleasure. 'Come and meet a new friend of mine,' he said, and took Paul over to where Teddy was standing talking to a very tall woman in a scarlet dress.

The woman in the red dress smiled and moved away as they approached, and Oliver introduced Paul to Teddy.

'Hi,' said Teddy, and shook Paul's hand.

'Charlie's going to let Paul help out at the gallery for the rest of his school holidays,' explained Oliver.

'Great,' said Teddy, whose dark hair was hanging loose over his shoulders and who wore a soft blue cotton shirt and linen trousers. Paul felt very schoolboyish beside him in his Kickers and new jeans. Charlie had stipulated informality of dress, but most people had ignored this, and Paul wished he'd dressed up a bit more. 'We can razz about town together,' Teddy was saying, raising his glass in a friendly salute to Paul. 'Charlie's got a new mini-van that he's terrified to let me drive, but I got the keys this morning.' He grinned at Paul.

Oliver watched happily as the two young men chatted. He had loved the previous evening spent with Teddy. His cooking had turned out well, and Teddy had wolfed down his moussaka and salad and wine with gratifying relish. They had talked and talked, they had looked at Teddy's pictures (which Oliver, his critical faculties by now undimmable by any incipient shades of love, thought rather promising), and when Teddy had left, Oliver had gone to bed with a light heart and the feeling that here was a promising beginning. He knew his own susceptibility; he had lived too many years not to be aware of his fatal weakness for the attractive and worthless. But Teddy, he told himself, was such a *nice* young man, so pleasant, so well-read, so unaffected and gentle in his manner. If only, thought Oliver, I was as lovable. But they had got on well together, and that was all that mattered for

153

the moment. He liked having young friends, he mused, as he left Paul and Teddy talking and went in search of some more of that delicious smoked salmon pâté.

Paul, as he talked to Teddy about England and about Charlie's pictures and about all the galleries that Teddy had been to over the past weeks, felt as though he were in another world, far away from Ampersand and its brown corridors and its reek of adolescent intolerance. There was no one at Ampersand like Teddy, not even among the masters, no one so assured and friendly and who knew so much about the things that were worth caring about. It was, he thought, going to be good fun working with Teddy in the gallery. He didn't care about next term. His heart expanded with joy at the prospect of the next few weeks.

In the flat in Caversham Place, Richard and Helena lay in each other's arms under the cotton sheet of Helena's bed. The duvet and their clothes lay in a heap on the floor. They whispered wordlessly to each other, their ears closed to the world and its everyday sounds, floating in some lovers' limbo as the dusk outside turned to dark and the shadows of the leaves ceased to shift upon the wall.

Five miles away in Richmond, Montacute stood by his mother's bed, looking down at her inert body that seemed to have taken on the ponderability of utter exhaustion, her limbs limp and heavy, her jaw slack, her iron-grey hair loose upon the pillow, her breathing rasping and deep. The doctor straightened up from his examination and sighed.

'A mild stroke,' he said. 'That is to say, not massive, but enough for me to want her moved to hospital. It's difficult to say whether her motor functions are significantly impaired, but I'd say from the facial indications that she may be suffering some temporary paralysis of the right side of her body. Yes, hospital, I think.' He smiled a faint, reassuring smile at Montacute, whose face was expressionless. 'Nothing to get too worried about, though. A stroke of this kind can happen with people of your mother's age, but let's hope it's not too bad. Where's your telephone?'

Montacute told him, and the doctor went downstairs to the hallway. What a frightfully gloomy place, he thought as he picked up the receiver, eyeing the dark bulk of the grandfather clock that ticked monotonously in the shadows by the coat-stand.

Upstairs, Montacute stood gazing down at his mother's face, noting the strange rigor that seemed to have gripped one side of it, pulling the corner of her mouth stiffly down and her eyebrow into a distorted slant, so that she seemed to be frozen into a spasm of prolonged durance of pain. He hoped that she would not open her eyes. He would go with her to the hospital, of course. Looking down at her, he was acutely aware of a sense of his own indomitability; her helplessness, her inertness seemed to sap her of malevolence. Hospital. That would teach her a thing or two.

He suddenly thought of his projected trip to Roffey at the end of the following week; a grip of angry fear tightened his heart momentarily, then relaxed. No, he would go anyway. He could do nothing for her while she was in hospital. Besides, she would learn that things must be as they must be, and possibly forever. He thought of being with Marion, his mother lying in a hospital bed far away from him, unable to reach or affect him, and he felt as though weights were shifting within his heart, and the balance of his life tipping perceptibly.

Chapter fourteen

Ten days later, as he watched Marion delicately rip open the envelope with her slender, coral-tipped fingers, Montacute felt himself to be the very apotheosis of masterfulness. From the moment of his arrival at Roffey that Thursday, wearing his new, sharply creased tan trousers and the checked Viyella shirt whose choosing had put him through such agonies of indecision a few days previously, he felt that events were to be, as he had intended, gently but firmly controlled by him. The dispatch of his mother to hospital had oddly uplifted him, endowing him with a sense of purpose and freedom which quite exhilarated him.

'Well, mother,' he had said to her as she lay in her hospital bed, conscious now, but still with the right side of her body rigid from the stroke, 'I have to go away for a day or two, I'm afraid, but I'm sure that the doctors and nurses here will do everything to make you comfortable. I shall come to see you on Saturday.' Her speech was still unintelligible, and in her pride she would not permit herself the indignity of struggling with it, even to utter a reproach; she had only been able to turn the dull, hard gaze of her eyes upon him as he strode away.

And now she was far from him, beyond his caring.

Apart from buying several new items of clothing for himself, including underwear and pyjamas, and even a blazer whose cut and colour suggested a carefree, irresponsible nature quite out of keeping with Montacute's own, he had taken pains to research the area around Roffey through Harold Strange's copy of *The Good Food Guide*, and had booked a table for two at the best and most expensive restaurant in the area. They were seated there now, over coffee, and Montacute had chosen this moment to deliver to Marion her surprise.

She pulled the cheque, drawn on Coutts Bank, from the

envelope, stared at it and then at him. From the expression on her face it seemed for an absurd moment as though she were about to breathe, 'How beautiful!' Instead she said, 'Geoffrey, what on earth . . . ? Why are you giving me a cheque for one hundred and fifty-four thousand—' She glanced at the cheque again. '—three hundred and eighteen pounds? I can't take this from you!' It was the prettiest of charades. Whatever she might say, someone had just given Marion a hundred and fifty thousand pounds, and she had no intention of parting with it.

But the wide-eyed protest allowed Montacute to pursue his masterful theme and embellish it with a few loving touches. 'Of course you can,' he said. 'It's your money. Or rather, if it is not yours, it certainly doesn't belong to anyone else.' He motioned to the waiter to bring them more coffee.

'But how did you . . . ? I mean, it's wonderful, of course, especially since you know how I'm pinching and scraping . . .'

Montacute leaned back. 'Oh, I moved a few investments here and there. The fund that produces your annuity – it really was a most uninspiring portfolio.' He smiled. 'I had a little information from a friend.'

'But, Geoffrey—' She leaned forward, as though anxious that no one should overhear her. '—you told me that you weren't supposed to run risks with trust money!' She was not in the least concerned whether or not Montacute overstepped the bounds of legal propriety in dealing with the trust, but the particular part which she was playing called, she felt, for some innocent protestations. Besides, she was intrigued to discover that his integrity was not so inviolable, after all. 'It's certainly not worth taking risks like that on my part.' She looked appealingly at him.

He leaned forward and cupped his hands over hers. The large brandy he had just consumed removed the last of his inhibitions. 'I would take *any* risk for you, Marion – absolutely any. You know that, don't you?' he said in a low, fervent voice.

Although she was faintly amused, she was taken aback by his tone; he was sincere, and his gaze for that instant was more earnest and honest than many she had seen. She dipped her head prettily, letting the soft light fall on the sheen of her blonde hair, which was pulled back from her head in a black velvet bow, and fixed her eyes on the big, pale hands that covered hers.

'I know you would, Geoffrey,' she murmured, looking up at him hesitantly. 'And it's terribly, terribly sweet to hear you say so.' Her blue eyes were large and lustrous and her face, he thought, was like some lovely flower. His heart felt as though it would burst with love. Should he ask her now . . . ?

Marion was thinking that a hundred and fifty thousand pounds in two – no, three – months, was pretty good going. She looked at Montacute in a considering fashion, still smiling. She had, she saw, been right after all. And the words he had just spoken showed her that there was more, much more, to be gained. He would do almost anything for her, because he wanted her. Very badly, she guessed. It was a delightful tease. If he could do that with the fund that produced her annuity, just think how much he could make with the rest of the trust fund. All that lovely extra money, without anyone's interests being hurt. She wondered, as she looked away from him – for she found the ardour of his gaze just a little unsettling – how he justified it to himself, how his spotless, professional conscience bore the commission of such an indiscretion. Not that she cared. She was merely interested in how best to play the next move in this intriguing game.

She took her hands away from his and folded the cheque carefully, thoughtfully, and put it into her bag. 'I think it's one of the nicest surprises I've ever been given,' she said, looking at him brightly. 'Am I going to get any more?' she added archly.

For a moment Montacute was uncertain what to say. He had ventured a little on her behalf, and was pleased that she was so gratified by the results, but he had not intended that it should be repeated. After all, it had merely been one friendly tip from his acquaintance at Overly Other. But the thought that such a reply might dash the cup of her gratefulness from his lips was too much, and with a faint smile he said, 'Oh, well, we shall have to see. One never knows.'

So that is the way the land lies, thought Marion, watching as he paid the bill.

She offered to drive back, since she knew the roads and had drunk less than he, but Montacute would not permit it. He was not prepared to relinquish his role as the dependable male, the provider, the doer, the wooer. It was not a role he had ever played before, except on the occasions when he was with Marion. He enjoyed driving along the dark, tree-lined roads, with Marion at his side, feminine, compliant. He was glad that he had not, in that momentary surge of love, proposed to her in the restaurant. He smiled to himself in the dark at the thought of such ineptness. Of course, a woman like Marion would laugh at the idea of being proposed to before she had been made love to. The apprehension of this made Montacute feel quite worldly. Perhaps tonight, he thought, as he swung the car neatly between the gates and up the long drive to Roffey, would be the night. Why else had she asked him down here? Away from London and his mother and all the influences that otherwise restrained him, he felt that tonight he could be Marion's lover.

As he sat in the long, lovely drawing room, watching as Marion poured more brandy for both of them, Montacute's heart did admittedly quail somewhat. Kissing her, embracing her, all that was all very well. But getting from here to her bedroom – or should it be his bedroom? – was another matter. And what did one do? How was the thing managed, taking off clothes and so forth? He was glad he had on his new underpants. Did one converse? Would she expect him to undress her, as he had read somewhere that women did? He sipped and watched as she kicked off her shoes and lit a cigarette, before curling up at the other end of the sofa.

He felt that they talked, oddly, much more easily than they had ever done before. He asked her about her childhood and, surprised, she told him – normally it was not a thing she ever talked about. She did not imagine that anyone would care to hear. Origins, since she had met and married Alexander, were not things that people seemed to be interested in, so long as the accent, the attitude, the clothes and the money were right. She felt curiously softened as she told him little bits and pieces of her girlhood in Chislehurst. And when she had finished, she naturally asked him about himself. She found herself genuinely curious.

Montacute hesitated. He never thought about his early years, that dark tangle of school and loneliness and boredom, of a silent mother and few friends. Whenever anyone used the word 'childhood', an image of the dark laurels and shrubs and evergreens, matted and knotted together in clumps in the rainy garden of Innisfree, would enter his mind. It did so now. He tried, unsuccessfully, to laugh it away.

'I doubt,' he said, with a vestige of his habitual stiffness, 'if it was as carefree as your childhood.' He paused, looking down at his brandy, and suddenly decided, for once in his life, to tell someone. 'I do not think that my parents liked me very much, or even wanted me.' He looked up. 'They certainly did not like one another.'

'What were they like?' asked Marion, watching his long, heavy face as he groped for words.

'They were – well, that is, my mother is still alive. I live with her.' He looked at Marion, waiting for some reaction to this humiliating revelation. But she did not say anything. He continued. 'My father was a doctor. I don't remember him very clearly. He died when I was seven. I have this difficulty – my mother, you see, has always spoken of him so little that I have only a distorted idea of what kind of man he was. She does not speak of him very kindly.' A thought occurred to him suddenly, and he voiced it. 'I have no pictures of him. There are none in the house. He – ah, I think he must have been a very private man. I do not remember him sitting with us in the evenings. He always seemed to be in his – well, it wasn't a study, it was his surgery, really . . .' Montacute gazed vacantly at the air, at the past. 'I remember sitting on his knee once, in his surgery. He was showing me things, things that he used for his work. His stethoscope, I suppose, that sort of thing. I can't properly remember. But I think . . . it was, it felt . . .'

'What did it feel?' asked Marion softly.

'Kind.' Montacute looked at her. 'Yes, I think he may have been a kind man. How curious, that I should only realise that now. Perhaps he did like me.' He smiled as if in embarrassment. 'Perhaps my mother never gave him a chance. She is a very unforgiving woman.'

'What was there to forgive?'

'I don't know,' replied Montacute vaguely. 'I don't know what it was between them. Perhaps I supposed it was . . . me. That I was the trouble. Certainly,' he added with a sigh, 'my mother bred in me a sense of guilt. Perhaps I *was* guilty.' He gave another uneasy little laugh. 'I remember long stretches of time when she would not talk to me. Whole afternoons. Sometimes a day. Taking me to school in the mornings, bringing me home again in the afternoon, and saying – nothing. Some kind of punishment, perhaps. I don't know. And then . . . when there wasn't silence—' He stopped.

'What?'

'Oh . . . it's hard to say, really. Just making me feel . . . worthless, I suppose. Just little things. Oddly, it may have made me more determined to succeed, to prove that I could do something.' He smiled, and drank a little more of his brandy. 'Not that she seems to think much of me now. Still. Everyone goes on trying to please their parents, right to the end – don't they?'

'Not all,' murmured Marion. 'And perhaps those that do, shouldn't.'

'You may be right,' sighed Montacute. He sat quite still for a few moments, as though listening to music from far away. 'I often feel . . . I often feel—' He spoke with difficulty. '—that I must have done something unforgivable, that I must have – maybe . . . something as a child . . . to explain the way she is. When we are together, I often think how – how *alone* we both are. Perhaps I would be less . . . alone if she – if it had been different, when I was a child.' He broke off, wondering why he was talking in this way. What a weak simpleton she must think me, thought Montacute. He smiled stiffly at her and finished his brandy.

Marion, not moved, but oddly excited by curiosity that anyone should have lived such a bleak, sterile existence, looked at him, at his sallow face and heavy eyes, his thin mouth and long nose, his greying, rather oily dark hair, and at his new clothes. She felt a sudden impulse of tenderness. 'She sounds a frightful old cow, if you ask me,' she said, and reached towards him and laid her cheek against his, perhaps

161

the kindest gesture she had yet shown him. Touched, Montacute essayed a kiss, a rather gentle one, lacking in his customary fervour.

Time to change the subject, thought Marion, unfolding herself from his embrace and leaning back against the sofa. 'We mustn't be so gloomy,' she said, 'especially after such a lovely evening. You do spoil me, Geoffrey,' she added, toying with his tie while he gazed at her adoringly.

'It was the least I could do, to take you to dinner – as a thank-you for letting me come here,' he replied. In his imagination his mouth was on that golden curve of her shoulder and he was pushing aside the straps of her dress.

She laughed. 'Oh, heavens, I meant being given all that money. It was rather unexpected. And very naughty of you.' She tapped him roguishly on the chin.

He leaned forward to kiss her again, this time more passionately, murmuring that she was worth it, worth anything. He was beginning to get the hang of doing it properly, Marion noticed, which wasn't necessarily all to the good. Still, at least what he said was reassuring. She returned his kiss, putting one soft hand upon his neck.

'Am I, Geoffrey? Am I really?' she murmured, quite pleased with her performance thus far. It was mainly a question of keeping the man under physical control, which was difficult, given that he was so large.

'Yes,' he replied, gazing at her. Strands of his lank hair had fallen over his forehead. How old-fashioned his haircut is, thought Marion idly, as she looked at him dispassionately. He leaned heavily forward to kiss her again, but she drew back as though trying to fathom a puzzle, and bestowed a light kiss upon his nose to be going on with. She had on her best perplexed, childlike expression.

'What I don't understand is – if you can make so much money with one bit of the trust, why can't you do it with the rest?'

'Because it's a risk,' replied Montacute, wishing she would leave the subject of money alone for the evening.

'But it's not,' said Marion, twisting her neck to look at him. 'You've shown it's not. You can make lots of lovely money . . .' She allowed him to draw her towards him and to kiss her neck. '. . . and not harm anyone.' She dropped her voice and added a slight breathlessness to show that she was paying attention to what he was doing. 'It would be so wonderful . . .' She arched her back a little and tilted her head back, letting him kiss her throat '. . . to have some more money. It would make such a difference—' She felt his hand slide down from her neck, as she had known it would. God, the things one did. '—to everything,' she breathed, running her hand lightly up and down his arm. The tips of his fingers slid tentatively into the bodice of her dress, and suddenly the change in him became quite alarming. He moaned and buried his face against her, his fingers, damp and slightly trembling, caressing her breast, his body trying to rise up against hers. She allowed a few seconds of that – no more, really, because (although she would scarcely admit it) his touch was a little more disturbing than she had expected.

'Oh, Geoffrey,' she whispered, her voice carefully poised somewhere between mild passion and maidenly reproof, and pulled herself away. He lay back, lost, anguished (it was quite amusing, really, how susceptible his lack of experience made him; as Sally had said, just like a schoolboy), and she leaned lightly over him to say, 'Couldn't you do that – for me?'

'Do what?' he said eventually, his hands limp at his sides.

'Just make some more money for me,' she whispered, keeping her voice gay. 'After all, you're such a clever old thing, and I would be so grateful . . .' She tapped his nose lightly, lovingly, and he reached up and caught her wrist. She expected him to make another lunge, but instead he just sat there, breathing heavily, looking straight at her. She was wondering what he was going to say, when suddenly they heard the kitchen door slam.

'Helena,' murmured Marion, raising her eyebrows ruefully, but in her heart faintly relieved. She straightened her dress and moved a little distance from him on the sofa. He pushed back his hair and sat up, his face a mask of solemnity.

Helena put her head round the door. 'Hi,' she said, glancing at Montacute. 'Oh, hello, Mr Montacute. I forgot you were coming. Listen, Mummy, I'm just going to make myself some supper. We didn't get anything to eat beforehand and I'm starving.'

'All right. How was the film?'

'Good. Rubbish, really. I'll say 'night.''

They both said goodnight to her and she disappeared. Marion sighed. 'I never know when she's coming or going these days. She spent all last week in London at the flat. Paul's up there, staying with Oliver and working at some gallery.' She drained her brandy glass. Montacute pondered the desirability of letting an adolescent boy keep company with Oliver and his set, but said nothing. 'Still,' went on Marion, rising and taking Montacute's empty glass from his hand, 'she seems a lot happier these days. If there's one thing I cannot bear, it's Helena when she's sulking.'

Montacute was scarcely listening. He had not counted on Helena's presence in the house. His dim hopes of making love to Marion that night seemed dashed. What had he expected? The brandy, a sudden tiredness, and the wretched aftertaste of having talked about his mother, all combined to produce in him a sense of hopelessness.

Marion glanced at him, at his silent, gloomy face. Oh, dear, she thought. Had he got his hopes up? Well, there was a lot of work to be done before things could go that far, she told herself grimly. Or maybe it was just the business of talking about his family – heavens, no wonder he was such a dreary prig, with parents like that.

'I think we should say goodnight, don't you?' she murmured, kissing him lightly and taking the glasses over to a tray. 'You'll find towels in your room, in the little chest by the wardrobe.' He rose stiffly from the sofa and came to stand by her. 'And there's a flask of water and some lovely detective novels by your bed.' She gave him her warm hostess smile.

I do not want detective novels, he thought, gazing at her face, at her shoulders, suntanned from Greece, rising from the bodice of her dress. I do not want flasks of water and kindness and smiles. I want you. But these words – although they were not words, merely disjointed thoughts barging together in his tired head – did not find their way to his mouth.

'Yes, thank you,' he said. 'I am rather tired. I'll see you in the morning. Goodnight.'

'Goodnight,' she called as he went into the hall. 'And thank you for a lovely evening.'

She stood for a moment, troubled. He had not tried to kiss her again. She wondered why not. Well, thank heaven for small mercies, she supposed.

In his room, which he had divined was some distance away from Marion's, Montacute sat on the edge of the bed. The spell woven throughout the day had been broken. He no longer felt masterful and assured; he felt defeated, disappointed in himself. Why, instead of making love to Marion and capitalising on the promise of the evening, had he begun to talk about his mother? The image of her, conjured up by their conversation, seemed to hang around him like a poison cloud. How tedious Marion must have found his ramblings. It was as his mother had always said –he was dull, virtuous and boring. He sat there sadly, gazing at his new pyjamas with their smart paisley pattern, neatly folded next to his pillow, where he had laid them that afternoon.

After a while he sighed, got up, and went to wash and brush his teeth in the bathroom that adjoined his room. Then he put on his pyjamas. He buttoned them, as was his habit, up to his neck. The taste of toothpaste seemed to have a refreshing antidote effect on the quantity of brandy that he had drunk, and he decided, as he emerged from the bathroom, that he felt a little better.

He picked up one of the detective novels by the side of his bed and examined it. Was this the kind of thing Marion read? He went over to the window and opened it. The window overlooked the long terrace, from which shallow stone steps fanned down to the lawn. As he looked out, he caught sight of a shadowy figure seated on the balustrade of the terrace; it was Marion, sitting alone, holding a glass and gazing out at the dark shadows of the shrubs and trees. Her back and shoulders seemed to gleam against the black of her dress. She will catch cold, thought Montacute. He watched her, wondering whether he should go down. Suddenly he pictured himself standing on the terrace in his new pyjamas. How ludicrous he would look. He had not thought to bring a dressing gown. Even then, what kind of a figure would he make in the old maroon felt dressing gown that he wore at home? I was not made for love, Montacute told himself as he closed the window.

Alice Montacute lay in the half-darkness in her bed in Elsie Mather Ward, motionless except for her left hand, which fretted feebly at the bedclothes. It was night, but still the sounds seemed to go on and on. The creaking of beds, the occasional shuffle of slippers on the floor, the coughing, the groaning, the sighing – all the shifting sounds of old women in sickness and misery. Every so often someone at the very end of the ward would call out for the night nurse in a thin, plaintive voice. The first two times, the nurse had gone to her, thick-soled shoes squeaking on the floor. Now her calls went unheeded. Perhaps they would stop eventually. Perhaps she would just die quietly in the dark.

It is like hell, thought Alice Montacute, a wardful of tormented, frail old souls, whining and moaning together in our pitiful condition. Perhaps we should all be put down. We are so useless, so wretched. And then she thought – no. Not I. I shall get over this. People do. I am a strong woman, not a tottering old wreck like some of those here. I am better already. I can think. I am not confused any more. They started my therapy today.

The paralysis was the worst thing. The stupidity of it. It was not so much that she could not lift her right arm – she could not even feel her muscles attempting to make an effort. It was as though something, somewhere between her useless limbs and her brain, which still tried to send its little messages, had been severed. At least she had discovered the pointlessness of trying. She had not thought that anything could be so tiring as that constant mental effort that she had at first made, to make the muscles on the right side of her mouth move when the nurse fed her. It had quite exhausted her; and so frustrating, feeling the food slip over one's rigid, stupid lip. Like having been to the dentist, but worse. There was no way to overcome the indignity, she realised. Those horrible, guttural sounds

166

that came out when she tried to speak to the nurses, they were her voice. She could no longer command – she could only long to be understood. Pride did not come into it. It was simply a question of necessity.

She lay and stared at the ceiling, thinking this over. If I succumb, she thought, if I allow myself to descend into indignity, then it is all over. I will become no more than the thing that they see when they look at me, those doctors and nurses. A wretched, half-paralysed, unintelligible old woman without any point, without any hold on life. But I *have* a hold, she told herself – I have a hold on Geoffrey. He is my son and he does as I ask him; he works so that I may live, so that we may live together. All that must mean something. I shall get better and go home with him.

She did not think now of her former unkindness, of the petty slights and cruel words with which she had tormented her son over the years. She saw only the utter necessity that he should salvage her from among the pathetic debris that filled Elsie Mather Ward, that she should be taken home and made strong and indomitable again. It was a conation which exhausted her. At last her mind slipped away from it, to a confused and rambling anxiety as to his present whereabouts. Who was he with? Was he with her, the woman he had been seeing? What were they doing, what did they talk about? Not her, she knew that. Geoffrey would never talk of her. Why would he wish to? As she realised this, she felt her place in the order of things slipping, her grasp on his life, all life, fading away.

She lay alone in the dark, until sleep descended upon her like a thin, grey shroud.

Chapter fifteen

More than a little daunted by the prospect of spending all of Friday alone with her guest, Marion had invited Sally and Hugh Howard to lunch the next day. Since Hugh, so far as Marion could recall, did something in the City, she had previously assumed that he and Geoffrey might get along together. Now, as she reflected upon Hugh's ruddy, thick-fleshed bonhomie and compared it with Geoffrey's bland stuffiness, she had her doubts. As for Sally, she would just have to hope that, as a close friend, she might be able to steer her away from any undesirable speculation and gossip that Geoffrey's presence might excite.

She was somewhat taken aback when, after breakfast – a stiffish affair, since Montacute tended to react to Helena's casual exuberance with a chilly reserve – Montacute appeared with a copy of Pevsner and announced that he was taking himself off for the morning to look at the local churches.

'I understand there are some very fine examples of Norman architecture in the vicinity,' he said with his lofty smile. 'Besides, I can imagine how tiresome it must be to have house guests who simply hang around all day. Can I fetch anything from the village on the way back?'

'Yes,' replied Marion, when she had overcome her faint surprise; what unlikely inner resources some people had. 'You might pick up a couple of bottles of white wine from the chill cabinet at the off-licence, if you wouldn't mind. There are two bottles in the fridge already, but it's always wise to have a bit of back-up when Hugh's around.'

She watched his tall, bulky figure as he made his way to his car. 'Well,' she remarked, 'that's something of a relief. I hadn't the least idea how I was going to amuse him all morning.'

'If that's how you feel about it, I'm surprised you invited him down here,' observed Helena rather rudely. 'What's for lunch?'

'Lobster salad,' said Marion. 'And passion fruit sorbet.'

'Don't tell me *you're* making *that!*'

'Good grief, no,' murmured Marion, gazing vacantly into the fridge and wondering if they had enough lemonade for Pimm's. 'Some girl who runs a catering thing in Hindhead is doing it. You know,' she sighed, thinking wistfully of Greece and the delights of being cooked for and waited upon, 'it would be *so* wonderful to be able to afford a cook again.'

'Well, maybe I'll buy you one when I come into my fortune,' said Helena. 'I'm off to Milly's for the day. Her little sister has a new pony. I might stay the night.'

'Well, if you do, for heaven's sake ring me,' said Marion.

When Montacute returned from his tour of Surrey church architecture, a bright red Alfa Romeo was standing gleaming in the August sunshine on the gravel driveway of Roffey. He parked his blue Austin Montego carefully next to it and got out, conscious of nervous apprehension in the pit of his stomach. Normally his social encounters were set within the framework of his legal world, and he could behave with all the aplomb of the senior partner of a leading law firm. But this was different. He was on intimate territory, staying in Marion's own home, and these were close friends of hers. He had not the least idea of their understanding of matters, nor what she might have told them of her relationship with him. It was a novel situation indeed for Montacute.

He went round to the side of the house and into the kitchen, where he put the bottles of wine into the fridge. From the window he could see past the terrace and down to the lawn, where Marion was sitting with a man and a woman. The woman had red hair and wore sunglasses, and he could hear the man's loud, confident laughter carrying faintly on the air. Montacute sighed and looked round at the large, airy kitchen, at the scrubbed wooden cupboards and shelves, the cream-painted walls, the Aga, the dried flowers and copper pans hanging prettily from a beam, and thought of his own dingy kitchen in Richmond, of the narrowness of his life. Two different worlds, utterly unconnected. How could he possibly hope to move from one to the other? He had only Marion's affection to trust to; no other compass. If it was genuine, as he felt and hoped it to be, then perhaps he had nothing to fear. So he told himself, as he made his way out across the terrace and down to the lawn, lifting his chin slightly and preparing his unctuous smile.

Marion introduced him, first to Sally, who smiled from behind her sunglasses and put out a plump, freckled hand, sliding with golden bracelets, to shake his; then to Hugh, who raised his Pimm's glass by way of salute. Montacute took him in in a second. Grizzled, iron-haired, with a face like rare roast beef and an easy, satisfied air. Montacute knew the type well; they filled the City. Company directors, corporate analysts, share dealers, syndicate heads; men with the trappings of wealth and the loud, languid voices of success. He wondered how long it would take Hugh Howard to be rude to his wife.

He sat down next to Hugh in one of the sun loungers (in which he felt distinctly uncomfortable, since his long, digni- fied person was not given to lounging) and took the glass of Pimm's which Marion offered him.

'So,' said Hugh, leaning back at his ease and studying Montacute, 'Marion tells us you've been having a little flutter in the market recently. Done quite well in Twentyfirst Holdings, she tells us. Very clever, that. Very astute.'

Montacute glanced at Marion stiffly, wondering just how indiscreet she had been. But no – she wouldn't mention the trust; of course, she wouldn't. Not that it was any of Hugh Howard's business, anyway. He turned to Hugh and murmured that the amount had been only trifling.

'Even so,' said Hugh, 'I wish I'd put my money there. I admire that; not many people realised that takeover was coming.'

Sally, bored with talk of the stock market, began to murmur to Marion. Hugh Howard leaned forward confidentially to Montacute, tapping his arm lightly with a hairy finger. Montacute did not like to be touched by other men, and flinched slightly. 'Tell you where the money is now,' continued Hugh. 'Weather insurance. Chaps underwriting risks of rain at Lord's, Wimbledon, that kind of thing. Clever stuff. That's where to put your money.' He took a large gulp of his Pimm's and then leaned forward to the jug to pour himself some more. 'You?' he said to Montacute, who declined politely. 'Platinum,' went on Hugh. 'There's another certain winner. Now, if I had to pitch my tent anywhere, that's where I'd pitch it. Can't bloody well go wrong. You know why?'

Montacute said no, he didn't.

'Catalytic converters,' said Hugh triumphantly, and struck Montacute's thigh lightly with his hand. 'Know what the Western world supply and demand figures were for platinum last year?'

Montacute looked enquiringly at the man Howard with a polite display of interest.

'Over four million ounces,' said Hugh. He finished his second glass of Pimm's, then said, 'Come on, girls! Drink up!' Marion did not look at him, but carried on talking to Sally. Hugh turned to Montacute again. 'Catalytic converters. All cars are going to have to be fitted with them in the next few years. Some bloody EEC directive. And what do catalytic converters need? Platinum. Price is going to rocket. Now, if I had a few hundred thousand to spare, I'd be buying. You look at those Johnson Matthey boys. They're no fools.'

Realising that Hugh Howard could probably go on in this vein indefinitely, Montacute said gravely that he really knew very little of commerce, beyond the kind of company dealings which his legal work demanded. He was about to take the opportunity to regale Hugh Howard with an account of the case of *Edelmann und Gützweig Montage GmbH v. Reckitt and Others*, feeling it was about time he had his say, when Marion said, 'Shall we have lunch out here? It's so pleasant. No, Geoffrey and Hugh, you stay here. Sally and I will fetch things.' She stood up. She had changed into a halter-neck blouse and linen shorts. Montacute's eyes followed the suntanned line of her thigh and felt his stomach fall away with desire. He longed for the evening; he was determined that something should happen. Marion was looking doubtfully at the table on which the Pimm's jug and glasses stood.

'I'm not sure if that's big enough for everything. Geoffrey, would you be a dear and fetch that other table from the terrace?'

Montacute obediently leapt to his feet, hoping that the stiffening of desire did not show, and went to fetch the table. Hugh Howard leaned back in the sunshine, closed his eyes, and thought about himself and platinum.

In the kitchen, while Marion fetched plates and cutlery, Sally stood at the window, her sunglasses pushed up into her red hair, and watched Montacute carrying the extra table down to the lawn.

'He's rather nice, in an odd sort of way,' she said. 'I mean, rather on the large side – sort of droopy, isn't he? – but not bad-looking.'

'Don't get the wrong idea,' said Marion, putting the lobster salad and plates on to a tray. 'He's purely business. Now, where's the bread?'

'It is possible to mix business and pleasure, you know, darling,' said Sally; then she added grimly, 'Hugh does it all the time.'

'Well, he's not really my type,' said Marion firmly. 'Can you take this, and a bottle of wine? Now, we need napkins . . .'

'But don't you always wonder what any new man you meet would be like in bed? I know I do.' Sally ducked her head to make her glasses drop down on to her nose. Then she looked up through them at Marion. 'Anyway, I'll bet he fancies you. Any man would. Hugh does.'

Marion picked up the tray and steered it and Sally determinedly out through the door. 'Come on,' she said.

To Montacute's relief, the conversation at lunch slipped along easily enough. It was largely dominated by Hugh, who drank a great deal of wine and grew redder under the sun with each glass. Every so often, Montacute would glance at Marion, and occasionally he was rewarded by her sweet, private smile. It warmed him deliciously. Of course, he told himself, she must love him in some degree. Why else would she ask him here?

Hugh Howard finished his sorbet and sat back slackly in his chair, gazing around appreciatively at Roffey's gardens stretching out to the woods.

'Bloody lovely place, Marion.' He took a small case from his back pocket and fished out a stubby cigar. 'Bloody lovely. I've always thought so.' He lit the cigar as Marion watched him carefully, sipping her wine. 'Tell you what you want to do with this,' he said.

Marion murmured a faint enquiry.

'Get some of those TV boys to use it for one of their series, or whatever. Miss Marples, that kind of thing. This is just the kind of location they're always after. Beautiful house, beautiful grounds—' His stomach billowed slightly with a noiseless belch. '—beautiful owner.' He laughed and drew on his cigar. 'Don't you think, Geoffrey?'

'Don't I think what?' asked Montacute coldly. He disliked this man, had disliked him on first meeting him. There was a loutishness about him, despite his accent, his clothes and his well-bred wife, that Montacute despised. He particularly disliked the man's familiarity with Marion.

'Oh, oh!' exclaimed Hugh, sitting up and smiling round at the company. 'No need to take the needle, old man! Merely remarking how well Marion fits into her surroundings. Don't tell me you haven't noticed, eh? You wouldn't be here otherwise, would you?'

It was only then that it occurred to Montacute that the man Howard was faintly angry, and that he was angry because he was jealous. Unused to this sort of drunken conversation, Montacute turned his head away and looked out across the lawn. Howard putted his cigar, laughing in grunts under his breath. 'What are you looking so po-faced for?' he suddenly asked Sally, whose mouth, beneath the blank, unreadable gaze of her sunglasses, was set in a tight line.

'Shall I give you a hand with the coffee, Marion?' she said in a light voice. 'I rather think Hugh could do with some.'

Hugh merely laughed again and glanced at Montacute's averted head as the two women got up and went into the house. He had caught the faint, but unmistakable contempt in Montacute's eyes and felt caught between irritability and a drunken desire not to be disliked. After a pause he said, 'Sorry about that, Geoffrey. Spoke a little out of turn. I'm a great admirer of Marion's. Have been for years.'

Slightly surprised by the man's tone of voice, Montacute merely said, 'Please don't apologise.'

Hugh rubbed his rubicund face and both men remained silent until Marion and Sally reappeared with the coffee. The rest of the time until the Howards' departure passed awkwardly; in an attempt to reassert himself and bring the conversation with Montacute round again, Hugh reverted to the subject of stocks and shares.

'You know, Geoffrey, if you ever cared to dabble again, the word is that Garter Cross is worth looking at. It's that Greek chap – oh, Lord, what's his name?' He paused for a second. 'Melanakis. That's the one. Giannis Melanakis. The word on the quiet is that those shares are set to rise in a very big way.' He nodded his head. 'A very big way.'

Montacute was not especially interested, but given the recent awkwardness in conversation, he felt he ought to respond to the man. 'What kind of business is it?' he asked.

'Oh, import-export, that kind of thing. Can't say he was particularly well-known in the City when he started last year, but he seems to have a bit of backing from his government. That's always good for confidence. He started off buying up companies at home and turning them round, and now he's doing the same thing here. Quite an entrepreneur. That's the kind of operation where, if you get in on the ground floor, well . . . As I say, if I had a few hundred thousand to spare—'

'If you had a few hundred thousand to spare,' interrupted Sally, 'we would have been able to buy that château in Languedoc.' She turned to Marion. 'Oh, you would have loved it, Marion. Just heaven. Far too expensive, but I couldn't resist getting the particulars and going to look over it when we were there.'

'I thought French property was relatively inexpensive,' said Marion.

'Well, it is, on the whole,' replied Hugh. 'That is, the kind of thing that the average suburbanite with a bit of spare cash goes in for. You know, falling-down farmhouses in need of doing up . . .'

The talk drifted to property prices and at last, after an hour or so, the Howards took their leave.

Montacute watched as Marion walked with them to their car. A curious sense of unease seemed to have settled over the garden. The birds still sang, the sun shone through the haze of cloud, and only the faintest of breezes stirred the treetops. Nonetheless, he was aware of an imbalance, a sense of something out of place amid the tranquillity. Marion waved goodbye to the Howards and watched as their car, driven by Sally, slowed at the end of the driveway, and then turned off and out of sight. She stood for a few moments, acutely aware of Montacute sitting alone behind her in the garden.

As she turned to walk back, she felt suddenly swept by irritation. Somehow, through Montacute's presence, she had felt obliged to acknowledge to herself that which she had always suspected. Hugh Howard was a bit of a boor. The knowledge had always been there, underlying the flattering attention which he customarily paid her, and now she felt that, in an unspoken way, her own good taste in choosing such a companion had been brought into question. She felt annoyed with Montacute, though she could not have said why. She did not even remember feeling the same annoyance with her husband, years ago, when he had managed, with scarcely a word and only a few looks, to betray his contempt for the friends that she acquired with her gathering prosperity.

'Well,' she said with icy brightness, as she came back across the lawn, 'that ended on something of a sour note, didn't it?' She began to put the coffee cups on to the tray.

'Please, let me,' said Montacute, taking the things from her.

Irritated by the fact that Montacute had obliquely avoided her brittle little challenge, she pulled the tray away from him. 'Please don't,' she said. 'I think you've already done enough for one day.'

Montacute was alarmed and dismayed by the tone of her voice. He did not think he had offended her friends. He simply had not liked the man Howard. He had been unable to pretend to. The smiling deference with which he was able to treat an objectionable client in his office was not something he could manufacture in a social context, where there were no trans-actions to effect, no comfortable roles to play. He was at a loss as to how to respond to Marion.

'I am sorry,' he said in a heavy, cold voice, 'if you think I have let you down in some way.'

'Geoffrey,' she replied in the sweet-and-sour voice which her children so detested, 'if you find it difficult to behave politely to my friends, then – then what can I do?' She picked up the tray and made for the house.

Montacute felt that this was unjust and rose to pursue both her and the subject; had he been a man of greater experience, he would have let the matter go and trusted to a brief lapse of time to improve her temper. But Montacute knew nothing of women.

'I hardly think that I was rude to your friends,' he said, following her across the lawn, but still speaking in a calm voice. 'I can think of nothing I said that might have offended them,' he added, annoying her even more by being right and by opening the kitchen door for her with a ponderously courteous gesture.

'Geoffrey, you didn't have to say anything! It was perfectly obvious from your manner that you didn't like them.' She began to stack the cups and saucers crossly in the dishwasher.

'I found Mrs Howard perfectly agreeable,' replied Montacute with equanimity. 'I cannot say the same for her husband. He was quite insolently suggestive,' he added unwisely.

'Insolently suggestive?' Marion stared at him, then smiled scornfully. 'You really do say the most ridiculous things! You must be the most pompous man I know!' He looked in surprise at her contemptuous face. He had no idea why she was speaking like this; he had no notion that she might be cross with herself for some reason and was taking it out on him. 'Anyway,' she went on, 'was it asking too much of you to make your dislike of my friends a little less obvious? There is such a thing as tact, you know!'

Montacute was by now thoroughly confused and disconcerted. He was appalled to find that Marion was arguing with him; he had never argued with a woman in his life. He did not care about the justice or injustice of her words, merely that he should stem their angry flow.

'Please, Marion,' he said as earnestly as he could, but unable to shake off the stiffness of tone which his consternation had produced, 'you must know that I would never knowingly do anything to – to upset you—'

'Well, that's just the trouble, isn't it?' she interrupted snappishly. She was feeling peeved, aware that this argument was going nowhere, that Montacute was an unsatisfactory opponent. 'You never do things "knowingly", do you?' She laid a scornful stress on the repetition of his word. 'You don't seem to "know" anything, certainly not about the way people behave, the way they try to oil the social wheels instead of indulging their – whatever it is they feel. You're so busy being stiff and proper and just so, that you can't see past the end of your dignified nose! I sometimes wonder if you're human at all!'

The disjointed irrelevance of this was lost on him. He was too distressed by her words, the tone of her voice so like his mother's, to be aware that her little storm of temper was, in fact, petering out. He could feel nothing but a sense of confusion and rejection.

He groped for words, for something to stop this bitter unpleasantness. 'Of course I am human,' he said, his voice cold with unhappiness. Suddenly he found himself saying, 'I love you, you see.' His voice was flat and sad.

'Well, you have a funny way of showing it!' replied Marion tritely; she was nonetheless thrown by his words and by the tone of his voice. She was uncertain how to respond, now that she had given vent to her brief anger.

There was a silence, during which she put the rest of the plates in the dishwasher and Montacute stood fingering the edge of the kitchen table dismally. I have told her, he thought; I have told her, and that is all she can say in reply. She has no use for me. She has no heart. How had all this happened?

'Perhaps it would be best if I were to leave this afternoon,' he said at last. Pride had not entirely deserted him. He did not see how he could remain in such an atmosphere, with his own unhappiness betraying itself minute by minute.

That which was for Marion the most trivial piece of bickering was for Montacute, with all his inexperience of emotional tussle, a catastrophe.

Marion was about to say, 'Oh, don't be so silly,' but did not. She, too, had her pride and she did not feel like cajoling him into staying. She did not much want him to stay, in any event. If he chose to overreact in such a pompous fashion, let him. At least she would be spared any more groping this evening. It might do him good to cool his heels for a while. She could always turn him around again when she needed to.

'If you think that is really necessary,' she replied airily, 'then do as you like.' She felt a tiny pang of conscience as she remembered that he had told her that he loved her, that it must have been painful for him, and that she had virtually dismissed it as of no consequence. She added, 'It all seems rather silly.' But her voice was cold, and Montacute was not the man to capitalise on the moment. He stood uncertainly for a few seconds while she made a show of being busy around the kitchen, studiously saying nothing more to him; then he went to his room and began to put his things together.

As he zipped up his leather shaving case, he paused. This is absurd, he thought. But there was nothing he could do.

He took his belongings downstairs and put them in the car. He hesitated for a moment, then went in search of Marion. She was lying on a sun lounger on the lawn. She had on sunglasses, and when he looked down at her he could read nothing on her face.

'I'm sorry that we had this needless misunderstanding about your friends,' he said stiffly, wishing he knew how to do that which he wanted to do – laugh it off, apologise facetiously, winningly, make her laugh in spite of herself, let them be friends again. It was not within his realm of competence. She knew it. She knew it all. She simply shrugged her shoulders by way of response. She knew that he was being driven away unnecessarily, unhappily, by the fact of her own little tantrum, with which he had not known how to deal. Well, there it was. If he was going to be such a great, over-stuffed, pompous fool about everything, let him.

When she said nothing, he merely added, 'Thank you, anyway. Perhaps it is as well that I am going back a little early, since my mother is unwell.'

The sunglasses were a blank.

'Goodbye, Geoffrey,' she said, and he went.

It was while he had been packing that the thought had occurred to her. What Montacute needed was a little more encouragement, a little feverish spur to push him to the point where he would do whatever she wanted him to. His over-reaction to the little scene in the kitchen was just the thing. He could pine for a few weeks in London – it had been quite unnecessary, really, for him to tell her he loved her; she knew that much, and more – and then she would sweeten him up again, lead him along a little further. She smiled to herself in the sun. A hundred and fifty thousand pounds. That had been a very nice beginning.

Chapter sixteen

For Paul, each day of his time in London was as precious as a drop of water to a thirsting man. There was, as his own mother had discovered some twenty years before him, little active work to do around an art gallery, but he simply enjoyed being in London, away from school and from Roffey, tasting the newness of the city. He liked staying with Oliver, who neither patronised nor interfered, but let him do exactly as he wanted. He spent most of his time with Teddy, and some of it with Charlie and Oliver and their friends, and was endlessly amused by their conversation, their attitudes and opinions. They gobbled up everything that was new – films, clothes, plays, exhibitions, gossip – and seemed to Paul to be ageless in their curiosity, their thirst for life. He tried not to think of Ampersand, which loomed nearer with every day that passed, but he found himself talking about it to Teddy in one of their many conversations concerning their different backgrounds.

'I suppose it's not very different from most schools,' said Paul in response to a question from Teddy over lunch one day.

'But – gee, stuck away in this big place with all these other guys all year. Don't you think that's a bit weird?'

Paul laughed, pushing his plate of pasta away from him. 'I suppose it is,' he said, and sighed. 'But it's what we do. It's the way public schools are.'

'No wonder British guys are so uptight with women,' said Teddy, musing.

Paul shrugged. 'Charlie went to Ampleforth. That's a big public school.'

'There you go!' exclaimed Teddy.

'What about you?' asked Paul, not wishing to talk about Ampersand. 'What was your school like?'

'Like a high school, I guess,' said Teddy, picking the little book of matches out of an ashtray and toying with it. 'Pretty tough. But like, you know, it had real atmosphere. Lotta drugs, though.' He shook his head. 'You do drugs at your place – whatsit? Ampersand?'

'No,' replied Paul. 'At least, I don't. I think some chaps do, but you get expelled if you're caught. It's really bad news.' He pushed his hair out of his eyes and looked at Teddy. He wished he were spare and muscular like that, and looked good in a T-shirt, instead of all thin and weedy. 'What did you do after high school?'

'Oh, art school, stuff like that.' Teddy paused, fiddling with the matches, breaking them off at the stem, then laughed. 'I dropped out, I guess you could say. I didn't really go a bundle on the stuff they were teaching. Real airheads, a lot of the teachers. So I got a job doing paste-up on a magazine, a sort of crummy street handout. That was really dead. But at least I met Errol. That was one good thing.'

'You met Errol in New York?'

'Yeah. At some party of a guy I worked with. He told me to get in touch if ever I came to London. So I did. He and Drew have been real good to me. Got me my job with Charlie and everything.'

'Errol and Drew are gay, aren't they?' said Paul nervously, uncertain why he was nervous. There it was again, that sense that sometimes you were grown up and sometimes you were really young.

Teddy threw back his head and laughed. 'Yeah, I'll say they are! Boy, you'd have a hard time missing that one!' He chuckled and looked at Paul, who was resting his chin on one hand. A waiter took their plates away. 'So what's your next question?' said Teddy.

Paul looked up at him. 'Are you?' he asked.

Teddy was looking at him with his clear gaze, half-smiling. He made a curious little rocking motion with his hand in mid-air. 'So-so. You know.' Paul just looked at him. 'It doesn't bother me one way or the other. Hey, you want some coffee?'

'It doesn't? No, no thanks.'

'Like my dad used to say, you play it as it lays. Depends

what's at stake. You know – times get tough . . .' He looked away and called for the bill.

Paul sat, turning this over in his head. Maybe he should tell Teddy, tell him of his fears about himself. No, that would mean talking about Oakshott; the thought was too appallingly intimate. He didn't know Teddy well enough. Teddy wouldn't want to hear. There was really nobody. Anyway, the way Teddy talked, it didn't seem as though it was important to him. But it was, he felt, dreadfully important. You only had to see the sadness far behind the camp, laughing behaviour of Drew and Errol, who were in their late fifties and who had been through much in their time, to know that it was important.

It was, at any rate, a relief to be able to talk to Oliver about the wretchedness of Ampersand, because Oliver understood in a way that Teddy could not. Oliver asked him directly one evening how he was coping at school.

'I don't know,' replied Paul simply. 'I was stupid to agree to change schools, but I didn't know.'

'No, you didn't. I'm afraid it was more or less a *fait accompli* by the time I got to hear about it.'

'My mother was very keen. I think she likes telling her friends that her son's at Ampersand.'

Oliver sighed. 'I rather think that Geoffrey Montacute put the idea into her head. Bloody man.'

Paul tried to describe his life at Ampersand. It was no different from most boarding schools, but he managed to convey to Oliver his isolation, his feeling of remoteness from whatever ethic it was that the school possessed, his difficulty in keeping up with the academic pace.

'It sounds just like my own wretched school,' said Oliver. He glanced at Paul. 'At least you're not fat,' he added with a smile. 'You don't get called Billy Bunter and ragged something stupid.'

'No,' agreed Paul, returning his smile, 'but I still don't fit in. It's going to be – it is – lonely.'

'Look, if you can hang on for just another year or two, then it'll be over, and you can do what you want to do. That's not such a long time, you know,' he added. Paul dropped his head and stared at the carpet, his hair falling over his eyes. He's not convinced, thought Oliver. And neither would I have been at his age; he remembered those long days, those endless terms, all too well. 'Do you want a beer?' he asked, trying to sound more cheerful.

'Yes, thanks,' replied Paul, and got up to follow Oliver into the kitchen.

'Anyway,' said Oliver, taking a couple of cans of beer from the larder, 'have you thought what you want to do when you leave school?'

'I don't know, really – art school, I suppose.' Paul had become more than a little disenchanted with the teaching he had received so far, and spoke without enthusiasm.

'Mmm.' Oliver sounded doubtful. He handed a can to Paul and went to the cupboard for glasses. 'I wonder . . . if that's such a good idea.'

'Why?' asked Paul hopefully. 'Oh, I won't bother with a glass, thanks.'

'No? Well . . . The thing is,' said Oliver, frowning, '—and I may be wrong; I am a middle-aged fogey, after all – one can't be very impressed with what comes out of art schools these days. Not only is there no technique, but there seems to be a virtual visual illiteracy amongst many young artists.' He poured out his beer and took a sip. 'It is the fault of the teachers, of course. They have utterly discarded the old, valuable principles and put in their place this notion that the artist should be allowed to express himself freely, that technique puts artificial restraints on him. It's nonsense, of course. It's only when you've learned some basic disciplines, when you've studied technique, that you can hope to develop properly.' He paused. 'That's my view, anyway. Still,' he sighed, 'you can't exactly blame the young. Standards of success are – well, naturally commercial. Everyone wants to get on. They think there are no objective standards – and if you go by a lot of contemporary criticism, there aren't. They look at what has made others rich and famous and they think, if I paint like Malcolm Morley or Gerhard Richter, then I can be rich and famous, too.'

183

Paul smiled and looked down at his beer can. 'Or like Alexander Laing,' he added.

Oliver laughed. 'Well, yes, that's true. The difference is, though, that no one can paint like your father. No one can replicate genius. Anyone can follow a vogue, jump on a bandwagon, trust to the gullibility of those who purchase art nowadays. They can always count on a Saatchi somewhere, someone who will buy dross and call it art. There's no integrity there. Worse still, there's no one brave enough to tell them that their work is poor, derivative stuff. So many of them actually come to believe in themselves as artists. The whole process becomes circular.'

'You make it all sound pretty depressing.'

'It is, I'm afraid,' replied Oliver, pouring out the rest of his beer. 'Still, you may live to see the end of it. There were real standards not so long ago, and they will come back, I hope, in time. There's too much talent out there for them not to. Anyway, that's why I don't see that art school is going to be much use to you. Not if you're going to be a serious artist. Which I think you will. I think you already are.'

Paul sighed. 'Yes, but what happens?'

'What happens? Oh, I see what you mean. Well, you just keep working and – what more can I tell you? Keep working. You're lucky, remember. In a year's time you'll have your own income. And if you don't behave like a blithering idiot – which is always possible – then perhaps you won't have to compromise yourself or your art.'

'Oh.' Paul smiled. He felt he had had enough of thinking about the future; school seemed to loom over everything, and he wanted to make the most of the present. So he said, 'Are you going to Helena's birthday party?'

Oliver nodded. 'I am, as a matter of fact. Your enchanting sister even sent me an engraved invitation. I was rather surprised, I must say. I should have thought that she would want a lot of hoorays, not ageing agents such as myself.'

'Well, she told Mummy she just wanted to invite special friends. Mum was really all set for some terrific big do. Just so's she could invite all her own horrible friends, I suppose. But Helena wouldn't let her. She said she didn't want anything big, and only the grown-ups *she* chose. They're taking over some restaurant by the river for the evening.'

'I'm flattered to think that your sister counts me as a special friend,' said Oliver dryly, although inwardly he was delighted. He did like to be liked; and he *did* like parties, particularly full of lots of young people.

Helena spent the few days before the party by herself in the Chelsea flat, having persuaded her mother that she could conduct the arrangements with the restaurant perfectly well herself.

'After all, Mummy, it is *my* money that's being spent,' she pointed out to her mother. This was true, and the truth of it rather infuriated Marion. Her daughter was becoming a creature beyond her control, a rival – prettier, younger, independent. And wealthy. It merely added to the mounting irritation that she had felt since the little row with Geoffrey. She doubted now her wisdom at having let him go off like that. He wasn't like ordinary men. For him, everything was grand opera. Experience had not yet taught him to trivialise emotional matters. She might have done some irreparable damage just at the very point where she was beginning to control things.

Helena was oblivious to her mother's black mood. She was nearly eighteen, she was in love, and next week she would come into her own private income – a hundred thousand pounds a year was the dizzying figure that Richard had come up with, possibly a little optimistically, and forgetting to mention the small matter of tax – and she felt that the possibilities of life were limitless.

'It's going to be such bliss,' she said for the hundredth time, as she lay in Richard's arms in the quiet flat.

'You're going to be quite beyond me,' he said with a smile, tracing the line of her collarbone with his finger, pushing back silky strands of her hair. 'An heiress. Just think of all the men who'll be after you.' He leaned over and picked up his watch to look at it. 'And they won't be articled clerks, I can bet you. I'm going to have to go. I've got to do some stuff for Montacute for tomorrow.'

'Oh, forget about that old windbag,' she murmured, her hand drifting across his stomach. 'Stay just a little longer, please?'

'I can't!' he said, laughing and pulling her hand away; she managed to resist. 'Ever since he turned up here with your mother and found me, he's been working me like a bastard. He doesn't like me, I can tell you.'

'That doesn't bother you, does it?' she asked, stroking gently.

'Well, it does, actually,' he said, turning to kiss her for a long moment. 'I may not want to stay there for the rest of my life like Clive, but I would like to finish my articles. So would you please stop that?'

'No,' she murmured. And he stayed just a little longer.

On the evening of Helena's party, Oliver dressed himself with particular care and stood looking at himself in the mirror. He wished to look especially well that evening, for he had decided that he was in love, and he hoped forlornly to sparkle somewhat in Teddy's eyes. He had procured some lucrative work for Teddy recently, and Teddy had professed his gratefulness – not that Oliver dared to hope that anything might come of this gratefulness. How could it, when Teddy was so young and lovely, and he, Oliver, was so much like a bespectacled Paddington Bear? Still, as with all people in love, he enjoyed making the hopeful effort.

Paul knocked and came into Oliver's bedroom and gazed at Oliver's plump little form in its peach-coloured dinner jacket and turquoise bow tie. He was reminded, startlingly, of Elton John. How could someone with such instinctive good taste in all other matters fail to apply it to his own appearance? Paul wondered.

'Very nice,' he said, and nodded; Oliver beamed happily at the mirror, then at Paul.

'How very grown up you look,' he replied. And Paul did; his tall, willowy frame looked well in evening dress; his face was losing some of its puppyishness and had a slight gauntness that reminded Oliver of Alexander.

The party was crowded with Helena's friends (and some of

Marion's) by the time they arrived. They had picked up Teddy on the way. Helena had told Paul to invite a few of his own friends, but there was no one from Ampersand whom he cared to ask, and he hesitated to bring anyone from his old school. So he had said he would just bring Teddy.

Helena's own friends consisted mainly of her school chums and their boyfriends, and a motley crowd of childhood companions, with whom she had shared prep schools, children's parties and gymkhanas. In short, a happy band of what Oliver called 'hoorays', all giving full tongue and all hell-bent on enjoying themselves at Helena's expense.

Richard, who Helena thought looked by far the most sophisticated man in the room (especially when compared with her schoolfriends' rather juvenile escorts), knew no one, but then, they were not exactly a difficult crowd to get on with. He very much enjoyed the attentions of one or two breathless seventeen-year-olds, who thought it terrifically typical of Helena to have a real man for a boyfriend, and he talked easily to the young men. In fact, he felt quite cynical and worldly wise, and thoroughly enjoyed the novelty.

Marion, who had decided to try and look as chic as possible among such a young gathering, was quite taken aback to realise that the well-built young man with the amused mouth and attractive eyes was Richard Ranscombe. She reflected that he really was, perhaps, a little old for Helena. Still, all that was slipping beyond her control now. Helena was eighteen and could do as she pleased. Montacute had even sent her a very charming, formal letter on the notepaper of De Vaut, Montacute & Strange, congratulating her on reaching her majority and enclosing her first income cheque from the trust. Marion took a savage little sip of her champagne. She and Montacute had not spoken for two weeks; she would have to do something about that. If she could. Of course she could, she told herself. She watched Helena, bright-eyed and lovely and happy, dancing with Richard, and felt suddenly a cold little flash of fear. Why didn't Arios Vourlides ring?

Paul rather enjoyed himself; he knew most of Helena's friends and felt proud of Teddy as he introduced him to them. Teddy, Oliver thought, looked utterly divine. Where had he got those beautiful clothes from? And he had his hair tied back in that rugged way that Oliver loved. But he felt more than a little wistful as he watched Teddy with Helena's guests. They were all so young, and so beautiful. It was quite, quite hopeless. Still . . . Shaking off his wistfulness, he helped himself to another glass of champagne and set off beaming into the throng to enjoy himself.

The party wore on, food was eaten, drink consumed in vast quantities, and the music and the voices grew louder. By eleven Marion felt exhausted.

'Darling,' she said to Helena, catching her in a quiet corner where she was giggling with Oliver over some extremely rude and expensive silk underwear which he had given her for her birthday, 'I think your poor mother has had it for this evening. I'm taking June and Philip back to the flat for a quiet nightcap. Oliver, will you make sure she gets back safely?'

'Mother, I'm eighteen now!' said Helena. 'And none of us are tired yet. Don't worry, Richard will make sure I get home safely and am all tucked up in bed. So night, night – don't wait up.'

'Poor old Mummy,' she added sweetly, when Marion was out of earshot. 'It must be awful to conk out before midnight.'

'She's only thirty-nine,' said Oliver, who was beginning to flag a little himself but, determined to enjoy whatever there was to enjoy, told himself that he would get his second wind in a minute.

'I think she's getting too used to early nights with Mr Montacute,' said Helena, and giggled. She had had a good deal more champagne than she was used to.

'Oh! Oh?' said Oliver.

'No, actually, I think it's all very proper. I mean, can you imagine Mr Montacute without—'

'Helena,' murmured Oliver in a warning voice.

'Actually, I think she's worried about money. She's always going on about it. Never mind, she'll get some from some-where. She always does. Come and dance.'

Around midnight, someone suggested going on to a night-club, which was greeted with rowdy enthusiasm. Helena, who was dancing slowly with Richard, murmured, 'I don't really want to go – do you?'

'No,' he said, feeling a little drunk and rather randy. 'I can think of things I'd much rather be doing.'

'Such as?' she whispered, smiling up at him. And he told her, at length and in murmured detail.

'We can't go back to the flat,' said Helena. 'My mother's there with some of her friends.'

'My flat isn't likely to be terribly civilised,' said Richard. 'My flatmate went to a concert in Hammersmith and he'll still be up and about. Not exactly the atmosphere.'

He thought for a moment as they danced, then bent his head to whisper to her. She looked at him in surprise, her mouth stretched in a smile, then nodded; a few minutes later they left, unnoticed by the rest.

Helena giggled as Richard switched on his desk lamp in the offices of De Vaut, Montacute & Strange.

'Do they always let you have a key?' she whispered.

'God, no,' he replied. 'I had to stay late a few nights ago. I haven't got round to giving it back.'

'What if we're caught?' said Helena, childishly excited by the illicitness of the venture. Richard, too, found something particularly titillating about the idea of making love in the hallowed offices of De Vaut, Montacute & Strange.

'Don't worry,' he replied. 'That's one of the advantages of not being in a decent, air-conditioned modern building. No alarms, no security guards.' He took her into his arms. 'Just us.'

He kissed her for a long time, enjoying the growing urgency of her body's movements against his. Then he lifted his head and, with one finger, slipped the thin straps of her evening dress from her shoulders, unzipping the back a little so that it fell down to her waist.

The curve of her breasts was outlined by the glow from the desk lamp, and he traced around her nipples with his finger as she reached up to kiss him again. His mind was drifting thoughtlessly, deliciously, into some blind realm of sensuality, when suddenly it froze. He looked up and saw, watching as if in slow motion, the handle of the door turn, then open; a hand snapped the light on. Standing in the doorway was the figure of his senior partner. Like Richard, he was in evening dress. On his way up Chancery Lane from a Law Society dinner, it had occurred to him to pick up some papers for a case the following day. He had seen the faint glimmer of Richard's light through the frosted glass panel of the door and had gone to investigate. Now he stood, gazing dumbstruck.

The couple stared at him, and he at them, for what seemed like a long moment. Then Helena hoisted her dress up gently and said foolishly, a little drunkenly, 'Hello, Mr Montacute.'

I don't believe it, Richard was thinking to himself. I don't bloody well believe it. Not a second time. And then he thought – I'm done for. I've had it. Unconsciously, his eyes still fixed on Montacute, he slid his hand round to Helena's back and zipped her dress up.

Montacute's initial expression of astonishment had given way to one of grim disgust. He looked at Helena and said, 'I think you had better go home, Miss Laing,' and then looked away. She felt suddenly very sober and very cowed, and not a very grown-up eighteen. Then he looked straight at Richard, whose heart was beating horribly fast and who was feeling distinctly juvenile himself. 'Mr Ranscombe will find you a taxi. I shall speak to him tomorrow. Goodnight.'

They made their way out sheepishly past him, and left the building. Montacute stood motionless in the doorway for some time, staring at the place where the couple had stood as though he could see them still, before going over to Richard's desk and switching off the lamp.

Chapter seventeen

When Richard recounted the episode to his flatmate, Peter merely remarked that it was just as well Montacute hadn't come in ten minutes later. Richard, as amused as someone can be when their heart is in their bowels, admitted that there was something in this.

As he waited in his room the next morning, trying to get on with some work but with his stomach churning and his mind fixed on the coming interview with Montacute, he felt that nothing Peter said would ever amuse him again. Clive, who had, through office telepathy, got wind of the fact that something of dire note had happened and that Richard was at the root of it, kept shooting him covert glances of ferret-like curiosity, *schadenfreude* glowing within him.

At last, at half-past eleven, when Richard was in a state of breaking-point tension, the summons came via a stony-faced Miss Reed. She, too, was aware from the ominous manner of the senior partner that wrath was about to descend, and she bore her message with grim satisfaction. Richard followed her to Montacute's room, his eyes fixed on her thick leather sandals squeaking righteously along ahead of him. Why, he thought, couldn't he treat this all with airy cynicism? Why should he be afraid of a middle-aged, anally retentive solicitor in whose firm he didn't particularly wish to work, anyway? He knew the answer. It was a matter of pride, of face-saving. He wanted to finish his articles here. He did not wish to be dismissed ignominiously from De Vaut, Montacute & Strange, and be forced to transfer his articles to some other firm; that in itself might be difficult, if Montacute chose to make it so. For that reason, his stomach was like ice and his palms were sweating, conditions not helped by the amount he had drunk the night before and his lack of sleep.

'Wait here, please,' said Miss Reed, pointing to one of the chairs that stood against the wall of her outer sanctum. Richard sat down. He watched Miss Reed going about her work with all the tight-lipped complacency of the virtuous anticipating the come-uppance of the wrongdoer. At last the buzzer buzzed, and she looked up at Richard. 'You may go in now,' she said.

Richard went into Montacute's room and closed the door behind him, quaking. Usually when one went in to see Mr Montacute, he would make a show of self-important industry and write for a few moments before deigning to bestow his attention on one. Today he was sitting back in his chair in his shirtsleeves, his gaze fixed on the doorway, all work put to one side. Richard stood in front of him for a moment, and then Montacute, in a cold voice, said, 'Sit down, please.'

He sat down. Still there was silence. Then Montacute leaned forward, his hands folded in front of him on the desk. 'What I saw last night,' he said, 'seemed to me utterly beyond belief. It seemed so then, and it seems so now.'

Richard felt his stomach relax a little as he kept his abject gaze fastened on Montacute; it was rather like plunging into cold water after standing shivering on the brink. It was better once you were in.

'I cannot think of a more outrageous, a more disgusting and irresponsible piece of behaviour, than for one of my articled clerks to bring a young woman to these offices late at night. For what purposes, one can only conjecture. It is as scandalous, as contumelious an act as any I can imagine.'

There was a long pause here, as though Montacute could hardly bring himself to speak in his displeasure, and Richard sought to take advantage of it by saying, 'I really do wish to apologise, sir. I have no excuse—'

'Your excuses, Mr Ranscombe, will avail you little,' interrupted Montacute frostily. Blimey, thought Richard. 'Apart from the impertinence of your behaviour, which must rank as an insult to myself, my partners and to every member of this firm—' (Richard wondered whether Miss Reed's intercom allowed her to listen in on this; if so, she must be loving it.) '—apart from that, I regard it as a signal breach of trust that you

192

should abuse your position here, that you should flagrantly violate the fiduciary obligations imposed upon you when keys to this office are entrusted to you. We cannot tolerate that kind of behaviour in this firm, Mr Ranscombe.' Here it comes, thought Richard. 'I must ask you to take a month's notice of termination of your employment here.'

Richard drew in a deep breath, glanced down at his hands, and then up at Montacute. 'Yes, I do understand that, sir. You said you don't want any excuses, so I shan't offer any. I do see that what I did was stupid and irresponsible, and I apologise for that.' He paused; Montacute was still looking at him. Not a hope, thought Richard. Still, it was worth a try. 'The thing is, sir—' He hesitated, then went on. '—I will have completed my articles in three months' time. It is going to be rather difficult to transfer my articles for that short period. I mean, it will look—'

'You should have thought about that earlier,' said Montacute, drawing back in his chair as though preparing to terminate the interview.

'Yes, I realise that, sir, and I don't expect you to keep me on here. It's just that, if you could allow me to finish my articles here—' He stopped, thinking he had probably said enough.

Montacute rested his elbows on the desk, pressing the tips of his rubbery fingers together. He had not yet plumbed the depths of his heart, had not yet acknowledged to himself that the sight of Helena and Richard together had been wormwood to him, bringing sharply into focus his own fumbling failure, thus far, with Marion. He was envious of Richard, of his youth, his looks, his ability to find love and take it as he pleased. Instinct told him that he wanted the boy out of his sight, so that he would not have to contemplate his own pathetic amorous struggles in the light of Richard's success.

There was, however, another, more professional instinct at work within him, one which told him that, at whatever slight cost, it might be as well not to offend Helena, future heiress and possible future client, further than was absolutely necessary. He had no doubt that Helena would react to Richard's peremptory dismissal with fury at its injustice – no matter how sensibly and equably Richard might treat the matter. Anyway, it had long been understood by all parties that Richard had no permanent future with De Vaut, Montacute & Strange. He was not their type, nor they his. Three months, one month; what difference could it possibly make? He wondered wearily, the slack of his anger now let out, his bombast spent, whether he cared. He did not feel as though he had cared about a single thing since the day of Marion's outburst at Roffey and the curtailment of his visit there. His life had become meaningless without her, the thought of her, the promise of her. To Richard's surprise, Montacute suddenly buried his face in his hands for a moment, then rubbed wearily at his features, blurring their customary dignity into tired resignation.

'Richard,' he said, unconsciously dropping the severe formal mode of address, 'you have been a fool. No more, no less.' He sighed. 'That does not lessen the gravity of your offence. But we shall take it that you are to leave us at the end of your articles. I think, on the whole, that is best for both parties.'

Richard's shoulders sagged with relief. It would be hard enough finding a new firm without a decent reference from Montacute, but to have been booted out with only a couple of months left to go – that would have made things much harder.

'Will you please go now,' added Montacute, with a return of his grim expression.

'Yes. Thank you, sir,' murmured Richard, and left, giving Miss Reed a smile and a wink as he passed her desk. Just to keep her on her toes.

He returned to his room, marvelling at the way in which Montacute had spoken at the end of the interview. It was as though he had, for a solitary moment, decided to become human. But he did not ponder Montacute's susceptibilities for long, only waiting until Clive had left the room before ringing Helena at the flat.

'What happened?' she asked anxiously.

'Given the boot,' said Richard airily.

'What? That's so unfair!'

'No, it's not. We did a really daft thing. Well, I did. If I hadn't been pissed I never would have dreamt of it. Montacute didn't really have much option. Anyway, one good thing is that he didn't seem to have told the other partners about it, so I may get a decent reference from Harold.'

'But I can't believe he sacked you! He's really foul.'

'He's letting me stay until the end of my articles, which is another three months. Under my contract he could have had me out after four weeks. Anyway, I hadn't intended to stay on here, you know. I'll start looking around for something else in the next few weeks. Chancery's not really my scene. I rather fancy a spot of litigation, I think,' mused Richard.

'Well, you don't sound too bothered about it, I must say. Do you want to come round tonight? Mother's going to the theatre with some people, then she's going back to Roffey tomorrow. After that, you could stay all weekend. Then I'll have to go back home and get all my gear ready for college. God, I'm nervous about starting there.'

'Nervous? You? You'll be a star from the word go.'

'I don't know about that,' said Helena wanly. 'I'm not that talented, you know. Not like Paul. I really just want to get this foundation course so that I can go on and do fashion.' She bit at the edge of her thumb. 'Oh, Richard! I won't know anyone! What if they're all brilliant and all have their own friends in London already?'

'I will come round tonight and soothe your fears,' replied Richard, feeling quite paternal. 'Anyway, you'll make loads of friends. You'll see. Then how much time will you have for me?'

And, of course, Richard was right. After the uncertainties of the first couple of weeks, Helena felt exhilarated and happy in her new environment. The fact of the flat had made her feel grown up in an outward sense; inwardly, she still felt like a child playing at house. Art school made her feel properly her own person. There was a freedom, an allowance for individuality, that had not existed at school. No one made you do anything. If you didn't want to show up for a class, if you decided to skip part of a project, no one came thundering at you with threats and punishments. No one cared. If you couldn't look out for yourself, that was your affair. It was this sense of personal responsibility that Helena found so novel and charming. Charge of one's own destiny. And the teachers and lecturers treated you as though you were grown up, the young ones in a gritty, laconic fashion that was a little intimidating, the older ones affecting a sort of street-credible mateyness, as though they were still eighteen and au fait with the music, the jargon and the fashions. In a desperate way, they were. The students, children that they were, were accustomed to being tolerant of the middle-aged, and smiled along.

If anything intimidated Helena, it was that the students who had not been to private schools (and there were very few of them) seemed to possess a sophistication of dress and attitude, and a working knowledge of London, that made her feel very provincial indeed. She knew little beyond her mother's terrain of Mayfair and Knightsbridge, and the handful of pubs and wine bars Richard had taken her to. These people knew everything.

She rapidly discovered those things that were acceptable, and those that weren't. She was careful, for instance, never to mention her old school or who her father was. And she was to cringe for months at the recollection of having, in the midst of a discussion of awful moments in one's life, mentioned her pony and how dreadful it had been to sell him. She had seen the flicker of glances and the ghosts of smirks across the canteen table and had wanted the ground to swallow her up.

She began to dress differently, too. Orthodoxy of any kind, she realised, was out. It didn't matter how you dressed – funereally, outrageously, in drag – so long as you didn't conform to any recognised standard. If you made your own clothes or bought them all from Oxfam and the 'Help the Blind' Shop, so much the better. Personal style was all important.

Helena threw herself into all of this with intense enthusiasm. Her gaffe about the pony made her reticent concerning all the other middle-class trappings which she felt gave her away, but she soon discovered that there were two sides to this coin. Her new friends were more than happy to polish up her provincialism and to show off their metropolitan erudition by initiating her into all the secrets of the London scene. They carried their wisdom airily and coolly. Far from regarding the revelation of her wealth with disdain, as she had fearfully expected, they accepted the existence of her Chelsea flat and her new Golf convertible gleefully, rather as children might fall upon unexpected gifts, and absorbed the usefulness of these things into their lives and doings. Helena was very popular, and too happy to care whether people loved her for her flat, her car and her money. Even if they did, it seemed perfectly natural to her, given their straitened circumstances. Just so long as everyone had a good time.

And everyone did have a good time – except Richard. He had known that Helena would find new friends and new interests at art school. But he had not expected it to affect their relationship so suddenly and so drastically. He sensed a new shift in her mood and attitude every time they met. She had begun to dress differently, startlingly, and to talk about things and people remote from him. He suspected that many of the views she expressed were not her own, that she was trying on various images for size, like a child dressing up, but he knew, too, that with each new experiment she moved a little further away from him, from the way things had been.

Up until now their relationship had existed almost without context; time spent together throughout the summer had been a delicious, haphazard affair. Now it was set against a background of daily and weekly routine, and the differences in their lives and personalities had begun to emerge. Richard played rugby almost every Saturday afternoon, and at first Helena had gone along after the matches to join him for a drink before they went out together. But as each weekend went by, she began to find the company of his rugby crowd and their girlfriends tedious; she did not enjoy the effort of plucking him away from his sporty, matey friends in the clubhouse. She considered them utterly pedestrian. She could not help thinking of her new image-conscious, art school friends, wondering, knowing, how they would view Richard and his friends. She had begun, fatally, to see and judge everything through their eyes and on their scale of values. She told herself that she still loved Richard, still clung sentimentally to the first ardour and bliss of being in love, but just as she was changing from a naïve and exuberant schoolgirl, so her perceptions of

Richard were changing, too. He was no longer Richard of the charming smile and delightful body – he was of a type, a world that she did not care to belong to, she saw. Helena had a new vision of herself, and it was not as the girlfriend of a rugby-playing, beer-drinking solicitor who bought his clothes from Next and Marks & Spencer. She saw herself as outrageous, unconventional, free-thinking. Richard was lovely – but very ordinary. Too ordinary.

For his part, Richard was careful not to make any complaint about the gradual changes in Helena and their relationship, about the cavalier and thoughtless way in which she sometimes treated him. All he could do was watch and wait, hoping for a return of the fresh-faced, enthusiastic child he loved, instead of the restless, aloof and unpredictable creature who had taken her place.

He felt this hope slipping when, one Friday early in October, while he and Helena were having a brief drink in a pub in Chelsea, she announced that she wouldn't be able to see him the following evening.

'Why not?' he asked.

'Well, some people from college are going to this transvestite party at a club in Victoria. It's just for a laugh. Everyone dresses up as outrageously as they can . . .' That which had sounded such idiotic fun when discussed with her new friends now sounded, it seemed to her, vaguely silly. This annoyed her and, for some reason she could not fathom, made her annoyed with Richard. 'Anyway, I really want to go. We weren't doing anything special tomorrow after all, were we? I mean, just a drink with boring old Alec and Lisa.'

'Well, they may be boring to you,' replied Richard, 'but they are my friends. And we have made an arrangement.'

'Oh, stop sounding so stuffy! "An arrangement." It's only a few drinks. You're beginning to sound as dull as they do.'

'I didn't know you found my friends so boring,' he remarked.

'Well, I do,' she replied with a little scowl at him and then at her glass. 'Those awful little suppers where she keeps trying out her latest Delia Smith recipe and talks about bridesmaids' dresses and house-hunting. Engaged couples are positively stifling.'

'That's not a very nice thing to say about Lisa when she cooks for us so often. I can't say that you've ever done the same for them. I was beginning to think it was about time we returned the hospitality.'

'My God!' she retorted, feeling coiled up inside like a spring, as though she wanted to argue. 'That's exactly what I mean! You're going on as though *we're* some sort of engaged couple! I don't *want* to have cosy little suppers with other couples! I don't *want* to listen to you and Alec talking about rugby while Lisa witters on about Laura Ashley fabrics!'

'At least she makes conversation,' murmured Richard, 'and can cook.' It was a mistake to say this, and he knew as much as soon as he had spoken. He had not realised that Helena was capable of yelling at him in a public place.

'Conversation! You call that conversation? She hasn't got a single original idea in her head! And neither have you! And as for cooking, I don't bloody well care if I can't! I'm *glad* I can't cook! I'm glad I have more interesting things to do with my time! Go and find yourself someone who *can* cook!'

And she slung her bag over her shoulder and left, her hair streaming out from beneath her floppy red velvet hat. Richard coughed lightly and waited for the murmur of conversation in the pub to recommence before looking up and surveying the empty chair opposite him.

There was, of course, more to it than just Helena's restless dissatisfaction with the way that she and Richard spent their time out of bed. A small, dark being had entered Helena's happy life of popularity and ease in the shape of one Con Aaranson, a student in his third year at the art school. Although slightly built – barely taller than Helena – he had one of those dramatic and distinctive personalities which flourish so well when permitted the eccentricities and affectations of youth. He rarely smiled, dressed in outfits which were only ever entirely black or entirely white, with gold or silver jewellery accordingly, and possessed the kind of hauteur and saturnine good looks which women found irresistible. He was a guru to the first-year students who, in spite of their anarchic and fearless manner, had still not lost their sense of school hierarchy and were somewhat in awe of him. He had class. He had style. He had mystery. He was not impressed by Helena. She had not had any direct encounters with him, for he hovered only on the fringes of her group of friends and had more important things to do than hang around with first-year students, but it came to her ear, as chance rumours will, that he didn't think much of public school darlings who didn't even have to think to stay alive, and who had flats and cars to cushion them against the real world. Helena was stung by the thought that such a god should think so little of her.

After that, whenever she saw him, it was as though she could see faint contempt in his glance. Such a glance. She became vividly conscious of him. She found herself eyeing his girlfriend of the moment, a sleek, enigmatic blonde who wore a great deal of ethnic jewellery and army fatigues, and wondered what it must be like to go out with someone as brutally lovely and intellectually peculiar as Con.

She became aware of a certain magnetism in him. He had a habit of lifting his chin and lowering his fine eyelids in conversation, before throwing back his head and looking away dismissively, that gave most of his utterances a peculiar depth. Helena watched for this trick in his conversation, for she had gradually edged herself nearer and nearer to his circle of friends, and when he did it, she realised that she found it heart-stopping. Such are the materials of infatuation.

He had not spoken to her or smiled at her (Con never smiled), but by the time of her argument with Richard she felt he was aware of her, that she had won a little of his precious attention. She badly wanted to dispel the impression that rumour told her he had of her. She was, without openly admitting it to herself, fascinated. And in her fascination, since the image of him had begun to fill many of her waking moments, she could not help but compare him with Richard. Of course, Richard suffered by comparison. There was no mystery, no challenge about Richard. Kind, sweet and safe he might be – but Helena was beginning to feel the attractions of something a little more dangerous.

The argument with Richard gave her, she felt, every excuse now to do exactly as she pleased. Their quarrel, like all lovers' quarrels, had been strangely liberating. Or so she told herself as, on the following evening, she carefully dressed and made herself up with the sole aim of appearing desirable to Con.

She had embarked upon a spiral descent into unhappiness. He paid some attention to her at the club in Victoria, but it was so scant in comparison to her own longings that she felt humiliated when he swept off into the night with his girl-friend, Gabrielle, and a small party of acolytes, all bound for some new place of adventure to which she had not been invited.

Three days later, her infatuation fuelled by Con's indifferent treatment of her, she was astounded when he came and took a seat next to her in the canteen, sitting very close, hunched inside a billowing black jacket, smoking and cupping his hands around his coffee.

'So?' he said quietly, glancing at her impassively and then taking a drag of his cigarette. She felt her heart pounding at the proximity of this deity; she wondered if her face was as pink as it felt and if everyone was watching her. She flicked her hair back nervously, trying to appear nonchalant. She couldn't think of a thing to say in response. He carried on smoking in the silence between them. At last she managed to murmur, 'I'm sorry?' To her own ears her voice sounded horrible, flutey, like that of a debutante.

He glanced at her again, not smiling exactly, but with an expression sufficiently relaxed to make him appear quite benign.

'So when are you and I going to get together?' he said quietly.

She stared at him, then at her coffee. 'I don't mind,' she replied, quite terrified. She had so magnified him in her imagination that she regarded him as some sort of superior being, not quite earthly. And here he was, asking her out.

'Whenever,' she added, with a little struggle.

'OK,' he said, lifting his chin and regarding her through half-closed eyes and a haze of cigarette smoke. 'I'll see you at the Three Tuns tonight. About eight.' And he rose and left, his coffee mug standing empty on the table and his cigarette end crushed and smoking in the ashtray.

There had been nothing friendly in the arrangement, but that did not trouble Helena. Con wasn't a friendly man. He was above that kind of thing. He just knew what he wanted and took it. He was magnificent.

The rest of that day seemed interminably long to her, and she was unable to concentrate on anything except the prospect of seeing him – what she would wear, what she would say. She had been careful not to answer the phone for the past few days, not wishing to speak to Richard, letting her friend Sissy, who now occupied the spare room in her flat, field calls for her. When Sissy mentioned that evening that Richard had called, Helena brushed him aside in her mind as a minor irrelevance. She had forgotten that she had once believed that she would love him forever. Any charm he might once have had was now dimmed, if not entirely extinguished, by her new, bright, particular star.

The evening, to which she looked forward with such delight and apprehension, was later to stand in her memory as an embarrassment, an occasion she did not care to think about.

She arrived at the pub at ten-past eight, not wishing to appear too eagerly punctual, and he was not there. A little hand of terror clutched at her heart; what if he had been there at eight, and had gone? She saw a couple of third-year students at the bar and asked them if they had seen Con.

'No. He hasn't been in since we got here. Why?'

'He said he'd see me here, that's all.'

The boy smiled, which made Helena feel uncomfortable, and she bought herself a drink and went to sit by herself at a table. A few more people from art school drifted in as time wore on and she said hello to them, her smile feeling wobbly with unhappiness. It was half-past eight. No one had ever done this to her before. How *could* he arrange to meet her and then not show up? That it was unbearably rude was not a thought that crossed her mind. The normal rules did not apply to Conrad Aaranson, she felt. Her emotions, her longing that he should come, were all that concerned her at the moment. At a quarter to nine, just as she felt she must go before her misery tipped into tearfulness, he arrived.

He came in suddenly through the door, a raw gust of

autumn wind whipping the black cloak he wore. He glanced around the bar, noted that she was there, waiting, and then went over to the bar to get himself a drink. Helena sat at her table uncertainly. He had not said hello, but she knew he had seen her. Should she get up and go over? No, that might look too . . . She watched as he bought his drink and leaned back self-consciously in her chair, taking a sip of her drink and trying to compose her face to look as though she had always expected him to be late and was not in the least concerned. He stood talking to some people at the bar for what seemed like ages. She glanced at the clock. Five to nine, and he hadn't even spoken to her. In spite of her awe, her infatuation, she felt a little spurt of rage. She would get up and go, she told herself. It was too much.

But just as she was about to rise, Con sauntered over from the bar with two of the young men he had been speaking to, still talking to them. He did not give Helena more than the most fleeting glance, but threw himself into the chair next to hers, draped his arm across the back of her chair, and drew her close to him with a wordlessly proprietorial air.

He did not speak to her or look at her, but the closeness, the warmth of his small body and the ease of his gesture in claiming her made her feel calm and, literally, possessed. She sat within the embrace of his arm, listening to him conversing with his friends. It was not so much a conversation, however, as a dissertation by Con on his beliefs and views on matters of intellect and style, studded with occasional murmurs of assent or approval from the other two young men.

Apart from asking her if she would like a drink and then buying it for her, Con did not speak to her at all. She simply sat there like an object of possession, feeling only faintly absurd, but trying to behave with as much composure as silence would allow.

The lack of any verbal communication between them made her feel distinctly awkward when they at last left the pub together, alone. But it did not seem to trouble Con. They walked along in silence, his arm still around her. She turned to look at him, and it occurred to her how much taller Richard was. Con really was quite small, now that they were walking together. Not that it mattered.

When he stopped in the half-darkness under some trees and leaned her back against some railings, she was not really surprised. He kissed her rather fiercely, and then a little more gently, for quite a long time. It felt wonderful; the lack of conversation, however, of any preceding intimacy, lent a detached sort of air to it all. Was he kissing her, Helena, or just some figurative creature, like the one he had wordlessly taken possession of in the pub earlier?

He pulled away from her after a while and surveyed her face unsmilingly. She could see the outline of his nose and cheekbone, and the tumble of dark curls upon his forehead, etched silver by the streetlamp a little way down the road. The light gave his face a faintly demonic look as he gazed at her.

'I'm sure there's quite a lot to be done with you,' he murmured at last, leaning forward to kiss her again, his words lightly touched with the arrogance that she found so seductive, so dangerous. She accepted his kiss gratefully, as though it were a gift, thankful just to be able to worship him, even if she could expect nothing in return.

'I don't think I'll come to your flat this evening,' he said, as he stopped kissing her for the second time. His words sounded so cool, so considered, that she wondered for a fleeting moment if she had actually invited him back. 'No,' he went on, lifting his chin so that he might look lazily down at her, since his height made this impossible otherwise, 'I think we'll save that particular pleasure for another time.' He kissed her lightly. 'See you around,' he said, and walked off down the road, leaving Helena leaning against the railings under the trees, too happy, too besotted, to question his manner of leaving her. He was Con Aaranson. He did things differently. He was not like other people.

Chapter eighteen

During these weeks, as late summer turned to autumn, the pain that Montacute had felt since his argument with Marion grew, rather than abated. He knew, as he sat viewing matters from the lonely perspective of his office, that the incident had been trifling, but he did not know how to recover the lost ground. He felt hurt and bewildered and impotent. He did not know what to do about anything, now that Marion had so summarily dismissed him from her life. She had become the focus of all his thought, and without the prospect of his enchanted meetings with her he felt as though he were merely groping his way through the days; stale, lifeless days. Before Marion, it had been a supportable existence; if life at home with his mother was a miserable affair, at least he had had his work and the pride which he took in its excellence, affording him the self-esteem and sense of purpose that he found nowhere else. Now the same work seemed burdensome, monotonous, the clients importunate and vexatious, the company of his fellow partners tiresome. He found he could scarcely pay proper attention to any of it and began to farm out work to Clive and the other assistants.

His mother had been out of hospital for a few weeks now. A district nurse called regularly, as did a social worker, and, of course, Mrs Carmichael was there each day, swelling and chirping around her invalid charge like an important sparrow. Mrs Carmichael adored illness and all its trappings. Montacute observed his mother's progress gloomily. She seemed to be fighting with all her strength to regain that of which the stroke had robbed her. Her speech was stilted and guttural, but she used it only sparingly and to effect. She had managed, in her son's hearing, to dismiss the social worker's tentative suggestions concerning mobility and disability allowances, giving her to understand that their financial circumstances were not so straitened. He could only silently agree with Mrs Carmichael as she marvelled daily at his mother's strength of will. He witnessed her gradual recovery with a heavy heart and a sense of guilt. He should have been pleased, he knew, to see her regain her health, but the process merely seemed to sap all his lately won confidence, confidence Marion had given him. Sometimes, as he lay wakefully in the dark of night, it was as though his mother had returned to claim him as her lost territory, as though she had spiritually overwhelmed and driven out the threat to her contained existence with her son. Marion was being exorcised.

In the light of day it was all much more mundane. Each morning he would help her to her commode, and then assist in dressing her. He would make some breakfast and help her to eat it, though at this point Mrs Carmichael would generally arrive, fussing and clucking around Mrs Montacute, who would eye her silently and balefully. Mrs Carmichael had gained a powerful ascendancy since the stroke, and talked continually as if to prove it. Then Montacute would leave for his office and the bleak monotony of his work. And in each day there was always a long interval during which he would stare out across Lincoln's Inn Fields, wondering what emasculation, what dismal repression, made him unable to pick up the telephone and ring Marion. It was not strength of pride, he knew, but some awful weakness of spirit.

He now returned punctually each evening, no longer staying late at his office or dropping off at his club. Above all, no longer returning late in the dark from evenings spent with Marion, no longer slipping the key gently into the lock of the front door for fear of waking his mother, no longer treading softly and happily on the stairs towards his room and thoughts of his love. The evenings with his mother passed even more slowly now, unenlivened by their former bitter, inconsequential exchanges. She still complained, still issued commands, but with such painful slowness that he could not respond in his usual manner, but merely bowed his head to it in silence.

Sometimes he tried to talk about the day's affairs, about snatches of news, imagining that she might welcome some conversation, but since she invariably moved her head away from his words with a show of impatience, he ceased even to try. He still poured for her her customary two glasses of sherry each evening, which she sipped with trembling but determined difficulty. He knew now that when he made his way upstairs to change his clothes, his mother could not even manage her former little luxurious deceit of him in the matter of the sherry, and he felt almost sorry for her.

In this atmosphere, with this sense of dragging penance as he helped his mother back to health, Montacute felt as though some creeping black blanket of suffocation was being drawn over his life.

Such was the pitch to which Montacute had been brought by the time Marion decided to call him and put him out of his misery. The last few weeks had been dreary enough for her, with Helena in London and Paul back at Ampersand. Paul had insisted on spending every last day up to the end of the summer holidays at Oliver's, which she felt was rather hurtful, in theory at least. So she had been prompted by the money produced by Montacute's inspired piece of investment to engage a new housekeeper, an act of conspicuous extravagance which had led in turn to a series of dinner parties and weekend parties of similar extravagance. These, however, had brought home to her the fact that all the most amusing people seemed to be eking out the last days of summer and the first of autumn on their yachts or in their villas, those symbols of a permanence of wealth which did not exist for Marion. Above all, and to her chagrin, Arios Vourlides had not called, even though she had discovered from friends that he was in London.

She was reflecting gloomily on this fact as she reviewed her finances in late September. To be the mistress of someone so enormously wealthy would have helped on the money front. Still, someone else's money was not the real solution.

Marion was sitting at her dressing table, painting her nails and going through her bank statements at the same time. It was a messy and dispiriting operation. Repairs to the house, some new furnishings and redecorations had, together with her own relentless personal spending, eaten a large hole in the proceeds from the sale of the paintings. If she invested what was left now – as she should have done at the outset, she realised, it would produce only a wretched amount of income. And then there was tax, the new cook-housekeeper, Leonie . . . She wouldn't last long unless things improved drastically financially.

No doubt Montacute could be cajoled into performing another little investment trick, but she realised that the one hundred and fifty thousand which had seemed such a delightful windfall when Montacute had presented her with the cheque shrivelled into nothing in the face of the economic realities of the future which stretched ahead. She could not live on hope, on occasional pieces of good fortune, on petty little subterfuges such as fabricated schooling expenses. She needed something substantial, something which could be invested and relied upon to produce an income on which she could live properly. Time, she thought, to take some serious steps with dear Geoffrey. Besides, she felt she had rather missed his devoted, if lugubrious attentions. It was nice to be adored.

Her mind, as she contemplated the crimson sheen of her nails, flickered away from the memory of his damp, fervent touch upon her naked breast and the surprise of her response to it. She blew gently upon the second coat of varnish and picked up the telephone.

At the very moment that Marion chose to make her call, Christopher Twysden, legal luminary and senior partner of the firm of Twysden, Chine & Grove, solicitors, was sitting in Montacute's outer office preparing to engage in settlement negotiations with Montacute in a case concerning a failed company merger. Several millions were at stake, and clearly only minds of the most lucent probity, such as those of Montacute and Twysden, were capable of resolving the issues.

As Twysden sat in Miss Reed's sanctum, polished and patient, utterly confident of his line of attack, Montacute sat miserably within, flicking through the file and the many bundles of documents, aware not only of his lack of enthusiasm for the business in hand, but also of the fact that he was probably insufficiently acquainted with the issues to do a decent job for his clients. What was wrong with him these days? He was beginning to feel slipshod and incompetent, as though something were being pulled away from under him. Sighing, he rose and slipped on his jacket and straightened his tie. At that moment the telephone rang. He picked it up and began to say, 'Not now, Miss Reed, I am about to –' when the name that Miss Reed had uttered came home to him. He sat down, paused for a moment, and then said, 'Please apologise to Mr Twysden and tell him that I shall only detain him a few minutes. Put Mrs Laing through.'

His heart lurched as he heard the familiar voice. 'Geoffrey? Is this a dreadful time to call? If you're frightfully busy I can always call back.'

'No, no,' said Montacute hastily. 'It's very good to hear – to hear from you.' He picked up a freshly sharpened pencil that lay on his desk and began to scratch nervous lines with it on his blotter.

'It's been such a long time since we spoke – I had rather hoped you would call me.' She sounded soft, reproachful.

He hesitated. 'I would have. I just rather thought, after our last meeting, that you might not care to – to—' He realised that he was speaking with the awkward uncertainty of a callow youth. All his dignity and his aplomb had deserted him in his joy at hearing from her. He was terrified that he might say some wrong thing, incur her displeasure again.

'To what?' She gave a low laugh, watching her face carefully in the dressing-table mirror. 'To talk to you? Oh, you are an ass.'

The gentle insult sounded to his ears like the sweetest of endearments. It was going to be all right, he told himself, closing his eyes and listening to her voice as she went on, 'I was rather bad, wasn't I? Getting so cross about nothing . . .'

'No, please,' he interrupted. 'I'm sure it was all my fault.'

'No,' she said firmly, staring straight at herself in the mirror and thinking how wonderfully clear and blue her eyes still were, just like a child's. 'I was simply dreadful, and I can't think why I was so silly.' She paused. 'Do you forgive me?' She bit her lower lip gently. She was rather enjoying this role, that of a penitent charmer, since it was one she had never played before.

'Forgive you?' gasped Montacute. 'You? Oh, Marion,' he said fervently, 'there is absolutely nothing to forgive. I was an imbecile not to ring you. I have missed you – dreadfully.'

The sincerity in his voice was so evident that Marion smiled. He really seemed to have suffered.

'Well, now that we're friends again, why don't we—' She hesitated, adjusting her voice to the perfect blend of mischief and enticement. '—kiss and make up properly?'

'Yes,' said Montacute. 'Yes, we should.' He could feel himself perspiring and shrugged the shoulders of his jacket back a little. He put the pencil down and opened and closed his damp palm.

'Well, I have to pop up on Friday. I'm attending a charity ball on Saturday and I simply *must* get a new gown. Why don't we meet on Friday evening?'

'Wonderful,' breathed Montacute. 'Where shall I pick you up?'

She hesitated. 'I don't know – I might stay with Helena—' Montacute's heart sank a little. 'But . . . well, anyway, why don't you pick me up there at eight?'

Each was smiling as they put the phone down. Marion's smile faded to a frown as her gaze strayed to the bank statements and then to the edge of one of her nails, where the polish had not quite dried and had become rubbed and dragged. She would have to do it again.

But Montacute's smile lingered as he wiped his brow with his handkerchief, then leaned forward to examine the thoughtless sketch he had made on his blotter of a little tree, some grass, and a shining sun. He sat smiling for a long moment, then pressed his intercom.

'Miss Reed, please show Mr Twysden in.' He stood up, a large, commanding presence, serene in mind and countenance, ready to do battle on behalf of Kirkbrooke & Handen (Leasing) plc.

Marion spent the better part of Friday in a variety of couturiers' fitting rooms, trying to find a satisfactory gown for the ball. She spent an enormous sum of money on the one she eventually chose, and a less significant – though still large – amount on a pair of shoes and a bag. That she could not afford to keep buying clothing at such an extravagant rate scarcely troubled her. She always found spending money on clothes enormously uplifting. She arrived at Helena's flat around teatime, laden with bags and parcels, and, seeing Helena's car parked in the street, rang the bell instead of using her key.

Helena answered the door after a few minutes, appearing rather flustered, barefoot, with her blouse wrongly buttoned. Marion seemed not to notice this, but leaned her scented cheek forward for a kiss before bustling through with her packages. Helena followed her through to the living room. Her mother paused in the doorway. The room was a shambles, cushions on the floor, tapes, CDs, magazines and a couple of empty wine bottles strewn around, ashtrays full. It did not appear to have been dusted for a week or two. And sprawled on the sofa, fetchingly attired in Helena's towelling bathrobe, was Con.

'Mummy,' said Helena quickly, 'this is Con. Conrad Aaranson. He's a friend of mine from art school. He – he's got simply rotten digs, so I said he could come back here and use the shower.' This was true. In between berating Helena for her personal wealth and her upmarket lifestyle, Con availed himself of everything that Helena had to offer. He used her shower, he ate the food she bought and cooked, he criticised her taste, read her books and listened to her music, never putting a book or a tape back in its place, he spent her money, and was rude to Sissy. In less than two weeks he had so far asserted himself that she let him make love to her, insult her, stand her up, and keep her constantly in a wound-up state of fear lest this beloved being should desert her. She thought that she loved him; she knew that he treated her abjectly. She thought herself lucky.

'Well,' said Marion, eyebrows raised. 'How do you do?'

Con merely nodded, did not offer to shake hands, did not even rise from his lounging position on the sofa. He regarded her with his cool, lidded gaze. Appalled, Marion could not help thinking how devastatingly good-looking he was.

'Well,' she said again, while Helena hovered anxiously in the doorway, 'I just dropped in to see how everything is . . . going.' She turned and glanced at Helena without expression. 'Although I had rather thought that I might stay with you for the next two nights.'

'Oh, Mummy!' exclaimed Helena. 'If you'd just rung and told me! You see, I'm letting my friend Sissy stay in the spare room for the time being, because it's really so difficult finding somewhere decent to live, and to be honest, it was a bit lonely here on my own. If you'd rung, she could have gone somewhere else for the weekend—'

Marion raised her hand to stem the flow. 'Please, darling,' she murmured. 'It doesn't matter in the least. It's your flat, and of course, I should have rung. I'll call the Connaught. Be a sweet and make me a drink, would you?' She reached into her bag for her cigarettes.

Helena gave her a look of blank surprise. She had expected an irate onslaught from her mother, to be taken to task for having someone to stay in what was, theoretically, her room, and for the general state of the flat. But Marion, aware that Con was watching her as he lit a cigarette, was not prepared to make a scene under the insolent and seductive gaze of that young man. She was more than a little startled when, rising from the sofa and tossing his dark, curling hair back from his face, he took his cigarette from between his lips and offered it to her before she could light the one she had taken from her bag. She hesitated, and then said, 'Thank you,' taking the cigarette and turning to follow Helena into the kitchen.

'I'm afraid we've only got red wine, Mummy, and it's not very good,' said Helena over her shoulder. Con had finished all the gin.

Marion winced. 'Please don't bother, darling. I'll get something at the hotel.' Marion picked up the phone and pressed the number, as well known to her as those of the Savoy and the Ritz, then turned to lean against the wall, taking a drag of her cigarette and pulling off the velvet bow that tied back her hair, so that it tumbled loose to her shoulders. I must ring Geoffrey as well, she thought. When she glanced up, Con was standing idly in the kitchen doorway, Helena's robe tied slackly so that his bare chest was exposed; his dark gaze was fastened on her face. Not very tall, she noticed; really quite diminutive. Still, a little of that young man probably went a very long way indeed. She wondered what had happened to that nice young man Richard Ranscombe. One never knew with girls these days . . . For a brief moment, as her eyes met Con's, Marion envied her daughter more than just her money.

It had come as a shock to Alice Montacute when her son informed her on Friday morning that he would be out that evening – out late – and had arranged for Mrs Carmichael to stay with her until he returned.

'Where – going?' she demanded with difficulty, stung to asking that which, in her pride, she had never before asked him.

'I am going, Mother, to have dinner with Mrs Laing,' he replied. Since his conversation with Marion he had felt a serenity, almost a sense of gusto, in all his doings. Mrs Carmichael came into the living room with a tray of tea and toast. Montacute turned from his glowering mother and remarked to Mrs Carmichael, 'I have just been telling my mother that you have very kindly agreed to stay with her this evening while I am out.'

'Ooh, yes, Mr Montacute. Do you good to get out and about for a change, won't it? Mrs Em and me will have a *luvvly* evening, won't we?' She patted Mrs Montacute's large arm with her own spry little hand, something she would never have done before the stroke, and gave a little chirruping laugh of proprietorial satisfaction. 'There's that Michael Barrymore chap on – 'e's always a bit of a laugh. We can watch it together!'

Montacute did not stay long enough to hear his mother's response to this.

While he was waiting for Marion in the lobby of the hotel that evening, he was accosted by a circuit judge with whom he occasionally came into contact, and with whom he had been at Oxford, Bernard Bessant. Bessant had rather disliked Montacute in earlier days, but time and professionalism had dimmed the recollection, and he always greeted Montacute now with bonhomie. They chatted for a few moments and, to Montacute's gratification, Marion arrived while they were still talking. He introduced Marion to Bessant with pride and watched and listened with proprietorial pleasure as she sparkled conversationally at him for a few moments. When they took their leave, Bessant watched with admiration Marion's elegantly clad figure going into the dining room on Montacute's arm. Amazing, he thought. Who would ever have thought that someone like Montacute could manage to find someone as delightful as that? A dark horse, Montacute. Perhaps there was more to him than met the eye. There would have to be, God knows.

This little encounter had done much for Montacute's self-confidence. His charm was still as heavy-handed as ever, but his conversation was easier than it often had been with Marion. He felt marvellous, reborn.

For Marion, dinner – indeed, the whole evening – had about it an inevitable air of *déjà vu*. She listened to Montacute's lofty discourse, she smiled, she ate, she drank, she looked amused, felt bored, talked about the children, and glanced discreetly at her watch from time to time.

When, over coffee, Montacute took her small, well-manicured hands in his own large, white ones, she had the distinct feeling of having been there before, many times. She smiled patiently into his ardent eyes, wondering why his hands were always so damp.

'Marion, darling,' he said in a low voice, 'you cannot imagine how wonderful it is to see you again. To be with you. The last few weeks have been – have been desolate.' He groped for a word that might sufficiently describe the utter bleakness of his recent miserable existence.

'I'm sorry,' she murmured, casting her gaze down. 'I would – I should have rung you earlier . . . It's just – well, things have been getting a little difficult lately. I've had to spend quite a bit of money on the house, and other bits and pieces—' She did not mention the new cook-housekeeper, nor the fact that she had bought herself a brand new dark-blue Porsche convertible. '—and frankly, I'm beginning to wonder how to make ends meet . . .' She smiled up at him bravely, and managed to disengage her hands from his moist clasp on the pretext of picking up her coffee cup.

Wine, and the sense that he had somehow reclaimed his love this evening, made Montacute bold. He took a deep breath. 'You know, Marion, there is no need why you should ever worry about money again.' His voice was grave, earnest, and his choice of words made Marion glance up at him in surprise. He went on, lowering his eyes to the tablecloth, his voice husky with emotion. 'I know – I feel that it is a great presumption – but I must ask . . . Please, Marion, I have more than enough for two – if you married me, then—' He broke off and looked at her. He did not quite know how to continue. His heart was almost bursting with dread that she might refuse him, refuse him the thing that he wanted more than anything else in life. His eyes met hers in mute appeal.

Faintly appalled, Marion mustered all her resources and produced a sweet, tremulous smile and a voice that seemed laden with both gratitude and sorrow. 'Oh, Geoffrey,' she said, and laid a hand on his, thinking quickly, 'how sweet you are. But I couldn't . . .'

'Why couldn't you?' asked Montacute earnestly. One lock of greying, dark hair slipped over his waxy forehead. He clasped her hand anxiously. 'I earn more than enough money. You could keep Roffey, we could have a house in London—'

'Geoffrey,' she interrupted in a quiet, kind voice, a voice full of sad wisdom. 'Geoffrey, do you think I could come to you on those terms? Do you think I could be so mercenary as to let you marry me just to ease my financial worries? It is a very noble, a very generous offer, but I couldn't let you do that.'

'But it would not be like that!' exclaimed Montacute. God, he wished they were away from this table, alone in her room, so that he could press kisses upon her, take her, make her want him, plead with her to marry him. He looked around. 'For God's sake,' he muttered, 'we can't discuss this in here. Please, Marion, let us go somewhere else. I must speak to you about this. Darling, please!' In his fervour, he picked up her hand and kissed it.

Marion thought for a moment beneath her sorrowful smile. She really had no alternative; besides, the few moments spent going up to her suite would afford her some space in which to consider her tactics. She nodded.

When they reached her suite, Marion suffered him to embrace her passionately for a few moments, then moved away from him, as though burdened with anxious thoughts. Montacute followed her, clasping her clumsily from behind and kissing her neck with passion. 'Say you will marry me, Marion,' he whispered hoarsely. 'Say you will.'

She turned herself in his grasp to face him and put her arms gently around his neck; this caused him to stoop slightly, and as he bent over her he reminded her of some oversize, loyal dog.

'Geoffrey,' she said in the sweet, earnest tones which she had adopted for this part, 'if I come to you, it can only be as an equal. I told you that downstairs. I have my pride, and I could not bear to think . . .' She pulled away from him and paced the room a little, plucking at her fingers. He looked after her helplessly. It was all very theatrical, but Montacute, deeply absorbed by his own emotions, could see none of this. 'You see, Geoffrey,' she resumed, 'this wretched money business is more than I can bear. What kind of future do I face? How am I to get from day to day on a mere pittance of an annuity? The children, of course, want for nothing . . .' She put a hand to her eyes, as though tears were close.

Montacute listened to this in bewilderment; something of the lawyer asserted itself in him, and he could not help saying, 'But the money that I gave you—'

Marion dismissed this with a dry, unhappy little laugh, and a motion of her hand which swept aside any ghost of a shiny new Porsche convertible that might have been hovering in the air. A slightly sharper note crept into the assumed sorrowfulness of her tone. 'Geoffrey, a sum such as that, given the upkeep of a house such as Roffey, hardly goes very far for very long. Oh, I know that my own lifestyle is hardly an economical one, but when one is used to certain things, scrimping is so hard, so demeaning . . . And yet there is that trust, all that money. If only you could help me.' She drooped her head, then fell into his embrace as he advanced upon her. She hoped she hadn't overdone it.

He hushed her, murmuring to her, and she allowed him to fondle her, to kiss her, to slip aside the straps of her dress and caress her. A mixture of thoughts and emotions assailed her at this point. She had intended, as usual, to let it go no further than a little tantalising foreplay; but there was some disturbing quality in his touch, something that made her want to prolong things. It had been a long time . . . And at the same time, she sensed that he would no longer be content with the tempting little morsels of herself which she had offered so far. If there was to be a bargain, it had to be sealed.

With this thought, she broke away from his embrace and led him, with a gentle, knowing smile, to the bedroom. As she crossed the room to switch on a lamp, so that the room was gently bathed in its glow, Montacute stood on the threshold, his heart pounding. Absurdly, he suddenly thought of his mother and Mrs Carmichael, and glanced covertly at his watch. Ten to ten. He had no idea of what was about to happen, or should happen, next. Seeing this, Marion went to him and slipped his jacket from his shoulders, pulled his tie loose, unbuttoned his shirt, and slid her hands across his pale, hairless chest. He kissed her clumsily, relentlessly, as she endeavoured to undress him and lead him to the bed at the same time. Sally was right, she thought. There was something rather novel and exciting about taking to bed someone who was an entire novice. It was something she had never done before – how many Montacutes could there be in this day and age? Perhaps thousands, she supposed, smiling in spite of herself as the last of Montacute's clothes landed on the floor and he stood, naked except for his socks, a monument to passion and acute self-consciousness.

Realising she would have to do this for herself, Marion unzipped her own dress and divested herself of underwear, then led him to the bed.

Montacute was not quite certain what was going through his mind. The whole experience was so new, so startling, and so unlike his imaginings, that he felt he could not quite focus properly. The getting off of clothes and getting into bed was the bit that he had always glossed over in his fantasies, and now that it was accomplished the thing felt almost clinical.

Was this quite how Marion should be behaving? It seemed very bold.

But the touch of her body against his beneath the chilly bedclothes drove every thought and instinct but one from his mind. Marion, who had been expecting to have to continue the initiative in everything, was rather overwhelmed by the suddenness of his lovemaking, but the surprise was agreeable rather than otherwise. When it was all over (with the speed which she had anticipated) he lay back, panting, as she ran her hands over his large, slack body, thinking how extraordinarily soft and white his skin was, and how pleasant he smelled, an old-fashioned smell of soap and loofahs and masculinity. No cologne, no after-shave.

'I'm sorry,' he said at last, appalled at the violation, at his own lack of control. He lay back on the pillow staring at the little hotel bedside light, unable look at her.

She glanced in surprise at his miserable face and smiled. 'What on earth for?' She leaned over and kissed him, feeling something like a vague affection, then ran her hands down across his stomach. 'You haven't done anything dreadful, you know. Perhaps a little fast, but that will get better . . .'

He let his glance slip slowly to her face. It was all right. It was going to be all right. He took her in his arms again. 'Oh, dear heaven, you must marry me,' he muttered. The intimacy, the fact of lying naked next to her, in love as he was, moved him unbearably. He had never felt so close to another human being before. She sighed and stirred against him; really, this was all unexpectedly relaxing. Still, one had to remember priorities.

'Oh, Geoffrey, I think I would, I could, if only . . .' She kissed his cheek softly several times, moving against him with gentle urgency. He felt himself engulfed, flooded with longing. If their first act of lovemaking had passed in a mindless flash, this time he seemed to feel every single sensation as it grew upon him, was conscious of every touch, every curve and fold of her body. He could never have imagined such pleasure.

'If only . . . what?' he murmured hoarsely, closing his eyes, giving himself up to the joys of anticipation.

'Oh, you know,' she replied, moving away from him lightly.

'The money. Help me as you helped me before – you know how. You're so clever. Just enough to end my worries, enough to make me feel—' She caressed him lightly and he groaned. '—secure. My own woman. I just want my independence again, so that I can come to you—' She slid one leg over his and moved it up against his hip. In for the kill, she thought. '—as you come to me . . .'

It was too much for Montacute. He knew what she was asking and he did not care. Nothing mattered except Marion, and that he should have this, keep this, on any terms.

'Anything,' he muttered, goaded beyond endurance as she arched her back away from him. 'Anything! Whatever you want – however much you want. I can get it for you. I promise. Only love me, marry me!'

As he fell upon her, Marion hoped he was too lost to feel the little shudder of suppressed laughter that rose within her. What an absurd great booby he was. But really rather surprisingly well-equipped.

Chapter nineteen

Paul realised, on his return to Ampersand after summer, that the pattern of his life there was set now. He knew his role – that of the quiet and unsought. At least the boredom and the loneliness held no surprises for him – no terrors lurked. He was one of them now, one from whom not much was expected; he, in turn, neither expected nor feared anything from them. He was without hopes or ambitions.

The days unfolded in dull monotony. He thought often of Teddy, of his bright, charming face and his lazy laughing conversation, of the things they had done together, of the fun he had had at Oliver's. It was another world, a world from which he was now locked away like a prisoner. Sometimes, in the first two weeks, he would walk down the corridor past Oakshott's old study and pretend in his heart that Oakshott still lived within, that he would see him again in assembly or catch sight of his blond head as he strolled across the quad. But that dream faded, too.

At least, he thought, his lot was not as dreadful as that of some of the younger boys. No one bullied you in the lower-sixth; they were beyond that there. They all had a kind of rugged independence. No, there was no question of anything like that –there never had been. But then, no one was particularly kind. They just left him alone.

Being left alone, he gradually realised, would probably have come as a merciful release to some of the poor little sods in the lower forms. There was one in particular, an overweight kid in the first form called Cowan, whom he saw going about from time to time. He always walked in a cowering, balled-up sort of fashion, Paul noticed, and he invariably looked as though he had been crying. Paul, infected with the ethos of the school, which crept inevitably upon every soul in the place, from old to young, regarded Cowan's obvious plight with a detached callousness. This plight seemed to range from miserable (when Cowan was allowed to slink around on his own) to utterly bloody miserable (when a taunting cabal trotted at his heels).

There was one occasion, however, on which Paul felt obliged to intervene, when he found Cowan crouched over on the ground behind the swimming pool building, filthy with dust and blubbering, surrounded by a small knot of his peers, who were shouting, 'You are a fat bastard, Cowan, aren't you? Yes, you are!'

'Go on, say it, Cowan! You're a fat little wanker, Cowan!'

'Yes, we've seen you! Wanker Cowan!'

And so forth.

He strolled over, wishing he hadn't come across this. 'Oh, come on, you lot!' was as much as he could find it in himself to say, but since he was a sixth-former, this was enough, and the culprits fled, leaving Cowan howling among the grit and weeds. Paul stood there for a moment, looking down. He felt a distant sympathy, but his heart was so hardened by his own hatred of the school that it was very distant indeed.

'You all right?' he asked, since Cowan seemed set to cry forever.

Cowan nodded, stopped crying, and looked up. He was, Paul acknowledged to himself, a pretty disgusting sight, and a fat one at that. Fat and objectionable though the child was, Paul suddenly saw him, not as yet another wretched first-former who was unfortunate enough to be bullied, but as a sad little boy who was being tortured beyond endurance. He helped Cowan to his feet and dusted him down as best he could. Cowan muttered thank you and was about to take himself off, aghast at the ignominy of having been found so by a sixth-former, when Paul took his arm and said, 'Hold on, it's all right. Let's have a talk.'

And so they talked, leaning against the wall, Cowan occasionally wiping at his runny nose with his blazer sleeve, reluctant to look Paul in the eye. But eventually Paul coaxed from him the full and horrible extent of his misery, the catalogue of repeated and exquisitely refined torments inflicted upon him by his classmates.

'But doesn't anyone know?' asked Paul, astonished that all this should go undetected in a junior form. 'Doesn't your form master know? Doesn't Matron ever get wind of this?'

Cowan shook his head in silence. He was sure that his form master, Mr Whitehead, did know, must know, but he assumed that everyone, boys and teachers alike, were all together in some hellish conspiracy in this hateful place to persecute him and make his life unbearable.

Paul stood looking down at the boy, appalled and perplexed. 'Can't you write to your parents?' he asked. Cowan said nothing. Paul thought of his own letters to his mother that first term, which now seemed a lifetime ago, and understood the silence.

'Oh, well,' he said at last, 'you'd better go off to prep.' And Cowan trotted fatly off to the next bout of degradation and humiliation, which he now accepted as his lot in life, while Paul gazed after him.

He went to see Mr Whitehead the following day. He had lain in bed after lights-out, thinking about Cowan, one moment telling himself that it was nothing to do with him, the next reluctantly feeling that someone should do something about it. Boys were bullied all the time, he knew, sometimes overtly, sometimes insidiously. What difference would it make if he managed to make it a bit better for Cowan? It would probably just start all over again after a while.

Nonetheless, next break time found him seeking an audience with Mr Whitehead. He waited until the first form had left, then stepped into the room. Mr Whitehead was busy gathering up exercise books. He was a tight-lipped, sallow man of thirty or so, a disappointed academic who disliked Ampersand and the job he did there, and only barely tolerated his pupils. He eyed Paul in a chilly fashion and asked him what he wanted.

Paul explained, hesitantly at first, how he had found Cowan the previous day and what Cowan had told him. 'I mean, sir, even if only half of what he says is true, it's enough. I think he's really having a very bad time of it.'

'Thank you – Laing, isn't it?' said Whitehead, who had remained silent and expressionless. 'I must say I find it a little presumptuous of you to come to me in this manner.' Paul gazed at him in astonishment. 'There is, of course, as you are aware, a degree of social interaction, commonly involving victimisation of one by the group, amongst any number of small boys. It is regrettable, but inevitable. If there were any question of serious bullying, such as you suggest, I am sure that I would be aware of it. I hardly think the kind of horseplay which is common among first-formers warrants serious investigation.'

'Well, look, I think that bogging – I mean, having your head put down the lavatory and the chain pulled several times amounts to a bit more than horseplay, sir,' retorted Paul. 'And that's the nicest thing they do.' Mr Whitehead was silent for a moment. He did not like Laing, he did not like Cowan, and he did not like the school. He was already looking around for some new position. He cared about none of this.

'Thank you, Laing,' he said at last. 'I shall bear what you have told me in mind. If anything were seriously amiss, I rather think that, as I am his form master, it would have come to my attention before now.'

Paul felt both savage and helpless as he left the room. Tough luck, Cowan, he thought. Your parents sent you to the wrong school.

He was determined to put the thing from his mind, and went off to see if there was a letter for him from Teddy. He looked every day. So far he had written several letters to Teddy, describing life at Ampersand and demanding news of the outside world, of things Teddy had seen and done. Teddy had obliged and had written back three times, jerky, spirited letters telling him of London, and Oliver, and people they knew. It was all more than Paul felt he could bear, that there should be that world only a train journey away, a real, breathing world that was denied to him, while he spun out his dreary days at school.

So he made his way to the pigeonholes. It was not that he expected Teddy to write very frequently, it was merely another of those little rituals that Paul went through, part of the web of life that he had constructed for himself at Ampersand, like devising ways of getting out of rugby and

223

CCF and wangling free periods that he could spend in the art room.

Today, however, there was a letter. With a glowing heart, Paul carried it back to the study which he now shared with Horsman, a lofty, intense boy with whom Paul had absolutely no common interests, and Beasley, with whom Paul was still tolerably friendly, but who regarded Paul as a bit of a drip and so didn't have much to do with him.

Horsman was there, reading a George Eliot novel and picking his nose, which he continued to do, covertly, while Paul read his letter. The letter was short, even cheerful, but the news that it contained stunned Paul. He looked up at Horsman's bony profile, then looked back down at the letter, feeling chilled to the centre of his being. Teddy was going back to the States. The news was casually and happily conveyed. It shouldn't have surprised him, he knew, but he had not realised how bereft such a thing could make him feel. A sense of desperation welled up within him. The Christmas holidays – he had so much looked forward to seeing Teddy then, had even hoped that his mother would let him invite Teddy down to Roffey for a few days. And now his friend was going back to New York, and he might not see him for years – or forever.

Paul looked out, above Horsman's head, to the grey autumn sky and the desolate line of poplars, a few scattered leaves still clinging to their branches, and felt as though some wind was blowing every love from his life. First his father, then Oakshott – now Teddy. It seemed more than he could bear.

At lunchtime in Kensington the following day, Teddy sat with Oliver in a snug, expensive restaurant – Oliver loved to spoil Teddy, loved to buy him costly, clever little presents and charming lunches which Teddy would never have been able to afford himself – and gave Oliver the same news which Paul had received in his letter the day before. Oliver's round face, previously beaming with satisfaction and happiness, went slack. He took a drink of his mineral water and looked down at his plate. His brioche with bone marrow sauce, one of his favourite starters at this particular restaurant, had suddenly lost its relish. He looked back at Teddy, who had already finished his ravioli.

'That's really good pasta,' Teddy observed, breaking off some bread and wiping it in the sauce. He met Oliver's eye. 'Hey, listen, man, don't look like that,' said Teddy with coaxing brightness, popping the piece of bread into his mouth.

Oliver picked up his fork and prodded at the brioche, then laid it down again. 'Well, I must say it's something of a shock,' he said. 'I hoped – I thought you were staying in London indefinitely. I thought you liked being in London.'

'Yeah, well, the thing is—' Teddy leaned back in his chair; Oliver looked at the lithe, muscular young body and the pretty, careless face, and felt a knot of grief in his stomach. '— it's getting kinda heavy at Drew and Errol's. They fight too much. I don't like that kind of stuff . . .'

'But you could stay with me,' said Oliver. 'Why don't you stay with me? You know I've always told you that you may.'

Teddy looked away uneasily. 'I know. That's real kind of you. Everyone's been real kind . . . It's just that I want to get back. I can't explain. London's great, but it ain't home. Now that you've given me some contacts and helped me sell a couple of my paintings, I really feel I could *do* something over there now. You know?'

Oliver knew. He had been useful, had been used, and was now discarded. He let the waiter take his unfinished plate of food away.

'I'm glad that I've been of some help to you, at any rate,' he said sadly, a little huffily. His face looked so comical in its chubby despair that Teddy had to check a smile. He laid a hand on Oliver's sleeve.

'Hey, c'mon! You've been great! You've been a real friend and you've helped me make a few bucks. I don't know what I woulda done without you. You and Charlie.'

Oliver pressed his lips together in a thin line and told himself that he would not humiliate himself; he would just accept the fact of Teddy's departure with good grace. Then he looked up helplessly and said, 'But I thought we – mattered to one another?'

Teddy looked uncomfortable and glanced sideways, hopeful of an approaching waiter to interrupt things. Then he looked back at Oliver.

'There are mistakes we make,' said Teddy gently. 'I'm sorry – I didn't mean it to sound that way. I mean, it should never have happened, Oliver. I'm grateful to you and all, but that's it.'

That's it, thought Oliver. I have helped you make money, I have given you some influential contacts, presents, my love. And that's it. But he said none of this. And when the waiter came with a plate of red mullet for him, and poached salmon for Teddy, he was glad of the opportunity to smile again and make an effort at cheerful conversation to mask the pain in his heart.

Montacute sat in his office in the late afternoon. Dusk was beginning to fall. The hum of the City traffic had risen in pitch as the working day's end drew near, and outside he could hear the clanking of the scaffolders dismantling materials around the John Soane Museum, preparing to leave for the day.

He sat in the fading light in his curiously old-fashioned room, with its dense velvet curtains and picture rail, its dark panelling, chandelier, and heavy furniture, and gazed fixedly at the window, his large frame motionless except for the fingers of one hand, which stroked the polished edge of the desk over and over again.

For all the calm detachment of his manner, his mind was seething with thoughts of Marion and what was to come. He knew many things. He knew that he loved her, that without her his whole existence must founder. He knew – he felt, too, that he was close to having her, that she would marry him if things were as she wished them to be. He did not fathom her desires, could not construe her greed or even name it as that, but he knew that she had bargained with him. He had told himself that he could not do as she asked, and she had seen this, and had fed him small morsels of herself, careful handfuls of her flesh, over the months. He knew all this and he knew, too, that now he had possessed her, he could not bear to lose her. He had had few chances of happiness in his life, and if he lost this one, he might as well die. It was not the getting of love, he now saw, not the gratification that was important, but the giving of love, the inspiring of affection. He wanted to matter to someone, as never before.

And so he turned his eyes away from the melancholy afternoon light and fastened them on the papers on his desk. Then he picked up the telephone. He did not ask Miss Reed to make the call, but did it himself.

He had not spoken to James Ackland, of stockbrokers Appin & Ackland, for some months, and so he was obliged to engage in a preamble of pleasantries and conversational trivia before reaching his business.

'I – ah – rang with regard to some reinvestments I propose to make, James,' said Montacute in his professional tones, his voice as smooth as a tallow candle. 'Yes, I felt it was about time to pitch into the market. It's actually more of a variation of investment. Yes . . .' He nodded at some little jest of Ackland's, his eyes still fixed on the papers before him. 'Yes. Ha, ha! You could say that . . . It might be nice to make a little sudden money for a change. What I had in mind was a company called Garter Cross . . . Yes, well, an acquaintance of mine, actually . . . Well, I don't know about his judgement – it was just a tip, if you like. What's your view?'

Ackland, in reply to this, elaborated on that which Hugh Howard had already told Montacute. 'Well, let's see. Garter Cross is this chap Melanakis, Greek fellow. He's not a known name in the City, but he seems to have got some solid backing from his government, which is good for confidence. The word is he's a very good bet. He's been expanding at a pretty steady rate – started off with import and export businesses at home and is diversifying abroad. Got quite a touch. The banks like him.'

Montacute listened, nodding.

'I take it that this isn't trust business, Geoffrey?' continued Ackland. 'Because, of course, he's still too much of a new-comer for that kind of thing. Hasn't been quoted for long enough. But I don't need to tell you that.'

'No, quite,' said Montacute quickly, his hand over his eyes. 'Nonetheless, it's quite a large amount. I'm looking for a fast, substantial return.'

'Well, Garter Cross is a good risk reward investment. I think it should answer, providing confidence keeps up and the banks are happy.'

And so Montacute gave Ackland instructions for the disposal of a large quantity of admirably safe, but financially unimaginative investments, and the purchase of a considerable quantity of Garter Cross shares.

'If the price takes off in the way it should, you should make a very healthy return on that sum,' remarked Ackland. 'You could, if it stays bullish, clear something in the region of eight hundred thousand – possibly more, depending on when you sell. Mind you, the other holdings were safe . . . Still, if no one takes any risks these days, where's the fun? And the profit? Ha, ha!'

'Quite, quite,' chuckled Montacute. When he put the phone down, he let out a deep breath. He felt reassured by what James had told him. It was just a matter of keeping one's eye on the market. If the thing was as good a risk as James seemed to think, then he had nothing to worry about. No one need know. Marion would be safe, paid for, his.

Helena sat in the flat in Caversham Place, waiting. She had been waiting for so long that she had even beguiled the time by clearing up a bit and making a stab at dusting and cleaning. But the hoover bag was full to bursting and she had no new ones, so the results of her labours were not spectacular. She switched the television on, couldn't concentrate, and switched it off. She thought about some of the work she should be putting together for tomorrow, and pushed the thought aside; she was so far behind that it wouldn't make any difference, anyway. Where the hell was he?

The pattern was so familiar by now, she told herself, that she shouldn't get agitated. He never showed up on time . . . But when he said eight o'clock, she started to watch the clock at ten minutes to, and so an evening would drag itself out, until Con deigned to show up.

If she was honest with herself, it wasn't he who had said eight o'clock. She had. She had found herself, humiliatingly, accosting him as casually as she could at lunchtime, and asked him if he wanted to come round that evening. She had seen the flicker of irritation on his beautiful, sullen face and had felt a little stab of fear, but he had nodded, impatient to get back to his friends. She had tugged at his sleeve as he turned away, saying, 'When, then?' And saying it too loudly. 'Eight? Is eight too early?' she had added. God, the thought of it made her cringe now, that she should allow herself . . . But she couldn't help it. She could help nothing where he was concerned. She realised that she probably shouldn't much like Con, that there was little between them, and that it had no future. But she was so in love, so obsessed, that only the moment mattered. Only this night, and only the next day, the chance that he might be kinder, that magic would touch it all and she would become happy, instead of abjectly miserable. She did not understand how she could see all this, know how hopeless it was, and yet still find herself watching and waiting throughout another evening.

She crossed the room and checked that the phone was not off the hook, in case he should be trying to ring to say he would be late. This was so improbable as to be utterly fantastic, but she did not admit it to herself. She told herself so many little lies, made so many excuses for him, trying to regularise matters, to create of him a decent, ordinary creature, to make their relationship a happy and equally balanced one.

No, the receiver was in place. She thought of picking it up to check that it was still working – but what if he should be trying to ring just as she picked it up? Her hand hovered. She picked it up and heard the familiar dialling tone, and put it down again, suddenly feeling dreadfully lonely.

She was just about to sit down with a magazine when she heard footsteps in the street, unmistakably turning off up to her door, and flew out into the hallway with joy in her heart.

It was Richard. She stared at him for a moment, naked disappointment on her face, and said nothing, the beginnings of a small, wretched, guilty feeling inside her.

'Hello,' he said, when she didn't speak. 'You haven't returned any of my calls, and you never seem to be in when I ring, so I got tired of speaking to Sissy and decided to come and see you. I want to know what's up.' He stood there in his

229

raincoat, its collar up, his brown hair lifting in the autumn night air, his blue eyes unhappy but determined.

Helena took in nothing he said; she was revolving in her mind Con's likely reaction to finding Richard in the flat when he arrived. It could be a good thing, or it could be a disaster. 'You better come in,' she murmured, and turned away, going back through the hall into the living room, where she dropped down on to a large cushion propped up against the sofa. Richard stood in the doorway of the dimly lit room. It was just about the kind of disorder and general mess that one expected in girls' flats, but somehow the expensive furniture and decorations made it look rather worse. He saw, glancing to the french windows, that the large green palm which he had given Helena as a flat-warming present, and which he hadn't really been able to afford, had been allowed to shrivel, unwatered for weeks. Then he looked at Helena, who sat cross-legged on her cushion, gazing at the floor, the expression on her face quite unreadable. She looked as lovely as ever, but tired; he could almost feel the nerviness radiating from her. The very set of her body made him feel like some unwanted intruder.

'Waiting for someone?' he asked, making an unlucky guess. He had suspected that there must be something more to her long silence over the last few weeks than mere huffiness. There had to be someone else. She glanced at him, then looked away.

'I am, as a matter of fact.' It was not said coldly or proudly, but sadly, faintly. He sat down on the sofa next to where she was, so that he was looking down at the back of her head and could not see her face. 'I've met someone else.'

'I see,' he said, despair tightening his throat now that he heard it spoken. 'I see.' There was a long silence. 'I wish you'd told me. Rung me, or something. I haven't known where I stood for a while, you know. I didn't think our argument was that bad. I didn't really think it was an argument . . .'

She said nothing. Sitting as she was, she longed just to lean her tired head against his thigh, to be held, to have a friend. It was a friendless, strange region which she inhabited these days. All the things that she loved, that mattered to her, she had had to cast off or hide away from Con's remorselessly critical gaze; she could not allow herself to do, feel, or like anything or anyone with which he might find fault. And he found fault everywhere. She was estranged from many of the things that had been happy and familiar in her life. Richard had been one of those things.

The best thing, she thought, would be if Con would come now, so that this wouldn't have to be prolonged, so that she would stop feeling weak and miserable. He would be here any moment. And then Richard would see. Then he would see . . .

'Can I make myself a cup of coffee?' said Richard at last, getting up from the sofa and away from the overwhelming temptation to reach down and caress the soft silkiness of her honey-blonde hair.

She glanced up, her face troubled. 'I don't know if that's a very good idea . . . really.' For a moment she hated herself, even more than she usually did these days. 'Oh, yes, go on. I'm sorry. Please. You know where everything is.'

He wandered into the kitchen, still in his raincoat, and filled the kettle. 'Do you remember,' he called through to her, feeling he should at least lighten the atmosphere a bit, 'when we came back and found old Montacute and your mother here?' He laughed. 'God, his face . . .'

'Yes,' she said faintly. Richard talked, rambled on from the kitchen as he made them both some coffee, and she began to feel better, just listening in silence to his voice. Maybe this was all stupid. She had no future with Con, she knew. Maybe she should just end it all now. Maybe it would still be all right with Richard. He would have her back in an instant, she knew. He loved her. She knew that without a doubt, but did not even pause to ponder its value. All she could think about was how devastated Con's pride would be if she did that . . . oh, just think. To be strong enough to do that, not to care. But she did care. She cared passionately. And so she would not – there was no question of her doing that.

Richard brought the coffee through and they drank it. Their conversation was stilted. He asked her how art school was, and she said, oh, okay. She asked him how work was, and he said, oh, you know. Richard longed to say, 'Tell me – tell me about this new person. Tell me what he's like, why you like

231

him more than me.' But he did not. He finished his coffee and rose to go, aware that Helena's mind was far away, that she was listening for some unheard footstep outside, her eyes darting anxiously around the shadows of the room, as she sipped her coffee.

She walked wordlessly with him to the door. Before he opened it, Richard turned and took her in his arms. She did not resist, let him hug her, grateful for the warmth and kindess. But when he bent to kiss her she turned her head away, her mouth unsmiling. He took his arms from around her and hesitated for a moment. Then he said, 'I'm always there, you know, if you ever need me.' She said nothing, and he left. She stood for a moment in the doorway, not watching Richard as he walked away, but scanning the street for Con's slight, unmistakable figure. The street was empty. She turned and went in, closing the door, and mechanically went through to the kitchen and washed the coffee mugs.

Then she went back in to the living room and sat down on her cushion to wait in silence.

Chapter twenty

At first Montacute hesitated about telling Marion of his bold investment; his natural prudence and discretion prevented him for a few days, until at last his desire to please her became too strong. But he referred to the matter only obliquely, with a sense of satisfaction not even tinged with guilt.

'I have taken a very large plunge on your behalf,' was how he put it when he telephoned her at Roffey. 'Something which I think should pay – ah – an extremely handsome dividend.' He smiled as he heard the little gasp and pause at the other end, and waited for her approbation.

Marion was, in fact, considerably more surprised than she had expected to be. When she heard it from Montacute's own lips, phrased in his rotund tones, she realised suddenly what he was risking on her behalf. It was, she knew, something which might put his entire career at stake, to gamble with trust funds. And such a trust. Such funds. But he was a clever man. In his hands it could not be called a misappropriation. If he intended to make money for her, then he would. He could not fail her. So after a moment's pause she said, 'Geoffrey, you are a most daring, darling creature. But isn't it very naughty, all this?'

He smiled to himself. 'I would commit the most cardinal of sins for you, Marion.' It was spoken lightly, and any faint sense of personal anxiety on Marion's part disappeared.

'Well, I shan't ask any more about it, because I'm sure you shouldn't be doing it—' It never once occurred to Marion that she, too, was a trustee with responsibilities. '—so I shall simply reward you by asking if you would like to come down to Roffey for the weekend. I'm having a dinner party on Saturday evening and then people for lunch on Sunday, but we can have all the rest of the time to ourselves.' It was important now to keep Geoffrey as sweet as possible until the benefits of their little bargain had materialised. After that – well, after that would take care of itself. At least with lots of other people around at the weekend she would only have to endure Saturday night alone with him. And the novelty of sex with a novice – such a willing, ardent novice – had not yet worn off.

Delighted with the arrangement, blissful in anticipation of those physical pleasures which he recalled countless times throughout the day, Montacute said that he would come down on Friday evening. Two nights with Marion at Roffey . . .

'No, darling, not on Friday,' said Marion quickly. 'I have rather a lot to do before the dinner party on Saturday. Oh, do bring evening dress with you. Let's say Saturday – early afternoon, perhaps?' The thought of spending an entire Saturday with him was too much.

He agreed, consoling himself with the thought of Saturday night, and when he had put the phone down flung himself into his work with all the energy of one happily and newly in love. He had the added satisfaction of knowing, from his morning copy of *The Times*, that Garter Cross was up six points that day, a steady rise since his recent purchase.

He had brooded on the problem of his mother and what to do with her over the weekend all the way home. He was determined that she should not stand in the way of his visit to Roffey. But when he had gone upstairs to change, he heard – he was absolutely sure he heard – the sound of the sideboard door creaking open in the living room below. He tiptoed out on to the landing, leaned over the banister and listened. Sure enough, a little muffled clinking, a creak again, and then her footsteps, slow yet furtive, making their way back to her chair. If she was well enough to do that, he thought indignantly, she would be perfectly all right on her own. He would ask Mrs Carmichael to look in – or perhaps spend Saturday evening here. It was only one night, after all.

With these thoughts, he put on his slippers and went downstairs. He rubbed his hands together briskly as he came into the room and picked up his whisky and the evening paper from the table where he had left them.

'How has your day been, mother?' he asked with the chilly brightness which was his most intimate mode of addressing her. She disliked his cheerfulness, was suspicious of it. Nonetheless, she tried, in a halting way, to tell him of her day. It had been detestable. The ambulance had come to take her to the day-care centre for therapy classes, even though she had told the social worker that she did not wish to go to therapy classes.

'They *made* me go!' she muttered.

'Nonsense, mother.' How childish her speech was, now that she was gradually regaining it. It prompted him to speak to her in a more condescending fashion than normal. 'I'm sure it's very good for you to be with other old ladies, with something to occupy your time.'

Alice Montacute plucked at the sleeve of her cardigan with the fingers of one hand, its joints painfully swollen, as she tugged out her words.

'Old – ladies? Pah!' She glared at him in disgust. The exclamation had left a little drop of spittle suspended from her lower lip, and he eyed it with distaste, thinking also that she did not dress her hair very tidily these days. It must be difficult, he supposed. 'Old bitches – is what they are,' she continued. 'Old bitches.' She wagged her head, looking away from him, powerless to convey to him in her fractured speech the deadliness of the place. The bright, spilling, articulate voice of Mrs Raines, the occupational therapist, still drummed in her mind like rain on a roof. She talked so fast, smiled so brightly, and yet Mrs Montacute knew that all her apparently kind chatter masked the repeated taunt – 'See? I am young! I can move quickly and easily! My fingers work, my tongue works! I do not shuffle! I am not old, I do not fumble and forget things, like you silly old women!' She hated Mrs Raines. She hated, too, the young man who taught pottery. She hated the echoing cleanliness of the day-care centre, like a transit camp for the old, the old being hustled along by the bright, smiling impatience of the carers towards their inevitable deaths. She hated the tea ladies, and she hated the other old women who shared her fate. They talked, they cackled, they clapped their hands and tried to join in with reedy, piping voices in the old-time singalong. In the ambulance on the way home, she had sat with a face as grim as granite, vowing never to allow them to take her there again. Otherwise she would be dragged down further and further, nearer to the dreaded institutionalisation, the nursing home, loneliness, and death. She had never felt so lonely, and so afraid of death, as she had among that awful, gregarious group of old women.

But she could say none of this to her son. It would enfeeble her in every sense.

'I will not – go back!' she exclaimed, as Montacute scanned the radio and television pages of the newspaper. He looked at her and raised his eyebrows.

'No?' He looked back to the paper again. 'Oh, I am sure you will. You'll get to like it there. It's hardly very good for you to spend all your time cooped up here with just Mrs Carmichael for company.' The smooth flow of his words – how easy it was for his tongue to slip them out effortlessly into the air! – incensed her. 'Anyway,' he added, 'that kind of thing is very important to ensure that you regain all your – your old abilities. So Dr Parry said, don't you recall? Radio Three looks good this evening. There's a repeat of that Somerset Maugham broadcast on his eightieth birthday, and then choral music from Eton.'

No, she told herself, she would not go back. The next step would be a home – that was what he was preparing her for. She would show her son that she did not need to go to that place to get well. She *was* well. She collected her strength and rose from her chair.

'Mrs Car—' She could not finish the name, dismissed it. '— has left some,' she hesitated. 'Gammon. I shall grill it – for us. Perhaps—' She mumbled her mouth, turning away from him as though merely pausing, trying to hide the uncertainty of her speech. 'Perhaps you would peel – potatoes.' She was proud of the firmness of her words. He would see that she was as able as ever. She made her way slowly to the kitchen, nerves sharpened by her sherry, and began to prepare supper. She had expected her son to demur, perhaps, but he followed her through in silence, fetched some potatoes from the vegetable basket, and began to peel them.

Something about the soapy moistness of the potatoes' flesh as he peeled them reminded him, absurdly, of Marion's firm body beneath his fingers. A warm, giddy sensation spread through him, the delicious charge of suddenly recollected love. He realised as he stood at the sink, comparing his lover's breasts to peeled potatoes, that he was happy. About the money, he cared nothing. He had every confidence. He felt reckless with passionate ambition. He glanced sideways at his mother, who seemed to be managing the matter of the gammon steaks with tolerable competence (practice counted for a lot in these things, he supposed), and wondered what she would say if she knew about the money. She would consider him a fool, he imagined. But she had always done that. Or perhaps she would admire him for his boldness? This thought struck him quite suddenly. Perhaps – perhaps she might have thought more of him throughout his life if he had taken more risks, if he had been careless of her, less anxious to please. He wiped his hands and put the potatoes in a pan. Well, too late to think of that now. That was all past. He had a new life to look forward to now.

Later that evening, after they had listened to the radio together in silence – hardly companionable, but marked on Montacute's part by a serene happiness, and on hers by a grim satisfaction at her competence that evening, showing him that she did not need those wretched carers and fussing therapists – he told her of his plans for the weekend.

'I can arrange for Mrs Carmichael to spend Saturday evening with you, if you wish. She is always grateful of the extra money.' He paused as she stared stone-faced at her hands. This was the reward, she thought, for her cleverness this evening. To be left alone while he gallivanted off with that Laing woman. 'Or perhaps,' Montacute continued, 'you feel that you can cope alone? It seemed to me this evening that you have made very good progress. You see how much the day-care centre helps you? It is clearly an excellent place for you to go.'

She said nothing, was evidently displeased, and so to ease

the little burden of his guilt he cleared his throat and went on, 'It is only for one night, mother. I shall go after lunch on Saturday, and I will make sure there is something for your evening meal. I can even make up a bed for you downstairs if you are at all worried about the stairs.' She shook her head angrily; words refused to come; her body, her tongue would no longer work for her. 'I shall be back on Sunday evening.'

She declined to speak to him for the rest of the evening – not an unusual proceeding when she was wrathful with her son – and eventually they took themselves off to bed, Montacute to the luxuriance of thoughts of Marion and the coming weekend, and his mother to a dark contemplation of the future. She lay listening to the silence of the house – the house which she had never liked, in all its drab dreariness, but which she had never sought to brighten through the years – and now feared the loss of it. He was going to her again. What if the unthinkable should happen, and he should marry her? She saw a future stretching ahead of her which consisted of days passed in the way that today had been passed at the day-care centre, deadeningly, from now until the end. Bright, cheerful, punishing days, until at last there was only death.

Marion had two reasons for inviting Montacute to Roffey that weekend. One was to keep him in a state of hopefulness, and the other was to play him off against her shipowner, Arios Vourlides, whom she had met with his wife at the charity ball in London and invited to dinner on Saturday. She still had high hopes in that direction, and felt that a little spice of rivalry might help matters along. Arios had behaved towards her at the ball with quite unmistakable attentiveness. It had been worth spending a couple of thousand on that dress after all, even if she might never wear it again. All these investments paid dividends.

Montacute, when he arrived at Roffey, noted with his customary perspicacity the fact of the new Porsche standing next to the BMW (with which Marion had decided not to part – one never knew, after all, when a second car might come in handy and, anyway, Leonie, the new housekeeper, used it to go shopping). Montacute noted the existence of Leonie, too –

238

Marion referred to her as 'my new, my absolute treasure' – and certain touches throughout the house, some elegant new furniture in the conservatory, and new carpets, curtains and decorations in all the downstairs rooms. 'I was even thinking, you know, that an indoor swimming pool might be nice. It's one thing I've always rather thought Roffey lacked,' she murmured to him as she led him through to the drawing room for a drink after his journey, 'Not that I particularly swim . . .' she added, pouring his whisky.

For just a second, Montacute's pragmatism rose to the surface; her expenditure was way beyond her means, surely, even though she had admitted to him the fact of her own natural extravagance. But when she turned and came towards him with his drink, folding one slender arm around his large body and drawing him to her for a few seconds, such considerations were forgotten. He took the opportunity to try to embrace her more closely and kiss her with his wonted passion and new confidence as her accepted lover, but she drew smilingly away.

'Not now, darling. Drink your drink and make yourself comfortable. I must just go and speak to Leonie. I still have masses to do before this evening.'

All that had to be done, however, seemed to be done by the admirably efficient Leonie. A handsome woman in her forties, she moved about with silent competence, arranging the dining table, attending to everything in the kitchen, decanting the wine, arranging bowls of flowers. As she glided in and out of his purview from time to time, Montacute began to suspect that she was an absolute treasure in a very literal sense. Marion's lifestyle would require no mean income indeed if it was to be maintained. She clearly expected a good deal from the bargain which had been struck. But then, so did he.

When Marion's guests began to arrive around seven-thirty, Montacute, now attired with dignity in his evening dress, slipped into the persona of the affable City lawyer, which was the only one he knew how to use, socially, and made conversation with his usual lofty blend of pedantry and complacency. He noted that Marion did not treat him with any special affection, did not mark him out with any fond glances or secret smiles – in fact, she seemed to pay rather a lot of attention to some stocky, grey-haired Greek – but he was pleased to think that she was merely exercising a natural discretion, and thought warmly of the night ahead.

Marion had seated Montacute several places away from herself at dinner, next to a particularly vivacious and frivolous middle-aged woman given to a love of intimate gossip, who Marion thought might benefit from an unrelieved diet of prosy legal tedium for an hour or so, and on the other side to an elderly sculptress, a friend from the days of her marriage to Alexander, who could bore just as consistently as Montacute on any subject without paying the slightest attention to anything her listener might interject. There was no conspicuous spitefulness on Marion's part in all this – she was simply accustomed to regarding other people as a means to her own amusement, and this arrangement afforded her some.

She watched Montacute as he held forth to the vivacious woman, now glassy-eyed, on the subject of legal reform, and thought how perfectly worthy and incorruptible he looked. The very epitome of the blameless, scrupulously honest lawyer. If only they all knew what this monument to virtue was perpetrating on her behalf; she smiled at the thought of it.

Montacute was impatient for the evening to end. People lingered over their coffee and brandy far longer than seemed necessary; he was almost willing them out into the night by the time eleven o'clock came. He had long ago exhausted the possibilities of conversation with the strange woman on his left, who had seemed quite animated at the beginning of the meal but who, on discovering that he knew none of the people she knew, had eventually turned her attention to her neighbour. As for the old woman on his right, with whom he had latterly had to content himself, it seemed that she spoke in a sort of braying monotone that brooked no interruption; besides, he had not the faintest notion what she was talking about for most of the time. He watched Marion sparkling with conversation and laughter at the end of the table, the stocky Greek on her left, and wondered how she managed to do this kind of thing so often. It quite exhausted him, all this social effort with people whom one didn't know. When they were married, perhaps she would be prepared to do a little less of it. He stifled a yawn at the thought of yet another gathering at luncheon the next day. He longed for the comfort of bed and the solitary intimacy and intense delight of making love to Marion.

It was not over until well past midnight. The last guests trickled off to their cars and Montacute smiled in a happy, conspiratorial fashion at Marion as she came back into the drawing room, unclasping a bracelet from her wrist and yawning. She gave him only a faint smile, however, and when he reached out to detain her as she brushed past the chair where he sat with his brandy, she murmured something about Leonie and went out in the direction of the kitchen. Montacute sat nursing his brandy, enjoying his solitary possession of the room. Such a room. Such a house. He gazed at the fire that now burned low in the large grate and pondered the pleasure which it would be to share such a life and a home with Marion. He would buy them a house in London, too. She could spend as much money as she wanted – well, within reason – when this investment paid off, and they would be happy together. As for his mother (although he did not care to think of her at such a time, the problem had to be faced), she would be content in a nursing home. It was only a matter of time, in any case. Somewhere quiet, expensive, where he could be sure that the care was excellent. It would be good for her to spend her time with people of her own age, instead of cooped up in that house in Richmond. That house. He would sell it for her, invest the money. It would pay for the nursing home. He sighed and gazed into his brandy. They would all be so much better off, so much happier.

Marion came back into the room and, switching off the central light at the doorway so that the room was lit only by table lamps, stood gazing across at Montacute. The shadows caught his long, pale face in a way that made it look almost handsome. Still, she thought, she hardly felt like sex after such a long evening. She had definitely made considerable head-way with Arios, in a flirtatious, unspoken fashion . . . Ah, well, needs must, she told herself, and advanced softly across the room to Montacute, who looked up at her as she drew near, as guileless and loving as a boy.

241

'Bed?' she said softly, and smiled. He nodded, tiredness forgotten, and let her take him by the hand and lead him upstairs.

As they lay in bed together, a wave of ennui suddenly swept her. He had obviously been reliving their previous lovemaking and had decided to be more assertive, she realised, as he attempted to indulge in some inexpert foreplay. Or maybe he had been reading it up. The thought of this made her smile, and this turned into a giggle. Montacute stopped and looked at her in surprise.

'You tickled me,' she explained, pushing a lock of his lank hair back from his forehead. 'Please do go on,' she added politely, which made her giggle again. He gave up and looked hurt. He felt that some of the magic of their previous encounter was lacking, but did not know why. Marion looked at his face and decided that she had better inject a little of her own enthusiasm into all this.

'Tell me,' she whispered, snuggling closer to him, 'tell me how much money you are going to make for me.' He was surprised that she wished to discuss finances at a time like this. Then she began to caress him, to run her hands over his pale flesh. 'Tell me – tell me.' His mouth felt dry with longing as he guided her hands.

'Well –' he said uncertainly.

'Go on,' she murmured, pushing herself against him.

'Um – several hundred thousand.' It wasn't the kind of thing one could murmur as a tender endearment, exactly. But the words seemed to have the desired effect upon Marion. She smiled at him and let out a low breath. 'Possibly millions – well—' Even in the throes of passion a sense of strict accuracy asserted itself. '—a million, perhaps.'

Nothing, thought Marion as she let him climb on top of her, was quite as exciting as the idea of a great deal of money; it was a positive aphrodisiac.

Six minutes later, Montacute lay back on the pillow, breathing rapidly, a sense of fading exhilaration being replaced with one of contentment. He felt that he was really getting rather good at this. Marion, drawing the bedclothes over her shoulders in preparation for sleep, hoped that it wouldn't be long before this investment paid off.

Waking up next to Marion the following morning was a curiously embarrassing novelty for Montacute. He had never woken up next to a woman – or anyone else, for that matter – in his life. His first sensation was that it was a mistake for him to be there and that he must get out as quickly as possible; and then he realised that she was not yet awake, and so he leaned on one elbow and looked at her. Her pretty face had a slightly slack, worn look, but still she looked very charming, breathing gently, her blonde hair loose upon the pillow. Then he wondered how he must look, and rose in alarm and padded to the bathroom. He had left his robe in his own room, so he tied a bath towel hastily around his thick waist and gazed at himself in the mirror. Not a pretty sight, he thought to himself; his eyes were slightly red-rimmed, his face was pasty, and the bristles of his beard showed iron-grey. He pushed his hair off his face. Maybe Marion loved him enough not to care how he looked in the morning. When they were married she would see him thus every day. He looked with doubtful depression at his reflection, went back into the bedroom and stood looking down at Marion's sleeping form for a moment, and then, with something like relief, crept back to his own room to bathe, shave and dress.

When he met Marion at breakfast he could see that she was not, for some reason, in the best of tempers. Although she flung him the occasional sweet smile, she was off hand and irritable. He decided that he had better make himself scarce until lunchtime, although he had previously had an idyllic vision of Marion and himself strolling hand-in-hand through the autumn stillness of the woods around Roffey. It was what he imagined lovers did.

Marion gave him a brief, incredulous look when he said that he thought he might 'take in' the morning service at St Olaf's in the village, and then shrugged her shoulders. A little disconcerted, he hung around the conservatory for a few moments while Marion breakfasted, rubbed his hands, and then remarked brightly that he didn't know how Marion could endure the amount of entertaining that she seemed to do.

243

'One has to have people, you know,' she replied, looking up at him with a frown. Clattering and splashing came from the kitchen, where Leonie was beginning the task of scrubbing and peeling vegetables for lunch. 'Sometimes,' she added reflectively, buttering some toast, 'I feel that unless there are people around, I'm not really there. Don't you ever feel that?' She thought she had made rather a philosophical remark, really.

Montacute looked at her and smiled uncertainly, stiffly. 'I'll be off, then,' he said, and went. The man has no soul, thought Marion as she finished her toast; he is a hollow, dreary lawyer without any concept of how I really feel.

Montacute pondered her remark as he made his way to church. The truth of what Marion had said did not entirely escape him. Marion was a woman who fashioned herself for other people, lived for their approval and admiration. Looked at in the charitable light of love, she was someone who lived for the pleasure and happiness of others. Looked at in a less charitable light, she was someone who possessed no inner core, who came to life only when playing out the part in the little dramas she created out of daily life. Montacute wondered if he would ever be enough for her, if she would be content to play the role of a City solicitor's wife. It was not exactly an absorbing one he admitted to himself as he entered the comforting coolness of the church. The worry of this little doubt threatened to spoil his pleasure in the weekend, and he tried to dispel it by leaning his forehead against the ledge of the pew in front and offering up a small prayer that Marion might slow down a little.

Sunday luncheon was altogether a more casual and light-hearted affair than the previous evening, with more people, much more alcohol, and a lot of laughter and noise. For all that, Montacute did not enjoy himself any better. He felt out of place amid the frivolity and gossip of Marion's local acquaintance, and withdrew into a stiff reserve. Marion noted this, but would not help him out. He was a grown man, after all. If he did not like her friends, then he should go. It irritated her to think that Montacute in any way despised her friends, and in particular because he did not say so outright – he would never be so discourteous – but merely suggested it by his look, his manner. Alexander, she recalled, had felt the same, but at least he had made no secret of the fact and had taken himself off to London whenever she insisted on entertaining people he did not like.

Aware that he was not acquitting himself well with Marion's set, and unhappy at this, Montacute was almost relieved to see Hugh Howard's rubicund face amongst a roaring, laughing crowd drinking out in the conservatory. Howard noticed him, excused himself from the group, and came over. Man was a bore, but he looked a bit spare standing all alone with half a pint of bitter and that look on his face. Someone had to talk to him. What Marion saw in the chap, God alone knew.

'Good to see you again, Geoffrey,' said Hugh, pumping Montacute's hand, the atmosphere of their previous encounter entirely forgotten. 'Just saying to some of the fellows over there how excellent these buffet luncheons of Marion's always are. Very easy. Just help yourself, wander around. Bit like Sunday lunch at the pub, only the food's better!' He laughed, took a drink of his beer, dribbled some down his Lacoste sweater, wiped it off, and then said, 'Funnily enough, I was talking about you to a chap the other day. That Garter Cross thing. Doing very well. Told him I'd given you a bit of a tip in that direction. What did I tell you? Hasn't stopped rising. You do anything in that direction?'

Montacute looked uncomfortable. 'I – ah – have ventured something.'

'Very wise,' replied Hugh. 'He's a flier, that Melanakis chap. Great businessmen, those Greeks. Look, come and say hello to Sally – she'll be delighted to see you again, I know.' And so he shuffled Montacute off on to his wife and some others, and made his way back to the chaps, feeling he had performed a small social duty.

Montacute felt dispirited as he drove back to Richmond in the fast-gathering dusk. He had a headache and a touch of indigestion which had begun in church and had been troubling him ever since. He reached into the glove compartment for some Rennies. He had not enjoyed the day. He did not like being with all those chattering, silly people. He simply wanted to be with Marion, to be alone with her. But she had scarcely even left her friends to say goodbye to him. Did she love him? Of course she must. When they were together, just the two of them, she was utterly devoted, charming, attentive. Of course, it was natural that she could not pay much attention to him when she had so many guests to entertain. So many. He yawned at the thought of them, switched on the car radio, and the strains of the Northern Sinfonia reminded him that he had forgotten to mention the tickets that he had bought for them both for that concert at the Wigmore Hall in three weeks' time. He would ring her tomorrow. She would come up, he would stay with her at her hotel . . . It would all be wonderful again. At this, he suddenly wondered how his mother was. He felt uneasy all the way home and drove rather faster than usual. Reaching home, he put his key in the lock, opened the front door, and called out to her.

There was no reply. He could hear faint sounds, and when he went into the living room, it was with a fearful heart. But she was in her chair, dozing, rasping the air lightly with her snores, the wireless tuned into the same concert that he had been listening to in the car. He looked down at her heavy form, her face set in its accustomed frown, and felt a mixture of pity and guilt, and something like relief at finding her there in her usual chair. He would not wake her, he decided, until he had made them both a pot of tea, perhaps even a plate of sandwiches and some of the bourbon biscuits that she liked. He hung his dogtooth tweed jacket in the hall and went into the kitchen, feeling gradually more peaceful as the shades of his gloomy, familiar home closed around him.

While Montacute and his mother ate their sandwiches and drank their tea, Helena and Sissy sat close together on the floor of the living room of the flat in Caversham Place, Sissy's arm around Helena's shoulders. A bottle of wine and two glasses stood on the carpet before them, and the sound of Suzanne Vega, turned down low, scratched out from the CD player.

'How sure are you?' asked Sissy. Helena drew up her knees and bowed her head upon them, sighing.

'Very sure,' she replied. 'It's three weeks since my period was due and I've begun to feel really queasy, as though I'm going to be sick all the time.'

'Well, why don't you do a test?'

'I will. I'll get one.' She raised her head, then picked up her glass and drained it. 'It's just that – well, I had this idea that if I didn't get a test, and didn't find out for certain, then it could be as though it wasn't really happening.'

'Oh, you are daft,' murmured Sissy in a kindly way. 'I thought you were on the Pill?'

'I was,' said Helena, 'but I kept forgetting and, anyway, it didn't make me feel very good, so I stopped it.'

'Well, why didn't you tell Con to use something?'

Helena stared at Sissy and laughed. 'Can you imagine me telling Con Aaranson to use a condom? I mean, can you? No one tells him what to do.' She sounded only faintly bitter.

'Have you told him?'

'God, no.'

'Well, you've got to. It's his responsibility, too.'

'Oh, but Sissy, how can I? I mean, what's he going to say when I tell him?' There was a note of fear and panic in Helena's voice.

'*I* don't know. But you have to tell him.'

'Why? He's just going to be furious!' she wailed, and bowed her head on her knees again. She knew how he would react. She had seen how things were going the last few weeks. He hadn't been round; he was short with her when he spoke to her, and she felt a faintly jeering atmosphere if she spoke to him when his friends were around. And, heart-stoppingly, deadeningly, she had seen him going into the Chelsea Cannon with his arm slung round the shoulder of some other girl the previous night. She had run all the way home and had lain weeping on the sofa, feeling as though her heart was shrivelling. She was being – had been – discarded.

'Well, anyway,' said Sissy after a long silence, 'whatever he's going to say, you still must tell him.'

Although Helena spent two days thinking of reasons why not to tell him, she realised, after the test bought from the chemist's proved positive, that she had to. Maybe, she told herself, with the last reserves of hope and fantasy, he won't be angry. Maybe he'll help me. Maybe he'll want it. With a quaking heart she accosted Con in the corridor at art school the next day.

'What?' he said shortly, looking at her without interest as she caught his sleeve. He paused. 'Look, haven't you got the message by now? I'm not interested any more.'

'Please, Con,' said Helena, tears pricking at her eyelids. 'I just have to talk to you. I have to tell you something.'

'Well, if it's "I love you" again, don't bother.' Helena felt as though she had been struck a sharp, shaming blow. She stared at him. 'Look,' he went on, 'I don't know if I need to hear whatever it is. We had a thing, now it's stopped. OK?'

'I'm pregnant,' she said quickly, as he turned to go.

He sighed and stopped. 'You're pregnant,' he repeated, looking her up and down. 'Congratulations.'

'But it's yours, Con – it's your baby!' She tried to keep her voice low, but it trembled with urgency.

'Well,' he replied, looking directly at her with his dark, lazy eyes, 'even if it is, I don't see what you expect me to do about it.'

'Even if it is! What's that supposed to mean? Even if it is! Of course it is!' As he shrugged away from her, she held on to his sleeve. 'Oh, please, Con! You could at least help me!' She felt both humiliated and desperate, already knowing the pointlessness of all this. 'I mean, what am I supposed to do?'

'Whatever it is you have to, I suppose,' he replied. 'You can afford it.' And he walked away, a small, assured, arrogant figure. She stared after him, and wondered how she could ever have thought him such a divine spirit, such a wonderful creature. He was simply an inadequate, cruel little monster. And yet if he had turned and beckoned her to him, she would willingly have gone.

Chapter twenty-one

Richard sat opposite Helena in the middle of a very packed and noisy Italian restaurant at the top of Kingsway. Very cheap, very cheerful. He looked at Helena's tired, drawn face as she hunched over her cappuccino, into which she was dipping the remains of a breadstick, and wished she had never told him. Thinking this, he sighed and said, 'Why have you told me this?'

She shrugged. 'I don't know. Because of what you said. Because you're a friend.' She seemed cool, not overtly miserable; her voice, her attitude, all had a flattened, resigned quality. 'Not to involve you – don't worry about that,' she added quickly, looking up from her coffee.

He passed a hand over his face. 'Of course I'm involved.'

'No – no, you're not. I know what I'm going to do. I've got it all worked out. I've been to the PAS, I've had all the counselling rubbish. I've just got to go back and see two more doctors there.' She shrugged. 'It's purely a formality, that. They all seem so bored. Makes you feel bored yourself. Then off I go, get rid of it.'

'That's a very cold thing to say, Helena. I mean, you are pregnant.' Richard felt indignant that she should pretend to be so amoral, so detached; it was a pose she had begun at art school and one he disliked.

'You don't have to remind me!' She glowered for a moment. 'I'm sorry if I sound brutal about it, but that's the way it is. Con doesn't want to know, I certainly don't want to have a baby right now, so I don't see that it helps to get all emotional and overwrought about it. There's nothing else to be done.'

'That may be so,' replied Richard, leaning back in his chair, 'but you don't have to speak about it as though you're going to have a wart removed.'

Having kept up the front for as long as possible over lunch, Helena gave way a little and tears rushed to her eyes. 'Oh, for God's sake!' she sobbed, as he grabbed a paper napkin from an empty neighbouring table and gave it to her. 'Don't you see that I *have* to talk about it that way if I'm not going to go out of my head? Do you think I like myself for all this? I loathe myself! I wish I'd never been born! But I can't deal with it in any other way. I have to pretend that it's nothing, that nothing exists. And then when it doesn't, it'll be . . . all right.' She snuffled a bit into the napkin.

'I wish you'd found someone else to tell,' he said. He felt –he knew that if he went on from here, helped her, supported her, then there would never again be the possibility of anything more than friendship between them. If that. He supposed, looking at her tear-stained face, that she was too young to understand that. Just wipe it all out, start all over again, and everything would be – all right, as she put it. She knew nothing about the deep, indelible little marks that would be left, about how some shared things divide human beings from each other forever.

'I – I couldn't think of another friend to turn to. I couldn't tell Mummy – she'd hit the roof. And then she'd just tell me to do exactly what I'm going to do, anyway, only she'd be there all the time making it ghastly and much worse and wholly memorable.' He smiled in spite of himself. 'I don't want to remember,' she went on. 'I just want to get it over with. I need someone – someone who is a friend, but—' She stopped. 'I mean, I've told Sissy, and she's great, but – well, she doesn't think I should have an abortion. She's Catholic and very scared of all that stuff . . .'

And what about me? thought Richard. What about what I think? He gazed at her. But she didn't care what he thought – no, not that, only that she trusted his love so absolutely that she knew that he would not let whatever he felt get in the way of helping her, would not let her down. She expected so much from him. She had learned to.

'Of course I'm your friend, and of course I'll help you if I can. But what do you want from me? Do you need money?'

'Oh, no. No.' She sniffed and smiled faintly. 'You know

that. A hundred and forty pounds is nothing.' She shook her head, then balled up the tattered remnants of napkin and raised her face to stare at the ceiling, sniffing back the last of her tears. 'I think I just want someone – you – to be with me. To look after me.' Her brown eyes looked huge, wet. 'Please.'

He put his hand over hers. 'Poor Helena,' he said. 'Just tell me where and when and all that stuff.' This is a death sentence for us, he thought.

'Thank you,' she said. And then there was silence for a while.

One week later, Richard was sitting in Helena's car somewhere in Twickenham, watching the October rain course down the windscreen, listening to LBC Radio and waiting for eight o'clock to arrive. He had expected the traffic to be much worse than it had been and had arrived at the nursing home early. He looked again at the information folder which Helena had given to him the day before. It was calm and bright and clinical, as though these things were a matter of course, something for which helpful leaflets were produced much as if for a savings bank.

Such things *were* now a matter of course, he mused, turning it over and avoiding the bit about vacuum aspiration, perusing the different maps for getting there, depending on who you were and where you were coming from and how much money you might (or might not) have. Helena had insisted on going by bus to the nursing home that morning on her own. 'How can you come and pick me up in the evening if I take the car?' she had pointed out. 'Anyway, the idea of just pulling up there in one's car, parking, and hopping out as if one were going shopping seems a bit – easy. Cheerful.'

So the bus ride was your penance, thought Richard, turning on the windscreen wipers briefly so that he could see up the avenue, watching the few figures scurrying back and forth under umbrellas. He gazed at the nursing home, glanced at another car parked on the other side of the street, in which a man was sitting reading a newspaper. He wondered if the man was waiting for the same reason he was. Then he wondered if the man had seen him sitting here in the Golf GTi and thought

251

the same thing about him. Well, if he had, he was wrong. But then, maybe he was wrong about the man.

He sighed, listening to the traffic reports, got fed up with some political commentator droning on and on, and switched the radio off. Ten minutes to go.

What if this baby had been his? How would he feel? He thought he knew how he would feel. The idea was so close to home that he could, without any effort, imagine the hollowness, the horrible pain, the sense of impotence and loss. Would she have done the same thing if it had been he who was the father, and not this creep called Conrad? Probably, seeing how ruthlessly, how single-mindedly she had behaved about this. A few tears in the restaurant, but apart from that, so far as he could see, all business. Then again, how far could he see . . . ? But if it had been his baby, if it had been someone who loved her as much as he did, then it might have been very different, she might not be doing this. Why, he wondered, rubbing his hands over his face, might it make a difference depending on who the father was? Why should women care about that? Why should they be allowed to be so illogical? It wasn't the baby's fault. The foetus was still the same, another being, one whose fate was directed by the emotional whims of the mother. Only it wasn't a baby by this time, he thought, glancing at his watch. It had for some hours now been just a disposable piece of rubbish.

He got out of the car, relieved to have something to do instead of sitting thinking morbid thoughts. As he turned his collar up against the rain he saw the man in the car opposite getting out, locking his door. The man glanced at him. Co-conspirators, thought Richard. Only there was, technically, no crime.

'You've left your lights on,' he called to the man, who hesitated, raised a hand, and said, 'Thanks,' and then went back to switch them off.

Richard trotted across the road through the rain towards the nursing home; the other man was walking quite close behind him on the pavement. Funny, thought Richard, that in any other circumstances, like if we'd both realised we were heading for the same party or something, we'd be chatting a bit. Matey. Blokes with a shared purpose. But this was different. Just being there, with other men in the same boat knowing what you were there for, was somehow an admission of guilt, of failure, of an inability to let life take its course. It was like admitting you were afraid. Just as afraid as the women, who wanted to keep their lives intact, didn't want to let a baby change the status quo. But, of course, the status quo would be changed forever, anyway.

Wishing that he had a sign he could hang round his neck saying, '*I am not the father. Don't judge me. I am not guilty*', he made his way to the reception desk, and a nurse told him to take a seat.

He sat there for another ten minutes or so, leafing through a copy of *Hello!* until Helena appeared. She looked extremely normal, a little pale, and she smiled when she saw him. They walked to the car in silence.

'You all right?' he asked as he opened the car door for her.

'Yes.' She nodded and smiled, the same thin, watery smile. 'I'm fine. I just want to get home.'

He was struck by the pattern of her behaviour during the journey home. At first, as they made their way through Richmond, she did not speak, but sat as though quietly relieved. Then, as they crawled through a traffic jam on Putney High Street, which was bright with lights and reflected rain, she began to talk in animated detail about the nursing home, about how the nurse had missed her vein when she took a blood sample, about how she hadn't known who to put for 'next of kin' and so had put his name, about the other women and how they had all chatted together as though it were some sort of club. She talked about being woken up from the anaesthetic by some big black nurse shouting in her ear – 'Why do they do that, I wonder?' she asked, without waiting for his reply – and about how she had got on really well with some girl who hadn't known she was pregnant until her boyfriend, who was a doctor, said he thought she was, and how they hadn't given you any decent food afterwards, just a cup of tea and some disgusting cheese sandwiches. She chattered on and on until they were halfway up the Fulham Road, then she fell silent for a moment or two and burst into tears.

Richard stopped the car, comforted her, stroked her hair, and wanted to turn the clock back two months and never let any of this be. When she stopped crying, she said, 'I don't want to go home. I can't bear to. Can we go for a pizza?'

And so they went for a pizza, and split a bottle of wine, which Richard suspected wasn't a good idea after the anaesthetic. But it seemed to do Helena good rather than otherwise, and by the end of the meal she was a good deal more composed and happy than she had been.

'You're very tired,' said Richard, watching her face, her lovely, weary face, as she nibbled at the remains of his pizza crust. He never ate his pizza crust; she always finished it for him.

'I'm not,' she assured him. 'I know I should be, but I'm not. I'd really like to go somewhere, do something . . .'

Anything not to have to lie on her bed and think. Anything not to have to have to look at the depressing mess in the flat, and to meet Sissy's nervous, reproachful eyes. If she could just make herself so tired that she would be able to fall asleep without thinking once of today, she would be fine.

Richard divined something of this as he looked at her anxious eyes, then at her restless hands plucking at the torn edge of the label on the wine bottle.

'Why don't you come back to my place and we can watch a video? Peter's on a rugby weekend, so you can have his bed.'

She nodded, grateful for the company and refuge from her thoughts.

So they went back to Richard's untidy, comfy flat and lay on the sofa together, watching *Jagged Edge*. Long before Jeff Bridges had shown his true colours, Helena was fast asleep, her head in Richard's lap. He sat there until the end of the film, stroking her soft hair, remembering other times not long ago when she had lain thus, and when it had all been very different, and she had not been like some errant younger sister. He glanced down at her face and realised, sadly, that he was still as much in love with her as he had been when she walked into the office on that summer's day. He put a hand beneath her shoulder to lever her up and gently shook her awake.

'Come on,' he said, 'you can't sleep here.' She sat up groggily and he went into Peter's room and switched the light on. The bed was made, at any rate, and only a few items of clothing were strewn around the floor. Helena staggered in behind him, yawning.

'Thanks for looking after me today,' she murmured, and put her arms around his neck. He laid his cheek against hers; it was amazing, he thought, how she expected his responses to be attuned exactly to meet her own feelings. Every platonic, sisterly gesture that she made – no matter how affectionate, how physical – he must accept in an equally platonic fashion.

'Sleep well,' he said, and left her, closing the door behind him.

It was half-past two when he was woken by the sound of Helena moving about in the flat. He got up, slipped on a T-shirt and some pyjama bottoms, and went through to the kitchen. Helena was standing by the cooker, watching over a pan of milk which she was warming.

'Hello,' she murmured, turning to glance at him.

'Can't you sleep?' he asked.

She shook her head. 'My stomach hurts a bit. I thought I'd make myself some hot milk. Have you got any paracetamol, or something?'

Richard went into the bathroom, rummaging fruitlessly in the cupboard, and came back. 'Sorry, no.'

She shrugged and came over to the table with her mug of milk, and he drew up a chair and sat down opposite her, watching her face as she tucked back her hair and sipped at her milk.

'It seems so strange,' he said with suddenness, 'to be with you, and for everything to be so different from the way it was before. We've never even talked about it. I don't understand what happened to us.'

'Oh, Richard, don't. I just want to drink my milk and try to get some sleep.'

He stared at the table, at a small transparent yellow stain on the pine surface left by Pete's last chicken madras takeaway. 'No, it's all right for you,' he replied. 'You seem to know what happened. You seem to think that as long as everything is the way you want it, then no one else's feelings matter. Well, that's not the way things go, in case you didn't realise. You don't just discard people and then – and then pick them up again, asking whatever you want of them.'

She looked at him bleakly. 'I don't know what happened. If I did, I'd tell you. Lord,' she muttered, 'why do people always want to have intense conversations in the small hours of the morning?'

'Perhaps it's because they hope the truth might be more likely to come out.'

'What – after dark?'

There was a silence.

'I thought you loved me,' Richard said at last. He had not wished to say this, to expose himself to the threat of humiliation and further pain, but the need to know was too great.

'I did. I think,' murmured Helena, bowing her head slightly. 'It's just . . . Oh, I don't know . . . I feel everything has changed so much since Easter, or whenever.'

'You've changed, you mean.'

'Yes, well, maybe I have changed. I can't help that. It certainly hasn't made me any happier, if you want to know.' She drank some more of her milk. 'But I don't think we're the same kind of people, Richard. Come to that, I wasn't really *any* kind of person when I first met you. I was just a schoolgirl.'

'And now?'

'Oh, I don't know!' she replied crossly. 'I'm not pretending I'm so terribly grown up now, or anything. But – let's face it – it wasn't what I wanted. I mean, you get up, you go to work, you come home, you go out to the pub with your mates, you play rugby at the weekends or go to rugby matches, and afterwards you have a few beers with your friends and their girlfriends.' She paused. 'I can't fit into that kind of life. I mean, there's more to relationships than just the individuals involved, isn't there? There's a whole load of things . . . I can't really explain it.'

'No, no,' said Richard, 'I understand what you're saying. But when it comes down to it, it's me you're talking about. My way of life.'

256

She sighed. 'I suppose so. Maybe it's going to art school, meeting different people. It's exciting! You see all kinds of new possibilities, not just doing the same safe things week after week, year after year, just *being* a solicitor, going to work in the morning, coming back in the evening . . .'

'I suppose Conrad – or whatever his name is – is never going to be so dull and predictable, is he?'

'Oh, don't bring him into it.' She paused. 'But, yes – maybe that's right.' She looked away across the room, her gaze nowhere.

'You're still in love with him, aren't you?' he asked quietly. Another question he did not want to ask, but had to.

She looked faintly ashamed, said nothing, and he knew it was true. How could she? How could she still feel anything for someone who had treated her as he had done?

'Look,' he said, trying to sound as kind and rational as he could, 'I'm not saying this for me, but don't – don't become the kind of girl who falls for complete bastards. I've seen it happen. It's like a drug habit with some people. It's unhealthy.'

She laughed and looked down into her milk, her hair falling forwards. 'Thank you, Richard.'

He felt a sensation as though his heart was sliding away from him. He was landlocked, cut off from her and from love by being the person he was. He could not change for her. Why did nature work this way? Why did it make you fall in love with someone without any regard for whether they were the right person for you or not? Why couldn't it match everyone up better? He sat opposite her, watching her, and knew that there was no way back.

Two weeks later, Oliver was sitting cosily in the dining room of his flat with Teddy and Charlie Vereker, at the end of an excellent dinner of Oliver's own preparing. He blinked at his glass of wine, enjoying the argument he was having with Charlie.

'No, no, no,' said Charlie vehemently, 'how can you say that? Cubism eclipsed the Fauvists, and Matisse lost his predominance entirely.'

'Merely because he became a more reclusive figure,' replied Oliver, sitting back in his chair and pushing his glasses back up on his nose, 'does not mean to say that his work was in any sense diminished. If anything, I would say that the excessive self-promotion of someone like Picasso—'

'Picasso was admittedly an exhibitionist,' interrupted Charlie, splashing more wine into Oliver's and Teddy's glasses, 'but at least he still tried to engage himself with real themes, with Surrealism, Guernica . . . "He best can paint who shall feel them most", you know.'

'I take your point,' said Oliver. 'I simply meant that the restrictions of privacy don't mean that one's art necessarily ceases to enlarge itself.' Oliver, who had drunk a good deal, suspected himself of wandering, and stopped.

Seeing that the life of the argument was spent, Teddy leaned forward and remarked that he would be able to see the Picasso retrospective at the Museum of Modern Art as soon as he got back to New York.

'Yes,' murmured Charlie, scratching his chin with long bony fingers. 'I should like to see that. When do you leave us, dear boy?'

'A week Wednesday,' said Teddy, smiling at the thought. Oliver got up and went through to the kitchen, murmuring that he would make coffee. Even though he had thrown this little dinner party as a farewell to Teddy, and had taken particularly careful pride in his preparation of the chicken stuffed with mango and ginger and the damson sorbet, he did not wish to discuss the painful fact of Teddy's departure. It left him feeling – ransacked, he told himself, spooning coffee into the cafetière. That was the word. Teddy was making off to America with his spoils – his contacts, the money he had made through Oliver, and Oliver's heart. Perhaps he was over-dramatising things, he told himself. That one night with Teddy – well, even if it had been a mistake, as Teddy said, it was too little to build so much upon. But he always did that, he knew. He could give his heart on the strength of a single glance, plant his faith in one kind smile. I am so wretched and so weak, he thought, carrying the coffee pot through to the dining room, preparing a smile for his two friends.

'I'm only sorry that Drew and Errol couldn't come this evening,' said Oliver, going to the cupboard for coffee cups.

'Well, I'm not,' replied Teddy dryly. 'Those guys just bitch all the time. I couldn't stand to live like that!'

'Drew is a darling,' murmured Charlie, unknotting his cravat, a sign that he was preparing for brandy and gossip, 'but I rather think that Errol is having some sort of mid-life crisis.'

The three of them drank their coffee and dissected the relationship between Drew and Errol with care. In the pause that followed Charlie said musingly, 'How is that young friend of yours, Oliver? The sweet boy who helped at the gallery. Paul.'

'I don't know really,' replied Oliver, shifting his bottom in his chair under a small weight of guilt. 'I should have been down to see him this term, but this Claude Rogers thing has kept one rather busy . . . You get letters from him from time to time, don't you, Teddy?'

'Yeah. Yeah, I do,' said Teddy. 'If you want to know what I think, I think someone like Paul shouldn't be at that school – whatever it's called. I think he finds it kinda stifling. I mean, he tells it in his letters in a light sort of way, trying to make it sound amusing and all, but I don't think he's happy.'

'No,' said Oliver thoughtfully, tucking his several chins in. 'I'm afraid you may be right.'

'Ghastly things, public schools,' said Charlie, waving the idea away with his hand.

'I blame that bloody man Montacute,' said Oliver, pouring out glasses of brandy.

'Who's he?' asked Teddy.

'One of my co-trustees,' said Oliver with faint bitterness. 'We manage the trust fund that Paul's father left when he died. It was Montacute who talked Paul's mother into sending him to Ampersand.'

'Mmm. Alexander Laing's trust fund. What a wealthy young man Paul is going to be,' murmured Charlie.

'Really?' Teddy glanced at them both with interest.

'Yes. Quite a tidy fortune,' replied Oliver.

'When does Paul get it – the money, I mean?' asked Teddy,

sipping his brandy and then swirling it thoughtfully in its glass, holding it towards the light of the candles on the table; Oliver noticed that Teddy's eyes caught the light with the same golden warmth.

'When he's eighteen,' said Oliver. 'Which isn't all that long away, as I recall. June next year, I think. That is to say, he gets the income then, and that's quite a considerable amount for an eighteen-year-old.'

'Lucky guy,' said Teddy.

'Perhaps, perhaps not,' said Charlie thoughtfully. 'A little wealth can be dangerous to the young – positively inimical to hard work, you know. How is it? – "His best companions, innocence and health—"'

'—"And his best riches, ignorance of wealth",' finished Oliver.

Teddy glanced from Charlie to Oliver, and laughed. 'You guys! If I had money, I'd want to know all about it! Yeah, I wouldn't mind being Paul,' he added wistfully. 'I wish someone would start handing out a fortune to me tomorrow, that's all.'

When Paul came into the room he saw Beasley, Horsman and Horsman's friend Jacklin at the window. Beasley was craning out into the cold, dark night, peering down at the flagstones.

'It's just some old clothes,' said Horsman, pulling himself off the sill and leaving the window. Paul went over to join the others, curious to see what they were talking about.

'Who's going to be chucking clothes out at this time of night?' said Jacklin.

Paul leaned out of the window next to Beasley. 'What is it?' he asked. Looking down, he could see a dark, crumpled heap on the flagstones, although it was difficult to make out because of the shifting shadows from some nearby trees. Beasley ignored Paul, replying to Jacklin, 'Probably the first-formers ragging about. Their dorm's above us. I remember chucking all Renfrew's stuff out of the window the first term he was here.'

Beasley came away from the window. Paul stayed there, looking down, a sickly feeling in his stomach.

'It's not clothes,' he said. 'It's a boy.'

'What!' exclaimed Beasley, and came back to the window. 'Jesus!' He stared down, and his face paled. 'Christ, you're right. Oh, Christ! Let's get someone.' And Beasley and the others raced off to the safety and comfort of someone in authority, while Paul looked down, the chilly wind lifting his hair, staring at what he knew to be Cowan's fat little form, lying dead upon the flagstones.

Long after the ambulance and the police car had left, and the whispering, horror-stricken waves that had eddied round the excited school had died away, there was still a potent sense of drama within the walls of Ampersand. Rumour and conjecture crept round the dark dormitories, from bed to bed. No one fell asleep with any ease. In his bed Paul lay wide awake, his mind going over and over that pitiful conversation he had had only weeks ago with Cowan – Cowan who was no more, who would never again have to suffer and snivel and slink his way through his wretched little life again – and his subsequent conversation with Cowan's form master. There was more I could have done, he thought. I gave up. I didn't care enough. Nobody did. He turned over and pressed his face into the pillow.

He heard Beasley stir uneasily in his sleep, and Horsman give a light, shuddering snore. Paul lifted his head, gazed at the curtained window, then rose. He put on his dressing-gown and slippers and crept downstairs, past the silent library and common room, where the moonlight fell in silver squares through the windows, and to the kitchens. They were dark and hushed, the moonlight picking out the gleaming curves of metal pans and basins. A bowl full of hard-boiled eggs left over from tea stood by one of the sinks, and Paul picked one up, rubbing his thumb over its smooth, cold shell as he lifted a large key from the row of hooks next to the range, and slid it into the keyhole. It turned with a dull scraping sound, and he held his breath for a moment. Then he opened the door and stepped out into the cold darkness, closing it gently behind him. He drew in deep lungfuls of night air as he made his way past the boiler house and down across the grass towards the line of trees that stood near the cricket nets.

His slippers were soaking by the time he reached the trees. He leaned against one and began to chip flakes of shell from the egg with his thumbnail, shivering, his breath pluming the air. He stared out across the dark, silent playing fields and remembered how he had stood there last term, under the same tree, in the warm shadow of its summer leaves, and watched Oakshott bowling, ball after ball. He remembered, too, how this line of trees had looked, etched against the soft summer sky in the evening, from Oakshott's study window. And he closed his eyes and wept.

He thought of Oakshott and of Cowan, he looked into the future at the days that must follow and knew he could not face them. Too much that was irretrievable was being lost. Did I become like this, or was I always like this? he wondered, brushing the last of his tears away with the back of his hand. Not that it mattered now. He must start here, he must face the fact that he could either be the person he had been in London, happy and free and in his element, or he could continue to let this place and the people in it bear further and further down upon him, crushing him, rubbing all the lustre from his spirit.

He glanced down at the egg in his palm as he picked away at the shell, peeling back the soft membrane until it lay naked, soft and moistly white in his hand. He felt as though he, too, after this night, had lost his shell, as though the little pieces of his boyhood had all been chipped away over the past year, leaving him vulnerable and new. They cannot touch me now, he thought. I won't let them. I will not deny myself. And with that he lifted his pyjama-clad arm and flung the egg as far as he could, watching the small white oval rise against the night sky before it fell noiselessly out of sight into the cold grass.

Chapter twenty-two

It was with disappointment, and not apprehension, that Montacute noted from the *Financial Times* that Garter Cross had slipped a couple of points. Nonetheless, the shares had been doing remarkably well over the past few weeks, and he seemed well on the way to realising the significant profit which he had anticipated. He folded up the paper and tapped his lip. It crossed his mind that he might sell today, but he knew that the company was on the brink of acquiring an important contract that could only improve the share price. He would wait a couple of days, he thought – maybe he should have a word with James and see what he thought. Before picking up the phone, Montacute jotted down some calculations on his blotter. If the price improved as a result of the contract – which, of course, it must do – then the investment could realise a profit of one million four thousand, roughly. He smiled to himself, then sat back in his chair and drew in a deep breath. Taking risks such as these was not in his character, but Marion's delight would be the most gratifying part of the whole business.

As was his happy habit these days, Montacute's normally businesslike mind slipped off into the pleasurable realms of speculation that had nothing to do with finance. In a few days, he thought, she could have her financial independence, meet him on equal terms, as she saw it. Marry him. He had taken a gamble for her, for her love, and it was going to pay off. He almost laughed aloud as he thought of the cold, cautious creature which he fancied himself to have been before he met Marion. Love had changed him. Love had made him reckless, daring.

From thoughts of marriage, his mind slipped inevitably to thoughts of his mother, and how to deal with her. He had given a good deal of consideration to this over the past weeks, and although he had not yet discussed the matter with her (an almost superstitious reluctance prevented him from broaching the subject of his marriage just yet), he felt the problem to be solved already. There could, he knew, be no question of his mother living with himself and Marion. She would have to go into a home. He had relieved his guilt at the starkness of this notion by obtaining particulars from several private residential homes near – but not too near – to Roffey, and had quite convinced himself that the comforts of these places were such that his mother could only be happier and more comfortable than if she remained at Innisfree. Besides, he felt it had grown apparent to both of them since her stroke that she was no longer capable of managing by herself, even with the help of Mrs Carmichael and the attendance of various offshoots of the social services that had manifested themselves since her illness.

No, he was convinced that any opposition on her part would soon disappear when she saw how bright and comfortable and sociable such places could be. Expensive, too, he had to admit –alarmingly expensive – but money would be no object where his mother's welfare was concerned. Anyway, the proceeds of the sale of Innisfree would cover much of the expense. And then he would be free, at last, to live his own life.

His thoughts returned to the Garter Cross shares, but as he was about to pick up the telephone and call James Ackland, it rang. Miss Reed announced, in tones indicating that such calls had become a regular feature of daily life, that Sir Reynold Cazalet was on the line. Montacute was swept with irritation. *In re Cazalet's Will's Trusts* had been one of Montacute's weightiest, dreariest cases over the past five years. The late Sir Frederic Cazalet had seen fit to dispose of a considerable fortune by will, consisting of land both in England and Scotland, investments, houses, pictures and antiques, in a manner that precluded any certainty as to the identity of his intended beneficiaries and which had resulted in protracted litigation involving the entire Cazalet family.

Sir Reynold Cazalet was the late Sir Frederic's eldest son by his first marriage and was as importunate and demanding as only a man obsessed with litigation and with family wrongs can be. A further important hearing in the case was due to commence in Chancery the day after next, and for the past month or two Montacute had been inundated with calls and visits from Sir Reynold. The man's mind seemed to be so deeply immersed in the minute particulars of the case that Montacute had begun to think that he was becoming slightly unhinged. He troubled Montacute constantly with new thoughts on the matter, with irrelevant suggestions as to this or that document, hints as to the base and intriguing motives of parties not remotely involved in the case, or not born at the time of the late Sir Frederic's testamentary dispositions, and generally pestered Montacute with all the tenacity of the most troublesome of clients.

Today a new threat to the success of their case had occurred to Sir Reynold in the shape of the Inland Revenue. He held forth on their base designs to Montacute for a full half hour, while Montacute tried vainly to reassure him. Montacute's insistence on the present neutrality of Her Majesty's Inspectors of Taxes in the matter did not satisfy Sir Reynold. He had long suspected that Montacute, whose bland affability and unruffled temperament he disliked, was in some sort of collusion with his younger half-brother's solicitor (he had seen them talking together after the last hearing eighteen months ago), and now he found the man taking the part of the Inland Revenue.

'Montacute,' he announced, 'I begin to suspect that you are losing your grip on this case. I think you are deliberately trying to ignore the points I am making. I have my doubts as to whether you and this – this – who is this new counsel we have on Thursday? Why do we keep chopping and changing?'

'Crispin Potts,' said Montacute patiently. 'He is very senior and a most capable man.'

'I don't like the fella. Why can't we have the chap we had before? He knew his stuff! He knew all about the case!'

'Terence Brook is now a High Court judge, Sir Reynold. I have explained all this to you.'

'Well, I am not happy, Montacute. Not happy at all. If I felt that you were not attending properly to my interests, and indeed to those of my children, then I might seriously have to consider taking advice elsewhere.'

This was a threat which Montacute had heard from Sir Reynold before, but it was always one of which he had to take note, for the affairs of Sir Reynold formed a useful part of the business of De Vaut, Montacute & Strange.

'I can assure you, Sir Reynold, of my most conscientious personal attendance to your affairs at all times,' sighed Montacute. 'I was merely trying to reassure you that the Inland Revenue has no *locus standi*—'

'In that case, I shall look forward to seeing you personally at the hearing on Thursday. It is vital that we follow every aspect of the case in the most scrupulous detail . . .' Montacute sat nodding through all this, annoyed at the thought of having to put in more than a token appearance at the hearing. Did Sir Reynold think he was the only client the firm had? 'And, Montacute,' added Sir Reynold, 'I have made a few pages of notes concerning the points I have put to you this morning. Since you hardly seem to be aware of their significance, I shall call this afternoon on my way to my club and give the notes to you personally, so that you may study them fully before Thursday. They may make all the difference. We must not be taken unawares.'

When Montacute finally managed to get Sir Reynold off the phone, his former good temper had almost entirely evaporated. He had also quite forgotten his intention of ringing James Ackland.

It was not until late in the afternoon that he thought again of the shares. He had concluded another tedious interview with Sir Reynold, this time in person, and had only just managed to dissuade him of the necessity of going through Sir Reynold's handwritten notes there and then, assuring him that he would do so that very evening. When his client had gone, he picked up the telephone and asked Miss Reed to get him Appin & Ackland.

'Oh, Mr Montacute, I was just about to ring through to say that I have Mrs Laing on the line.'

Thoughts of James Ackland fled. He smiled. 'Please put Mrs Laing through,' he said to Miss Reed. He was delighted that

266

Marion had called him. He felt that he had hardly seen enough of her in the past weeks, and no doubt she felt this, too. She had been unable to come with him to the concert at the Wigmore Hall – he had given the tickets to Miss Reed and her sister – and he had only seen her once, briefly, for a drink in town since that weekend at Roffey. His nights had been filled by the most startlingly voluptuous longings. Now they could arrange to meet properly.

But Marion was in no mood to arrange intimate trysts. 'Geoffrey,' she snapped, 'I have rung because I am at my wits' end! Paul has run away from school. The headmaster rang me ten minutes ago. Apparently he has been missing since this morning, but for some reason they have only seen fit to tell me now.' She sounded extremely annoyed, rather than in any way worried. 'I simply don't know *what* to do!'

Montacute hesitated, startled. 'Paul? He has run away? From Ampersand?'

'Yes!' exclaimed Marion, who found Montacute's lugubrious tones particularly irritating at a time like this. 'Yes, he has run away,' she repeated.

For a moment Montacute wondered what on earth he was expected to do about this, but he did not say so. Instead, he asked, 'Why?'

'Oh, for heaven's sake, Geoffrey!' snapped Marion. 'Do you suppose I know? The point is, what am I to do?'

'Well, does anyone know where he has gone? Do you know where he might have gone?'

'No, of course no one knows! And neither do I! Do you think that if I knew where he was I would bother ringing you? Honestly, for a supposedly intelligent man, you are sounding positively dim-witted!'

Montacute was faintly offended by this, but thought it best not to rouse Marion's ire any further by taking issue. He paused, considering what best to do.

'You are naturally dreadfully upset, my dear,' he began; she gave a snort at the other end of the phone. He went on hastily, 'But I doubt if there is much that can be done today, late as it is. No doubt the school and the local police are doing everything they can. I suggest that we both go down to Ampersand tomorrow morning, see Dr Whatley and find out exactly what has happened. After all,' he added with gravitas, 'the school is *in loco parentis*, and largely responsible for this kind of thing.'

Marion pondered for a moment. 'Yes,' she said. 'Yes, very well. Perhaps some of his friends at school have some idea where he might have gone. God, the trouble that child is to me!'

This arrangement concluded, Montacute then hopefully offered to go down to Roffey that evening to keep her company, since she must be quite distraught, but Marion declined this offer rather tetchily and said she would see him in the morning.

As Marion and Montacute talked, James Ackland sat in his spacious, handsome office in St Katharine's Dock, talking to one of his firm's senior and most trusted advisers, Tom Abbott. Tom sat with his backside resting against the edge of Ackland's mahogany drinks cabinet, one thumb sliding up and down his braces strap.

'. . . the word is – mind you, it's only a word – that the Serious Fraud boys have already been to their offices,' said Tom. He eased himself off the cabinet and paced up and down in front of Ackland's desk. 'Some time early this morning.'

'Heyworth is a connected company.' Ackland rubbed his jaw with his forefinger and thumb and leaned back in his chair.

'As you say, a connected company. I can't be the first to have got wind of it.'

Ackland leaned forward in his chair and glanced at the screen on his desk. He frowned. 'Well, we'll have to see how prices go. Could just be one of those scares.'

'Even if it is . . .' murmured Tom Abbott.

'Quite. Even if it is.' Ackland paused. 'I know someone who's in rather deep with Garter Cross . . .' He mused for a moment, then looked up at Tom. 'Interesting, anyway.'

'Interesting,' agreed Tom, and he smiled and sauntered out.

When James Ackland rang Montacute, Miss Reed told him that he was engaged. Ackland wondered for a moment whether to ask her to interrupt him, then thought better of it.

'Tell him I rang, would you? James Ackland,' was all he said. When Miss Reed saw from the intercom that Mr Montacute had finished talking to Mrs Laing, she buzzed through. But his line was already busy; he had rung Ampersand to speak to Dr Whatley. By now it was five-thirty, and so the ever-punctual Miss Reed tidied up her things, put her coat on, and left. She would give Mr Montacute the message in the morning.

By the time Montacute had rung Dr Whatley and then sat digesting the import of this fresh trouble for a while, it was almost six. He suddenly recollected his earlier intention of ringing Appin & Ackland and did so, but the only answer he got was a courteous, pre-recorded message telling him that the offices of Appin & Ackland were closed and would he ring again in the morning after nine o'clock. There was nothing more to be done that day – such a day as it had been – and so he put on his overcoat and scarf and made his way home to Richmond. At least he would see Marion tomorrow; there was always that pleasure to look forward to.

The journey from Roffey to Ampersand with Marion the next day was not as pleasant as he had anticipated. She met the attempts at light conversation, with which he sought to improve her temper, with icy dismissiveness. He was even faintly reminded of his mother's tone, a little hint of impatient contempt. He grew depressed. They then had a brief argument over the map, which Marion failed to read properly, and this was followed by a prolonged and disagreeable grumble from Marion about the unsuitability of Ampersand – how she had always known it was not right for Paul.

'I should never have allowed you to talk me into it,' she said at one point, lighting yet another in a long chain of cigarettes. Montacute could not let this pass unchallenged.

'That is hardly fair, Marion. I do not think I can be held accountable for the negligence of the school in failing to prevent this kind of thing. They are *in loco parentis*, after all.'

'Oh, stop saying that, will you? All I know is, you were the one who recommended this school. Now look what's happened.' She spilled ash on to her skirt and rubbed at it furiously. He took this opportunity to reach out and squeeze her hand; it grieved him to hear her speaking in this tone to him. It was – dare he think it? – almost shrewish. But, of course, she was overwrought, she was desperately worried about Paul. It was with this in mind that he made his sympathetic gesture. Irritated beyond measure by the damp clutch of his hand, Marion almost pulled away. But she recalled to herself how things presently stood between them, realised that she should perhaps soften her tone, and let out a sigh. After a sufficient few seconds had passed she disentangled her fingers from his.

'I'm sorry, Geoffrey,' she said as sweetly and contritely as possible. 'I am being horrid. Of course it's not your fault. It's no one's fault.' Flicking her cigarette end out of the car window, she pulled down the visor to examine her face in the mirror. She flipped it back up. It wasn't true, she thought. This was entirely Paul's fault; the thankless, spoilt child. She rejected quickly and entirely the notion that he might have run away because he was unhappy. He must have done it simply to get attention.

When he met Montacute and Marion, Dr Whatley conducted himself with a carefully prepared blend of tactful regret and deep concern. The tact was mainly directed towards ensuring that the matter should remain as private as possible, without being made public to too many parents. Following as it did on the heels of that dreadful accident of the first-former falling from his dormitory window, the absconding of a boy from Ampersand did not make for good publicity. Having assured Marion that everything, in conjunction with the help of the local police, was being done to ascertain Paul's whereabouts, he and Montacute and Marion conducted a series of interviews with some of Paul's classmates, most prominently Beasley and Horsman, concerning Paul's disappearance. These were not helpful.

'He was pretty sick about the business over Cowan,' said Beasley, obliging Dr Whatley to explain the matter of Cowan's death to Marion and Montacute. But that was all. No one had any notion of why or where Paul might have gone. His locker and wardrobe had been searched, but no clue found. If it was any consolation, Dr Whatley said, no boy in such circumstances went missing forever. It was certain that Paul would be found.

When it seemed that there was nothing more to be said for the time being, Marion and Montacute made their way back to Montacute's car.

'Did Helena have any idea of his whereabouts?' asked Montacute, as he held open Marion's door for her with his customary ostentatious courteousness.

'Oh, I haven't spoken to her yet,' replied Marion, tugging her coat about her against the bitter wind. 'I can never seem to get hold of her – the child is constantly out. One would think that she and that girl she shares the flat with hardly ever speak to one another.' She got into the car. Montacute closed the door carefully and went round to his side and got in. They both sat for a moment in silence. In a way, Montacute rather wished that Marion would break down in tears of despair so that he could put a protective arm around her, soothe her fears, and take masterful charge of the situation. But her attitude throughout had been one of anger and impatience; she was quite without the vulnerability that he had expected. In any event, he could think of nothing masterful to do. Marion, far from being grief-stricken and in need of comfort, seemed to regard the whole episode as an annoying inconvenience.

'That boy has no consideration for others,' she muttered, then fished in her handbag for her cigarettes. She had smoked the last one. She closed her bag and glared ahead. Montacute started the car. 'I *had* planned to go to the opera tonight,' she observed.

'Oh, really?' asked Montacute in distant tones. He felt he might have been informed, included.

'Well, I don't see why I shouldn't still go,' she went on, paying no heed to Montacute. 'It won't help to sit at home. Perhaps if you wouldn't mind driving me back to London, Geoffrey, I can call on Helena and talk to her about Paul.'

'Certainly,' replied Montacute, and drove huffily back to London.

When they arrived at the Chelsea flat and found Helena in, Montacute announced that he would go back to his office.

Realising that it had been imprudent to mention the opera and that Montacute's tone was chilly, Marion laid a detaining hand upon his sleeve as he turned to go.

'Oh, please, Geoffrey, do stay for a moment. You've been such a dear so far, and I'm rather depending on you. Besides, you haven't had any lunch. I'm sure Helena can make us something.'

Montacute hesitated; the thought of the hearing tomorrow was preying on his mind. If Sir Reynold ran true to the form of all clients, he would have called the office several times that morning already and would be apoplectic at the absence of his solicitor this afternoon, too, on the very eve of the hearing.

As Helena turned and walked back through to the kitchen, Marion stretched up and kissed his mouth. 'I'm sorry if I've been beastly, darling,' she whispered. He stayed.

Helena greeted the news of her brother's disappearance with a doleful lack of surprise. 'It's a wonder he didn't run off earlier,' she remarked, preparing bacon, lettuce and tomato rolls for her mother and Montacute with ill grace.

'I think you might have told me he was so very miserable, Helena,' said Marion. 'It might have made all the difference.'

'What difference?' replied Helena, dumping the rolls on to a plate. 'I haven't got any mayonnaise, sorry. Anyway,' she added, 'you're his mother. You should know about these things.'

It struck Montacute that Helena had changed somewhat in the past few months. She appeared sullen and dispirited and was being extremely disagreeable to her mother. Perhaps this was what too much money at too young an age did to one.

'Be that as it may, Helena,' replied Marion evenly, 'can you think of anywhere that Paul might have gone? Anyone he might be likely to go to?'

'Well, why don't you try Oliver?' said Helena and picked up one of the rolls.

'Oh, for heaven's sake, Helena!' replied Marion in exasperation. 'If he had gone to Oliver's, Oliver would have rung me! He would realise that I was dreadfully worried!'

Helena raised her eyebrows, then smiled. 'That wasn't what I meant. I meant, he was staying with Oliver for most of

August, so maybe Oliver has some idea where he's gone. I'm sure he made all kinds of wonderful new friends there.' Helena picked up her coat from the back of her chair and went out into the hall with it, still eating her roll. 'Now, if you don't mind, I have to get back to college. Let me know how the hunt goes. See you.'

And she left.

'I suppose she has a point,' said Marion with a sigh. She picked up the telephone and rang Oliver's office, but Oliver's secretary said that Mr Pocock was out at lunch – no, she didn't know where and had no idea when he might be back. Perhaps Mrs Laing should ring back after three.

'Three?' said Marion.

Well, said the secretary apologetically, sometimes Mr Pocock took quite long lunches. She was only saying three to be on the safe side.

'Thank you,' said Marion. She put down the phone and stared at the rolls Helena had prepared. 'Do you want one of these?' she asked Montacute. He shook his head. There was something about the silence of the flat, the strangeness of the territory, that made Montacute approach Marion quietly and gently, as if for the first time, and slip off her coat, then unbutton her dress, kissing her all the while, with a calm and absolute assuredness that surprised them both. Aroused by Geoffrey's astonishingly forceful intentness and the illicit thrill of behaving thus in her daughter's flat, Marion succumbed wordlessly. And so Montacute made love to Marion Laing for the very last time in his life.

Having dressed, they left Helena's flat and drove in silence for lunch. Marion was astonished to find herself bound to Geoffrey in a kind of shared euphoria. There had been no puffing or panting, no sham; it had been wonderful, and she felt wonderful. He turned to smile at her from time to time, and she found herself smiling back, in spite of all her troubles.

As for Montacute, he did not know what to think. If he had been happy before, he knew that it was as nothing compared with now. He felt as though he had reached some kind of completion, that he and Marion were utterly at one. And yet they had spent the morning bickering. He marvelled at this. He did not care, he decided, as he drove through the West End to the best restaurant that he could think of, about Sir Reynold Cazalet or his wretched family dispute. He could fume all afternoon if he cared to. Tomorrow morning would find Montacute bright and smiling and attentive to all Sir Reynold's business. But for now he was taking the woman he loved, and to whom he had just made love, to lunch.

In Lincoln's Inn Fields, Miss Reed placed the third note on Mr Montacute's desk asking him to call James Ackland, and the fifth demanding that he call Sir Reynold. On the Financial Times Stock Exchange Index, Garter Cross had fallen eighteen points to stand at 312. Half the City knew that the Serious Fraud Squad had called at the offices of Heyworth Mercantile, of which Mr Melanakis was the executive chairman, and was behaving accordingly.

After lunch Montacute and Marion went to Oliver's office and found him back from lunch. He looked perplexed when Marion told him of Paul's disappearance, then angry.

'This is dreadful!' he muttered. 'Dreadful! Can you imagine how miserable the boy must have been?'

'Of course I can!' retorted Marion. 'I am his mother. I'm practically out of my mind with worry!'

'That bloody school!' said Oliver, rising from his chair and walking to the window. 'I told you, Geoffrey, that it was quite the worst decision.'

'I hardly think,' replied Montacute with dignity, 'that there is any point in attempting to lay personal blame for this – this misfortune. We are all merely anxious to ascertain Paul's whereabouts, so that he might be brought back to his mother safe and well.' His voice had taken on a sonorous tone.

'Good God, Geoffrey, the boy is nearly eighteen – practically an adult! You talk as if he's a lost child. He has clearly made a decision to leave Ampersand, and I for one applaud that decision.'

'Oliver!' exclaimed Marion.

'Well, I do!' replied Oliver, pursing his chubby lips. 'I don't mean that I don't want him to be safe and well – of course I do. It's just that I have every confidence that he can look after himself and will reappear in our midst as and when he wants to. What is dreadful is to think of how unhappy he must have been, and how isolated – feeling compelled to escape in this way.'

'I frankly find your attitude most remarkably unhelpful,' said Montacute coldly. 'Marion has come here, at Helena's suggestion, hoping that you might be able to give some help in finding Paul, and yet all you can do is to say that, as far as you are concerned, the boy can come home as and when he pleases.'

'Well, he can, can't he?' retorted Oliver. 'Just leave him alone for a change! Your interfering, Geoffrey, has done enough damage. That ridiculous school! None of us should be surprised that this has happened.'

'The point is,' said Marion, 'Paul stayed with you for the last three weeks of August. God knows what kind of associations he formed then, what kind of people he met! I don't know what I can have been thinking of—Do you think I want him walking the streets of London, turning into some – some kind of rent boy?' She was furious with Oliver's stance on the matter and vented all her rage on him.

Oliver gazed at her levelly. He said nothing. After a pause, he went back to his desk and sat down.

'I can ring Charlie Vereker and see if he can suggest anything.' he said quietly. 'And of course I shall call you, Marion, if I can find out anything that might be of help. It must all be very distressing for you.'

They left Oliver's office and walked back down Hay Hill in silence towards Curzon Street, where Montacute had left his car. Both were aware that the mood – whatever mood it had been – that had possessed them as they left the Chelsea flat had evaporated. Montacute felt unaccountably weary and the thought of the case the following day was nagging at him again. Marion had just realised that she could not go to the opera that evening with her friends, for she was in town without having brought anything to wear; she hardly cared, for she was aware that her initial anger at Paul's disappearance was now being replaced by a cold, growing sense of worry. She wanted to go back to Roffey and wait. She felt she could do nothing more.

When they reached Montacute's car, they found that it had been clamped. Montacute stood staring at it mournfully.

After a pause Marion, with a show of pretty sympathy, said, 'Geoffrey, darling, I know I shouldn't abandon you here, but I don't honestly think it will do much good for both of us to wait around in the cold. I'll get a train back down to Roffey. I shan't stay in town tonight.' He looked so forlorn and vexed, his face heavy with disappointment, that she reached up and kissed him. 'I'll call if I hear anything. Thank you for being such a dear about all of this.' A taxi appeared at the top of the street and she hailed it, and sped off through the rain which had begun to fall.

Montacute looked at the notice pasted to his windscreen. It told him not to attempt to move this vehicle. Why on earth should he attempt to move this vehicle, since it was clamped? He took down the phone number that he was instructed to ring in order to effect the release of his car, turned up the collar of his coat, and set off through the rain in search of a telephone box.

He did not arrive back at his office until just before five o'clock. It had taken the de-clamping vehicle an hour and three-quarters to arrive. He was soaked and was as close to the edge of his even temper as Montacute was ever likely to get. Miss Reed scuttled in behind him as he strode through her room and into his own. The telephone on his desk had just begun to ring.

'That will be Sir Reynold, Mr Montacute,' she said, quite unnecessarily. 'He has been telephoning all day and said that he didn't wish to speak to me any more. He told the switchboard that he insisted on being put straight through to you.' She hovered uncertainly as Montacute picked up the receiver with a savage glare, then she left. Montacute paused, lifted his chin, let his features slacken, then smiled slightly as he said, 'Good afternoon, Sir Reynold. I do apologise for being out of the office for the better part of the day. I was called away on urgent personal business . . .'

By the time that he got Sir Reynold off the phone it was six o'clock, and Montacute felt unutterably weary. He had sat through that telephone conversation in damp clothes, too, and was aware of an unpleasantly chilly, creeping sensation at the back of his throat.

He longed for a large whisky. Possibly two. He laid his head upon his folded arms and let out a long sigh, thinking for a brief, blissful moment of being with Marion in the flat in Caversham Place. Then he raised his head and gazed at the little heap of telephone notes which the punctilious Miss Reed had laid there regularly throughout the day. He flipped through the top three. Sir Reynold Cazalet, 3.13 PM, Sir Reynold Cazalet, 4.18 PM, Sir Reynold Cazalet, 4.45 PM . . . He swept the whole heap into the bin and stared across at the heap of files marked '*In re Cazalet's Will's Trusts*' which stood upon the floor and on chairs. He would go to his club, he told himself. He had not been there for weeks. He could do with some company, some peace . . . No, he should go home and see how his mother was. He should change out of these damp clothes.

And so Montacute drove off through the evening traffic towards Richmond, while James Ackland, who had left many of the telephone messages which Montacute had just swept into the bin, headed for his club for a couple of drinks – the club of which he and Montacute were both members.

Sitting at Hammersmith roundabout, waiting for the traffic to move, Montacute switched on the car radio. He decided to opt for 'Going Places' on Radio Four, instead of tuning into LBC, which at that moment was giving the latest City and financial update.

Chapter twenty-three

When she got back to Roffey in the early evening, Marion was weary in body and spirit. She ate the meal which Leonie prepared for her, took a bath, and tried successively to read, to watch television, and to answer some letters. But her mind was on constant alert for the sound of the telephone, and she could concentrate on nothing. During the daylight hours her thoughts of Paul had been of a lanky seventeen-year-old bunking off school to cause everyone worry and inconvenience. Now that it was night, the spectre of the loneliness and unhappiness which must have impelled him to run away rose up, and in her mind he was a frightened child, alone in the dark. But he would turn up, she told herself. Of course he would. It wasn't unheard of for children to run away from school. Then again, one read of children disappearing, never to return . . . She poured herself a drink and moved nervously about the drawing room. No, he would come back. How much money could he have had? Well, his allowance was generous . . . She supposed he didn't spend much.

She sat down on the sofa with her drink and tried to rearrange her thoughts, to rationalise her fears. Perhaps – perhaps he had gone to one of his friends from Hamilton House? He had been happy there, or as happy as Paul ever seemed to be. But no, she would have heard if that had been the case. There was nothing she could do but wait. If she had been another kind of mother, she would probably have been dashing all over the countryside in a state of desperation. Perhaps I'm the wrong kind of mother, she thought, and looked down in surprise at her already empty glass.

She poured herself another drink, finding that the alcohol slowed her mind down, if not exactly calmed it. Then she wandered through the house, whose air seemed shrill with the silence of the telephone. Pacing around the long, oval rose-wood table in the dining room, she caught sight of her own robed reflection in the window. She moved forward, drawn to her own ghostlike image. Unable to read her own face properly in the glass, she went over to the mirror which hung above the fireplace. Resting her arms on the cold marble of the mantelpiece, she studied her face, noted the fine lines and slight pouching around her wonderfully clear blue eyes, the faint dragging around her mouth, the way her blonde hair was a touch thin and wispy at the hairline. She was not young. In just ten years' time she would be nearly fifty. She felt a sudden pang of fear, of anguish almost, at the loss of youth. Everything that was important in life had probably already happened to her – yet what had happened to her? Perhaps she should have remarried . . . No, she had not enjoyed marriage, she had not liked any relationship which confined her, demanded of her. Being the mother of small children had been bad enough. She drew her eyes away from her reflection.

Thinking of men, she mused upon Geoffrey, and was surprised to find that the thought of him made her rather melancholy. Why was this? Perhaps because he loved her, loved her unconditionally and completely, with a love she could not return. What had been that feeling, that warm, elusive feeling she had had when she left Helena's flat with him at lunchtime? She tried to summon it back, but failed. How strange. It had been so pleasant. Anyway, it was gone. But the way he loved her . . . That was supposed to be a rare gift, she knew. She tried to see it in this way. But all she could see was Geoffrey, tall, pompous Geoffrey, with his leaden voice and expressionless face, those long, dignified features. It was an absurd, dreary picture. It was not a picture of love. She wished, for the most fleeting of moments, that she could be the kind of person who could endure the kindness and safety of such love as Geoffrey felt for her. But, she told herself, deciding it was time for a cigarette, she was not that kind of person. She was like her friends, like the silly, chattering people of whom Geoffrey thought so little. Well, it all ran too fast and too deep in her now, the need to be amused, the longing for change. The best she could do was make the most of such advantages and opportunities as his love might bring her. On that note, as she lit her cigarette in the hall, she wondered how those investments of dear Geoffrey's were doing, and when she was going to see some results.

Charlie Vereker's phone call, when it came, did not surprise Oliver.

'Paul is in New York,' said Charlie, 'with Teddy.'

'I might have known,' said Oliver with a sigh. 'I think I did know. Well, at least we know where he is. When did you hear?'

'Teddy called me a few minutes ago. I spoke to Paul as well. He seemed very cheerful, actually. He travelled up to London, went to Drew and Errol's – apparently he knew when Teddy was leaving – and asked to go with him. He already had a US visa in his passport. So Teddy took him. Paid for his ticket. And there they both are, duckie.'

There they are indeed, thought Oliver. He knew why Teddy had called Charlie instead of himself. He knew that Teddy would be slightly ashamed, too nervous to talk to him.

'He said he didn't mind speaking to his mother,' went on Charlie, 'was sorry to have worried everyone and so forth, but simply couldn't stand to stay at his school for another minute. Poor child. I have Teddy's number, if you want it.'

Oliver took the number and thanked Charlie for letting him know.

'Boys will be boys, eh?' said Charlie cheerfully.

Oliver agreed that this was so. He put the phone down and stood in thought for a moment. Should he ring Marion now, or speak to Paul first? The latter, he decided. He glanced at his watch. Nine-fifteen. Which meant it was four o'clock or so in New York.

Teddy, when he answered the phone and heard Oliver's voice, merely said in apologetic tones, 'Oliver, none of this was my idea, honest. He just wanted to get away. What could I do? Anyway, I'll put him on. Hold on.'

In the pause, Oliver pondered this. What's in it for you, Teddy? Nothing like a soon-to-be-wealthy young friend to help things along. He sighed. Perhaps he was being unfair.

Paul's voice, when he came on the line, seemed rather breathless. 'Oliver, I'm really sorry if I've had Mummy and everyone worried. I just couldn't stick it there any more, and I knew if I asked to leave everyone would just have said what you said – you know, hold on, it's only another year or two, but honestly . . .' His rapid apology tailed off. 'Anyway, I'm here now.' His voice was a mixture of contrition and jubilation.

'Yes, well,' said Oliver with a sigh, 'it's not perhaps the cleverest thing you've ever done, Paul. Your mother and Mr Montacute have been backwards and forwards trying to find out where you'd gone. I've been more than a little concerned myself.' He felt that he was under a grown-up's obligation to reprove, even though it was quite futile.

'Okay, I'm sorry. But, Oliver, it's so good to be away. It's so wonderful to be with Teddy and be – be somewhere different. It's a brilliant place, New York. I mean, the apartment is a bit small, but Teddy's taking me out to get something to eat in a couple of hours. I can't wait to see it all. We're going to the Picasso retrospective next week.'

'Paul, that is all very well, but you can't stay there forever, you know. You have no money.'

'I will soon enough,' replied Paul quickly, with a touch of belligerence. 'I'll be eighteen next summer, and then I get my income from the trust.' He hesitated. 'They can't stop that, can they, just because you're in America?'

'No,' replied Oliver with a slight smile. 'No, they can't. But there's rather more to it than that. You can't stay there for more than six months, you know. Your visa will expire.'

'Oh, well,' said Paul lightly, 'then I'll come back. But I won't need to go back to that awful bloody school. I'll be able to do what I want, won't I?'

And just what is that? wondered Oliver. He decided, however, that it was best not to go into that on a transatlantic call.

'I shall have to ring your mother now and tell her where you are. Can I give her this number?' It seemed only courteous to ask.

'Yes,' said Paul. 'Of course. I have to say sorry to her and all that. Causing her worry. That was the only thing that really bothered me. Just so long as she doesn't come over here.'

'Knowing your mother, I can't make any promises,' said Oliver. 'Anyway, look after yourself. Enjoy yourself while you can. Bye bye.'

'Bye,' said Paul happily.

Oliver decided to have a largeish drink before ringing Marion. The sharp note in her voice as she picked up the telephone and said hello told him that she had been waiting anxiously for news. When she heard where Paul was, her reaction was a mixture of anger and relief.

'In New York? My God, that boy is driving me to distraction! And you say this is with some friend he met at that gallery?'

'Yes. Teddy. You met him at Helena's party. The American.'

'Oh, the rather handsome one with dark hair?'

'Yes,' said Oliver sadly, 'that one.'

'Oh, good Lord! Well, at least we know where he is now.' Marion lit a cigarette, digesting the information. 'But heavens above! Why go all the way to New York? Does he expect me to go over there and fetch him back?'

'I – ah – don't think that was quite the idea, no,' replied Oliver. 'I think he just wanted to get as far away as possible from – from things. For a while, at least. And I think he wanted to be with this friend. You know.'

Marion smoked and thought, her mind growing calmer. 'He can't stay there,' she said eventually. 'I mean, what's he going to do? He's got no money.'

'Not yet,' said Oliver.

'Oh, good grief, of course. He'll be eighteen next June. Well, well.' She thought for a moment. 'Can he just ask for the money? I mean, is it given to him, just like that?'

'Yes. It's his money. He just tells Montacute where to send it. But no, you're right, he can't stay there forever. Look, I have the number of the friend he's staying with. Why don't you call and speak to Paul? He sounded quite – jolly, really.'

'Did he indeed?' said Marion darkly. 'Yes, give me the number please, Oliver. Look, I'm going to come up to town tomorrow and talk to you about this, if you don't mind. Work out what best to do. I'll ring his school in the morning. Heavens, all this to-ing and fro-ing!' Relief was giving way to a headache.

'What about Montacute? Shouldn't he be told?' asked Oliver.

'Oh, I suppose so,' said Marion.

'I just thought you might have his home number.'

'Good heavens, no! Don't you? I thought he was a friend of yours.'

'No. That is, I don't have his number. It will have to wait until tomorrow, then.'

After he put down the telephone Oliver finished his drink, washed up, and went to bed. He lay there for a while, too accustomed to his solitude to feel lonely, and thought with envy of Paul and Teddy, young and free and in New York.

Montacute's day started as it was destined to go on. Badly. He had to listen to his mother's fractured grumblings and protests at having to go to the day-care centre again, until at last he lost patience and said, 'Very well, mother, don't go. I frankly do not care one way or the other. But let us hear no more of the matter.'

But he had to hear more of the matter, since his mother's imagined sufferings at the hands of the hospital and social services seemed to be her chief preoccupation these days. Besides which, Mrs Carmichael failed to show up at her usual time. Montacute stood fretting at the window, lifting the net curtain from time to time, muttering angrily, 'Where is that wretched woman? I have an important hearing today and will have to go straight to court at this rate! Why does she pick today of all days to be late?'

Eventually Mrs Carmichael did show up, twenty minutes late, chattering her apologies and explanations. Montacute brushed these aside, picked up his things, and headed for the front door, leaving his mother to listen to Mrs Carmichael's breathless account of how her husband's car had broken down and she'd had to get a minicab. 'An' 'e wos black, of course, and didn't know any of the streets . . .' was the last thing he heard as he closed the front door and hurried down the path at a brisk, striding walk. Montacute never ran.

He realised, as he glanced at his watch on the train that he would have to go straight to court without stopping at the office. And he had assured Sir Reynold that he would meet him at the office and go with him to court. He would be furious. Well, it could not be helped. He would be late as it was. Sir Reynold would just have to content himself with raving at Graham, Montacute's assistant in the case, all the way through Lincoln's Inn.

Sir Reynold, who was already at the law courts with Graham when Montacute arrived, was stony-faced with displeasure. He greeted Montacute stiffly. It was as he had suspected. The man simply did not attend to matters as he should. He could not even be bothered to turn up at his office at a decent time. If this hearing went against them, he would certainly change solicitors.

In the courtroom, Montacute subsided into his seat and drew towards him one of the bundles of documents which Graham had brought down from the office. He felt hot and flustered and took a few slow, deep breaths. Then he leaned forward and murmured something inconsequential to counsel to show Sir Reynold that he was in control of things, then sat back, grateful as ever for the reverential courtroom calm which always preceded a hearing, waiting for events to proceed. As he glanced round, his eye fell on Sir Reynold's copy of the *Financial Times*, resting on the wooden ledge next to his notes. Montacute's mind flew with a jerk to the Garter Cross shares. He had not thought of them in forty-eight hours. One event seemed to have piled on top of another, and he had simply not had the time. He longed to reach out and pick up the paper, but he knew he could not. He had no doubts or apprehensions; he just wished to know whether the company had secured that contract. He longed to know. He was sure it had. Well, he would just have to wait until lunchtime.

As Her Majesty's High Court of Justice, Chancery Division, sat listening to counsel unravel yet another tangled skein in the woolly case of *In Re Cazalet's Will's Trusts*, Miss Reed was busy fielding telephone calls on Mr Montacute's behalf.

'I'm very sorry, Mr Pocock, Mr Montacute is in court this morning. I had expected him in the office, but he must have gone straight there. I don't expect him back until the end of the day. Yes, I'll tell him. Yes, thank you. Goodbye.'

Good gracious, thought Miss Reed, as the telephone rang again almost as soon as she had put it down, this had been the most frightful two days. And hardly a sign of the man. Really. She picked up the telephone.

'Mr Ackland? I'm sorry, Mr Ackland, but Mr Montacute has been away on personal business. Yes, I did leave all your messages. No, I'm afraid he's in court all day today. Yes, yes, of course I shall. As soon as he comes in. Goodbye.'

Now, she thought, putting the phone down and scribbling out notes recording the calls of Oliver and James Ackland, perhaps we can have a little peace.

James Ackland put down the telephone in his office in St Katharine's Dock and swivelled round in his chair. Well, it was all too late now, anyway. The DTI had been called in, and the shares in Garter Cross suspended. Poor old Montacute. Or whoever.

When the court rose for lunch and Sir Reynold and Montacute put their things together in preparation to leave, Sir Reynold already commencing a harangue on the morning's proceedings, Montacute reached out a hand towards Sir Reynold's newspaper.

'Might I?' he murmured. Sir Reynold stopped mid-flow. The man did not even have the courtesy to listen to what he was saying! Wanted to read the paper instead! 'Here, take it!' he snapped, and thrust it into Montacute's hand, striding off ahead out of the courtroom. Montacute unfolded it. He had not expected to see what he saw. In fact, it took him almost a minute, during which time he read the headline twice, then the opening paragraph, and then the headline again, to comprehend it. Trading in Garter Cross shares had been suspended. Something about a connected company offering bribes for that contract, a company of which Mr Melanakis, the infallible Greek, was also an executive director. The shares were worthless. It was all gone. Everything. Every single penny. All this must have happened in a mere forty-eight hours – the investigation by the Serious Fraud Office, the collapse of the share price, the suspension of trading . . . all without his knowing. If only he had picked up a paper . . . He stared around him at the empty benches, at the piles of paper, at his world. He stood for a moment, then folded up the paper carefully, and went out into the corridor, where Graham was talking to a glowering Sir Reynold in an attempt to assure him that the hearing was really going quite well for them. Sir Reynold buttonholed Montacute.

'Now look here, Geoffrey, we must talk about this! I have some—'

But Montacute barely glanced at him. 'Graham, would you be good enough to take Sir Reynold to lunch? Rules, I think –or perhaps Luigi's. You have your Diner's Card? I may join you later, but I rather doubt it.' He paused. 'I may not be back in court this afternoon. My apologies, Sir Reynold, for having to disappear again so abruptly. A pressing personal matter. I am sure Graham will look after you.' And he handed Sir Reynold his copy of the *Financial Times*.

'Damn it, man, I do not need looking after by some clerk! I wish to talk to you!' roared Sir Reynold. But Montacute was already striding off down the corridor and out of the law courts.

He walked up Bell Yard and through the archway past Wildy's bookshop, and into New Square. His pace slowed. Why hurry? What was there to hurry for? The wet weather had passed, he noticed, and the November sunshine was unseasonably warm. It shone gloriously on the gardens and buildings of Lincoln's Inn, on the flowerbeds behind their neat railings, on the trim white paintwork of the casement windows of chambers, on the smooth, ancient flagstones. He wondered how many times in his life he had walked back and forth from his office to the law courts. He walked, this time, as one in a dream.

As he came into his office, Miss Reed scuttled out from behind her desk.

'Oh, Mr Montacute, there have been any number of calls for you – a Mr Ackland rang several times yesterday, and again this morning, and of course, Sir Reynold—'

He regarded her blankly; it struck her that his face wore a distracted, absent look – quite unlike himself, she thought.

'Would you just give me a few moments alone, please, Miss Reed?' And then he went into his room, closed the door, and sat down at his desk. After a moment or two he leaned his elbows on its smooth mahogany surface and put his hands over his face.

It was almost eleven by the time Marion reached London. She would see Oliver, she told herself, and do a little shopping to ease her mind of the worries that had been piling up in it over the past two days. Really, coming backwards and forwards like this was dreadfully tiresome. When Geoffrey's investment yielded its fruits, she would have to see about finding herself a place in London. The original project of using the Chelsea flat as a bolthole had rapidly fallen by the wayside. The child was a domestic catastrophe, as her visit the other day had shown. Thinking of this, it occurred to Marion that she would do her shopping first, then drop off her purchases at Helena's at lunchtime in the hope of catching her in, so that she could tell her about Paul. Then she could have lunch with Oliver and discuss Paul's predicament at Oliver's expense. Oliver always lunched well.

After she had whiled away an extravagant hour in Knightsbridge, Marion arrived at Helena's flat to find it empty. Not surprising, she supposed. She set down her parcels and carrier bags and wandered from room to room, reflecting silently on the mess that she found everywhere. In Helena's own bedroom heaps of clothes, many of them new and expensive, were flung carelessly over chairs; the surface of her dressing table was littered with make-up, and piles of magazines lay on the floor among scattered drawings. There was nothing cheerful about the disorder; everything had an air of discarded excess, of uselessness.

She heard the front door slam and came out into the hallway to meet her daughter. Helena looked tired, sullen, and neither surprised nor pleased to see her mother.

'I wish you'd ring before coming, Mummy,' she said, dropping her bag in the hallway and taking off her coat. Joseph, thought Marion, eyeing it expertly; labelling clothes and possessions was second nature to her. 'What were you doing in my room?' added Helena.

'Surveying the appalling mess that you have let this place get into,' replied her mother.

'It is my flat,' retorted Helena, and brushed past her on her way to the kitchen. Marion followed, puzzled and disturbed by the recent change in her daughter. What was wrong with her children? Were they deliberately conspiring to make life difficult for her?

'Helena, I am merely worried about the state that you seem to be letting things get into . . . And look at yourself! You used to take such good care of yourself—'

'Oh, drop it, Mummy. I'm a big girl now. If you don't like the place, don't come here.'

This was more than token rudeness, Marion realised. She hesitated, watching Helena taking bits and pieces from the fridge for her lunch. 'Helena,' she said, trying to make her voice even and gentle, 'is something the matter? Is there something I can help you with?'

Helena sighed. 'No, there isn't. I'm sorry if I'm rude. I'm just a bit tired and – things.'

'Is it that boy who was here before?' pursued Marion. 'That Conrad person?' She wondered vaguely what had ever happened to Richard Ranscombe.

Helena laughed. 'God, no! Nothing like that. Nothing's the matter. Honestly.' She turned round. 'You didn't just come here to quiz me about my personal life, did you?'

'Oh, Helena, I only want to—' But Marion decided she had neither the energy nor the inclination to continue in the role of the concerned mother. She sighed. 'As a matter of fact, I came to tell you that we've found Paul. He's in New York with that American boy who came to your party. I can't recall his name. Good-looking boy with his hair in a pony tail.'

Helena looked at her mother in genuine surprise. 'With Teddy? Heavens!' And she laughed and turned back to the sandwich she was making. 'Who would have thought it?'

'Quite,' said Marion, subconsciously relieved to hear her daughter laugh. 'Though why he had to go halfway round the world with that young man, just because he didn't like his school, I do not know.'

'Perhaps they're lovers,' said Helena, and took a bite out of her sandwich, watching her mother's face carefully.

But Marion decided to ignore this as a joke in bad taste. 'Now,' she said, 'I must ring Oliver.' She picked up the telephone as Helena murmured, 'Be my guest,' and sauntered with her sandwich into the living room. She was secretly relieved that Paul was safe and well. Lucky Paul, being in New York.

When she had rung Oliver and arranged to have lunch with him, Marion came through to take leave of Helena. 'Oh, I forgot,' she said suddenly as she pulled on her gloves, 'I haven't told Geoffrey yet about Paul. I must ring him.' She disappeared into the kitchen again.

When the telephone rang in his office, it startled Montacute so much that his hands jerked involuntarily away from his face.

'I have Mrs Laing for you,' said Miss Reed's voice. His leaden thoughts suddenly disturbed, he felt as though woken from a sleep. He hesitated for a moment. No, it did not matter. He might as well tell her. There was no point in waiting. He could only hope that it would not matter to her. What a ludicrous hope.

'Please put her through,' he said.

'Hello, Geoffrey?' Her voice sounded bright and sweet. 'I thought I should ring and let you know that we've found Paul. Or rather, a friend of Oliver's did. He's in New York with a friend. Tiresome, but at least we know where he is.'

'I'm so glad,' said Montacute.

'I'm going to have a talk with Oliver about what best to do – he seems to know this boy that Paul has gone off with. Honestly, that child really is the end. I hardly think he had to go as far as New York to make a point. Still, there it is.' She lit a cigarette with her free hand, then put down her lighter and dragged a finger through the dust on the kitchen window sill. Sunlight fell in bright, clear strips through the blind.

There was a long silence as Montacute wondered how to say what he had to say. 'Geoffrey? Are you still there?' asked Marion.

289

Montacute roused himself. He leaned back in his chair. 'Yes. Yes, I am. Listen, Marion, I have something to tell you. About the investment. I'm afraid it's – it's all been a bit of a disaster.' He laughed faintly. 'An utter disaster, in fact. The company I invested in ceased trading this morning.'

Marion stared at the pattern of sunlight. Everything seemed to stand very still for her in that moment. 'Geoffrey,' she said in a low voice, 'I don't understand what you are saying. What has happened?'

'I have lost everything.' His voice was quite calm with the relief of saying it. Saying it outright. 'Everything. I was so busy with – you, and the problem of Paul, that I did not even know what was happening.' He talked as though to himself, ruminatively. 'I was too busy, too inattentive.' He passed a hand over his face. 'I'm afraid I've rather ruined myself.'

In the flat, Marion stood rigid with disbelief. 'How could you have been such a fool?' Her voice came out in a low hiss as the truth of what he was saying dawned upon her. Appalled, she put the phone down.

Helena appeared in the kitchen doorway and stopped, startled at the sight of her mother's face.

'What on earth's the matter?' she asked. Marion turned to look at her.

'The matter?' she said fiercely, relieved at having some vent for her wrath. 'The matter? The matter is that your father's imbecile cousin, Geoffrey Montacute, has gambled away every single penny in the trust fund! He has robbed and ruined us!'

Helena looked at her, then uttered a little laugh. 'What are you talking about?' she asked. 'He can't have! Why would Mr Montacute do a thing like that?'

Her mother had no answer for her. Helena stared at her. Hesitantly she asked, 'You're joking, aren't you? I mean, the money's still there, isn't it?' She thought of Mr Montacute, upright, unctuous, dreary old Montacute; the thing seemed impossible. Grown-ups didn't do things like that, did they?

'I'm afraid I am not joking,' said Marion stonily. A sudden fear had taken possession of her. This thing that Geoffrey had done could implicate her, too, she realised. She knew little enough about the law, but when it was discovered what Geoffrey had done, the fraud he had perpetrated, then it might be found that she had some hand in it. Fraud. She felt cold. How had things gone so dreadfully wrong? She had never doubted Geoffrey's ability for a minute – and now this! She would have to see him now, face him, find out the extent of the damage before matters went further.

'I'm going round to his office,' she said, and left, slamming the door behind her.

Helena stood in the silence of the flat. What on earth was going on? Her mother must have gone off her trolley, she told herself. Mr Montacute was a solicitor. Solicitors didn't do things like taking other people's money . . . But they did, she knew. They could. The reality of what her mother had said sank in. If it was all gone, then how could they get it back? She would have nothing! The easy, charming life she had thought stretched out before her – it simply didn't exist any more if the money wasn't there. She would be like other people. Like Sissy. The idea made her feel a bit panicky. No, someone would put this right, someone could set it straight. There wasn't just Montacute. Her mother and Oliver were trustees as well. Oliver would know what to do. He would set it all straight. None of this could be right. No one would take money – just like that. She would ring Oliver.

'Where's your mother?' asked Oliver when he heard Helena's voice. 'I'm expecting her for lunch.'

'She's at Mr Montacute's office,' replied Helena, who had begun to feel a little shaky before, but now felt better at the sound of Oliver's plump, bright voice.

Oliver gave a little sigh of annoyance. 'But I've got a table booked! Why on earth has she gone to see that bloody man?'

Helena told him. 'She says he's – he's gambled away all the trust money. She says he's lost it all.' She waited for reassurance, and it came.

'Oh, for heaven's sake, what *is* she talking about? Of course he hasn't lost the trust money.' He hesitated. This was all rather odd. 'What did she say exactly?'

At his hesitation and the question, fear lit up in her again. She started to cry with vexation. 'Oh, Oliver! I don't know! I only know she spoke to him on the phone a minute ago, and then Mummy got into a state and said he had robbed us . . . And then she went off! Oh, Oliver, what's happening?'

Oliver sighed again. Why was life full of problems?

'Don't get so worked up,' he said, trying to soothe her. 'Your mother, as usual, seems to have got hold of the wrong end of some stick and is going around alarming everyone.'

'But what if it's true?' wailed Helena. 'What if all the money *has* gone?'

'Helena, the money has *not* gone!' said Oliver in exasperation. 'Of that I can assure you.' Really, the notion of Montacute making off with trust funds was one of the most half-baked he had ever heard. Where did they get such ideas from? Didn't they understand anything? 'Look, I will go round to Mr Montacute's office myself and sort this mess out. Now, stop crying over nothing!'

Oliver left his office and trotted down to Berkeley Square in search of a taxi, grumbling at the unnecessary troubles that the Laing family seemed to have brought into his life.

When she put down the phone, Helena was struck by the awful silence in the flat, broken only by the sound of her own whimpering sobs. Such comfort as Oliver's voice had brought her slid away. There was nothing Oliver could do. What could he do? It had to be true – why else would Mr Montacute have said such a thing to her mother?

She paced from the kitchen into the living room, her knuckles pressed against her teeth, her face streaked with wet lines of tears. What would happen, now that the money was gone? She tried to bring it to real terms. All her life there had been enough money; Daddy had been a sort of golden presence – not there, but illuminating her life with his money, the security of its existence for her, now and forever. Without it, she became just like any one of her friends from art school.

She thought of them, the privations, scraping by in the awful kinds of places they lived in, no cars, no decent clothes, no money to do whatever you liked, whenever you liked. And Con – he would never look at her again when he found out that she had no money. He would laugh. Despite all he had said, Con had liked her being rich. She had hoped that gradually he would see that life had been more fun with a girlfriend who had money, and that he would come back. No money – no Conrad. But what did she care about him? she suddenly thought savagely. What help could he be to her now that this had happened? God, he wasn't even a friend. She was completely alone. No one loved her for anything except the things she had, the money that now didn't exist.

She stood in the middle of the room and stared at the shrivelled palm, Richard's present, standing next to the curtains. She felt a stab of anguish and guilt at the sight of its scrappy, dried-up fronds, lifeless as strips of brown paper. She could at least have watered it. Richard, she thought – he would help her. No – no one could help. What had happened must, it seemed to her, be beyond anyone's help. But he would comfort her. He loved her. He had told her – hadn't he? – that if she needed him, she must just call. The image of him struck her with tender relief as she went back through to the kitchen to ring him. She had been foul to him, she knew, but she would make it all right. She did love him a bit, she told herself. Of course she did. To think that she'd begun to despise him because he wasn't exciting, and because he was always there when she needed him.

'Hello? Can I speak to Richard Ranscombe, please? Yes, thank you.' She waited, and then after a few seconds heard his voice on the line. It sounded very dear to her. 'Oh, Richard, it's me!' She hoped she wasn't going to start crying again.

'Helena?' replied Richard cautiously. Something was up, he could tell from her voice.

'Richard, I'm sorry, ringing you at work. I – I just had to speak to you.'

'What's the problem now?' he asked. His voice sounded terse, reluctant.

'Oh, it's – it's—' If she began to tell him now, she would start crying again; she didn't want that. '—I just need to see you.' She discovered that she really did; in her fear and desolation she wanted the safety, the security of his love very much.

At the other end, Richard hesitated. He could feel Clive's beady, curious gaze fixed upon him. 'I can come round after work,' he said. He supposed she wanted to cry on his shoulder again; probably about this awful bloke of hers. 'But I can't stay,' he added.

'Can't you?' Her voice was small, miserable.

'No. I'm meeting someone.'

In the midst of all her anxieties, Helena felt a pricking of jealousy. She didn't want Richard to be seeing anyone else. He was hers. She needed him. She would make him stay. Of course he would stay for her.

'When can you come?'

He looked at his watch. He could probably get off early. Montacute was in court all day. No one would miss him. His heart lifted with pleasure at the thought of seeing her again, on whatever terms, for whatever selfish reasons she might have. 'I can be there about five-thirty, I suppose. Depends on the rush hour, though.'

She felt deep relief at the thought of his comforting presence, at the thought of sharing all this awful thing with him. And he was a lawyer, wasn't he? Maybe he could do something practical.

'Wonderful,' she said. 'About five-thirty, then.' They said goodbye and then, just as he was about to hang up, she added hastily, 'Richard!'

'What?'

'You will come, won't you?'

'Yes,' he said kindly. 'Yes, I'll come.' He put the phone down, turned to wink at Clive, who shifted his gaze hastily back to his work, and picked it up again to call his friend Derek and tell him that he might not be able to make it that evening.

Chapter twenty-four

Montacute was still sitting at his desk when Marion arrived at the office. He had not moved since he had put the phone down. In his mind he had been revolving the implications of his loss. Everything, he knew, would be gradual, the effects of the catastrophe slowly piling one on top of another, until he was buried beneath the weight of his own folly. He could not bear to think that the first blow to crush him might be Marion's defection. The loss of the money, with all its appalling consequences, was one thing, but to lose her, the one cherished thing in his now wretched life, was more than he could bear to contemplate. Was the money really that important? Would she discard everything that had been precious between them merely because of it? He could not allow himself to believe it.

It was with relief that he heard Miss Reed inform him that Mrs Laing was waiting to see him. So must prisoners feel, he thought, when a visitor comes. He looked up at her in hope as she came in. Of course, her initial reaction to the news had been understandable, but she would not let him down. She had come to reassure him of her love. He knew that. There must be one consolation in the midst of all this ruin.

But Marion, too, had been calculating her losses on the way to Montacute's office, and she was glowing with the white heat of anger. When he saw her face, Montacute felt his hope die within him.

He managed to smile, however, and say, 'Thank you for coming.'

Marion could not believe her ears. She advanced upon him, unable to contain herself. 'What are you talking about?' she almost snarled at him. 'How can you sound so – so calm, so polite after what you have done? You have stolen and cheated and swindled! How *could* you? The stupidity of it! How could a man in your position take my children's money and – and squander it . . . ? for whatever senseless purpose – my God, when I think of it!' Indeed, the thought of the loss of so much money incensed Marion, and she raged on. 'Well, don't imagine that you can involve me in this!' She kept her voice as low as her temper would permit, ever mindful of Miss Reed in the outer office. 'My children may have to suffer for your greed and hypocrisy and stupidity, but you will not drag me into it with you! You did this! I didn't ask you to! Don't pretend it was done for me!'

A mixture of fear and fury had brought her to this pitch, and she could not find words to continue. If she could weep, she would have wept, but she was beyond tears.

Montacute sat amazed at this outburst, but his astonishment slowly gave way to comprehension. He gazed at her, gazed at her pretty face and the harsh lines that this imagined disaster had brought to it. So that was what she thought. Was that why she had come here? Had she imagined that, at her smiling, wheedling behest, he would compromise his integrity, use trust funds for personal gain, commit an act not only of criminality, but one which was the grossest breach of his duty as a trustee and a solicitor? She must have thought, during all these weeks when they had been making love, when he had smiled at her and she upon him, that he was behaving as a cheat and a reckless swindler. And yet, having so misjudged him, she clearly had not cared – she had only hoped to profit from his imagined deception. And now she was seeking, in panic and anger, to absolve herself from any complicity. Every proper instinct in Montacute was repelled by this realisation.

And yet mingled with this was a sense almost of relief; she had misunderstood matters, had leapt to this awful, this base assumption, but when she realised the truth she would be ashamed, and they could both brush it aside. It was a horrible mistake, but it need not matter.

'No, no,' he said, his eyes still fixed upon her face. 'You are quite wrong. There is nothing like that.' His gaze dropped, and he could not help adding heavily, 'I am appalled that you should think so.'

She looked at him levelly, her breathing becoming less rapid now that her outburst was over, struck by his calm, bleak tone.

'What do you mean? What are you talking about? You told me – what were you talking about, then, when you spoke to me on the telephone? What about the trust money?'

Something of Montacute's cold aplomb returned for an instant. 'There is nothing the least the matter with the trust fund.' But it was only an instant, then his voice dropped. 'The speculation was with my own money. I thought you understood that. I was entirely foolish. And now I have lost it. So.'

She looked at him for a few moments. She had been standing, but now she sat down. 'Your own money?' she said. He did not reply, but gazed down at his hands, pleating his long, white fingers together. 'But I thought . . . I mean, the money you made from the annuity investment . . .'

'You thought that was some improper act on my part also? No, that investment was quite legitimate. It was not one which would have have been suitable in the long term, but for the immediate purpose – since you wanted money – it was . . . adventurous perhaps, but quite within my powers as a trustee. I think I see the source of your mistake.' His voice was as distant as though he were addressing a client.

'I see,' she said, after a pause. 'I see. How much was it? That you lost, I mean.'

He made a slight gesture of dismissal. 'That does not matter,' he replied. 'But I have failed. I have disappointed you. I am sorry.' They both sat in silence for an interval. Then, as if to expiate his folly, he could not help adding, 'If I had not waited, if I had sold just three days ago, then I should have made over nine hundred thousand pounds. Well over. I could have given that to you.' It somehow eased his mind, as in a confessional, to confront openly the consequences of his recklessness. He gazed absently at the wall, as if contemplating his own past actions with awe.

Any embarrassment which Marion might have felt at her own misjudgement had been quickly eclipsed by relief that the children's money was safe. Now, at his words, a look of pain crossed her face and she felt genuine anguish. So much money – and it would have been hers. Whatever his mistake, it still remained the case that she now had only twenty thousand pounds a year to live on. You fool, she thought, looking at him, at his solemn face; strands of his hair had fallen over his forehead, giving him an uncharacteristically dishevelled look, yet he still possessed in every feature that dull, unshakeable rectitude. What an absurd thought it now seemed, to imagine that he would steal and squander trust money, even for her. She surveyed him bitterly.

'If only you had told me what you were doing,' she said, thinking how it could all have been saved, how she would never have let such a loss occur, 'then I might have – have helped you.' She gave him a fleeting look of frustrated despair.

'Perhaps,' he said slowly. 'Perhaps you would have stopped me?'

She gazed at him, her lips parted as if to reply, but no words came. No. No, they both knew she would not have stopped him. She was too greedy for that. She would have let him risk all for her. Her mean spirit comprehended something of this. He had so far departed from his own careful principles that he had not been afraid to risk as much as he had on her behalf. She would have let him.

'I'm sorry, Geoffrey,' she murmured. 'I'm sorry this has happened.'

'But at least,' he said, 'you know why it has happened. Because I am a fool, and because—' He struggled with the words. '—because I love you.'

A little wave of anger rose in her, and she looked away from him impatiently. Were things not bad enough without Geoffrey having to drag this up? Any pity she might have felt was fixed on herself, and only slight contempt was left for him.

'Well,' she said, letting out her breath, 'there it is. I suppose it's done now.'

There was something final in her tone that was unbearable to him. He looked at her in anguish across the wide surface of his desk, longing to rise and hold her to him, but quite unable to do so.

'I know there is nothing – well, very little – left now. I cannot offer – that is, I cannot expect you to marry me. But—'

'Marry you?' She stared at him. 'Oh, for heaven's sake,

Geoffrey. We have had – well, we have had a fling, a pleasant enough time together. But let's not pretend there was more to it than that. Maybe we have both been extremely foolish. Perhaps you more than I.' She broke off, and frowned around herself impatiently. It was about time she went. She had a good deal of thinking to do. Geoffrey and his misfortunes no longer figured in her schemes. 'I don't think any of this is getting us anywhere,' she added, rising from her chair.

He watched her stand, watched her preparing to leave, appalled at what she had said. A fling? A pleasant time? He loved her, he would sacrifice – had sacrificed – everything for her, and she was able to turn her back upon him and leave him forever!

'Please, Marion!' His voice broke with emotion.

'Geoffrey,' she said calmly, interrupting him, determined to stand no more of this nonsense. 'You are rather overwrought. I think you need some time to think about things.' She hesitated. 'I am sorry I misjudged you so badly.' She paused again as she pulled on her gloves. 'But we both seem to have misjudged a few things, don't we?' She glanced at him; a tiny regret, a tiny recollection that he had not always been entirely pathetic and pompous and dull, touched her, and she leaned forward and kissed his pale, heavy cheek. 'Goodbye,' she added.

He looked after her as the door closed. He felt as though the breath had left his body. It was the most final goodbye, he thought, that he had ever heard.

As Marion came down the steps of De Vaut, Montacute & Strange, Oliver was emerging from a taxi. He caught sight of her as he paid the driver and hurried over, puffing and frowning.

'Marion! What on earth is going on? I've just been hearing some ridiculous nonsense from Helena about Geoffrey making off with the trust fund, and you believing it!'

Marion laughed. 'It is nonsense, isn't it? No, of course he hasn't done anything of the sort. I don't know where she got such an absurd idea.' She sighed. 'I'm afraid poor Geoffrey is in a bit of a mess, though. It seems he made some very bad investment and has lost most of his money.'

Oliver stared at her. 'Geoffrey? Speculating with his money? Oh, good Lord! Why would he do a thing like that?'

'Why indeed?' said Marion lightly, but thinking bitterly of the money that could have been hers. 'Dreadful, isn't it?'

Oliver frowned at the pavement, digesting this. 'When you say *most* of his money, do you mean—?'

Marion raised her eyebrows in eloquent reply. 'It appears so. One feels for him, but one can't help questioning his judgement . . . But look, we're meant to be having lunch together, aren't we?' she added cosily. 'I'm sure if we hurry—'

He glared at her with faint offence. 'I hardly think so, Marion. I must go and see Geoffrey, see what's happened and whether he's all right. Besides,' he added, 'you might go and reassure Helena. She seems to think she's lost every penny in the world. Silly child.'

'I might just let the young lady stew in that particular juice for a few hours,' murmured Marion, musing on this. 'Perhaps it will do her good to speculate on living a life not cushioned by money. Some of us do it all the time.'

'In any event – about lunch, Marion – we can discuss Paul another time, perhaps,' said Oliver, moving towards the steps. 'Goodbye.'

'Goodbye,' she replied, her mind already elsewhere. As she stood on the pavement, scanning Lincoln's Inn Fields for a taxi, she was pondering whether, given the material alteration in her prospects, it might not now be necessary to take a bold line with Ari Vourlides, and call him herself. She felt there was a significant enough understanding between them now to make this possible, even though she would start off with the disadvantage of having made the running . . . Still, that didn't matter. She saw a taxi, its yellow light on, and raised a gloved hand. One could always recover lost ground.

Miss Reed gave Oliver a keen glance as he came into the office. She was beginning to have the feeling that all was not well with Mr Montacute. He had been behaving rather strangely. Not only had he failed to go back to court, she was sure she had heard raised voices when Mrs Laing had been in with him. She had never liked that woman. Far too sure of her own good looks.

'May I see Mr Montacute?' asked Oliver mildly. 'Oliver Pocock.' He waited while Miss Reed went into Montacute's room, a feeling of genuine concern growing within him.

Miss Reed showed him in and he found Montacute sitting behind his desk, looking fairly normal, only slightly untidy and blank in expression.

'Hello, Oliver,' he said. 'Sit down, please.'

'I met Marion outside,' said Oliver, manoeuvring his plump frame into one of Montacute's elegant Georgian chairs. 'She said you'd had some money problems. Is there anything I can help with?'

'Not much,' replied Montacute with a faint smile. 'Thank you, though, Oliver, for enquiring. No, I hazarded a good deal of money in Garter Cross – you may have heard of it – and the thing has gone bust. It was—' He paused. '—a mixture of bad luck and bad management, you might say. But there it is.' He laid his hands flat on the desk and stared at them. She has gone, he was thinking. If she could leave me, just like that, then she could never have loved me. Of course she never loved me. So preoccupied had he become with drumming this dull truth home to himself, that he spoke of his money almost dismissively.

Oliver's face creased in anxiety. 'But – but it can't have been very much, surely?' he asked. Montacute's manner seemed to indicate that it wasn't the catastrophe Marion had suggested.

Montacute looked up. 'Oh, yes,' he replied mildly. 'I invested almost everything I had.' He tested his heart again for the little burning ache that came whenever he thought of Marion's soft, warm body beneath his, and stared back at his hands. He felt like a child probing a sore place, knowing it will hurt but doing it nonetheless.

Oliver drew in a breath. 'Good God, Geoffrey!' He found it hard to believe that someone of Montacute's unfailing prudence and dull pedantry could have flown such a kite. He spoke the question immediately in his mind. 'But why – why on earth did you do such a thing?'

Montacute looked up at Oliver as if surprised. 'To make money,' he replied.

'But you didn't need money – did you?' Oliver was

beginning to realise that there were depths to Montacute which, in all his years of knowing him, he had not even begun to plumb. He gazed at him, full of curiosity.

'No,' said Montacute. He raised his hands from the desk and then slapped his palms down lightly. 'But Marion did. She needed money to go on living as she has always done, and I had hoped – I had thought – that I could do it for her. I loved her. I *do* love her. I thought that if I did this, she might marry me.'

As he said this, he recalled how it had been to kiss her, how he had loved to draw his face away from hers and see her eyes still closed from kissing him. It was a new pain, this recollection, and he revolved it slowly in his heart while it was still fresh. Any sensation, even these small torments, was better than the empty bleakness which he had felt since she had left his office and his life.

Oliver's thoughts were still bound up with Montacute's material losses, and he could not understand the remote carelessness of Montacute's tone.

'But, for God's sake, Geoffrey! One doesn't do such a thing for – for love!'

'Doesn't one, Oliver?' Montacute's gaze met his, and they looked at one another for a moment. For the first time in his life, Oliver felt some spark of human understanding between them. Montacute's long, solemn face betrayed nothing of passion, but something in his voice told Oliver that it was there.

'But – everything? I mean everything that you had put up at Lloyd's?'

Montacute nodded.

Oliver digested this. In the region of several hundred thousand pounds, in that case. All that Montacute had diligently earned over the years. And all for Marion Laing! He could have told Geoffrey that she didn't care tuppence for him, or for any man. Of all the undeserving causes. Poor Geoffrey. This must have been the first, the one great love of his life. What a rotten choice. He sighed. 'Well, maybe it's not as bad as it looks—'

'It is every bit as bad as it looks,' replied Montacute,

302

recovering some of his briskness. 'When the annual revalua-tion is made at Lloyd's, I shall be found to be without assets, and I shall cease to be a member. Then – if not before – I shall be forced to declare myself bankrupt. Then,' he went relentlessly on, his voice as cold and matter-of-fact as though he were giving advice to a client, '—as I shall be bankrupt, I will be unable to give a receipt for monies and shall be unable to continue as a partner in this firm. Moreover, as a bankrupt, the Law Society will not grant me my practising certificate and I shall be unable to continue my practice as a solicitor. Not until I am discharged, that is. That,' he concluded, looking evenly at Oliver, 'is as bad as it gets. There is, of course, the question of future liabilities which I may have to meet at Lloyds, also.'

Oliver drew in a deep breath, and Montacute leaned back in his chair. At least when he was thinking about money, he was not thinking about Marion. It would be so with his work. If he had the solace of his work, then he would be able to get over Marion in time. But there would be no work, and there would be a great deal of time. He saw all this, as he sat regarding Oliver.

Oliver looked up. 'Geoffrey, this is all a hopeless mess. But I am very hungry, and you must be, too. Let me take you to lunch.'

And because there seemed to be nothing in the world that mattered any more, Montacute let Oliver take him to lunch.

Oliver made sure that they both got rather drunk, and when twenty to four came and the waiters in Le Poulbot were clustered impatiently around the till, Montacute and Oliver had reached a kind of empathy which neither would ever have believed possible.

'You see,' said Montacute, closing his eyes and taking another sip of his brandy, 'I have never known any women before – not like Marion. She made me feel – she made me feel . . .' He groped for words, his face plaintive with the force of his emotion and the drink. 'She made me feel worthy. As though I had some value, some meaning. Not just some meaning as a solicitor, as someone who busied himself with other people's affairs, but as – as a man! As a person! Do you understand that, Oliver?'

Oliver, resting one rubbery cheek on his hand, nodded. 'I do,' he replied. There was a pause, in which Montacute shook his head slowly in despair.

'And now I see that she can never have loved me. How could she? My mother was right.' He gazed at his brandy. 'Do you know my mother?' He looked up at Oliver.

Oliver, his cheek still resting on his hand, shook his head forlornly, and said no, he didn't.

'Well, she was right,' said Montacute. He thought for a moment. A waiter skirted the table, but neither man took any notice. 'God, what if she was laughing at me all the time?' He looked up at Oliver, shaken with the force of imagined humiliation added to his pain.

'Your mother?'

'No,' said Montacute morosely. 'Marion. I loved her so much.'

Oliver sighed and shifted his cheek to his other hand. 'It is,' he said, 'the most bewildering, the most unspeakably painful thing, to find that you have given your love, invested your entire soul in someone – only to find that they are worthless, that they have betrayed and deceived you.'

Montacute looked at him, drunk and admiring; the man was a poet.

'But,' went on Oliver, staring at the tablecloth, 'there is one consolation, one inestimable prize that can be salvaged.'

'What's that?' asked Montacute. He felt fleetingly, wildly, that he was glad to be drunk, to be able to forget about the money and Marion for just a few hours. He had not been drunk since he was an undergraduate.

'To have loved. To have tasted the ultimate delight. Bestowed the greatest gift. But to expect to be happy, too, is to ask a great deal. "For to be wise, and love, exceeds man's might; that dwells with gods above."'

Montacute considered this, grateful to Oliver for his sympathy. But it did not obliterate the deadening knowledge within him that something was gone which would never come to him again, and that before him stretched a vast tract of time when he would be entirely alone, when he had hoped to have her, and the warmth of affection. All would be cold now.

Oliver, realising it was time they should go, looked at Montacute's face. In its misery and thoughtfulness it seemed more open than ever before. Hitherto, Montacute had never revealed any emotions, concealing them behind an aloof façade of reserve and pomposity. All those years, thought Oliver. He's probably not a bad fellow, really. Just rather dull. He was suddenly struck by the awfulness of Montacute's predicament, as outlined by him in the office earlier. Wasn't there an invalid mother, too, somewhere? In his new rush of affection, Oliver decided then and there that if anything could be done to help Montacute, he would do it. He would find a friend in Oliver Pocock. Had they not pretended, for whatever reason, to be friends for all these years? Perhaps they really were, after all.

They came out together into the fading light of the November afternoon and stood together uncertainly on the pavement.

'Well,' said Oliver, 'I should be getting back to the office, I suppose. What about you?'

Montacute lifted his head and looked up at the sky, and blinked. 'I don't know,' he said uncertainly. 'I don't think I shall go back to the office now. No.' He paused. 'Thank you for lunch, Oliver. It was very kind.'

'Not at all,' replied Oliver, adding with determination, 'I enjoyed it. We shall do it again. I shall call you very soon.'

Montacute looked at him a little sadly. Then he said goodbye and set off for the nearest tube station, to make his way home to Richmond.

Chapter one

Anthony Cross woke suddenly in the grey half-light of morning and knew that he had been dreaming of Leo. He closed his eyes again quickly, trying to summon back the feeling of safe happiness, of intimacy recaptured, but already his mind was breaking the surface of his dream like a stone left by the tide. He lay nursing his sense of loss for a moment or two, then turned his head upon the pillow to look at the girl sleeping next to him, at her blonde, anonymous head, her hand upon his shoulder. He moved the hand gently away and rose, pulling on his robe, and went through to the bathroom.

There he stared briefly at himself in the mirror, at his own handsome features, slack with sleep, and wondered why he had these dreams. He passed a hand through his dark hair, yawned, and began to run his shaving water. The dreams occurred every few months, like strange, tender echoes. Although each dream left in him a small, hollow pain which he could not fathom, he welcomed them. They took him back in time as though to some forgotten country.

Anthony began to lather his face, remembering the closeness of the hours he and Leo had once spent together, working, talking, sometimes just dawdling time away. He dipped his razor into the water and watched the scum of lather and tiny black bristles float away from the blade. He wondered if Leo ever dreamt of him – and then pushed the thought away as absurd. What might have happened if the affair had not ended before it had even begun? Anthony often wondered this, often wondered what depths there might have been to their unexplored relationship. But now they worked together, side by side, barristers in the same chambers, and there was no hint that such intimacy had ever existed. They met only in the company of others now, and every encounter was hedged with a casual remoteness.

1

Perhaps, thought Anthony, as he rubbed his face with the towel, the dreams were a kind of compensation. Compensation for loss, the loss of Leo's company, smiles, attention, conversation. Perhaps the pain of losing such a close friendship had not died away in his heart after all; perhaps it was merely buried, so that the recollection of that which he had lost floated to the surface of his subconscious as he slept. Perhaps.

He went through to the kitchen where his flatmate, Adam, was already dressed and gulping down coffee.

'Hi,' he said. 'Want some? I'm off in a sec.'

'Yes, thanks,' said Anthony, and put a slice of bread in the toaster.

'I taped the cricket for you,' said Adam, then added, 'since you and Lizzie seemed to have gone to bed early.' He grinned at Anthony and handed him his coffee.

'Oh, thanks. Yes,' replied Anthony abstractedly, thinking with guilt and boredom of the girl still sleeping in his bed.

Adam studied his face, able to gather what was in Anthony's mind. Another one for the chop, he thought. Adam, with his sandy hair and pale, thin face, thought that if he was tall and good-looking like Anthony, and apparently able to have any girl he wanted, he'd manage to look a bit happier about it. He turned and rinsed his mug out under the tap. 'You in tonight?'

'I think so.' Anthony took his toast from the toaster, and rummaged in the fridge for the butter. 'Then again, I don't know. I never know.'

'Okay. See you later then.'

'Bye,' said Anthony.

He drank his coffee and ate his toast, then went back into his bedroom to dress. He moved about quietly, closing drawers and cupboards gently so as not to wake the girl. He was tying his tie when she woke; she simply opened her eyes and lay gazing at him sleepily. He looked wonderful, she thought, in the dim light, the raised collar of his white shirt framing his lean face, his dark eyes expressionless. He glanced at her, turned down his collar, and bent to fasten his shoelaces. His demeanour had a telling remoteness about it,

2

each movement was made with a brisk finality. But she was not sufficiently awake to read any of the signals.

As he came to the side of the bed to pick up his watch, she stretched out lazy arms to him. 'Do you have to go just yet?' she murmured, and kissed him gently.

'Lizzie,' said Anthony, a note that was almost one of pain in his voice, 'I'm going to be late.'

She merely smiled and drew him towards her again, but there was a stiffness about him, an impatient reserve, that made her drop her arms. She lay back and looked at him as he straightened up and took his jacket from its coathanger. Something in the atmosphere made her feel suddenly like an intruder.

'Will I see you tonight?' she asked. She knew the answer, but still she had to ask.

Anthony hesitated in the doorway. What should he say? 'Lizzie –' he began, then stopped. Say something final, he thought. Tell her. No, there might be tears and awfulness, and he'd be late. He glanced at his watch. 'Lizzie, look – I'm really busy for the next week or so. I don't know. I'll ring you, okay?'

She said nothing, merely lay there, feeling the space between them widen into infinity. Anthony added, 'There's some coffee left in the pot. Help yourself to breakfast.' And he went.

He clattered downstairs and out into the early September sunshine, hating himself. What did you do when the whole thing had become stale and lifeless, when there was no point in going on? Nothing, except let it peter out. Anything was better than tears and scenes. But every relationship seemed to end in this way. Perhaps it all came too easily. Perhaps it was just as well; he didn't want to become serious about anyone again, not after Julia.

In the train in took some papers from his briefcase and tried to concentrate on them, but the dream of Leo hung about him like a scent that clung to the air, imparting itself to everything, distracting him. He could not recall any detail of it, except that Leo had been there and things had been happy. The happiness of dreams, he mused, elusive and wonderful. The best kind of happiness. Am I happy now? wondered Anthony. He supposed he must be. He should be. At twenty-four, he had a new and flourishing barrister's practice in one of the best sets of commercial chambers in the Temple, he shared a decent flat in South Ken with his friend, Adam (which was a bit of an improvement on life in a tiny semi in East Dulwich with his mother and his brother), and he had a good social life, money to spend, girlfriends . . . I must be happy, he thought, and stared sightlessly at the window opposite, wondering why, in that case, he ever stopped to think about it.

The dream was still so present in his mind as he strode swiftly from the tube station through Temple Place that it came as a real shock when he bumped into Leo Davies hurrying up from the Embankment.

'Good God!' said Leo, steadying himself from the slight collison. 'Hello.'

'Hello,' stammered Anthony. 'Sorry. I'm in a bit of a hurry. Got a con at nine and a summons at half ten.'

'My bloody car broke down halfway along the Embankment,' said Leo and sighed, passing a hand over his hair. 'I had to leave it there. Must ring the AA from Chambers.' Although he was only forty-four, his hair was silver, lending his gaunt good looks a maturity they would not otherwise possess, for his smile was brilliant, boyish, and his blue eyes candid and restless. He was of Anthony's height, but more squarely built, and was expensively dressed, almost to the point of dandyism.

They fell into step together as they made their way to chambers. There was an uneasy silence between them. They were not accustomed to being alone in one another's company, these days.

Anthony muttered something inconsequential about a recent House of Lords judgment and Leo uttered some words in reply. He glanced at Anthony, feeling in his heart the faint pleasure he always felt when looking at the young man. Then he made some remark about his car and Anthony laughed. Leo loved to see him laugh. It's absurd, he thought, that we hardly ever speak to one another these days. Ridiculous. That business was all finished a long time ago. None of it mattered any more.

4

'Look,' said Leo, stopping at the foot of the steps to 5 Caper Court, 'what about a game of squash this evening? Ring up the club and see if they have a court free. Yes?'

Anthony was startled. Leo had not invited Anthony to spend time with him since the day he had got his tenancy.

'Yes.' he replied hesitantly. 'All right.' They went upstairs together. Anthony's room was on the first landing, Leo's on the second. Anthony paused at his door. 'I'll see you later, then.' And he smiled at Leo, his happiness so evident that the older man was touched, first with pleasure, then with a slight misgiving.

'Six thirty,' said Leo. 'Try to get a court around then.' And he passed on up the stairs to his room.

At six fifteen Leo was sitting at his desk itself was of pale ash, it, surface devoid of any other object save the document. All the furniture was of the same pale wood, quite unlike the old, dark, comfortable furniture favoured by most other barristers. No cosy Dickensian shades hung around Leo's room. All was austere, clinical. There was no friendly muddle of papers and briefs lining the shelves and windowsills; everything was neatly tidied away behind the doors of expensive, func- tionalist cupboards. Even the pictures that hung upon the wall were anodyne modern abstracts, and not the usual charcoal sketches of the law courts, framed watercolours of ships or landscapes, that hung in the rooms of other members of chambers. It all seemed of a piece with the man himself – one of them, yet set apart from them in unusual ways.

Leo was one of the most exceptional advocates in the Temple, with a mercurial personality and a ready wit, and was popular in chambers. Life always seemed to lighten up when Leo was around. He was charming, amusing, and although he moved within the well-defined codes of the Bar with deference and circumspection, there was a certain unconventionality about him; he was an elusive man, and few knew anything of his life outside work.

As he sat studying the document, all his customary energy and restless habit of movement seemed concentrated and contained. The evening light that fell through the window glinted on his hair, and the angular shadows beneath his brow and cheekbones lent his face a brooding, hawklike quality.

The document was headed 'Lord Chancellor's Department. Application for Appointment as Queen's Counsel'. Beneath the word 'Title' were five little boxes, mared 'Mr,' 'Mrs', 'Miss', 'Ms' and, slightly larger than the rest, 'Other'. Leo sighed and passed his hand over his head. 'Other'. That about sums me up, he thought.

He rubbed his hands over his eyes. At forty-four, he supposed it was about time that he did this. It was part of the plan, the next step up the golden ladder. There was almost an inevitability about taking silk which bored him. He would achieve this just as he had achieved everything else – his successful practice, his cars, his clubs, his houses in Mayfair and Oxfordshire, his polished circle of social acquaintances. All a long way from the Welsh mining village of his childhood, where he had struggled to free himself from his beginnings and to create a new identity. This would be part of that identity, part of the image which he had cultivated as assiduously as his own charm and urbanity. Leo Davies, QC. Another stitch in that tapestry of his life, the one behind which he could conceal himself from the rest of the world.

He sat flipping through the pages of the form, wondering how long it would take for his income to climb to six figures, once he had taken silk, when there was a knock at his door and Anthony came in.

'Hello,' said Leo, glancing up.

'Hi. Squash courts are all booked up, I'm afraid. They've got some competition ladder, or something, I don't know.'

'Pity,' said Leo. 'I could have done with a game. I'm right out of condition.' His voice still held an attractive Welsh cadence. He leaned back and flexed his arms above his head, studying Anthony. The young man's face was leaner now, and without any of the softness which had caused Leo to fall in love with him some eighteen months before. Nearly two years. It seemed like a lifetime ago. Well, thought Leo, that had all ended as soon as it had begun. They were friends now, colleagues, no need to let the slightest shadow of it hang between them. They never alluded now to anything in the past, and Leo had hidden away any lingering traces of his former love as easily and effectively as he hid so much from himself and others.

'What's this?' asked Anthony, coming over to the desk and squinting down at the paper. Leo was about to pull the document away and fold it up, but stopped. Why shouldn't Anthony know?

'Application to take silk,' he replied, and leaned back again. 'Have a look, if you like,' he added, and Anthony picked the paper up and flipped through it curiously.

'Listen to this,' said Anthony, smiling; he read aloud: "Have you ever had an action brought against you in respect of another matter involving you personally, or under your supervision, for professional negligence? Have you ever been subject ot the disciplinary process of the Bar without the matter having been dismissed? Have you ever been adjudged bankrupt, made a composition with your creditors, or been sued to judgment for any debt?" ' He looked up at Leo and laughed.

'Well quite,' replied Leo, dryly. 'Instead of "yes" and "no" boxes, they should put one marked "no" and the other marked "forget your application, in that case".' He took the document from Anthony, folded it up and put it into his breast pocket. 'Well, if we can't have a game of squash, a vigorous drink seems like the next best thing.'

They made their way downstairs and out into Caper Court, where a light drizzle had begun to fall; the flush of golden light at the end of the September day was beginning to be eclipsed by banks of grey cloud. They ran through the cloisters and over King's Bench Walk, out into the back alleys of Fleet Street. Leo paused in the doorway of the pub before going in and tapped his breast pocket lightly.

'I'd rather you didn't mention this to anyone. The silk thing, I mean.'

Anthony gazed at him and raised a hand to brush away the surface drops of rain from his dark hair. He nodded. 'Of course. But why did you let *me* know?'

Leo looked back at him candidly. All that ground was too well trodden. Anyway, he didn't really know himself.

7

Something to do with the slender thread of once-shared intimacy which he liked to feel still bound him to this young man, however loosely. He wanted Anthony to know things, wanted to share whatever hopes and disappointments there might be. But he could not acknowledge this.

'Probably,' he replied, 'because you happened to come into my room when I was reading the bloody thing. I was never a good dissembler.' No, never. At that moment someone brushed between them and went into the pub. 'Come on,' said Leo, and Anthony followed him in.

He was pleased to be alone with Leo once more. Tonight's invitation to a game of squash had seemed to him like a return to old times; perhaps the defences were coming down, and he could enjoy Leo's solitary company as he had once done. It struck him as strange and propitious that he should have dreamt of Leo that very morning. For these reasons, he was conscious of a vague disappointment when he saw Stephen Bishop, a fellow member of chambers, sitting alone at a table with a pint of beer and the *Financial Times*. He looked pleased to see Leo and Anthony, and folded up his paper.

'What will you have?' he asked them.

'Large Scotch, please, Stephen, since I happen to know you can afford it,' replied Leo, settling himself into a chair. 'William told me this afternoon about your disgustingly fat fee for that Harvey case.'

Stephen smiled and took his glasses off to polish them with a large handkerchief. 'Yes, well, you know, some of us are just born to greatness. But I have to admit it's nice to get the odd moneyspinner.' Stephen was a portly, cheerful man with an easy manner and a mild nature. His practice was steady but unremarkable, and he never let it interfere with the harmony of his life at home with his wife and four children. He was liked and respected at the Commercial Bar, but he never brought to his cases the energy and dedication that Leo did. Safe, but unexciting, was the verdict on Stephen. He put his glasses back on and turned to Anthony. 'What about you, Anthony?'

'Just a small Scotch, please,' said Anthony. 'I still have some papers to look at tonight.'

Stephen fetched the drinks and sat back down.

'So,' he said, 'how's the day been?' He glanced at Leo. 'Still plugging away at that supply contract dispute?'

Leo yawned and rubbed his jaw with his hand. 'Yes, unfortunately. But, surprise, surprise, Stott has to go off and sit on some judicial enquiry for the next four days, so it's been adjourned till next week. Since I don't have anything else in particular to occupy me, I think I'll absent myself from chambers for a few days.'

Anthony felt a little pang. It was absurd, he knew, but he liked to know that Leo was around, liked to hear him whistling on the stairs, to catch an occasional glimpse of him at tea or in the clerks' room. When Leo was away, life for Anthony, even though he was remarkably busy himself, became a little bit emptier. Leo just had that kind of personality, that was all.

'What will you do?' he asked Leo, and took a sip of his Scotch.

'Oh, go down to the country, I think, drink in the last of the summer in peace.' He thought briefly of his house in Oxfordshire, and of its present occupants. 'Relative peace,' he added thoughtfully. Without looking up he could feel Anthony's eyes on him, knew that he was wondering who would be there with him. Was he jealous? Well, thought Leo roughly, knocking back the remains of his drink in one, it didn't matter to either of them if he was. That was all water under the bridge. And why was he even thinking like this? It had been a mistake to ask him for that game of squash this evening. It just made life more complicated.

'I wish I had somewhere worth retreating to,' observed Anthony. 'I mean, somewhere like your place,' he added awkwardly. 'If ever I get anything adjourned, there's always another piece of work to plod on with.'

'Oh, what it is to be young and thrusting and ever so popular with solicitors,' laughed Leo. 'I remember being like that – don't you, Stephen? Never turning work down, working all the hours God gave, buttering up your clerk, trying to cultivate a worldly image.'

Anthony smiled, and Leo was charmed to see him colour faintly.

9

'Yes,' observed Stephen dryly, 'I understand that we're *particularly* popular with lady solicitors.'

'Oh, balls,' said Anthony. 'Anyway, no doubt it's all very well when you're middle-aged and established and don't have to keep chasing fee notes.'

'Less of the middle-aged,' said Leo. 'I feel quite coltish as I sit there in number five court, listening to Marcus Field enlightening us all on the official policy of the Government of Qatar towards brokerage commissions. Thank God I'm off the hook till next Monday.'

Stephen drained his glass and shook his head. 'I'm glad I'm not Anthony's age any more. Too much cut-and-thrust . . . You have to be so energetic, so determined. Exhausting, just to think of it.'

'Not thinking of retiring, are you, Stephen?' asked Leo jokingly, crushing out the butt of his cigar.

Stephen smiled. 'The fees at Marlborough won't permit it, I'm afraid. Got to keep slogging away. Anyway, see you chaps tomorrow. I'd better be making a move.' He rose and picked up his newspaper. 'Goodnight.'

When Stephen had gone, Leo sat in silence with Anthony for a few seconds, then picked up his empty glass. 'Another?' he asked Anthony.

Anthony hesitated. He felt tired. He had an interlocutory application in the morning and he hadn't even looked at the papers yet. But he wanted to stay. He glanced up and smiled. 'Yes. Okay, another, thanks.'

Leo brought the drinks and sat back down. Anthony looked on idly as Leo lit another little cigar, watching the lean, fine hands he had always found so fascinating. He enjoyed watching Leo, enjoyed his restless, elegant movements, the way he turned his head, the way the side of his mouth jerked when he made a joke. His mind strayed back to Leo's remark as they had entered the pub earlier and he asked, 'Isn't Stephen senior to you in chambers?'

'Yes. He joined two years before I did. Sixty-two.' Leo blew out a little smoke and looked at Anthony. 'Why?'

Anthony looked uncomfortable and turned his whisky glass

between finger and thumb. 'Isn't it . . . I mean, wouldn't you expect him to take silk first, or something?'

Or something. Still with that charmingly juvenile sloppiness of speech when embarrassed, thought Leo. He looked levelly at Anthony. 'In the normal course of events, yes.' He paused and leaned back. 'But one can't wait around for ever for Stephen to dither his way through life. He should have applied two years ago, if he was going to go for it.' Leo stroked the glowing edge of his cigar against the rim of the ashtray. 'Maybe he did. Maybe he was turned down. All I know is, one has to be loyal to oneself, not to the other members of chambers.'

'But don't you owe the rest something? I mean, we are all one set of chambers.'

'There is something you have to learn, Anthony,' replied Leo, and his voice was hard, the blue of his gaze quite cold. 'And that is, that you must put yourself first. Every time. Look.' He leaned forward. 'I've run every case for the past two years without a leader. And won most of them. The time is right for me. I'd be a fool to pass it up this year. I don't care what Stephen does or doesn't do.'

Anthony thought for a moment. 'But what effect will it have on Stephen's career if you're successful? Could he still take silk?'

Leo looked carelessly away. 'Probably not.' He drew on his cigar. 'Almost certainly not. If it were to happen, once could take it that the Lord Chancellor's Office had assumed that he wasn't going to apply – or that they were sending out a signal that he wouldn't get it if he did apply. Either way, the writing would be on the wall.' He did not look at Anthony as he spoke. 'Besides,' he added, 'even if he did apply next year, there wouldn't be enough work to justify another silk in chambers. There would be Sir Basil, Cameron, Roderick, Michael – and myself.'

You're so confident, thought Anthony. But of course you are. Why shouldn't you be?

He nodded and said, 'So that would be it – for Stephen, I mean?'

'Well, I suppose so,' replied Leo. 'Otherwise we'd be top-heavy. We might be, in any event. Unless Sir Basil retires.'

'That's not likely, is it?' asked Anthony in surprise. Sir Basil Bunting, the head of chambers, was, admittedly, in his sixties, but he seemed to be riding with magnificent serenity on top of a lucrative and immensely successful practice.

Leo smoked in silence for a few moments. This was something he had thought about. Poor old Stephen was one thing – well, he had had his chance and not taken it. Why should Leo care? Considerations of Stephen were easily dismissed. One was loyal to oneself. Sir Basil was a different kettle of fish. Leo knew that Sir Basil's practice wasn't quite as flourishing as Sir Basil liked to make it appear. Clients nowadays liked younger men – they liked people on their own wavelength. Solicitors were the same, too, and God knows they seemed to be getting younger by the minute. If Leo took silk, he was confident of mopping up a good deal of work from the juniors in chambers. Sir Basil could be squeezed out. And that, thought Leo, might be no bad thing.

Just when Anthony was beginning to think that Leo hadn't heard what he had said, Leo turned to him and flashed a wicked, attractive smile. 'You never know what pressure might be brought to bear on Sir Basil,' he murmured. 'We might just have to hope that the Lord Chancellor wants another High Court judge.'

Anthony drew in his breath and stared at Leo. Will I ever become as ruthless? he wondered. Leo glanced briefly back at him and wondered the same thing. He had detected a slight toughening in Anthony over the past year or so. That touchingly tender aspect of his character seemed to be rubbing away, as the work poured steadily in and the money increased. Or was that just a physical illusion, something to do with the fact that Anthony's face was older, less boyish, that he wore decent suits and shirts now, that he was more confident – even a little arrogant – as his practice grew more successful?

'Don't worry,' he said, and drained his glass. 'It's not as bad as it sounds. And don't feel too sorry for Stephen – he's doing very nicely. Anyway, you never know – maybe he's applying for silk this year, too.'

And we know which of you is more likely to get it, if that's the case, thought Anthony. One way or the other, Stephen was the loser, and Leo, it seemed, couldn't care less.

'Want a lift anywhere?' asked Leo as they left the pub. 'The AA seem to have remedied its little defect.'

'No, thanks,' replied Anthony. 'I'm going back to chambers. My papers are still there.'

Leo nodded, and the two men said goodnight and went their separate ways.

In the kitchen of Leo's Oxfordshire house, a young, blonde-haired woman was carefully laying sheets of pasta on the bottom of an oblong dish.

'It's not a problem for me,' she remarked over her shoulder to the boy who stood looking out of the window, arms folded, at the dusk falling on the rainy garden. 'I go back to Oxford in a month's time. It's just been another episode in my life.' She paused briefly to gaze at her handiwork before moving back to the stove to stir a white sauce. 'I like to think of my life as a series of episodes. Nothing final. Nothing static.'

The boy turned to look at her. Like her, he was blond, but taller, and his face wore a sullen, dissatisfied expression. The girl's face was airily serene as she moved about her tasks.

'Don't give me that. You love him.'

'Oh, of course I do!' she turned in smiling astonishment. 'He's divine, an utterly divine man. I love him to death. He's the most wonderful fuck, and he doesn't care in the least for me – that's why he's so attractive.' She turned back to her work, still smiling. Then she added, 'He doesn't care for either of us. We're just a – summer dalliance, you might say.'

The boy turned to look back out of the window. 'At least you've got something to go to. What have I got when it's over?'

'Oh, get a job, James.'

'That's a laugh.' He picked up a knife from the draining board and fiddled with it, running his thumb along the blade. 'Anyway, I don't want a job. I want to stay here.' His voice took on a plaintive, childish tone. 'God, Sarah, I really don't want to have to go.'

'You're just insecure,' remarked Sarah. 'Pass me that grated cheese, would you?'

'So what do I do? Go back to being a photographer's assistant? Let him drop me just where he picked me up? No thanks. He owes us something, doesn't he?'

Sarah flicked her hair back from her shoulders and licked at the finger she had just dipped in the sauce. 'Not a thing. Not me, at any rate. After all, he's paying us for being here – for being his . . .' She paused and laughed, then sighed. 'His companions. He's fun. He's amusing. This was just a holiday job – I told you. My parents think I'm working as a cook for someone.'

'Well, you are.' James's voice was sulky, bored.

'That's all they know.' She began layering mince and pasta together. 'Put it down to experience, James.'

He said nothing, and she turned to look at him. Seeing the forlorn expression on his face, she came across and put her arms gently on his shoulders. 'Come on, cheer up. We've had a good time, had a laugh, haven't we? Anyway, it's not over yet.' She gave the tip of his nose a soft, pecking kiss.

'That's not the way you kiss me when we're in bed with him,' said James, staring into her eyes.

She smiled back. 'No – but that's work, isn't it?' She watched his troubled face and her smile faded. 'Oh, James, what is it you want? Why can't you just make the most of it, and be happy?'

'Because it's different for you, Sarah! Your family have got money. You've got something to fall back on. What have I got? You'll just swan off back to Oxford and forget about all this –'

'Well, I wouldn't say that.'

He ignored the interruption. ' – while I'm just sort of – thrust aside!'

'Well, face it.' She took her arms from his shoulders and went back to the dish of lasagne. 'He doesn't need you. You can see the kind of man he is. We're just a little diversion in his life. Nothing special. He doesn't want anyone to come too close. There's nothing you can do about that. Anyway, let's change the subject. What do you want to do tonight? Pub?'

'That's just about all there is to do, isn't there?' said James angrily. 'He leaves us stuck here in this hole from one weekend to the next, expecting us to stick to his stupid rules, and be all bright and cheerful and eager to please when he turns up on a Friday night! I'm fed up with it. He's not the only piece of excitement around here, whatever he thinks.' James rammed his hands into his jeans pockets. 'I met this bloke when we were in Ryecot. I'm going to ask him back.' His voice was dogged.

'Don't be a berk, James. You know what Leo said.' Sarah began to pour the cheese sauce carefully over the last layer.

'What's the point of having a place like this for the whole week if we can't share it with a friend or two? I need a bit of company.'

'Thanks. What about me?'

'Well, like you said, that's just work, isn't it?' He looked at his watch. 'I'm going to ring that bloke now.'

'Fun for me,' murmured Sarah. 'I'd better see what's on telly tonight.'

'If you're very good,' said James as he left the kitchen, 'we might let you watch.'

'Ha, ha,' said Sarah to herself, as she stared admiringly at her lasagne.

She was watching the late-night film when she heard Leo's car pull up in the driveway, the beam of its headlights brushing the curtained windows with a faint arc of light. She thought of James upstairs in bed with his friend. Leo's bed. She knew she had at least thirty seconds in which to call up to them, warn them, and that James might just, possibly, be able to get him out through an upstairs window in time. She couldn't be bothered. She heard the car door slam, then his feet on the gravel, and snuggled a little lower in her armchair. She was fed up with James, anyway. Always whining round the place. And with him out of the way, who could say how things might develop? Maybe she could make her position that little bit stronger. A man like that. Life would become divinely simple. She'd never wanted to settle down, but if it could be someone like Leo . . . Some hope, she told herself, and smiled wryly at the television screen as Leo opened the front door.

'Hello,' he said, as he came into the room.

'Hello,' she replied, and smiled winningly, briefly, at him

15

round the side of the armchair. Then she stared at the television again. Her heart was thudding a little at the thought of Leo finding James. 'A midweek surprise,' she murmured. 'Just as well I made some lasagne this afternoon. I was going to put it in the freezer for Saturday.'

'Good.' Leo rubbed his face and gazed blankly for a few seconds at the television screen. 'I need a drink. No – I think I'll go upstairs and change first.'

'That's a good idea,' said Sarah. 'I'll fix you a drink while you're up there. You'll need it,' she added under her breath.

It was difficult to concentrate on the film with doors banging and voices shouting and feet thumping on the stairs, but at last they died away. She heard the front door close. Leo came into the room.

'I've poured us both a drink,' she said. 'Yours is over there.'

Leo picked it up. 'James is packing,' he said. He crossed the room and switched off the television, then turned with a sigh to Sarah. 'I'm afraid,' he added, 'that you're next.'

She smiled the impudent, tantalizing smile that he had always liked. 'Oh, well. All goods things come to an end.' She raised her glass. 'Cheers, anyway.' She took a sip. 'Can I at least stay tonight?'

Leo pushed back a stray lock of grey hair, then tugged his tie loose. He sighed, the anger gradually dying away. That bloody boy. He had known it was a mistake to let it all go on this long. It should have ended ages ago.

Sarah put down her glass and rose, moving forward to embrace him, pressing her body gently against his. 'After all,' she said softly, 'two's company. And three *was* a bit of a crowd . . .' She kissed him, parting his lips gently with her tongue. As he put his arms round her waist she felt some drops from his glass of whisky fall on the back of her skirt. His hand was shaking. She knew that his anger at the discovery upstairs had left a little legacy of excitement. Weird old Leo.

'All right,' he replied. 'Just for tonight.' He had always preferred her to James, anyway. She was far more inventive. He would be sorry to see her go, in a way. 'You go first thing in the morning,' he added, more firmly.

'First thing,' she agreed. Probably just as well, really. She

16

had enough saved for a couple of weeks in Cyprus with Alicia. And there was always tonight. 'First thing,' she repeated with a smile, before he closed his eyes to kiss her properly.